# Through A Glass, Darkly

ALSO BY CHARLOTTE MILLER

*Behold, This Dreamer*

# THROUGH A GLASS, DARKLY

♣

CHARLOTTE MILLER

NewSouth Books

MONTGOMERY

NewSouth Books
P.O. Box 1588
Montgomery, AL 36102

Library of Congress Cataloging-in-Publication Data
Miller, Charlotte, 1959–
Through A Glass, Darkly / Charlotte Miller.
p. cm.
ISBN 1-58838-054-8
1. Farmers—Fiction.
2. Alabama—Fiction. 3. Farm life—Fiction.
4. Rural poor—Fiction. 5. Depressions—Fiction.
6. Land ownership—Fiction. 7. Rural families—Fiction.
I. Title.

PS3563.I37649 T49 2001
813'.6—dc21                               2001044109

To Justin

When I was a child, I spake as a child, I understood as a child, I thought as a child: but when I became a man, I put away childish things. For now we see through a glass, darkly; but then face to face: now I know in part; but then shall I know even as also I am known.

*1 Corinthians 13: 11-12 (KJV)*

# PART ONE

# CHAPTER ONE

"Imagine him bringin' her here."

"Two more mouths t' feed, 'stead 'a just one."

"An' look at her, with her bobbed-off hair an' her skirt right up t' her knees—ain't nothin' but trash, I tell you."

Elise Sanders fled into the small bedroom that opened off the kitchen in the little sharecropped house, but the voices of the two old women followed her into the room, as she knew they had intended.

"Trash, I tell you—an' for us t' be throwed out 'a our room for them two, t' give 'em 'privacy,' I bet she's done with child, married only a few days or not; she's just th' type—"

Elise's face burned with embarrassment as she leaned her cheek against the cool wood of the door. She did not know how she would ever face the two old women again, even though she knew she would have to, for they were Janson's aunts, her new husband's aunts, and they lived here in the same house where she was now forced to live. It made it only worse that they were right—she was with child, a child Janson did not yet know that she carried. She could only imagine the smug looks the two old women would wear when her condition became obvious.

She made herself turn away from the door, her eyes moving around this room she and Janson had been given here in his grandparents' house, finding herself suddenly filled with a sense of homesickness she had not expected, but that had stayed with her from the moment she had left her home in Endicott County, Georgia. She moved further into the room, looking first at the hand-pieced quilts drawn up over the narrow bed, then at the whitewashed walls and the sagging cane-bottomed straight chairs, and at the washstand topped by its chipped pitcher and basin. This room was nothing like the one she had known through the sixteen years of her life, that room with its papered walls and the drapes and counterpane that had been a gift from her mother on her last birthday, its lovely mahogany furniture, its colors of pink and rose and white. She knew she would never see that room again, just as she would never see her family, or the home that had sheltered Whitleys for generations, even long before the war with the North that had ended six decades before. She had given up that room, just as she had given up her home and so much else in her life, so that she could be with Janson—he was all that she needed, she kept telling herself.

She hugged her arms for warmth as she moved about the room, the fire burning in the fireplace set into the far wall doing little to alleviate the chill in the air. There seemed to be dark shadows everywhere she looked, cast by the light of the fireplace and the single kerosene lamp sitting on the table beside the bed, moving against the far wall near the chifforobe, and even reflecting in the fading mirror over the dresser. She felt for a moment as if she had gone back in time as she stared around this room, back to a time and a place before electricity and running water, for the little sharecropped house had neither, to a time of superstitions and old-fashioned folk ways, a time and a lifestyle made worse by the knowledge that Janson's family was Holiness and did not believe even in jewelry or makeup. She felt as if her very presence here in this house was offensive to these people, for her hair was bobbed short in the style most girls were wearing now in the 1920s; her dress, though the most conservative she owned, low-waisted and coming well to her knees, was far shorter than those worn by any of Janson's female relatives she had met today. She even felt that more than one of those relatives had stared at her simple wedding ring—none of these people seemed to belong here in the last months of 1927, for they all seemed part of that other time, and, worse still, Janson seemed a part of it as well. He fit in here, as he never had during the months he had worked as a farmhand for her father.

She made herself move toward the bed to take up the white cotton nightgown she had left there earlier when she unpacked their things and put them away in the chifforobe, not wanting to change for bed, even though she knew Janson would be in shortly. Changing from her traveling clothes seemed too easy an acceptance of this new life.

She caught a glimpse of her reflection in the mirror over the dresser and she stopped for a moment to stare at herself, somehow surprised to see that she looked no different, though she was a married woman now and a mother-to-be. She was not Elise Whitley anymore—she was Elise Sanders now. She lifted her hand and stared at her wedding ring, then forced herself to turn away and begin to change for bed.

She quickly removed her dress and slipped into the nightgown, rushing more than she needed to, but she could not stop herself. She felt exposed, vulnerable here in this house that belonged to someone else, fearing that someone might take the notion to check on her before she was fully dressed. She lifted the quilts and got into bed, then moved to the far side, pulling the covers up over her breasts and hugging them tightly to herself as she stared at the dark shadows moving over the whitewashed ceiling. She felt so very alone and homesick, even as she told herself that she now had what she had wanted most in the world. She was Janson's wife; no one could hurt him anymore or try to keep them apart. She was Janson's wife—but she wanted her mother now. She wanted to be home, in a place that would be familiar to her. She wanted to feel safe—but she should feel safe, she kept telling herself. Janson would take care of her.

The door opened and he entered the room, then turned to close the door quietly behind himself. He was still dressed in the dungarees and work shirt he had been wearing when they had arrived in Eason County earlier in the day, but the clothes were wrinkled now even worse than from the long train ride, the dungarees and shirt both stained heavily in places from the work he had been doing with his grandfather. His green eyes came to rest on her where she lay under the quilts on the bed, and he smiled—but she could not bring herself to do anything more than stare at him, watching as the shadows played over his features, across the high cheekbones and the complexion darker than her own, the features that showed so clearly the mixed blood of his heritage. He began to talk as he undressed for bed, his words moving over her, but she could not listen to him. She could only stare as he removed his shirt and dungarees, and then hurriedly stripped off his long-johns in the chill room as he prepared to get into bed with her.

He lifted the quilts as Elise stared at him, and she burst into tears, turning her face from him toward the whitewashed wall.

Elise awoke slowly the next morning, her head hurting from having cried herself to sleep. She sat up on the straw tick of the bed, bunching the quilts in her hands as she stared around the room. She was alone, alone in the room, and alone with her thoughts.

She was embarrassed, feeling guilty over the bout of crying the night before. Janson had left their bed unsatisfied this morning as he never had in the times they had been able to be together in the months before their marriage. She could not understand her reasons for crying so when he had only wanted to do what they had done so many times before. He had been so kind even as she cried, holding her, seeming to understand as she cried herself to sleep on his shoulder—he must think he's married a child, she told herself, drawing her knees up to her chest to rest her crossed arms on top of them. She felt as if she'd driven him out of bed this morning, even for all his kindness the night before. He had a right to expect more than that from his wife, and he could probably not look at her now in the light of day without remembering the whimpering child who had spent the night crying her eyes out on his shoulder.

She lay back on the straw tick and looked around the room, realizing that it did not seem so frightening now, with the sunlight streaming in the window near the foot of the bed. The room was neat and clean except for their discarded clothes that were now folded over the back of one of the straight chairs. The whitewashed walls, fire burning in the fireplace across the room, and the colorful patchwork quilts beneath which she lay, now brightened the room up in the light of day.

She wished Janson had awakened her before he had left to do whatever work his grandfather might have for him this morning. She needed to apologize for her behavior the night before. She was not about to allow a moment's self-pity to ruin what she had worked so hard to have. Her father's words when he had ordered them from his land rose all too easily to haunt her—he had told her she would grow to hate Janson for her decision to marry him, and that Janson would grow to hate her as well. They had both risked so much, even Janson's very life, just to be together. She was dead to her family now, for she had chosen to marry Janson even though her father had forbidden it. William Whitley and Elise's oldest brother, Bill, had both been willing to kill Janson to keep them apart. They would have found murder preferable to seeing Elise marry a man who was part Cherokee, a man who was only half white, no matter how much she might love him.

Now she had what she had wanted, what they had risked so much for, what they had given up so much to have, and she had cried herself to sleep, pitying herself for having gotten the very thing she had wanted so badly. She felt herself a fool this morning, a silly, empty-headed fool who would see devils in friendly faces and cry at dreams she thought were nightmares.

She got up quickly, washed her face and bathed with water from the basin sitting on the washstand near the foot of the bed, brushed her hair, and dressed in a low-waisted frock that she hoped Janson's grandmother would not find too offensive. She wanted the old woman to like her, or at least to tolerate her; she already knew there was little hope that either Janson's Aunt Belle or Aunt Maggie would ever feel more for her than an absolute dislike. To have Janson's grandmother feel the same would be more than she could bear.

She sat down before the dresser and did her makeup and hair almost without thought, then she stopped for a moment and stared at her reflection in the fading mirror, smoothing a spit-curl of hair down against her cheek and thinking that she looked younger than she should. The memory of having cried herself to sleep the night before was all too fresh, and the knowledge of what Janson must think of her this morning spurred her to movement. She would have to find him, apologize, and show him that she was not a child. She had only gotten what she had wanted—she was not about to lose it now over a silly bout of homesickness.

The kitchen was warm and filled with the smell of baking bread when Elise entered it a moment later. Deborah Sanders looked up from the bread dough she had been kneading and asked how she had slept.

"Fine," Elise answered, then asked, "Where's Janson? He was gone when I woke up."

"Folks're usually up an' workin' around here about sunrise." She glanced up from her work again, leaving Elise feeling properly chastised for having slept so late. "Th' men had work t' do out back 'a th' barn. I 'spect Janson's out there with th' rest of 'em—now, you set down an' eat you some breakfast; we're gonna have t' put some meat on them bones 'a yours." She wiped her floury hands on the apron tied around her waist, then brushed a strand of gray hair away from her forehead with one hand and toward the heavy bun at the back of her neck. She put her hands on her hips and leveled a look at Elise, making Elise feel as if there was nothing the woman saw within her in that moment that she liked in the least.

Elise looked toward the pots boiling on the back of the woodstove, then away quickly. She was feeling queasy this morning, and the thought of food was almost more than she could bear. "I'm not really hungry. I think I'll just go find Janson. I wanted to—"

"Now, we'll have none of that," the old woman said, taking her by the arm and ushering her to one of the benches beside the kitchen table, making her sit down, then going to take a plate down from the warming oven over the stove, a plate piled high with biscuits, sausage, eggs, and grits. She set it down before Elise. "Now, you eat," she said. "Cain't go skippin' breakfast. It ain't good for a body t' start th' day without somethin' in their stomach." She turned back to her bread dough, glancing back up at Elise one last time.

Elise looked at the mountain of food before her, her stomach churning. She obediently picked up the fork the old woman had placed beside her plate and tried to do what she could with it. "You said Janson's working out behind the barn?"

"Yeah, but you don't want t' be goin' out there. Th' men're workin', my Tom, Wayne, an' Janson—"

"I won't bother them. I just wanted to talk to him for a second."

"Not out there. You leave him alone until he comes in for dinner, an' you can talk t' him then."

Elise looked up at her, thinking that the woman might make her eat, but she could not stop her from going to see her own husband.

"Olive an' her husban', Cyrus, an' their Daniel and 'Nita'll be here for dinner t' meet you," Janson's grandmother said, and Elise had an awful, sinking feeling at the idea of meeting any more relatives. She had had her fill of them already, but it could not be avoided. They all came along with marrying Janson, even though Elise could not quite make herself happy about any she had met thus far. Within an hour of their having arrived the evening before, she had already been introduced not only to Janson's grandparents, his cousin, Sissy, who lived with them and who was only a few years younger than Elise, but also the two old biddies who had gone out of their way to make her feel unwelcome, and Janson's Uncle Wayne, his wife, Rachel, and their brood of sons. Now it would be the snooty Aunt Olive that Janson had told her about, and her family. She could only imagine who might show up next, her mind going over all the people Janson had told her about.

She was making some headway on the breakfast that had been set before her. She had only picked at her supper the night before, and the morning sickness was easing off. At least the woman made good biscuits, Elise told herself, even if she did think she could tell everyone what to do.

"Janson's done got you with child, ain't he?" Deborah Sanders asked and Elise choked, her fork stopping midway between the plate and her mouth. She looked up at the woman, feeling her face grow hot with the blushes that answered the question as well as any words ever could. Elise looked away, certain at any moment that this woman—this extremely religious woman—would damn her to hell in a sermon within a few moments. Her face, down to her neckline, felt hot, her hands clammy, as she set her fork down, preparing herself for what she knew was to come.

After a moment she felt a gentle hand come to rest on her own, a kind, understanding pat, and she looked up into Deborah Sanders's eyes. "Don't be afraid, child. What's done is done, an' cain't nobody change what is. I'm your gran'ma too, now—you're with child, ain't you?"

Elise nodded, feeling the blushes still cover her face, and she cleared her throat. "Yes, but—but, how—"

"Child, there's many a baby in this county that I midwifed int' this world, an' I had enough 'a my own as well. I can pretty much tell when a woman's with child."

Elise nodded and looked away again. It did not help her embarrassment that this woman seemed so understanding. She was proud that she carried Janson's child, but she could not help but be embarrassed that this woman—Janson's grandmother of all people—knew that she had been pregnant when Janson had married her.

She heard a soft chuckle from the older woman, and she looked up, surprised to find Deborah Sanders smiling at her, even more surprised when the woman reached to pat her cheek before lowering her large frame to sit on the bench beside Elise. "My boy's gonna be a father," the old woman smiled and shook her head almost incredulously. "It don't seem like Janson ought t' be old enough, but I know he is. I must be gettin' old; seems like it was only yesterday that Nell told me that she was in th' family way. Her an' Henry'd wanted a baby for s' long that it was just like a miracle that they was finally 'spectin'. I'd been prayin' for them for s' long, an' then I prayed even harder that it would be a boy, for Henry's sake. Janson was all there was in th' world t' them two, 'cause he was th' onliest one they had; an' oh, but how they loved each other—can it be three years now that Henry's been gone?" the old woman said, almost to herself, her tone becoming quieter. "An' more'n two years since Nell—"

Elise moved to put her hand on top of the older woman's, and Deborah Sanders's eyes came back to rest on her, a smile returning to her face. "Listen t' me, talkin' about th' past; I am gettin' old. Well, I guess I got a right t' be old, don't I, child, since I'm about t' become a great-gran'ma again in a few months time—" Elise found herself smiling as well at the genuine pleasure on the woman's face—maybe living here would not be so bad after all. Maybe—

"I bet my boy's wantin' a son, ain't he?" Deborah said, moving to push herself up from where she had been sitting on the bench beside Elise, her eyes moving toward the wooden dough bowl on the table, and the bread dough waiting inside.

"He doesn't know yet. I haven't told—"

"Haven't told!" the woman's words interrupted her, her steps halting where she was as she turned back to look at Elise. "Why, you'd better be tellin' him! Child, you should'a done told him. That's somethin' a man's got a right t' know right off."

"I know, it's just—"

"There ain't no excuses t' be had about it; you best be tellin' him. My boy's gonna know, an' he's gonna know t'day—you hear me?" The woman leveled a look at her that allowed no argument.

"Yes, ma'am—" Dear God, she could not let him find out from his grandmother. Elise would have to find him and tell him first.

"I mean it—you best be tellin' him t'day," Deborah Sanders said as she returned to kneading her bread dough. "Now, you finish that food; you're way too skinny t' be havin' babies every year or two. We'll have t' get some meat on your bones." She looked back up at Elise again, giving her a stern look when she did not immediately pick up her fork and obey her words. "You heard me, eat—"

Elise tried to choke down a mouthful of food, any appetite that she may have had now completely ruined. She wanted to tell this woman that Janson was a man now and her husband, and no longer Deborah's "boy" as she kept referring to him. She wanted to tell her that she did not need fattening up, and whether she had babies every year or two was her own business, and Janson's, and none of the old woman's concern. She wanted to tell her that she did not want to eat, even as she tried to force herself to choke down another mouthful of food. She wanted to leave this hot room with all its cooking smells and go and find Janson, to tell him that she was carrying his child before this woman could—she would not let the old woman rob her of that, of being the one to tell him, of being the one to see the look on his face, a look she hoped would be of happiness. She wanted to do anything but sit here obediently and choke down food she did not want—but she stayed and ate, unable to make herself leave, no matter how badly she wanted to.

As soon as she had eaten enough to satisfy the old woman—and had washed the dishes for the first time in her life, just to prove to herself that she did belong here—she got her coat and left the house, hearing Deborah Sanders's admonition once again to stay away from where the men were working. Elise told herself silently, as she stood in the chill air on the small rear porch, the door now closed between them, that she had already had enough of the old woman's interference, enough of her meddling, and that she would go wherever she pleased to go, and that she pleased to go see her own husband.

She made her way down the slanting board steps and across the bare-swept yard, along the edge of the now-cleared winter garden, and toward the barn where it stood at a distance from the house with the cotton fields stretching away from it, feeling the wind pick up and begin to whip her skirt about her legs as she walked. She could hear the voices of the men as she neared the side of the structure, and she realized with a flush of embarrassment that Janson was enduring some good-natured jesting from his uncle and his grandfather at his supposed lack of sleep due to their being newly married. She blushed with embarrassment and stopped where she was, glad she had heard them before she had walked into the conversation.

"That's my business, an' Elise's—ain't nobody else's," she heard Janson say, a stern tone in his voice, and she felt a stab of guilt go through her. There was no reason he should not have gotten plenty of sleep the night before, that is, unless her crying had kept him awake.

She looked back toward the little sharecropped house, the sky low and gray beyond it, not wanting to return there, but knowing she could not walk into the discussion that had been going on, even as she heard the men fall silent for a moment. She sighed and tugged her coat closer about her shoulders, deciding she would have to return to the house, whether she wanted to or not, but then curiosity got the better of her as she listened for a moment, hearing the sounds of the men's breathing, and occasional words and phrases.

"He sure was a big 'un."

"Hope that gamblin' stick's good 'n stout."

"You got them pans ready?" she heard Janson ask.

Curiosity overcame embarrassment, and she moved around the side of the barn to see what they were doing, what she had been warned away from intruding on. At first she could not see, for Janson's grandfather and his uncle blocked her view of Janson and of what it was he was doing. She moved closer at the same moment the two men moved aside, and she saw—

Janson knelt on the ground before a hog strung up for slaughtering. There was a quick swipe of a butcher knife, and then Janson was turning, standing up, the creature's decapitated head in his hands—

Elise covered her mouth, vomit rising to her throat. The glassy eyes in the head seemed to look right at her, and she forced her eyes away— to the carcass that hung headless over a waiting pan. She did not want to look, but could not stop herself. She had known that animals had to be slaughtered for food, but she had never seen, she had never known—it was so barbaric, and the men could do it with seemingly no feeling, no emotion at all.

She finally forced her eyes away, and to Janson, who stood looking at her, a bloody apron tied around his waist. Her Janson—who had cut the creature's head off.

She felt the vomit rise into her mouth, and she turned and ran a few steps away, then fell to her knees, the breakfast she had just eaten coming back up. She hated this place, this barbaric, bloody, superstitious place. She hated these people, and everything about them.

She continued to retch long after there was nothing left to come up. Janson was kneeling beside her, saying gentle words she could not understand—but he did not touch her; he kept his hands away. She looked at his hands again, and thought of what he had done, and she began to retch anew, wishing he would just shut up, wishing he would just go away, wishing he would just leave her alone and never come near her again. The man who had rushed to her, the man kneeling at her side, the man she had married, seemed a stranger now.

The late afternoon sunlight slanted across the yard beyond the window, throwing it into stages of light and shadow. It seemed a familiar sight to Janson, familiar from all the times of visiting his grandparents' home over his years of growing up in this county. So little had changed in the months he had been away, so little—except for his own life. When he had left Eason County in those early January days of 1927, he had been responsible for no one but himself.

He had left, swearing never to return to the county until he could return as a man, until he could return to buy back the land that his parents had fought and died to give him, the land he had lost to the auction block so soon after they had died. Now, less than a year later, he was back, responsible for Elise, as well as himself—and he had not returned as a man should have returned. He had come back to live off his grandparents' charity, bringing Elise to a life he had known she could never understand, for it was a life so far different from the one she had always known in the white-columned great house the Whitleys had lived in for generations. All her life she'd had anything she could ever have wanted—and there was nothing he could give her now to compare to the things she had given up in order to marry him. They had no home, nothing they could really call their own—only each other. He had tried so hard to make her understand—but he knew now that he had failed miserably at getting her to see the kind of life she was choosing in deciding to marry him. He had failed miserably, and at more than making her understand.

He could hear the old floorboards creak behind him as he stared out the window, the sound of the rocking chair moving slowly back and forth where Elise sat in it, but he did not turn to look at her. The room had been chill, and he had built a fire for her, pulling the rocking chair closer to its warmth so that she would not be so cold, but she had said nothing. She had said so very little of anything all day. He stared out the window, feeling more helpless than he ever had before. He knew now that he had made a mistake, perhaps the greatest mistake of his life, to have brought her here.

This was no way of life for Elise Whitley; she was a lady, accustomed to grand and fine things, and he knew he had been a fool to have offered her any less. She could not live in this little house crowded in with so many of his relatives, with his aunts making her feel unwelcome, with Gran'ma's healings, and the country life and ways she could never understand—but he did not know what to do. There seemed nothing he could do now to set things right again. She was his wife, and because of that her father had disowned her. She could never return to her home in Georgia. Janson loved her, but knew already that he had failed miserably at being her husband. He only wanted for her to be happy, only wanted for her to love him.

He was surprised to find her eyes on him when he turned to look at her. There was such a look of sadness on her face, such a look of loneliness, that a stab of pain went through him. He wanted to go to her, but he could not. There seemed a distance between them now that he had never felt before, a distance much greater than that of the room between them, a distance of promises he had made to her that he was afraid now he would never be able to keep. He told her they would have a home of their own, that small, white house on those red acres he had been born to, a life that would have been something in exchange for all she had given up. Now he was afraid that would never be, afraid in a way he had never allowed himself to feel before.

There seemed a sadness in her eyes now as he stared at her, a sadness that broke his heart, and a longing that he was afraid he would never be able to fulfill.

"I'm sorry," he said, simply, staring at her. For a long moment, he could think of nothing more to say. He crossed the room slowly and knelt on the floor at her feet, reaching to take both her hands in his and lifting them to hold them against either side of his face as he stared up at her. "Forgive me for what I've done t' you, for bein' s' blind as t' bring you here—"

"There's nothing to forgive you for," she said, very quietly.

He released her hands and moved to wrap his arms about her legs, laying his head in her lap for a moment. "Don't hate me, please—"

"I could never hate you. You know I could never hate you. It's just that—" For a moment, she fell silent. "Everything's so different, so—" Again, the words seemed to fail her.

Janson squeezed his eyes tightly shut, feeling in that moment that she was slipping away from him, even though he held her, even though his cheek rested against her thigh. She had given up so much to marry him, so much. How could he ever expect—

For a long moment there was silence between them. He could think of nothing to say, even though there were a thousand thoughts and feelings moving through him. Words were so little compared to the things he felt, the things he needed, from her. "I love you," he said at last. "I just want you t' be happy. I just want—"

When he lifted his eyes to her face, he found that she was crying, and that vision tore completely through him.

"Please—oh, God, Elise, I would do anything t' make you happy. I'll work as hard as any man can; you know I will. I'll give you th' home I promised you; I'll give you th' life I promised you, no matter how long it takes me—oh, please, I would do anything. Anything—" For a long moment he stared at her, suddenly knowing, understanding. "Even if that means I have t' take you back home, back t' your folks. Even if it means that I have t' beg your pa t' understand this was all my fault, an' that you need t' be back with your people. Even if that means—"

"No," she said, quietly, shaking her head. "No, I'm not going back home. That's not my home anymore, and it never will be again. My home is here, with you, wherever we have to be to be together."

"But, you'll never be happy here. I know that now—"

She shook her head again. "I'll be happy because I'm with you; that's all that's important. That and—" She fell silent again, her blue eyes searching his own. "Janson," she said quietly, after a time, "we're going to have a baby."

He stared. "A baby?" he said at last, surprised to hear himself say the words, even after he had heard her say them.

"Yes," she said, nodding her head, her eyes never leaving his.

"Are you sure?"

"Yes."

His hands reached out, his fingers to touch her flat stomach through the fabric of her dress—Elise, his Elise, with a baby inside of her. His baby—he could only stare at his hands for a moment. Elise was going to have a baby. They were going to have a—

He looked up at her, finding her watching him closely. For a moment he was too dumbstruck to speak. "We're havin' a baby?" he heard himself say.

"Yes," she said, and he felt himself begin to smile a moment before he realized—

"You're happy about it, ain't you?" he asked, searching her eyes, needing to know.

But suddenly she was smiling, almost with what seemed to be a mixture of relief and worry, as well as with happiness. "You know I am."

"That's not th' reason you're willin' t' stay here, is it? Just because—"

"You know it's not. After everything we've been through to be together—" For a moment she fell silent. "There are a lot of things we both will have to get accustomed to. Everything is so different here, it will just take time for me to get used to it. You have things to get used to as well, you know—" She was suddenly smiling again, looking genuinely happy for the first time since they'd arrived in Alabama. "At least I've had a little time to get accustomed to the idea of becoming a mother—"

"A mother," he said, smiling, the worry leaving him for now in the face of concepts he had not considered coming to them so soon. "You're going to be a mother."

"And, you're going to be a father—the two things go together, you know."

He was grinning helplessly, and he knew it. He just kept touching her

stomach, amazed that inside of her was a new little person. "We're havin'
a baby."

"You're happy about it, aren't you?"

He looked up, surprised that she had even asked. "You know I am."

"I've just been worried, with everything else—"

He shook his head. "None of that's important. Don't even think
about it; I'll take care of everythin'. All you have t' worry about is takin'
care 'a yourself, an' our baby." He grinned, returning to touching her
stomach, amazed at what they had done. "How long have you known?"

"Since just before Daddy found out about us—"

"Since—Elise, that's been—" For a moment he could only stare up
at her. "Why ain't you done told me?"

"With everything that's been happening, having to worry about
getting away, and Daddy hurting you like he did, you almost dying—I
couldn't add even more to the burdens you were already carrying—"

"Burdens? Elise, this ain't no burden. A baby is the farthest thing
from a burden."

"You won't mind there being an extra mouth to feed? Three of us to
support, instead of just two?"

"Lord, woman, what kind 'a man do you think you married? A man's
got t' know children'll come along if he loves his wife th' way he's
supposed t'. I knowed there'd be more 'n two of us sooner or later. I guess
I never thought about it happenin' s' soon, since it took my folks s' long
t' have me after they got married."

She smiled at him. "It must have happened one of the first times we
were together."

He grinned to himself, then stretched up to draw her lips to his. After
a moment, he stood and pulled her up into his arms, to hold her close to
him, more content in that moment than he had ever been. "I love you,
Elise Whitley," he said quietly against her hair.

"Sanders," she reminded him, bringing her eyes to his.

"Mrs. Sanders," he said, looking at her for a long moment, knowing
in that instant what it was to be truly happy.

♣

Janson lay awake before dawn that next morning, having slept very little through the hours of the night. Elise's body lay warm against him, her head on his shoulder, as he stared at the dark shadows that played across the whitewashed ceiling. Daylight would not be long in coming, but there were decisions he still had to make, choices he had never thought to consider. There were three people he was responsible for now—three—and yet he had no job, no roof of his own to put over their heads, no future he could offer his wife or their child. In bringing Elise here to this life he had offered her, in bringing her to his grandparents' home to live off what amounted to little more than their charity for a time, he had been doing all that he had known to do in the circumstances in which they had found themselves. There had been no way they could have stayed in Endicott County, Georgia, and lived as man and wife. William Whitley would never have allowed his daughter to live openly as the wife of a dirt-poor, half-Indian farmer—they had both known that, even before her father had tried to kill him, even before her elder brother had thrown him, unconscious, down a well to die, even before that same brother had stolen the money he had worked so hard for and saved, money that would have brought them a much better life than any he could see for them now. Janson had not even known about the baby then—but he could never have left Elise behind in Georgia, could never have left her behind in her beautiful house and gone on to any kind of life of his own.

Now she was his responsibility, she, and the baby she carried—he was a husband now, and in a number of months would be a father. For the first time he understood how his own father must have felt, in struggling so long, and in finally dying, to try to give his son something that would have been his own. Now that son would have a son or daughter of his own—what could he give his child? And, what could he give Elise? In bringing her here, he had not allowed himself to think beyond the very fact of their being together, trusting that he would find a way for them to build a life—but he had to think beyond that fact now. He had to put a roof of their own over their heads, had to put his own food on their table, had to be the husband and father and man that his parents had raised him to be.

Elise moved slightly in her sleep, curling closer to him as she lay on her side, her soft hair brushing his neck as she settled again, sighing softly in her sleep before becoming quiet. He pulled the patchwork quilts closer about her, for the room was cold still in spite of the fire he had gotten up to put wood on twice already in the night. He moved to press a cheek to her hair, closing his eyes, and losing himself for a moment in the warm feel of her against him—but the thoughts would not go away. He owed her so much more than he was giving her now, so much, in light of all she had given up to become his wife. Elise Whitley's children were meant to be born to wealth and luxury, to a fine home, to a world of electricity and running water, of motor cars and radio and more money than you could ever need—not the things he could give them.

But she had chosen him, and now he had a choice to make, a choice he had never thought to be brought to, but a choice he could no longer see a way around.

He woke her gently in the hour before dawn, and loved her with his body for a time before they rose from the bed to go into this world he had brought her to. He could not help but to watch her as she helped his Gran'ma prepare breakfast that morning, realizing that she had probably never before cooked anything in her life—there were a great many firsts ahead for both of them, he realized.

He was not surprised when, as that day wore on, he found his steps leading him toward a path through the winter-quiet woods, and toward the land that he had been born to, toward the home he had known for the first nineteen years of his life, and the dream that both his parents had given their lives to have. The sky to the west was low and gray as he broke free of the woods at the edge of the winter-dead cotton fields, the air heavy with moisture. It would rain before this day was over, a hard, cold rain that would sit on the red land for days before seeping in.

His steps finally stopped as he reached a rise, where he could see the small, white house where it sat beyond the apple orchard and the clay road. He stood beneath the barren branches of the old oak tree that he had played in as a child, staring at the house where his mother had given him life, and where his father had given him a dream. He was unmindful of the threatening sky or the cold wind that whipped about him as his eyes moved over the yard and toward the Model T car that now sat pulled up before the front steps, his eyes coming to rest on the wide porch and the door to what had been his home. For a moment, he could almost hear the sound of an old, foot-treadle sewing machine, the sound of a woman's voice singing, the creak of a rocking chair, and feel the warmth of a fireplace and a time he knew would never be again. For a moment he could almost feel the presence of the tall, strong man, and the small, dark woman who had once been his world, and the little boy who had lived in their hearts and had somehow carried on their dreams. He stared toward the house, remembering all his father had told him about the struggle and saving, of all the hard work and worry, to have this land and to hold onto it—land that Janson had lost to the auction block.

He stared toward the fields, now barren, the dry cotton plants waiting to be turned under for the new year's cotton crop—fields that had once been burned black in a gasoline-ignited fire that had ended a part of Janson's life forever. He stared toward the edge of the field to the place where his father had died in his mother's arms in the midst of that hellish night, and he could almost smell the smoke, could almost feel the heat, could almost still choke on the smell of the burning lint and the taste of his own hatred as he remembered.

He stared toward the front of the house to the place where Walter Eason had stood little more than a year later, after those months of Janson struggling to try to hold onto the land, after Janson having seen his mother die the winter after his father, after the notice of foreclosure had finally been received—Walter Eason had offered him a job in the cotton mill in town, had told him there would always be a place for him there, for a "good, hardworking boy" like him.

Janson could remember that day so well, could feel the lowered, darkened sky, so like this day, and the hatred as he had stared at the man he knew was responsible for both his parents' deaths, and for his loss of the land. Henry Sanders had refused to sell his cotton crop in the county at the Easons' prices, for he had known that to do so would have meant the loss of the land—but they had lost the land anyway, and Janson had lost both his parents as well. He had thrown Walter Eason off the land that day, and had left Eason County shortly thereafter, knowing he could never work for the Easons, for Henry Sanders had worked and slaved and sworn never to see his son within the walls of that cotton mill, never to see him owned and sweated into old age for someone like the Easons.

Henry Sanders had worked in that cotton mill; he and his wife had saved and dreamed and done without until they could guarantee their son a better life. Janson had grown up with the red land beneath his feet, the first in his family ever born to his own land in a line of Irish tenant farmers, Southern sharecroppers, and dispossessed Cherokee. Janson had never once worked indoors, had never thought to work where he could not see the sun or sky, for he was a farmer, and that was all he had ever wanted to be.

But now there was something he wanted more. Now there was something that meant more to him than the red earth, more even than the dream of owning something that was his own—Elise. Elise and their baby. Now he had a reason to want the land more than for himself alone. Now he had a reason to want it more than as a home he could give Elise— it would one day belong to his son, to grandsons he would someday know. Now there was a reason to accept a roof and walls to work within, as his own father had done. He could not take Elise to a sharecropped farm, for that would be a life far worse than any in town, losing half a crop each year for use of mules and plow and earth, watching their own half eaten up by a store charge they would be forced to run, taking her to live in a drafty shack, for most sharecropped farms were far worse than the one his grandparents cropped on halves—no, that was no life for Elise, or for their children. The choice was made, a choice he would have to live with, a choice he had no alternative to.

He knelt and picked up a winter-brown leaf that had fallen from the branches of the oak tree, then straightened to stare toward the house again—this would be theirs again, one day, no matter how long it took him; one day he would give this to Elise, and to their sons and daughters. Until then he would work, he would slave, he would be sweated into old age if he had to—but this would be theirs.

He crushed the leaf in his hand as he took one last look at the land he had dreamed of through the last year, the way of life he had always known—at the red earth, the tall pines, the all-seeing sky. It was a way of life he would not know again for a very long time, locked within the walls and ceiling of a cotton mill, owned and worked by men he would forever hate. He looked, and he remembered. Then he turned his back and walked away.

# Chapter Two

"It'll kill him," Deborah Sanders said as she pounded the wash that lay on the battling block, using the heavy stick she held in both hands. "He ain't a man for workin' indoors—it'll kill him, sure as I'm standin' here." She pounded the wash even harder, staring across the narrow distance of ground beside her sharecropped home at the girl who was now wife to her grandson. Elise stood nearby, up to her elbows in steaming water, scrubbing clothes up-and-down over the rub board in front of her. The girl did not say a word as she stood in the cold air, a slight mist of steam rising from the washtub before her, and that made Deborah only angrier, even as she prayed again, for the innumerable time, for the patience to deal with the girl.

Janson had been back in Eason County for a little over a month now, having brought this one back with him after almost a year's absence from his family and home—Lord, but Deborah had been surprised to see the sort of girl Janson had taken to wife, with her bobbed-off hair and her short skirts, and—heaven help them both—she had already been with child when Janson married her. Deborah still did not know what to make of this Elise Whitley, except that she was a spoiled child who had never done a day's work in all her life. Deborah had no idea what sort of marriage this was going to be, since the girl had never cooked or cleaned or sewed or made a bed even once in her life for all anyone could tell of her. She had burned so many pans of biscuits and cornbread over the past month that Deborah had worried she would set the house ablaze over their heads if not kept away from the stove—Elise was never going to be able to keep house on her own, Deborah was certain of that, if Janson kept to this fool's plan he had announced to them only this morning. She had known something was coming, had felt it, over the past weeks as Janson had gone about the work that Tom and Wayne had found for him to do about the place—he had only been waiting, finishing up chores he knew would be easier for a younger man to do, even though she realized now that he had known all along that it had many times been make-work that had been given him.

She stared now at this girl through the haze of woodsmoke that came from beneath the black pot of boiling clothes nearby, setting her lips for a moment, then snapping: "You're gonna rub a hole in that shirt. If it ain't clean enough already, put it back int' th' pot t' boil some more."

The girl stopped rubbing the shirt, dunked it back into the wash tub, and reached in for another piece of laundry, coming up with what looked to be the same shirt again, which she then set about scrubbing vigorously on the board. Deborah sighed, exasperated, and reached to sling the wash she had been beating into the girl's tub as well, surprised when Elise only paused for a moment, then went back to rubbing the shirt without saying a word. Heaven help me, Deborah prayed silently, asking God to make her not dislike the girl so much, even as she knew that her own feelings stood in the way of any intercession from the Almighty, for she could find very little even likeable within the girl. Henry and Nell would have been surprised to have seen this little piece of baggage their son had wed, even more surprised to have seen what she had brought him to—Janson working in a cotton mill, Janson working in town, for the very people who had—

Lord, give me strength—first to find out the girl was already with child, then her absolute incompetence at anything wife-like, then, to seal forever what would probably be Deborah's unending dislike of her, the girl had burst into tears when Deborah had told her she would be the one to midwife her child at its birth. Elise had thrown herself on her bed and cried until Janson had promised her a doctor to bring the baby—a doctor, when money was so precious; a doctor, when Deborah had helped bring into the world more babies than anyone else in this county, when she had brought Janson himself into the world, and now she was not good enough for—

Deborah slung a new handful of wash onto the battling block and began to beat it even harder than necessary with the stick, considering the girl's figure, too flat-chested and still too skinny, even though she was already beginning to show with child. She was a pretty little thing, Deborah had to grant her that much, and she could see how Janson might have been attracted to her, with her reddish-gold hair and blue eyes, but Deborah would never have thought it possible that he would have had his head turned to such a degree by this sort of girl, so modern, not at all the sort of girl he had been raised to marry. She had even allowed herself the worry that the child the girl carried might not be Janson's—but she had voiced that concern to no one but Tom, and then only in the privacy of their bed in the night. Tom had told her to hush her mouth, that Elise seemed a good girl, and that Janson loved her dearly. Tom believed the girl loved Janson as well—men could be such gullible fools about some things, Deborah told herself. Such gullible fools.

She heard the front door of the house open and close, and a man's footsteps on the porch, and then descending the steps toward the yard. A moment later Janson walked around the edge of the house, coming toward them where they worked in the side yard. He was dressed neatly in his best dungarees and a work shirt that was neatly pressed, though worn and frayed both at the cuffs and neck. His shoes were knotted together at the strings and slung over one shoulder, and his worn coat was in his hands as he walked to where his wife stood working at the washtub.

Elise had paused in her work and was staring at him, a look on her face that Deborah had not seen there before. Janson stopped before her and dropped his shoes to the ground, then took his coat and wrapped it about her shoulders. "You ought not be out here workin'," he said quietly, but still she did not say anything. He turned to Deborah instead. "Gran'ma, she ought not be out here in the cold with her sleeves rolled to her elbows an' her hands in that water. With th' baby an' all, she ought t' be inside."

Deborah looked at the girl and actually felt a twinge of guilt, realizing she had been working her so hard simply due to her own anger. She herself had worked harder than this throughout each of her own pregnancies, but this girl was not accustomed to such work, to any work at all, and Deborah had known that.

"I'm all right," Elise said at last, drying her hands on the too-big apron Deborah had given her to wear, and then reaching back to take Janson's coat from her shoulders and hold it up for him to slip it on. Janson's hands closed over hers instead as she held the coat for him, and he looked down at her for a moment.

"I'll be back soon as I can," he said. "Don't be worried if it's late."

"I won't be. I just hope someone will stop to give you a ride into town, so you don't have to walk so far."

"Somebody probably will. If not, I'll walk it; I've done it before."

She nodded, and after a moment he drew her closer, holding her against him as his mouth came to hers. Deborah cleared her throat self-consciously, and, after a moment they separated, Janson finally moving to allow her to help him with his coat, and then turning back to look at her again.

"You go in an' rest in a little while, you hear me?" he told her, and she nodded. He glanced at his grandmother for a moment, but did not say anything more, then he turned to look about the yard, toward the sharecropped house one more time, toward the fields where the dry cotton plants had recently been turned under, his eyes moving over the red land in a way that Deborah had so often seen before. For a moment he looked torn. There was a longing in him that she could almost feel— and then it was gone.

He straightened his back and turned his eyes toward his wife again, a brief smile touching his lips as he looked at her one last time before taking up his shoes and starting toward the road that would take him into town and away from the only kind of life he had known throughout his twenty years. Deborah watched him go, seeing him turn back to wave toward them before the rise of the land could cut off sight of the house behind him. She saw the girl wave in return, but Deborah did not. She could only turn back to her work, thinking of the years her son Henry had spent in that cotton mill, and of how often she had heard him swear that his son would have a better life.

Walter Eason sat in his office at the mill that morning, listening to the words of his son, Walt, but his eyes never left the hands folded neatly atop the massive oak desk, his own hands—his knuckles were large, his fingers long and tapering. Dark veins stood out along the backs of both hands; his nails were neatly groomed. Here and there were signs of his seventy-plus years, but the aging did not bother him. His hands were steadier still than many a younger man's; they still held strength and assurance, as well as the wisdom he hoped that his years had brought him. They were hands that held influence far beyond this mill or Eason County, or even Alabama itself, hands that he was proud of, as he was proud of anything that was his own.

Walter sat looking at his hands as his son, sitting at the far side of the desk in a leather-covered armchair, delivered news that Walter did not want to hear. He listened, until long after the younger man had finished talking, but still did not say a word. He heard the shifting of his son's abundant weight in the other chair, the creak of the upholstery, the clearing of a throat, a waiting and then silence, then he lifted his gray eyes and considered the man opposite him.

His only grandson, Walt's only son and Walter's hope for the future of his family and of his county, was causing difficulties again—but Buddy had been causing difficulties almost from his birth. Only the family name had kept him out of trouble with the law on several occasions in his eighteen years, but even the Eason name could not go on protecting him forever. He had to grow up someday if he were ever to assume the responsibility that would one day come to him.

After a long moment, Walter spoke. "Will the other boy recover?"

"Dr. Thrasher said that he would, though Buddy would have killed him if someone hadn't pulled him off of the boy first."

Walter nodded his head, considering. "Over a girl, you say—one of Buddy's girlfriends?"

"No, the other boy's—Buddy was, well—"

"And the boy's parents?" Walter asked. He knew very well what his grandson was like; he did not have to be told, and he wanted none of the sordid details.

"The boy's father is keeping his mouth shut."

"Donner's a good worker," Walter said, nodding. It was his highest praise.

"But, Donner's wife—" He did not continue, and did not have to. Walter expected nothing less than complete loyalty out of a millhand, no matter the circumstances.

"When the shift's over, give Donner and his wife both their notice. I want them out of their mill house by day-end tomorrow—and make sure his wife keeps her mouth shut."

The last words were said with a feeling that Walter showed only on such occasions. He could not allow such talk in the mill or the village. Complaint bred nothing but discontent—the more people talked, the unhappier they were; the unhappier they were, the more they wanted, and there could be nothing more a mill villager could want than what Walter Eason provided for them. They were poor; they worked long hours in the mill, and lived out their lives in mill houses he owned. They married other mill villagers, and had children just like themselves, too ill-equipped to make more of themselves than what they came into life with, for it was not within Walter to believe that anyone would be poor in the first place if he had any drive or ambition within him. All they could do was complain and cause trouble if they were given the chance, gaining for themselves freedoms they were never equipped to handle. They should be content in their neat homes along their clean streets, content with their steady wages, and the food on their tables, content that their children would come into the mill just as they had—he guaranteed them work; he guaranteed them shelter; he guaranteed them existence. What more could any of them need?

A discreet tap came at the door, and Walter looked up to see the secretary enter. "Yes, Grace?" Walt asked, an annoyance evident in his voice that brought his father's eyes to him. Walter had stressed to both his sons never to show emotion, anger or annoyance, before any other human being. To do so only made one appear weak, and Walter Eason would have no member of his family appear weak before anyone.

"I didn't mean to bother you, Mr. Eason, but there's a young man here, and I knew there was an opening in the card room—"

"Well, send him on to the overseer, and don't bother me with hiring. What do you think I pay you for?"

Walter gritted his teeth, wanting in that moment to reach across the wide expanse of the desktop and grab his son by the shirt front. When he had reached the age of sixty-five, he had given Walt a form of authority over the cotton mill, but, in the more than five years since, he had not been able to bring himself to divest complete responsibility for the enterprise, still maintaining his office in the mill just as he always had. It was times such as this when Walter could see the wisdom in not having turned the complete control of the mill over to his son. Walt lacked the temperament to manage a business as vast and involved as the cotton mill, village, and the related enterprises.

"But, the young man, he asked to see you, Mr. Walter, personally, and I thought you would want to see him—it's Henry Sanders's boy, Janson."

Walter brought his eyes back to Grace quickly. "Janson Sanders is here, looking for work?"

"Yes, sir." There was relief evident on the woman's face that it had been Walter who had addressed her this time.

"We had enough trouble out of that boy's father," Walt began. "We don't need the son now bringing the roof down on our heads. Tell him—"

"Send him in," Walter said, and the woman moved immediately to obey his words, even as Walt, with his paper title, blustered in opposition.

"You know what trouble Henry Sanders was, selling his cotton out of the county, thinking he could do whatever he damned well pleased, when every other farmer in this county stayed in line and sold their crop here. He was so damn proud, and so damn stubborn, that if he hadn't died when he did he might have started others following him—and that boy of his was even worse. I tell you, I won't have him in this—"

Walter stared him into silence, seeing the anger in his son's face at having his orders countermanded. It had been a long time since Walter had struck his son, but at that moment he wanted to—he wanted to thrash him as he had done so many times when he had been a small boy showing his bluster in disrespect.

The door opened again and the secretary entered, followed by Janson Sanders. Walter turned his attention from the angry man who sat across the desk from him, to the angry one who stood now near the doorway. The boy looked older, much older, in fact, than the passage of a year should have allowed him, and, for having all the coloring and features of his dark, Cherokee mother, he reminded Walter in that moment of no one so much as the tall, reddish-brown-haired man who had made such a problem of himself those years before. Henry Sanders had concerned him as few other men ever had. There had been something in the man that could not be controlled, something that could not be broken—and that something showed in the eyes of the young man who stood before Walter now.

Janson Sanders held his head high. He looked at Walter, at Walt, then back to the older man, meeting his gaze with a pride in his eyes that showed a sense of self even beyond what had been in Henry Sanders. The boy nodded his head and addressed Walter directly, the green eyes, so odd in the dark face, never leaving his own.

"You told me once there was a place in th' mill for me if I wanted it." The boy met his gaze levelly, that indomitable pride in his eyes, as if demanding respect by his very bearing as few men ever could.

Walter looked at him, at the straight, black hair, the high cheekbones, the odd green eyes, at the worn coat and dungarees, and at the scuffed work shoes, remembering that day, more than a year before, when he had made the offer. He had gone to the Sanders farm after he had received word at last that the land was being foreclosed on. He had gone to offer the boy a job, and a decent house in the village. The boy had lost both his parents, and now he had lost his home as well; Walter had assumed that he was beaten, finished in life even as Henry Sanders had never been finished even in death—but the boy had ordered him from his land, staring at him with that same hatred that sat in his eyes even now. It took a great deal of character, or stupidity, for the boy to be able to come to him today in acceptance of that same offer, and Walter wondered as he stared at him what it had taken in the past year to bring the boy to this.

"As I recall, you told me to get the hell off your land," Walter said, watching Janson closely.

"I've got a wife now, an' a baby on th' way. I've got t' have steady work, an' a decent place for her t' live." His gaze never wavered.

"A baby, eh?" All the county needed now was another generation of these peculiar men. He considered Janson for a long moment, remarking to himself again how like the father this son was. There had been something within Henry Sanders that Walter had grudgingly respected, just as there had also been something within the man that Walter had feared, as he had feared few things in his life. Henry Sanders had not been content to be who and what he was, just as this boy before Walter now was not content. They both held a desire to have something that was all their own, not to be beholden to anyone or anything for their livelihoods or their dreams—and Henry Sanders's dreams had at last cost him his life, as well as his land. Walter knew this boy held him responsible for his father's death, as well as for the foreclosure that had taken his farm; the boy had made no secret of his feelings before he left the county a year before.

And now he was back, with a wife, and a child on the way, having reached a moment in his life that the boy would never have thought to see himself reach, and, as Walter stared at him, he could almost feel responsible—

"Go see the overseer of the card room," Walter told him, never once letting his gaze leave the green eyes. "Tell him you're on the night shift, and go see the house boss for your house assignment; the rent will be held from your wages."

Janson Sanders stared at him without speaking, and Walter returned the stare, not moving his eyes toward his son even as he heard Walt mutter angrily just beneath the level of his hearing. After a time, Janson nodded his head just once and left. Walter watched him go, not surprised in the least when the boy did not say thank you.

Less than an hour later, Janson left the white-painted office building that sat before the mill and made his way, following directions from a nervous little man in a tiny office, toward the place that would be home to him, and to Elise, for what could be many years to come. Row upon row of neat, white-painted frame houses sat on either side of the red dirt streets that led away from the mill. The houses all looked the same, with their small, neat yards and tiny, cleared garden patches, their stacks of cordwood against side walls, their chimneys with smoke drifting out, their tin roofs and gray porches—all the same. Most he passed were of six rooms, divided down the middle, he knew, for two families, an outside water faucet in the yard between every other structure. Occasionally he passed a four-room structure, one designed for the fixers on each shift, or a three-room shotgun house where no larger home would fit.

He stared at the houses, the structured sameness of the place seeming odd to his eyes more accustomed to the never-ending change of the countryside. God might not have made any two things alike, but Walter Eason had tried to, with these identical houses along these identical rows throughout the village. But, even here, touches of individuality did show through. Chairs and rockers sat on porches; flower beds and garden patches, neatly cleared for winter, were marked off in various yards; trees and plants grew and were tended. A dog was tied before one house, and a cat slept on the porch of another. Milk cows stared back at him from beneath houses that sat supported high off the hilly ground on one side by stone pillars; gaudy flowered curtains hung in one window, sedate lace ones in another.

Janson nodded to the few people he passed on the street, not recognizing a single face. He felt out of place in this village, and he found himself wondering how Elise would be able to survive here—but this was the best he could do. At least it would be a roof of their own, a home that he could provide. Something he could do. Part of him still resisted the knowledge that he would be working for the Easons, that he would be bringing Elise and their child under the Easons' control—but he had no choice. The events of the past year had left him with little choice in anything.

He could hear a train passing along the edge of the village on tracks that ran beside the mill, tracks that effectively cut the town in half. On the other side of those tracks lay the business district, the big churches and nice homes, the town schools and Main Street. On this side lay the mill and the mill village, the row upon row of mill houses the Easons owned, the small stores the Easons rented to proprietors, and the small Methodist and Baptist churches the mill villagers attended. On this side was the cotton warehouse that sat just behind the mill and alongside the railroad tracks, the village school for the children of the mill workers, the small power plant that supplied electricity to the mill and mill office, and the water plant and tower that supplied the faucets throughout the village—all owned by the Easons. The Eason family owned much of the businesses and property on the other side of those tracks as well, owned, or at least controlled, much of the county, but on this side, in the village, they owned all, down to the last thought, the last feeling, the last impulse they could lay hands on.

The noise of the mill followed him through the streets of the village, as did the lint that floated in the air. This was an existence so far from any he had ever thought to have, and so different from the one he had hoped to bring Elise to, that he was surprised at his own feelings as he finally reached his destination and stared up at the house that was his assignment. It was a house like any other on this street, divided down the middle to be shared by two families. It sat on a rise, sandwiched between two houses that looked very much the same, high off the ground on stone pillars in the front, flush with the level of the yard in the back. Its gray porch, smoke-blackened chimneys, tin roof, and twin front doors much the same as the others, its yard just as neatly tended—but, as he stared up at it, he felt a degree of satisfaction that he had not felt since before the money he had worked for and had saved to buy back his land was stolen. This half of a house would be something he could do, a home that he could give to Elise, could give to his child, and to other children who would one day come to them.

He looked at the place, memorizing every detail, wanting to take it in memory back to his grandparents' home so that he could tell Elise about it—he was going to give her a home; he was doing his job, the job of a man, of a husband and father. He knelt at the side of the road and took his shoes off, smiling at a little boy of about five who played, bundled in a coat much too big for him, in a yard nearby. In a few years his son or daughter would be playing here. Elise would make friends, and he would work hard—life would not be so bad, he told himself. He had the woman he wanted. He would be a father in a few months time. He had a dream to work for. The rest he would take care of himself with his own sweat and work, just as his own father had. Sweat and work were two things he did not fear.

He knotted his shoestrings together and stood, slinging his shoes over one shoulder as he looked up at the house once again. It might be a long walk before someone offered him a ride back toward his grandparents' place, and it would be even more difficult to get back into town late that afternoon in time for the night shift in the mill, but perhaps he could borrow his Gran'pa's wagon. He was hungry, and he wanted to see Elise, to touch and love her and tell her about the house, and maybe have her lie in his arms while he tried to get some rest before returning for his first shift in the mill. He would have to get at least a few hours sleep this afternoon, or he would be dead on his feet by the morning when his shift ended—but he would not worry about that just now.

He stared at the house—two weeks, he told himself. Two weeks, and he and Elise would move here. Two weeks, and this would be their home. The man who lived in half of this house now, the half that would be their home, had held the job that Janson would begin on learner's wages tonight. In two weeks he would be leaving this home he had held for ten years, just as he had left the job he had held for even longer. He had been fired—not for dishonesty or unsatisfactory work, the mill's nervous house boss had told Janson, not for a sharp tongue or trouble-making on the job, but because his children had started a fight with other children on the way home from the village school one day. Walter Eason tolerated misconduct from the children and families of his millhands no better than he did from the millhands themselves.

What a pretty hell I've bought for us, Janson thought, staring up at the house, realizing that no matter how satisfied he felt to be doing something on his own for his wife and for the family they were making, he had very likely gained that satisfaction by selling their souls to the devil in exchange.

The first night Janson worked in the mill, he saw a man mangled in the machinery.

It had been a careless movement, a moment's inattention, and the man's arm was jerked into the cards while he was stripping cotton dust out of a machine. From that moment, the sight of that mangled arm would not leave Janson, giving him a healthy aversion for machines that could cost him an arm, or even his life. There was too much talk in the mill of lost arms and broken bones, of women who had their hair ripped out by machinery in the spinning room, or of a card hand killed when he had gotten caught in the belt that ran from the machinery to the drive shaft near the ceiling. Janson could not afford to take chances; Elise was depending on him. He knew he was risking enough to be working for the Easons in the first place, for he well knew what they could be capable of doing to a man in Eason County—and, if he had not known, Walt Eason had given him a clear reminder on his first shift in the mill, coming into the card room only minutes after the bleeding man had been taken out, to stand staring at Janson for an interminable time, his arms crossed before his chest. The man had not spoken, but his eyes had never once left Janson—it had been a clear warning, a warning that Janson had understood. He was being watched, and it would take only one mistake to cost him home, shelter, livelihood, and much more in Eason County.

To Janson, the first weeks working in the mill seemed to stretch into forever. He saw Elise only for the short while between the long rides to and from town and an exhausted sleep, with what seemed almost too little time in the afternoons when he finally woke to dress, eat, and begin the long ride back to town to start the next shift. He found as the days passed that he hated the mill more than he had thought possible, but the time away from Elise was even worse. The twelve-hour shifts five days a week left little time for anything except eating, sleep, and the never-ending rides in the creaky wagon to and from work, rides ending in the walk across town from the wagon lot on Main Street to the mill village, since the town would no longer allow mules, horses, and wagons free roam of the village any more than they would the town area on the other side of the railroad tracks. Janson stole whatever time he could to be with Elise, even though his body was exhausted from both work and the wagon rides, his mind numb from the machinery and noise he had endured through the night, and his lungs choked on the cotton dust he had breathed in the card room. He told himself that things would be better once they were living in the village, even though he hated the thought of bringing Elise to live in this place. At least they would be alone, in half a house that would be their own, until the baby came. At least there would be no more endless hours behind the plodding mules to get to his shift—things would be better then.

On the last night of the two weeks, Janson sat on an overturned dye-can on the loading dock just outside the large doors that led into the opening room of the mill. He had chosen this place to take his brief, middle-of-the-night break to eat once he had his job caught up enough to take the time. The air was almost unbearably cold, chilling him through his worn coat and the legs of his overalls as he sat eating, but he would not go back inside until he had to. The open sky was far preferable over the noise and cotton dust within the confines of the card room, or even the stuffy atmosphere of the lunch room where he knew he could have gone to eat.

The sausage sandwich he ate, on thick slices of home-baked bread, was long ago cold, but he was so hungry that it did not matter. It was good to be hungry, good to be working, sweating and earning a wage, even if it was over machinery and not behind a plow or dragging a pick sack. He missed the sky, the sun and earth as he worked. It seemed so odd to look up during his shift to see the dark ceiling overhead, beyond the glaring electric lights that lighted the card room, so odd to have the noise of the machinery in his ears, a noise that stayed in his head even when he was far away from this place.

Janson bit into the cold, fried apple pie that was the last of his meal, listening to the sound of a train whistle as boxcars and a caboose moved down the nearby tracks and at last left his sight, then his eyes moved back to the darkness of the village. There was no light showing anywhere that he could see, except for the mill itself. A light burning at some unusual hour would bring a neighbor or even someone from the mill to investigate, to make certain there was no sickness or trouble, and, as Janson had already learned, most of the people who lived on these peaceful streets preferred not to bring attention to themselves.

By the next night Elise would be sleeping in one of these dark houses. It would be good to have her so close, to know he would be able to return to her once the shift was over, without the long wagon ride to get through, to be able to touch and love her and glory in the daily changes in her body that the baby was causing, without the worry that Gran'ma or Gran'pa or someone else would hear them. There might be neighbors on the other side of the house, but it would be more privacy than they had known under his grandparents' roof.

Janson closed his eyes and leaned his head back against the wall, thinking of having Elise all to himself at last, thinking of her hair, and the feel of her skin, the newly gentle rounding of her belly against him, and the knowledge that his child was inside of her. He could see her so clearly in his mind, more lovely now than when he had first met her—less than a year ago, and both of their lives changed so completely since then. It still amazed him that she was his wife, as he guessed it would amaze him to the day he died.

There was a sound from the doorway, and he opened his eyes and turned in time to see the dark form of a man starting back into the mill. For one brief moment Janson saw the man's face, and what he saw there in that instant was more anguish than he had ever thought to see in any man.

"Nathan, what's wrong?" he asked, recognizing the man as the night janitor of the mill, Nathan Betts, whom he had seen in passing over the last two weeks.

Nathan stopped, but did not turn back. It was a long time before he spoke, and, when he did, there was a choked sound in his voice. "We—" he stopped for a moment again, his eyes set on a place somewhere in the distance as he took a deep breath before he seemed able to continue, "we buried my wife this mornin'."

Buried—the word sat on Janson for a moment. He had no idea what to say. He rose from where he had been sitting on the dye-can and went to stand beside the older man, watching as Nathan pulled a handkerchief from the back pocket of his trousers to wipe at his wet eyes.

"What happened?" Janson asked at last.

"She had a boy, th' boy we'd been hopin' for after our two girls—but, after, th' bleedin' wouldn't stop. It hadn't been like that before, with th' girls, an' th' granny woman, no matter what she did, she couldn't make it stop. She sent me for th' doctor, but it was too late—"

Tears started down his cheeks again, tears he did not try to wipe away, as he looked at a memory that Janson knew he could not help but to unfold.

"She bled to death before we could get back. Th' granny woman had her covered over with th' sheet." His words trailed off as he stood in silence and cried, the tears rolling from his cheeks now and dripping onto hands that Janson could see were shaking.

"You don't need t' be here t'night, Nathan—"

But the older man shook his head, anger mixing in his voice with the grief. "I asked Mr. Walt for a few more days, t' give me time t' find somebody t' keep my girls an' th' baby while I'm workin', time t' just take care 'a things, an' t' give th' girls time t' realize their mama's with Jesus now and that she ain't comin' back—they're both s' little, they can't understand—"

"You need time, too. You lost your wife—"

Nathan wiped at his eyes again with the handkerchief, and then a look of forced and bitter determination came over his face as he folded the square of material and shoved it back into his pocket. "Mr. Walt told me that he'd done give me two days, that she was buried now, an' that there wasn't nothin' I could do t' bring her back. He told me I had a job t' do, children t' support, an' that I'd better start thinkin' about them an' not about me—as if even once since th' day th' first was born I ever thought of me over them, as if even once—" The bitterness seemed to fill him for a moment to the point there was no room for anything else. "I can't afford t' lose my job, even if it means leavin' my children with th' neighbor woman every night, an' her s' old she can't hardly walk, hearin' my youngest girl screamin' as I leave because she's afraid I ain't gonna be able t' come back since her mama can't ever again—" Tears started from the edges of his eyes again, but he did not seem to notice. "Sometimes you got t' find strength in you t' do things you never thought you'd have t' do."

Janson stared at him. "If there's anythin' me or my wife can do t' help, you let me know."

Nathan brought his eyes to him and looked at him for a moment. "You really mean that, don't you?" he asked. "Most white men wouldn't make a offer like that t' a colored man, no matter what's happened in his family."

"My pa was white an' my ma Cherokee," Janson said. "We're all one color or another—besides, it's what's inside a man that makes him what he is."

Nathan nodded. After a time he turned and started back into the mill. Janson watched him go, realizing in that moment that he had felt a degree of kinship with this man that he had felt toward few other people—Nathan Betts was here in the mill tonight not for himself, but for the sake of the family he had made with the wife he had buried today. He was here, not for himself, but for those he was responsible for. That was something Janson could respect far beyond the power or money of someone like Walt or Walter Eason.

He looked out over the darkened mill village one last time, then turned and went back into the mill, knowing that work waited for him.

❧

Within days of moving into the mill village, Elise hated the sight of the huge, red-brick mill with its white-painted office out front and its tall chimneys billowing smoke throughout the village. She hated the flying lint that floated in the air for streets away, that stuck to her hair and clothing. But most of all she hated the sound of the machinery. No matter where she went, it was always there, keeping her awake at night as she lay alone in her bed, grating at her nerves in the daytime as Janson slept alone in the front room of their house, following her from morning to night and to morning again.

She longed for quiet and peace during those first weeks in the village, longed for someone to talk to, for books to read, for something to occupy her time as the minutes of each day dragged by. She found herself wishing for her mother, even for the constant harping of Janson's grandmother— someone, anyone, to help her fill the hours of her days.

Most of all, she wanted Janson, but he seemed more distant from her than at any time since she had known him. He seemed driven to work, driven to earn, to prove something to her that did not need proving, accepting the shortened Saturday shift any time it was offered to him, sleeping through the days, waking only to hold her for a while, eat, dress, and return to that god-awful place that dominated life in the village—he hated the mill and the village even more than she did, and she knew it, though he never said a word. She knew he was working in a place he had never thought he would find himself because of her, and because of the baby.

He returned from his shift in the card room each morning, tired and hungry, covered with lint and cotton dust, and weary to his soul. He would eat whatever she had prepared for him, then fall into an exhausted sleep, no matter the hour. For the first week she tried to rearrange her sleeping so that she could lie beside him, but found that she could not sleep, no matter how tired she could make herself, so long as it was light outside. The only time she lay with him was for loving, and to watch him sleep afterward, before rising to try to find something she could do.

She tended their three rooms, doing housework for the first time in her life, housework she quickly decided she hated, in a house filled with mismatched furniture that had once belonged to his parents or that was borrowed from his relatives or given to them outright. She was determined to prove to herself, and to Janson, and to his grandmother as well, that she could be a good wife—the old woman had told her she was too spoiled to ever keep a decent house, which had made her all the more determined, and, it seemed, all the more doomed to failure. Each pan of burned biscuits now reduced her to tears; each meal that Janson did not compliment seemed inedible; each cobweb in a corner or hole in a sock seemed a slap in the face, until she sometimes thought she swung from crying jags to bouts of homesickness with nothing in between.

She could hear the neighbors' voices in the other half of the house during the days, the many Breedloves as they came and went, hearing the children's voices, even the parents arguing. She could smell their meals cooking, and hear their lives going on right here under the same roof as hers, and that made her feel all the worse. She could feel her body changing, the baby growing inside of her, and it had her mind in a turmoil. She was no longer the girl she had been, yet she was not sure who she was supposed to be. Life in the village was so different—and it was boring, so unendingly boring.

She wrote long letters to her mother and to her brother, Stan, and received long letters in return. Her mother's writings were falsely cheerful, prattling on about people she knew, gossiping about neighbors, and showing a genuine excitement over the grandchild that Martha Whitley had to know she would likely never see. Stan's letters were much more honest, and his honesty tore right through Elise's heart—her name could no longer be spoken in her father's house. Her room had been dismantled, her things either burned or given away to the colored families who lived at the edge of town. The people she had grown up with had been told that her father had thrown her out, that she was an ungrateful daughter who was at last getting what she rightly deserved. No mention was to be made of her, or of the "damned half-breed" she had married, and, when her mother at last told her father that she was pregnant, he said that he hoped that neither she nor her baby survived the birth.

She was dead to him, and he wanted every part of her dead as well, and, as Elise went through the days, she began to feel that a part of her really was dying, the part of her that had been Elise Whitley, the part that had been young and carefree and so excited just to be a young woman of the twenties. She could remember being that girl; she could remember being excited over new dresses and shades of lipstick, of wanting to be bold and daring and a bit shocking—but she wasn't that girl anymore, and she knew she never would be again. She was Janson's wife, and, though her entire world had changed because of him, she still wanted nothing else so much as to be his wife—she just wanted time with him, and something to do with the hours when they were apart. She just wanted to know who she was now, and to figure out her place in this new world. She had always had friends in Endicott County, people very much like herself, and she realized that she had defined who she was through those friends—but she had no friends here except for Janson himself.

She began to attend the Baptist church in the village, going alone, for Janson usually slept on Sunday mornings. She quickly became part of the choir, and was delighted when people made a fuss over her and told her how well she sang, until she realized she was valued primarily for her ability to drown out one of the other choir members, Helene Price, who sang loudly and usually quite off key, and who seemed to think that she could run the choir and the church and many of the other church members. Elise decided that she detested Helene, and it did not take long to realize that at least one other of the choir members felt much the same.

"Thinks she's somethin', don't she?" she heard someone say as she was putting on her coat after choir practice on a Wednesday evening late that February. She turned to find Dorrie Keith just behind her, the heavy-set woman taking up her own coat from where it had lain across the back of a pew. Dorrie was the only person Elise had met who was outspoken enough to tell Helene Price when she was flat or in the wrong key.

Elise followed her gaze, and found Helene standing near the front of the church talking to the preacher, Reverend Satterwhite.

"Thinks she's so high-and-mighty," Dorrie was saying, bringing Elise's eyes back to her. "I remember when she was just Helen, growin' up at the edge of town. Her family was about th' poorest I know of, 'cause my mama used t' feed them young'ns more than their own folks ever fed them—then she married Bert Price, and him th' boss of th' supply room, and she was suddenly Helene, all high and mighty, but she ain't nothin' but Helen, no matter what she thinks of herself."

Elise found that she liked Dorrie Keith as heartily as she detested Helene, and was surprised when she learned the two were distant cousins.

"She just about lived at our house growin' up," Dorrie told Elise one day, "though t' hear her talk now you'd 'a thought we were her poor relations—tried t' give me a old wore-out dress of hers not too long ago, as if I'd have some old rag she'd wore—"

Dorrie lived with her husband, Clarence, and their four sons only a few streets away from Elise and Janson in the mill village, and Elise began walking to church on Sunday mornings and afternoons and Wednesday evenings by way of Dorrie's house.

It was nice to finally have a friend in the mill village, even if that friend was old enough to be Elise's own mother, nice to have another woman to talk to about being pregnant, and about what having a baby would be like.

Elise sat in Dorrie's kitchen late on a Thursday afternoon in March. Janson had left for his shift in the card room at the mill and would not be home until early the next morning, and Elise had been looking for company when she had walked the few streets to Dorrie's house. Dorrie had just gotten in from the shift she worked in the spinning room, and was beginning supper for her family, but she had been uncharacteristically silent almost from the moment she had met Elise at the door. Dorrie was peeling potatoes for supper, her eyes going to the door repeatedly, until Elise at last asked her what was wrong.

"They sent for Clarence just as soon as we got in from our shift, told him t' bring Wheeler James t' th' mill office," Dorrie said, meeting Elise's eyes from where she sat just opposite Elise at the old table then looking away again. "Men—" she said, the word coming out almost as if it were a curse. She peeled viciously at a potato, taking away chunks of white with the peelings, "they think we got nothin' t' say when they go t' talk somethin' important. Women're there t' birth 'em, an' bury 'em, an' in between we get t' clean their bottoms an' bandage their heads an' put 'em t' bed if they've had a drunk—they sent for Wheeler James an' for Clarence with no mention 'a me, as if I ain't been in th' mill every bit as long as Clarence, as if I ain't Wheeler James's mama, as if I ain't got nothin' t' say, or even th' right t' know—"

"Why would they want to see Wheeler James at the mill office?" Elise asked. Wheeler James was Dorrie's oldest son, only a couple of months younger than Elise herself, very tall and thin, with a quiet manner that did little to show the brilliant mind that Elise had found behind his brown eyes and shy smile. He seemed to know something about almost any subject she could bring up, and could do mathematics in his head that she could never hope to do with pencil and paper and unlimited time.

"Mr. Eason offered him a night shift in th' twister room at th' mill, soon as school's out this year," Dorrie said, an odd tone in her voice.

"A night shift—for the summer?"

"No, permanent." Dorrie's eyes moved back toward the door, and Elise realized she was waiting for her husband and son to return from the mill office.

"But, there's no way he can work all night and go to school the next day."

"I know that."

"But, he shouldn't quit school; there's so much he could do with his life. He—"

"Don't you think I know that?" Dorrie asked, anger coming to her brown eyes and into her voice as she turned to look at Elise once again. "Don't you think I know how smart he is? Don't you think I know that he's got in him t' be anythin' he wants t' be—I've knowed it since he was talkin' in complete sentences at two, an' readin' books when he was only four. I've watched him grow up, thinkin' every day, dreamin' every day, about him finishin' school, not just the village school here, but goin' on beyond it, maybe even college—"

"Then, why—" But Elise's words were cut short as the door that led from the rear porch into the kitchen opened, and Clarence entered followed by Wheeler James. Clarence did not bring his eyes to his wife, but turned instead to take the battered hat from his head and hang it on a peg by the door. Wheeler James walked past him without a word, not looking at his mother or Elise. He crossed the room and went through the doorway into the middle room of their half of the house, closing the door silently behind himself. Elise watched him go, then turned her eyes back to Clarence and Dorrie, seeing a look of what seemed to be almost physical pain pass between them.

"Wheeler James comes int' th' mill just as soon as school's out this year," Clarence said, quietly.

For a moment Dorrie did not speak. She still held the small knife in her hand, the bowl of half-peeled vegetables now forgotten on the table before her. "What if he went t' live with Aunt Min? It wouldn't be th' same as livin' here, but he could finish school, an' then maybe—"

But Clarence was shaking his pale head. "It won't work, Dorrie. If he don't come int' th' mill this summer, Mr. Eason'll put us out 'a this house, an' out 'a th' mill—we got th' other boys t' think about. We can't be losin' our jobs an' th' roof over our heads."

"He wouldn't do that, not just because Wheeler James won't come int' th' mill. There's plenty 'a people willin' t' take a shift, grown men with families, an' women who are needin' th' work. One boy can't really matter that much—" But, even as Dorrie said the words, Elise could see she did not believe them.

Clarence was staring at his wife, a look of pity in his light-colored eyes, and Elise wondered who the pity was for: Wheeler James, who wanted nothing more than to finish school, Dorrie who was seeing her dreams for her son ripped apart before her eyes, or Clarence, who had dreamed of something better for his sons. "There's nothin' we can do, Dorrie. Mill houses are for mill workers, and mill workers' children are expected t' come int' th' mill in their own time—we've always knowed that. Mr. Eason ain't gonna let Wheeler James go against what's been done all these years, even if it means puttin' us all out in th' street."

Or burning a cotton crop, or costing a man the land his parents had fought and died to give to him, just to keep the same kind of control over the farming community that he had over the mill village, Elise thought. Her eyes came to rest on Dorrie and on the knife Dorrie still held only an instant before Dorrie's free hand closed over the blade.

Elise rose to her feet, seeing a flicker of physical pain pass across Dorrie's features, and then stopped as Dorrie opened her fingers outward to drop the knife and stare at the blood spreading across her open palm. Clarence was suddenly kneeling beside her, pulling a white handkerchief from his pocket to wrap it around her hand.

"We got t' accept it. We knowed it was comin'," she heard him say, but Dorrie seemed not to hear him. She had instead turned her eyes to stare out the window, and Elise turned to look out as well. "There ain't no other choices left," she heard Clarence say at last, and Elise wondered if those few words were supposed to explain the world in which they were living.

The sky was gray and threatening rain, the air chill, with a bite to it that said winter was not yet over as Janson left the mill on a Saturday morning in mid-March. He was tired from his twelve-hour shift in the card room, his feet aching from standing on them all night, but there was satisfaction within him, as there was each Saturday morning when he left the mill. The card room received their pay envelopes at the end of each Friday night shift, and Janson had his already counted, neatly folded away in the bib pocket of the overalls he wore beneath his coat. It was one more week's pay from which he might save even some small amount toward buying back his land one day.

He wanted nothing more now than to go home and hold Elise in his arms, and to count his pay again with her, so they could see how much they would have to use for food and for other necessities this week. With any luck, there would be at least a few coins they could put away in the fruit jar Elise had hidden in the old cupboard in the kitchen. Another week, a few more coins saved; it was a good feeling.

His stomach rumbled, reminding him that he was hungry. He could see other mill workers leaving from their shifts through the main entrance, the wide double doors set into the front of the building, doors that opened into the card room near the drawing frames, and that led to the staircase that rose to the twister room on the second floor of the mill, and the spinning room where Elise's friend, Dorrie, worked the day shift. Janson liked to leave through the picker and opening rooms, thus reaching the outdoors much sooner than the trip through the length of the card room to the main entrance would have allowed. Besides, it prevented him from being stopped by someone to talk; when his shift was over he wanted to go home, not stand around talking.

He smiled to himself, thinking about Elise. She would be up making breakfast for him now, having been awakened by the whistle the mill blew to wake the day shift workers who would work the shortened Saturday shift. He could imagine her in the kitchen, working at the woodstove, maybe still in her nightgown. He would not have to return to the mill until Monday night, and he would probably spend the afternoon and evening of this day asleep—but this morning he would spend with his wife. Perhaps breakfast could wait, and counting his pay with her as well. Perhaps there were more important things to share with his wife this morning than food and money.

He could see mill workers slowing as they reached the sidewalk before the small white office building that sat before the mill, some deliberately crossing the street, others staying on the sidewalk, but hurrying on with heads down and eyes averted as if trying to avoid something there. As he drew nearer, he could see several young men loitering near the front of the structure. One sat on the bricked steps that led up to the office door, saying something to a woman who seemed to increase her pace, as if trying to hurry by and avoid him. Another was leaning against a tree that grew alongside the sidewalk, occasionally, and it appeared deliberately, sticking a foot out into the path of workers as they left their shifts. The third made straight for Nathan Betts the minute the night janitor came around the corner of the office building, grabbing a sack from Nathan's hands and turning to keep it away from him as he rifled through it.

"What're you stealing, boy?" he asked, reaching out with one hand to shove Nathan back as the older man tried to retrieve the sack. "We can't let no nigger walk out of the mill without checking to see what he's stealing from honest white folks first, now can we?"

"Mr. Richard, give me back my sack, now. I got t' get home—"

"You ain't 'got' to do nothing, boy, not until I say you do—now, why don't you ask me again if you can have it, real nice this time, and don't forget to say please—"

Janson started toward them, ready to intercede on Nathan's behalf if necessary, but there was a quick movement from the young man leaning against the tree as he turned and stepped onto the sidewalk and directly into Janson's path, almost running into him. "Where do you think you're going?" he asked in a stink of alcohol breath just before he shoved Janson backwards against the tree. A jolt of recognition came across the man's face at the same moment that Janson felt the same recognition hit him—it was Buddy Eason.

He stared at the closely set gray eyes, remembering a day, two and a half years before, when he had tried to kill this younger man. He could almost smell again the oily smell of the carriage house that stood on the Easons' property at the end of Main Street, could almost see again Buddy Eason's sister as she sat in the open doorway of her grandfather's Cadillac touring car, the girl yelling encouragement to her brother in a fight that had begun after Buddy had found them together. He remembered his embarrassment, and then the rage as he had realized that Lecia Mae Eason had never wanted him, but only a diversion. He could feel the heat of the struggle with Buddy Eason, and then the cold shock of the knife blade Buddy had driven through his right shoulder—he could also remember the fear in Buddy's eyes when Janson had held the bloody knife in his own hand with the blade to Buddy's throat at last, and the strong scent of urine as Buddy wet himself because of the fear within him. He could see in Buddy Eason's eyes that he remembered as well.

A muscle worked in Buddy's jaw as he stared at Janson. "What are you doing here, you red nigger," he said, his voice low, filled with fury, his eyes never leaving Janson's face. The muscle worked again in his jaw. "I thought you'd been run out of this county for good—"

"You thought wrong," Janson said, returning his stare. He could see the rage building within Buddy Eason as Buddy shifted from one foot to the other, both hands tightening into fists at his sides, loosening, and then tightening again.

"You better get out of this village, boy. You got no right to be here; you get your goddamn ass back into the country where the rest of the stinking shit is—"

Janson could hear the others snicker at Buddy's words, but he did not turn to look at them. "I got all th' right I need; I live here."

"Only mill workers live here, and I know Daddy would never have hired a red nigger to work in the mill."

"He didn't," Janson said, seeing a momentary look of satisfaction come into Buddy's eyes, "but your gran'pa did—"

Buddy's expression was immediately one of a pure hatred. He took a step closer, crowding Janson even further back against the tree, and bringing his clenched fist up to hold it to within inches of Janson's face. "You listen to me, you goddamn half-breed son-of-a-bitch, I won't have you living in this village, or working in this mill. Do you understand me?" He stared at Janson, his breath hot and stinking in Janson's face. "You pack up whatever shit you have and get the hell out of here, and don't you let me see you in this town or near the mill again or I'll cut your balls off and stuff them down your throat for you—now, get out of my sight before I beat your ass just for being here." He stepped back, obviously expecting Janson to leave, but Janson only stared at him. "Did you hear me—get!"

His voice rose on the last word, his eyes never leaving Janson's face.

"You goddamn—" He moved toward Janson again, grabbing him by the front of his coat and trying to drag him closer. Janson reached up to tighten a hand round Buddy's wrist, twisting, digging his fingers into the exposed flesh at the underside until pain shot across Buddy's features. Buddy struggled to maintain his grip, then failed, releasing him with a shove that sent Janson back against the tree again. He rubbed at his wrist, his eyes never leaving Janson's face, his own expression a study in hatred. "You goddamn red nigger, I'll kill you one day for that. You wait, one day I'll blow your fucking head off."

Janson only stared at him, then, after a moment, he turned his eyes to the young man who had Nathan Betts's package. "Give him back his sack," he said.

The man looked at him, then back to Buddy Eason. Buddy did not speak, or meet his eyes, but just continued to stare at Janson. After a moment, Nathan reached and took the sack, and it was released without any resistance. Janson turned his eyes back to Buddy Eason, finding nothing but hatred on the man's face.

"You're dead," Buddy said quietly. "One day—but I'm gonna hurt you first. I'm gonna make you beg to die. I'll teach you what hell is before I send you there."

Janson stepped back up onto the sidewalk, intending to walk around him, but Buddy stepped out of his way.

"You're dead—remember that, you red nigger," Buddy said as Janson walked past. "You're dead."

# CHAPTER THREE

There was a rumble of thunder in the distance as Elise reached the railroad tracks going back into the mill village the last Saturday afternoon in March. She had waited out the storm in Brown's Grocery on Main Street, sitting in a cane-bottomed straight chair that Mr. Brown had brought out from behind his counter for her, he having refused to allow her to stand while she waited for the rain to slack off. She wanted to make it home before the downpour resumed, so she quickened her pace, going down alongside the loading dock there at the railroad tracks, and starting down the sidewalk before the mill.

The azalea bushes in the yards of the dayboss houses across from the mill were drooping and wet, their color catching her attention from across the street, and she felt a touch of disappointment as she saw that many of their blooms now lay on the ground, beaten from the plants by the rain. The sidewalk was wet, as were the trees around her, and she felt a drizzle hit her face but had no way of knowing if it was from the branches overhead or from the rain that looked ready to resume at any moment. She knew she could have bought the few things she needed from McCallum's Grocery there in the village. If she had, she would have long since been home. As the wife of a mill worker, she was supposed to do her buying from the stores the Easons rented out to proprietors there in the village; that was one of the unwritten but well-known rules of village life she had been introduced to early, but one she could not bring herself to follow once she learned that almost anything they might need could be bought for less money from the stores along Main Street.

Her trips uptown often brought stares and even comments from people on both sides of the tracks, but she did not care. The walks gave her something to do during the days while Janson was asleep, and they allowed her at least a little time away from the incessant noise and lint of the village—and, besides, they gave her a chance to avoid the smelly, tobacco-chewing old men who considered the village stores their domain, sitting around the pot-bellied stove in the cold months, and now, on warmer days, occupying sagging cane-bottomed chairs between the open barrels of pickles and crackers before McCallum's Grocery, oftentimes spitting tobacco juice on the ground almost at your feet as you passed. The old men seemed to be an accepted part of village life, but one Elise could not get used to. Their streams of tobacco juice made her stomach roll, and their habit of scratching themselves made her want to run away.

She felt rain spatter her again from the trees overhead, hearing the distant rumble of thunder even over the sound of the mill machinery so close at hand. She could hear voices as she neared the white building that served as the office for the mill, and she saw three boys, none older than eighteen or nineteen, come around the corner of the structure as she neared it, feeling their eyes rake over her only a moment later as they noted her approach.

"Hey, Buddy, look at her," one called out as they stopped before the steps that led up to the mill office, blocking the sidewalk as they stared at her.

"Look at that red-gold hair and them tits—my, oh my—" the one called Buddy said. "That's a fresh little piece if I ever saw one."

She kept looking straight ahead but shifted her grocery sack to her other arm, thinking they would see that she was obviously pregnant and then realize that she was married so they would leave her alone.

"Somebody's sure been at her; look at that belly—"

She felt herself blush to her hairline, but kept walking, telling herself that it would only be a few more steps and she would be past them. Only a few—

"Hey, I've seen her with that red-trash Sanders before, must be his wife—" one of the boys said, and immediately the one named Buddy, who had been standing at the edge of the sidewalk, stepped directly into her path, almost causing her to run up on him before she could stop herself.

"Sanders?" he said, staring down at her as she took a step back, moving again to block her path as she tried to move past him. "You're married to that red-nigger?"

She glanced up at him, but did not answer, trying again to get past him.

"Answer me—you're married to Janson Sanders?"

"Yes, I am—now, let me by—" But he moved to block her path again.

"What's a white girl like you doing married to red-nigger trash like him?" he asked, but she would not answer. "Answer me, girl, what're you doing married to that red-nigger?" He put his hand on her arm but she jerked away, almost dropping her sack of groceries. "Are you scared of white men, or something?" He stepped closer—too close, her mind told her as she tried to push past. "I bet you ain't never had a real man, have you—now, I've got something that could show you what a real man—"

"Leave me alone!" She tried to pull away, to run. She was shaking so badly that the sack rattled in her hands. She saw people in a yard just down the street, a man passing at the other side of the road, but no one offered to help her.

"Leave her alone, Buddy. She's gonna have a baby," one of the other boys said, seeming to have had enough.

"That don't matter. I've had them with bellies bigger than this one— right, little mama? Just because you've got a baby inside of you don't mean you don't need a man between your legs to—" He placed a hand on her stomach, over the baby inside of her, as only Janson had done before. It was not an intimate touch by any standards, but it went beyond intimacy to her. She drew her hand back and slapped him hard, seeing a stunned look come to his face.

"Keep your hands off me!" she yelled, wishing she had done it earlier.

"You little bitch!" He grabbed her and shook her hard, sending the sack from her hands and her groceries spilling onto the sidewalk and rolling into the road. Fear filled her, fear for herself and for the baby as well. Her eyes searched for someone, anyone who would help her. The yard down the street was deserted now, and the man just across the road was hurrying on as if nothing was happening within his hearing. "I'm gonna teach you to—"

"You get your hands off 'a that lady right now!" A voice came from the steps nearby, and Elise turned her eyes in desperation to its source, finding a tall black man standing on the steps that led up to the mill office, the door almost shut behind him now and a large wrench held in his hand. "You heard me; get your hands off 'a that lady!"

"You get back in that building, nigger. I'll deal with you later. This ain't none of your business."

"Let her go." He did not raise the wrench held in his hand, but its threat was clear.

"You stay outta this, boy—" His words were brave, but he released Elise. She took a step away and tried to calm her beating heart, feeling her knees tremble beneath her. She saw the look that passed between the man named Buddy and the black man, and she was almost certain she would see murder done before her, but then the office door swung all the way in and a heavy-set man in his forties with great jowls for cheeks stepped out to stare down at the group before him.

"Buddy, what's going on out here?" he demanded, looking at the boy who had shaken her.

Buddy looked quickly from the black man to Elise and back again, and that look had held clear warning. "Nothing," he said, staring up at his father.

The man looked at Elise, and then to the one person who had helped her. "Nathan, what're you doing out here? You're supposed to be inside working on the lavatory."

"I came out t' get Mr. Buddy t' come look at it, t' make sure everythin' was okay before I left," he answered, then turned his eyes to the three boys who had accosted her. "But Mr. Buddy an' his friends were helpin' this lady pick up her groceries she dropped so she could go on home when

I came out." His eyes met hers for a moment and she understood—for some reason he would not accuse this boy of what he had done, not even with her there to confirm his words. She remained silent and returned his stare, not understanding, but also not willing to contradict him when he had helped her when no one else had even tried.

"Yeah, that's what we were doing," Buddy said, looking at the black man, then slowly bending to gather up the few cans and parcels on the sidewalk. The other two boys moved to retrieve those that had rolled into the street. He refilled the sack and handed it to her. "There you go, lady," he said, holding onto the sack for a moment too long after she had taken it, his gray eyes boring into hers, causing a chill to move up her spine.

"Buddy, you go on in and look at the lavatory for Nathan. Make sure everything's okay before he leaves," the older man said, then waited on the top step until Buddy and his friends had gone through the door before he followed them inside.

Once the door had closed behind them, Elise brought her eyes to those of the man who had saved her. "Thank you," she said, feeling the words horribly inadequate.

"You're Janson Sanders's wife, ain't you?"

"Yes."

He smiled and nodded. "You tell him that Nathan Betts returned a kindness."

Elise found herself smiling. "I will."

"Now, you better go on, Miz Sanders, an' you best be careful walkin' past here again. Ladies got t' watch when Buddy Eason an' them two friends of his are about; most everybody else does, too."

"I will, and, thank you again."

It wasn't until she had walked a street away that she got the shakes and had to stop for a moment and calm herself. Eason—Buddy Eason. The boy who had attacked her had been the same one who had stabbed Janson, leaving the scar that still marked his right shoulder—but there was even more she knew of Buddy Eason from her months of living in the mill village. The mill workers and their families rarely spoke of anyone in the Eason family, but, when they did, it was almost always about Buddy

Eason. She had heard gossip, rumors, about his having beaten a boy almost to death, about another boy, not even a teenager yet, whose arm he had broken. She had been told about a daughter of a mill village family, a girl engaged to be married, whom he had raped, and another he had severely beaten when she would not give into his demands. There were whispers about a teacher he had struck when he had been no more than eight years old, and fires he had started both behind the Methodist church in the village and the school building up town, as well as in a trash barrel just outside the rear entrance to the police station.

She closed her eyes and tried to calm her breathing—Janson would not care about any of that. He would not care about anything but putting an end to Buddy Eason's life once she told him what the man had done and suggested to her today. She could still remember the look on his face when he had at last reluctantly told her about the fight all those years before that had ended in his stabbing, and she knew there was a hatred already within Janson for Buddy Eason that went far beyond anything she had known him to feel toward anyone else. He would kill Buddy Eason for what he had done; there was no doubt. He would kill him, or at least try to, and would either end up in jail, or dead himself, before this day was over—and it would all be her fault. If only she had not gone into town today. If only she had crossed the street when she had seen the three boys. If only—

But there was nothing she could do about that now. If she did not tell him, then certainly Nathan Betts would, and Janson would go after Buddy Eason anyway.

She trudged the remainder of the way home, feeling wearier than ever before. Fear would not leave her, not only of what Janson would do, but of Buddy Eason himself. A man like that could be capable of doing anything, to anyone, here in Eason County. He was above the law, above justice, and he knew it. He would never have to pay for whatever it was he did—and Janson would not care about any of that. Not any of it.

She could not make herself enter the house when she reached it. She stood on the rear porch, one hand on the doorknob, having gone to the back of the house to keep from waking Janson where he slept in the front room that overlooked the street. He would be up within a few hours, and she would have to tell him then—and her mind raced, trying to think of words she could say, or anything she could do, that might lessen the impact of what Buddy Eason had done today. She knew that he would go after Buddy Eason the minute she told him. And then—

She turned and walked down off the porch and back along the side of the house toward the street, realizing a moment later that the sack was still in her hands, but not turning back to take the groceries into the house to put them away. She reached the street and turned in the direction of Dorrie's house.

Dorrie Keith's smile changed to a look of concern the moment she opened her front door and saw Elise standing there. "Elise, honey, are you okay, has somethin'—"

Elise shook her head, realizing how she must look with her hair disheveled from the shaking Buddy had given her. "I'm okay, just a little jittery—"

"You're pale as a sheet, come on in an' sit down," Dorrie said, taking the sack from her hands and leading her into the house, then through and to the kitchen where Dorrie did most of her visiting. She made Elise sit down at the kitchen table, then went to chip ice from the block that cooled the icebox in the corner, bringing Elise a glass of ice water and not asking her what had happened until Elise had finished half of it.

Dorrie's husband, Clarence, came in the rear door from his gardening long before Elise finished her story. He stood listening as he dried his hands on a towel, and then continued to stand leaning against the wall near the rear door, his arms crossed across his chest long after Elise had finished speaking. His eyes at last went to Dorrie and the two of them exchanged a look before he voiced what was already Elise's worse fear. "Janson's gonna try t' kill him when you tell him," he said quietly as she felt Dorrie's hand come to rest on her own with a concerned pat.

"I can't let him do that. It was all my fault. I should have crossed to the other side of the street when I saw them, or—"

"No," Dorrie said with a shake of her head. "It weren't your fault; it was Buddy Eason's. Him an' them friends of his are a bad sort, an' Buddy's th' worse of th' lot. Th' world'd be better off without any 'a them three, though I'd 'a never thought Carl Miles would'a turned out like he has, 'cause his folks're good people, but I guess runnin' around with Buddy Eason'd do that t' anybody—"

"But, I can't let Janson—he'll end up in jail or killed or—"

"Shh—" Dorrie said, giving Elise's hand another pat, her presence helping to steady the girl's nerves. "Don't you worry about that none. You got that baby t' think about now, an' you been through enough already. Me an' Clarence'll come back t' th' house with you, an' maybe Clarence can talk some sense int' that man 'a yours when you tell him," she said, looking up at her husband, and Elise saw Clarence nod his head in apparent agreement with his wife.

Elise had already burned a skillet of cornbread in the old woodstove in her kitchen by the time Janson awoke. She had the rear door standing open to try to air the smoke out of the room. Clarence was sitting at the kitchen table and Dorrie trying to help her salvage what she could of the meal, when Janson entered the kitchen from the middle room of their three, his short, black hair messy from sleep, though he had dressed before he had left the front room. His eyes moved over Clarence and Dorrie, then went immediately to Elise, giving her the sudden and horrible thought that he would think something had happened with the baby, which made her blurt out the entirety of the truth before she could even consciously arrange her thoughts.

She watched his face drain of color as she told him what Buddy Eason had done and suggested to her today, realizing with a sudden clarity of thought that she was not censoring her words or the impressions of what had happened to her in the slightest way, though she knew she had earlier in speaking to Dorrie and Clarence.

Dorrie stood beside her now, though Elise could not tear her eyes from Janson's face—she could do nothing but stare at him, seeing the awful loss of color leave his face, being replaced suddenly by a redness that she knew was anger.

"Did he hurt you?" he asked at last, his words perfectly clear, though she could see his jaw was clenched, his green eyes in that moment harder than she had ever seen them.

"No, he frightened me more than anything—"

He stared at her as her words fell silent. "He put his hands on you." It came out as a statement, and the look in his eyes in that moment was worse than anything she had imagined. She could see murder in his expression. He was going to kill Buddy Eason for what he had done today. She was certain of it.

"He put his hand on my stomach, and, when I slapped him, he grabbed me by the arms and shook me, but he didn't—"

But he was already halfway across the room headed for the open rear door, and she saw happening exactly what she had feared. She ran after him, knowing that he intended to go out that door and cut across the back yard and the yard of the house behind them on the way to the mill to find Buddy Eason. He intended—

She grabbed for his sleeve, only to have her hands pushed away. "Janson, you can't—"

But he did not even look at her.

"Janson—"

Then Clarence was between him and the door.

"Get th' hell out 'a my way, Clarence."

But Clarence would not move. He met Janson's gaze for a long moment, staring at him even as Dorrie reached Elise's side and reached to draw her away.

"He'll kill you," Clarence said, conveying more feeling in his toneless words than Elise had ever seen in him before. "He'll kill you, today, or some other day, if you go up against him. Elise ain't hurt this time, but what'll happen t' her once you're dead? Who's gonna look after your wife an' your baby if Buddy Eason kills you because you came after him? From what Dorrie tells me, you're th' only family she's got now, you an' that baby, 'cause she gave up her own people t' marry you—are you gonna leave her behind now? You best think of your wife, boy, your wife, an' not yourself an' your own pride that you got t' avenge now by goin' after him."

Janson stared at him, and Elise felt her heart rise to her throat to choke her, certain that he would still go after Buddy Eason.

Then Janson took a deep breath, and Elise knew that he was struggling to control the anger that was still written plainly in every line of his body.

"One of these days somebody's gonna make Buddy Eason pay for all he's done," Clarence was saying as Janson turned at last to look at Elise again. "One of these days—but not today. You got your wife t' think about, boy, an' she's been through enough already. She's been through enough."

It seemed as if Buddy Eason was determined to make his presence known in the village, and most especially to Elise, as the weather grew warmer. He drove down their street so often in the afternoons that she took to locking the doors at night while Janson was at work, even though she knew the locks were of little use, for they opened with a large skeleton key that was readily available in the mill office. Janson had told her she was never to go near the mill again unless he or someone else was with her, and that suited her just as well—she had no desire to run into Buddy Eason.

As the days passed and she became larger with the baby, she no longer felt like doing so much walking anyway—oh, how she missed the luxury of having an automobile to take her wherever she wanted to go, as she had had when she had lived in her father's house. Back then she had never thought it a luxury that their family had owned three automobiles, her brother's Packard, her father's Studebaker Big Six President, and the ugly Model T Ford she had hated so much, as well as a number of trucks. She could not now think of any family she knew personally in the mill village, except for snooty Helene Price and her husband, Bert, who owned even a single automobile, and she was amazed sometimes when she realized how naive she had been never to realize how privileged her life had been as Elise Whitley. That life seemed so far away now, that life of easy transportation, of electricity in her home, of running water and decent bathroom facilities. Now there was walking if she had to go anywhere, kerosene lamps to light their three rooms, and that little room in the back yard that nauseated her stomach each time she had to use it.

She sat in the front room of their half of the mill house late on a Friday afternoon in June. Janson had left for his shift in the mill no more than twenty minutes before, but already darkness had begun to fall, an early darkness brought on by a storm she could hear approaching in distant and prolonged thunder from the west. The rain had not started yet, and she found herself dreading when it would, for that would mean she would then have to pull down the side windows in all three rooms, leaving as ventilation only the front and rear windows that were protected by the overhangs of the two porch roofs.

She sat reading again the letter she had received from her mother the day before, and tried to write a letter in response, but her mind would not stay with what it was she was trying write. She missed her mother terribly, and her brother, Stan, and now that the baby's due date was drawing closer she found herself missing them only more, and missing her home in Georgia as well. She got up and moved about the three rooms they had in the mill house, thinking how odd it was that her child would be born here and would grow up in such a place.

The house she had lived in as a child had huge verandas in the front and rear, and tall, white columns. Frosted panes etched with floral designs were inset into huge double doors that opened into the downstairs hallway. That hallway led to twin parlors at the front of the house, a library, sewing parlor, dining room, and downstairs bedroom, as well as a grand staircase to the second floor. The rooms were filled with plush, brocaded settees, with shelves of first-edition books, with mahogany furniture and expensive rugs. Lovely wallpaper covered many of the downstairs walls, and delicate designs much of the upper. Crystal chandeliers of electric lights hung from ceilings, and lovely Coalport china filled the glass-fronted cabinet in the dining room. Her mother had promised to give her that china one day, a day now that would never come.

When Elise thought now of growing up in that house, it was of a sense of grace and beauty that she knew her children would never know. Her children would never sit beneath a chandelier that hung over the dining room table in a house her family had lived in for generations. They would never sit around a table covered with her grandmother's antique lace tablecloth; they would never eat from her mother's cherished china, or drink from the pressed-glass water goblets her Great-Aunt Eunice had left to her father. They would never know anything of the life she had known, and that realization sat heavily on her that evening as she moved about the rooms of the mill house.

As darkness settled in, the storm finally hit, and with a ferocity that Elise had not expected. She pulled down the exposed windows, then sat in a rocker she drew nearer to the kerosene lamp on the table in the front room, hearing the thunder crash outside as she tried to occupy her mind with the volume of poetry she had been reading, but she quickly gave up as she was unable to concentrate on the words. She got up and thumbed the latches on the front and back doors, then blew out the lamps and lay down, though she knew there was little chance she would sleep with the storm now lashing rain against the windows, and with her cotton nightgown already sticking to her from perspiration.

It was in the middle of the night as she lay listening to the storm that the first contraction came, surprising her with its intensity—but the baby was not due for more than a week, she kept telling herself; that was what the doctor had told her. Dorrie had said she could expect to go even longer than that, because a first baby never came as soon as anyone thought it would.

But a second contraction came, and then a third, and she sat on the side of the bed in the darkness, trying to force herself to remain calm. It would be hours, even days, before the baby would come. Dorrie had said it took a long time for the first baby even once the pains started, and her mother had written she had been in labor for eighteen hours before Bill was born. There would be plenty of time for Janson to go for the doctor when he arrived home from his shift in the mill. That would be early morning—but still she got up and lit the lamps, feeling safer in the glow of the kerosene light. Janson had told her that a light burning in a mill house in the middle of the night would bring someone to check to see if there was trouble, so she expected—

But no one came, and, as she listened to the storm intensify outside, she knew that no one would. She thought things were going faster than they should—first babies were supposed to take a long time, but surely this could not go on for eighteen hours or more. She knew she would never be able to stand it.

She sat in the rocker and watched the lightning flash outside, trying not to hold her breath when the contractions came. She had already found out that doing so only made it hurt worse—she had to have help. She could not take the chance on the baby coming with her alone, or of something going wrong, and she realized she was almost crying as she got the oversized wrap Janson's Aunt Rachel had given her and wrapped it around her shoulders—all she had to do was walk next door, just across the length of the front porch, she told herself, and she could have the Breedloves' oldest daughter run for Dorrie. The girl would be watching her younger sister and brothers while their parents were working their night shifts. Elise would just have to be careful as she made her way across the front porch—she could have Dorrie here shortly to wait with her, and send Clarence Keith or one of the boys for Dr. Washburn if the time came before Janson got home. Dorrie would know when they would need the doctor; she had been through this six times herself, with her four boys, a little girl who had been stillborn, and twins, one having died in childbirth and the other only a few hours after—and Elise wished she had not thought about that now. Oh, how she wished she had not thought about it.

She had to stop halfway across the floor, catching hold of the foot of the bed for support as another contraction came, making her bend with the tightness that built into what she knew was coming. After a moment she straightened and made her way to the door. She watched her footing carefully as she stepped out onto the wet porch. Lightning flashed and struck something nearby, making her jump. Rain was pouring down, beating heavily on the porch roof and blowing in to wet the hem of her gown as she made her way across the narrow distance to the Breedloves' front door. She could hear the sudden squeal of frightened children from inside as lightning flashed again, followed by thunder so intense that it rattled the upper panes of the windows. She banged on the door, feeling the wind whip the rain under the edge of the porch roof, quickly soaking through the bottom edge of her gown and making it stick warmly to her legs. She banged on the door again, then reached down to twist the doorknob in her hands, finding it locked. Lightning flashed again, forking off into two bolts that seemed to hit the ground at the far edge of the village. There was the sound of the strike, then the clash of thunder so powerful it shook the boards of the porch beneath her.

She banged her fist on the door again, yelling out the name of the eldest girl. "Carolyn! It's Elise Sanders from next door—please let me in!" But, even as she yelled the words and twisted the doorknob in her hands again, she realized the children would never hear her over the sound of the storm. She banged again, calling out the girl's name, but stopped as another contraction started to build.

Elise leaned against the damp wood of the door, bending slightly as the tension built into the pain she knew was coming. She made herself breathe, riding the contraction to its peak—what am I going to do? she thought, raising her hand to bang at the door again, feeling so absolutely alone.

The morning was a dark gray, clouded and reluctant. Little light showed through the windows of the card room, and it was only the mill's whistle that told Janson it was time for the workers to come in for the shortened Saturday shift.

He left the card room that morning more tired than he had felt in a long time. He passed through the picker and opening rooms and stood in the wide double-doors that opened out onto the loading dock, staring at the rain. It was still coming down steadily, drenching everything outside, slacking up just to start down in torrents again only moments later. The clay road looked ankle-deep in red mud, the trees and bushes soaked and drooping. Pneumonia weather, Gran'ma would call it.

He looked up at the clouds that hung low and heavy over the village—then ducked his head and hurried out into the downpour, going down the sidewalk before the mill, and then along the sloshy mud streets, the action of his own steps, and that of the few automobiles that made their way down the slippery roads, quickly covering the legs of his overalls in red mud. The village had come to life in the gray, early-morning hours. There was the damp smell of woodsmoke coming from kitchen flues as biscuits baked in ovens and sausage, eggs, and bacon fried in skillets the village over. The mule-drawn wagon that was sarcastically referred to as the "ice-cream wagon" sloshed down a muddy street on its rounds to clean the outdoor toilets. The ice truck was parked in front of a house, Mr. Harper nodding a greeting as he hoisted a block of ice destined for use in someone's icebox, and Janson watched as neighborhood children crowded about him even in the rain for the treats of chips and slivers of ice that he always gave them.

He was soaked long before he reached the house, Luree Breedlove giving him a disapproving look from her open front door, making a pointed comment about muddy feet and tracking the porch, which he chose to ignore. He heard a soft sound from the bed as he entered the house, and he turned to see Elise lying there, the sheet twisted and knotted about her, her reddish-gold hair damp with perspiration and matted to her forehead.

"Elise—" He moved quickly to the bed and dropped to his knees beside it, taking her hand in his. Her face was drawn and tired, her skin even paler than usual. "It's started? Why didn't—" But he could not finish the thought as she suddenly tightened her hand in his, digging her nails into his palm. Her face twisted with pain, her breath catching in her throat for a moment before she seemed to force herself to breathe again. He waited through the pain with her even as she twisted his hand in hers, feeling helpless. At last the grip on his hand decreased. She took a deep breath and licked her lips, looking exhausted and so young for a moment that he could do nothing but look at her. "I'm sorry," was all he could say as he brushed the sweat-drenched hair back from her forehead. "I wish it didn't have t' hurt—"

She managed a weak smile. "I'm just glad it's finally time. I think you'd better go for the doctor; I don't think it'll be much longer."

"Will you be okay until I get back?" he asked, pushing himself to his feet, still holding onto her hand, unwilling to let go.

"I'll be fine—go and ask Dorrie to come wait with me until you bring the doctor back."

"I will." But still he did not let go of her hand.

"Go on, Janson. I'll be fine—"

He released her at last and moved toward the door, looking back at her one more time before going through out onto the front porch. Once free of the house he ran, almost stumbling in the front yard, but catching himself, and running on into the muddy, red clay street.

Dr. Curtis Thrasher rubbed his tired eyes and set about repacking his medical bag, going through the contents that morning with eyes and hands that were tired from lack of sleep. He had spent many nights with little or no rest in his forty years of practicing medicine in Eason County, but the past week, with Dr. Bassett bedridden with a back injury, and Dr. Washburn out of town on a family emergency, had seen him as the only able-bodied physician in the county, and had resulted in a state of exhaustion he had not known in many years. He had spent few nights as long or as distasteful as the one he had just been through, however, the one spent cleaning up after a poorly done self abortion on Clois Eason, working through the entire night just to try to save the stupid girl's life. Well, now he knew she would live, and there would be no child, perhaps no child ever, so badly had she done herself, and perhaps that was for the best. In Curt's opinion, there were more than enough Easons in this county already.

He stretched, trying to loosen the tight muscles in his back—I'm too old for this, he told himself. He'd become a doctor to save lives and help people, not to clean up after some stupid girl doing away with her child—but I ought to be used to it, he thought. It was not the first time he'd had to attend to the after-effects of an abortion, not even the first time he'd had to lend such care to one of the Eason girls, but, then he'd been called upon to do so many things for the Easons over the past forty years, things that medical school had never prepared him to do. It was just that he was so tired, so unbelievably tired, and not just in body alone.

He closed his medical bag, then stood for a moment staring down at it where it rested on his desktop. He needed sleep, and badly, but he knew there would be no sleep for him this morning, and perhaps not throughout most of the day. He would not be seeing patients in his office, but there were hospital rounds to make even on a Saturday, the occasional emergency, and at least one drive to a patient's house he could not avoid. After having worked through the night to save the life of Clois Eason, he would now have to spend the morning with her grandmother, as he had to spend almost every Saturday morning. There would be nothing wrong with Patricia Eason, at least nothing that sunshine and fresh air would not cure, but the weekly visit was obligatory—she was certain she was ill; she was always certain she was ill, and her husband, Walter Eason, demanded that Curt be there for her whenever she asked for him. Curt would make the perfunctory examination, prescribe his sugar waters and pills, and listen to her complaints—and the listening, he knew, would be the most effective medicine. He could almost feel sorry for the woman, considering the two sons she had raised, the younger of which she had buried before his eighteenth birthday, and her three grandchildren, the two girls being little better than alleycats, and her only grandson, Buddy, being—

There was a sudden, hard pounding at the exterior door that opened into the reception area of the office. Curt sighed, knowing it would be some emergency that would deny him any rest at all today. He made his way from his book-lined office and across the deserted reception area, wishing he had already left to make the visit on Patricia Eason, for that might have avoided this one extra burden.

He opened the door, preparing himself for some mother with a sick child, or mill hand with a bloody injury. The man standing on the doorstep appeared uninjured, however, and the sight of someone bothering him so early on a Saturday morning who was obviously in no dire need of help replaced Curt's exhaustion to a degree with anger.

"You're th' doctor?" the man asked, shifting impatiently from one foot to the other. He was soaked, his overalls muddy; he was dark, too dark to be a white man, and had to be from the mill or village, considering the amount of cotton fibers matted in with the wet black hair that was plastered to his forehead.

"Yes, I'm—"

"You've got t' come with me—"

"I don't have to go anywhere with you—" Curt snapped, then he forced a degree of control over his exhaustion, making himself speak in a more reasonable voice. "Is someone injured at the mill?" he asked, rubbing his eyes again.

"It's my wife—she's havin' a baby. You've got t' come—"

"Your wife? What's her name?"

"Elise—Elise Sanders. She's hurtin' real bad—"

"Well, of course she's hurting, man, she's having a baby," Curt snapped, then took a deep breath. "Her name's not familiar. She's not one of my patients—"

"She's been seein' Dr. Washburn. There wasn't nobody at his place, an' th' woman next door, she sent me here—"

"How close are her contractions?" But the man only stared at him. "Well, take her on to the hospital," Curt said, turning to start across the room toward his open office doorway, hearing the man trudging across the clean floor behind him. "I have a patient to see right now, but I'll come to the hospital to check on your wife as soon as I'm through. Labor can last for a long while—"

"I ain't got no way t' get her t' th' hospital." There was a sound of desperation to the man's voice.

Curt turned to find him just a few steps behind as he reached the door to his office. "Well, then get a midwife to help her. That's what most of you mill families do anyway."

"I promised her a doctor. I've got th' money. You've got t'—"

"I don't have to do anything," Curt said, losing his patience with the man. He had already offered to care for the woman; what more could he do? There were too many other patients needing his services today for him to spend the entire day waiting for one woman to give birth. It could be hours before she was ready to deliver—hours wasted, with hospital rounds to make, and no one else to tend emergencies. That was what midwives were for, when Curt had two other doctors to cover for, the hospital, and Patricia Eason still waiting for his visit. "Now, go on and find a midwife for your wife. There are many good—"

"She wants a doctor. I've got th' money. It's at th' house; all you got t' do is—"

"I've already told you I don't have time for this. Either get your wife to the hospital, or get a midwife to tend her. Now, I've got a patient waiting—"

"Elise cain't wait. She's bad off; there ain't no time for me t' get a midwife. You've got t'—"

"I've already told you—"

"I'll give you every cent I got, an' more when I get it." The look of desperation in the man's eyes made Curt feel all the more tired—the woman was probably hours away from delivery, and this man wanted to drag him out in the middle of a rain storm just to sit by her bedside and wait.

"This is just a waste of time. I've told you what you can do, and I have no intention of going over it again. Now, please leave my office; I have more important things to do."

A muscle clenched in the man's jaw. "Ain't nothin' more important than Elise. You're gonna come help her."

"If you don't leave, I will call the police and have you put out."

Curt reached for the telephone resting on the desktop, but the man's hand closed over his wrist before he could pick it up. "You're comin' with me—"

"Let me go, or I'll—" He tried to free his arm, but the man held it only more tightly. "Turn me—" There was a moment's struggle, and at last Curt managed to free himself, moving quickly to the fireplace set into the wall nearby to take up a poker from the stand at its side. He turned back to the man, holding it between them. "Now, go on, I told you."

The man stared at the poker for a minute, but did not move. The muscle worked again in his jaw, and then his eyes lifted to meet Curt's over the short distance.

"Go on," Curt warned again, raising the poker between them to make certain the man understood the threat. "I don't want to hurt you, but I will if I have to."

Still the man did not move.

"You're not doing your wife any good by just standing there," Curt said, watching the green eyes, feeling the uneasiness rise within him—the man was not going anywhere.

But suddenly he turned and strode from the office, and Curt heard the front door slam behind him as he left the building. Curt walked out of his office carefully, looking around the reception area to make certain the man was not simply lying in wait for him.

He moved cautiously to the exterior door, stopping for a moment to survey again the reception area before he reached to thumb the bolt that would secure the door against the man's re-entry.

It was not until after the door was locked and he returned to his office that he at last put the poker down on the desktop beside his medical bag. He stood for a long moment staring down at it, then reached to take up his bag, knowing Patricia Eason would be waiting for him.

Dorrie Keith felt as if she were in a nightmare that morning as she stood staring out at the driving rain where it beat against the side window of Elise and Janson's front room—but her nightmarish feeling could be nothing compared to what even now made Elise Sanders moan from where she lay on the bed. Dorrie made herself turn away from the window and move toward the bed to see if there was anything she could do for the girl, but she knew there was nothing she could do to help. Only time and nature could help Elise Sanders now; time, nature, and that husband of hers if he would only get here with the doctor.

Dorrie reached to take the cloth from the basin of water that rested on the table beside the bed, squeezed it out, then gently wiped Elise's sweaty face. She smiled down at the girl and nodded her head, but did not say anything, then she turned and paced across the room, toward the window again, then back toward the front door—where was that doctor?

She heard Elise moan again as another pain came, and she tried to shut her ears to the sound—Elise was little more than a girl; she ought to be worrying about new dresses and returning to school next year, not a husband, a house, and a baby so soon. Dorrie looked toward the bed, seeing Elise twist and knot the sheet in her hands as the pain peaked and then began to lessen—she just looked so young lying there, her reddish-gold hair soaked with sweat and sticking to her forehead. She was little more than a year younger than Dorrie had been when Wheeler James had been born, but she seemed so much younger, so unaccustomed to the way the world was. Her husband had done this to her, and now he was taking all the time in the world in getting a doctor here to her now, while this baby was getting ready to be born all too soon—where was he, and where was that doctor? If this baby should decide to come before they got here, Dorrie had no idea what she would have to do to help the girl. She might have had babies of her own, but this was altogether different. She'd had little choice in the matter when she had been the one giving birth, and little idea of what the old, black granny woman had done to help her in each birthing. In fact, she had even forgotten the feel of the pain, the hurt, the tearing, especially so bad with the first, in the feeling of holding her baby in her arms for the first time—but now, here in this sticky, humid room, those memories had come back, memories of twenty-seven hours of labor, memories of pain so bad she had thought she would die, and those memories would not leave her now. She looked toward her friend where she lay on the bed, her eyes closed, exhaustion on her face as she waited for the next pain to come. Maybe it was better that it was going more quickly for Elise; Dorrie did not think the girl would be able to survive many more hours of this.

But if the child should come before the doctor arrived—

She paced across the room again, then back toward the door, wringing her hands before her. She was not accustomed to feeling useless, but there was nothing she could do now other than be with Elise—oh, Lord, where was her husband, Dorrie wondered as she moved back toward the bed, bending again to sponge Elise's face off as another pain came and went. Elise took a deep breath and licked her dry lips once it was over. "He'll be here soon; I know he will," she said, reaching to take Dorrie's hand.

"Sure he will, honey," Dorrie said, making herself smile at the girl as she sat down at the edge of the bed. "An', don't you worry. Ain't nothin' t' havin' a baby. I was up cookin' supper only a hour or two after I had each one 'a mine."

Elise ran her tongue over her lips again, moistening them. "You're a terrible liar, Dorrie," she said, smiling for a moment.

"Ain't I, though," Dorrie said, and reached up to pat the girl's cheek. "But, don't you worry none. That man 'a yours'll be here any minute with that doctor, an' he'll make sure you an' that baby both have a easy time 'a it."

"I know he will," Elise said, moving slightly on the bed and releasing Dorrie's hand, and Dorrie knew that another pain was beginning to build for the girl. Dorrie watched her face until she could take no more of it, then got up from the bed and moved again toward the window to stand staring out at the rain: *I will cause it to rain upon the earth,* she found herself quoting silently, *forty days and forty nights; and every living substance that I have made will I destroy from off the face of the earth.* She looked back to her friend—Janson, for God's sake, please hurry, she thought, please hurry.

She paced away from the window toward the bed, to the chifforobe across the room, and then back to the window, until she felt she would wear a path in the floor.

The door banged open and Janson came in, wet, muddy to the knees—and alone. He started toward the bed, his face a study in fear, but Dorrie intercepted him half-way across the floor. "Where's th' doctor?" she demanded.

"He wouldn't come. Said he had a patient—" He looked past her, toward the bed and his wife.

"She's havin' that baby soon. You've got t' get somebody t' help her."

"Damn it—don't you think I know that!" he yelled into her face, then pushed past her and toward the bed, stopping to kneel beside it and take his wife's hand in his own. "I couldn't get th' doctor t' come, Elise. I tried—"

"I know you did." Her voice was quiet, almost too soft to understand.

"I've got t' go get Gran'ma. I got Mr. Brown's wagon an' team from up town; I tried t' get th' grocery delivery truck, but it was in a ditch at the edge of town because of th' rain—"

"Your gran'ma's too far off," Dorrie broke in, and Janson looked up at her. "That baby ain't gonna wait that long."

She could see his hand tighten over his wife's, and his worried eyes returned to Elise.

"Granny Alice from over in colored town delivered all 'a mine, an' she's closer. Mrs. Smith at th' edge 'a town is even closer than that. You got t' go get her, or, if she ain't there, Granny Alice—"

"I will, just tell me where—" He started to rise to his feet, but Elise stopped him.

"No." She held tightly to his wet sleeve, a look of near desperation in her eyes. He knelt again at her side, taking both her hands in his.

"Elise—I cain't get th' doctor t' come; I got t'—"

"No, no, not that—don't leave me; I don't want you to leave me. I want you here when—" The last word was gasped out between clenched teeth and Dorrie saw her face wrench with pain again.

"Elise—" Janson's voice sounded frightened. He held tightly to her hands even as she twisted his own, his eyes never leaving her pain-closed ones.

When it was over she licked her lips and looked up at him, the fear in her eyes almost more than Dorrie could bear. "You've got to be here. We'll be okay if you're here—"

"Elise, I cain't. I got t' get somebody t' help—"

"No, I want you here—"

"I'll go," Dorrie stated, knowing she could take no more of this helplessness, no more of the sounds of pain, no more of this hot, sticky room. "I can drive a team an' wagon just as good as you, an' I know right where t' go—"

"But, if—" Janson looked from her to Elise, and then back again, unable to put his fear into words. "What if—if the baby—"

"It won't get here before I can get back. You just stay with her—" She started for the door, looking back to the man's worried face for a moment before going out into the rain—he looked so young himself, so utterly lost and helpless, kneeling at the side of the bed, his wife's hands held tightly in his own.

She hurried as fast as her size would allow to the wagon, getting up onto the driver's seat as the horses moved skittishly to her presence. She closed her mind to the rain that soaked immediately through her clothes, making them cling warmly to her skin as she whipped the horses hard. They whinnied in protest and the wagon jerked forward, almost unseating her. Within seconds her dark hair was loose from its bun, hanging wet and heavy down her back as she whipped the horses even harder, hearing the protesting honks and curses of the driver of a car that she almost ran from the road and into a muddy yard alongside a village street. She knew that she had to get Mrs. Smith or old Granny Alice as quickly as possible, for she had lied again. Elise's baby was coming very soon.

Janson had never felt so useless, or so frightened, seeing pain that he could not stop or control, wanting to help Elise, but unable to think of anything he could do that might lessen what she was going through. He knelt beside the bed, wet and muddy still, and he prayed—please, God, don't let the baby come without somebody to help. Please, God—

She squeezed and twisted his hands when the pains came, digging her nails into his flesh until both hands throbbed. "I'm so sorry—" was all he could think to say over and over when each was finished. Though he did not know what it was he was sorry for.

He silently cursed the doctor for refusing to come, cursed Dorrie and the midwife for taking so long, and Mrs. Breedlove when she would not come to help—he should have made the doctor come, he kept telling himself.

He watched her face as another pain began to build, seeing her eyes close and her face set a moment before she wrenched at his hands again—please, God, help me, he prayed. Please, God—

It was over. After the hurt and the fear, after the cries of pain, and the scream of a new life—it was over. Janson sat beside the bed in the old rocker, moving only enough to keep the chair in motion slowly back and forth. He was exhausted, his mind dulled from lack of sleep and food throughout much of this day—but it was over.

He rocked slowly, his mind wandering over all that he had seen and learned today—he was a father now, the baby newly born and sticky still and screaming when Dorrie had arrived with the old midwife. Janson had been driven from the house immediately, told to go wait on the porch out of the way where he belonged until they called for him, but that did not seem to matter—he had seen his own son being born.

He rocked slowly, the warm baby wrapped in a faded hand-me-down blanket in his arms. The baby was quiet now, after his loud screams of protest at his entry into the world. He slept peacefully in Janson's arms, his little hands curled into fists against his chest, and Janson watched him, just as he watched Elise where she slept in their bed. Dorrie would be back soon, bringing plates of food for him and Elise from the supper she was preparing for her own family. Janson had not eaten all day, but that bothered him little. He just wanted to sit and rock his son, sit and watch his wife sleep.

Elise smiled briefly as she slept, her face peaceful now after the nightmare she had lived through. He wondered what she dreamed, and if she dreamed, after the treatment she had suffered under his incompetent midwifery—she had seemed to forget it all as soon as the baby was born. She was crying and laughing at the same time as she counted the little fingers and toes, even as Dorrie and the midwife came in and drove

Janson from the room—by the time they allowed him back inside, the baby was cleaned up and the bed changed. Elise was in a fresh cotton nightgown and the baby was in her arms. "He looks so much like you," she kept telling him. "Don't you think he looks just like you?"

She fell asleep holding the baby, and Janson took him gently from her arms so as not to wake her, then sat down in the rocker to watch her sleep, too exhausted to do anything but sit and watch the peaceful breathing of his wife and son. They had agreed months before to name the baby Henry Alfred if it were a boy, after Janson's father and Elise's brother, and Janson could not help but to think that his father would have been pleased when he heard Elise first use the name. "Hi, Henry—do you like your name?" she had said very softly, in a tone Janson had never heard her use before.

Before today he had never even held a baby in his arms, but it seemed such an easy thing to do now—he was a father, and Elise was a mother. He looked at the little face, seeing both of them there, the shape of Elise's nose and mouth, his own dark hair and coloring. Elise's child—he should have been born to the finest things in life, to the experienced care of a doctor, born in a soft feather bed, and wrapped in the finest linen blankets. Instead, her child had been conceived on the straw mattress of a narrow, sagging rope bed, and born into inept hands that knew nothing but hard work. He had been wrapped in a faded, hand-me-down blanket, never to know the comforts and luxuries of life to which Elise Whitley's child should have been born. He would never have the fine education, the nice clothes, and the gentle way of life that could have been his birthright. There was so little Janson could give him compared to all he should have known, so little, except for one thing.

At first he did not know he was speaking aloud, but he was not surprised at the sound of his own voice in the quiet room, a voice speaking of land rich and red, of rolling hills, green fields, and tall cotton, of land so fertile that it only needed a man's hard work to spring to life. He spoke, and he dreamed, with dreams that were as much a part of who he was as life or breath were, dreams that had known their birth in some time long past before Janson had ever known life, in a tenanted field in

Ireland, or along the Trail the Cherokee had marched to the West, and that had come to him along with the blood in his veins. He spoke, and he dreamed, sitting in half a rented house in a mill village, while his soul walked free on land that he knew would be his again one day.

When Martha Whitley received the letter from her daughter, the letter announcing the birth of Martha's first grandchild, she cried for half an hour. Elise was her only daughter, and Elise was a mother now. Elise was a mother.

She went to tell William as soon as her tears were dried, standing just inside the doorway of the library in her home, speaking to William where he sat looking over a ledger at the cluttered rolltop desk against the far wall. "We have a grandson, William."

A muscle worked in William's cheek, but he did not speak or even look up to acknowledge her presence in the room, keeping his head bowed over the column of figures in the book before him.

"Elise had a little boy two weeks ago." When he still did not respond, she took a few steps farther into the room. "William, we have a—"

"We have no grandson," he snapped, though he never brought his eyes to her, "and we have no daughter—she made her choice; don't bother me now with news about her when she's nothing to us anymore."

"She's my daughter, and she's yours, too."

He sat for a long moment, not moving. "She's nothing to me," he said at last, not looking up.

"I don't believe you mean that." She moved farther into the room, going to stand just behind a large, overstuffed chair near the desk, bracing her hands against its tall back for support. She always seemed to need support these days, her legs weak and easily tired from under her, her breath hard to catch. She looked at William's bowed head—he could not feel that way about his own child; he could not. He had to care about his daughter and his only grandchild, no matter what it was he said. "Elise said the baby's perfect—she sounded so happy in her letter, William." He seemed to be listening—he had to be. She leaned more fully against the chair back, wondering why her heart seemed to be beating so rapidly within her. "She says he has Janson's black hair, but that he's already got a Whitley temper—they gave him Alfred's name as his middle name, William, and his given name is Henry, after Janson's fath—"

"Damn it, woman!" He rose to his feet quickly, upsetting his chair. "Have you gone deaf, or just stupid in your old age—I don't want to hear it. I don't want to hear it—not about her, or her brat, or that half-breed son-of-a-bitch she ran off with. Do you think I want to know she was carrying his brat while she was still living under my roof? Do you think I want to know he was getting at her for months before I ever knew about them—I can count, woman. All you've done is tell me she was a cheap little whore in addition to being stupid and ungrateful. We don't have a daughter anymore, and we sure as hell don't have a grandson."

She stared at him, leaning more heavily against the chair for support. "You're a fool, William." She felt suddenly too tired to argue, too tired for anything—how could she have been so wrong, for so many years. She had thought she had known him—even after all she had learned because Elise had fallen in love with Janson Sanders, she had still thought she had known him. She had believed that buried somewhere within him was something of the man she had married all those years before. But there seemed to be nothing left of that man now. He was as dead to her as was her own beautiful Alfred, her son dead now more than this past year. "That baby is absolutely innocent; he hasn't done anything to harm anyone—how can you hate your own grandchild?"

"That Indian's brat is none of me!"

"You'd deny your own flesh and blood?" Why was the room suddenly so close, her breath impossible to come, her heart beating rapidly. "You'd deny—deny your own—"

The room went dark, her senses spinning about her. She dug her fingers into the chair back, but could not feel her fingers, could not feel anything—

When she awoke, she was lying on the sofa in the library. Disoriented for a moment, her eyes searched for Elise in the room—she had been talking to Elise; had been—

Then she remembered. Elise was not here. She was living far away, in Alabama, with her husband. And her new son.

Martha brought her eyes to William where he knelt beside the sofa. He patted her hand, a worried expression on his face.

"Martha—are you all right?—Martha—" His eyes held more gentleness than she had seen in years when she looked at him.

"Yes?" She wondered at the sound of her own voice. It sounded so small, so weak there in the room.

"What happened—are you all right?"

"I—I fainted—"

"I'm going to call the doctor," he said, rising to his feet and releasing her hand.

Martha started to sit up, to protest that she did not need a doctor, that she was fine, but found that she could not and sank back against the sofa as the room began to darken about her again. For a moment she could not remember where her daughter was, then it came back to her—she wanted to see Elise. She wanted to see her grandchild, just once. She wanted to—

♣

"She's going to die, William," Matthew Lester said for the second time, as if William had not heard him the first.

"She can't—" William spoke quietly, standing in the front parlor of his home with the doctor while Martha slept upstairs in their bed under the watchful eyes of Mattie Ruth Coates. Martha couldn't die—she was still a young woman, still very much the same girl he had married what seemed to him now so few years before. He could more easily believe that he would die than that she might.

"She is—there's nothing I can do to help her, William. I wish there were—"

"But she—" He could find no words. He could not even remember what he had been about to say.

Matt lay a gentle hand on his arm. "She knows, William. I didn't tell her, but she knows."

William turned his eyes back to Matt, his friend for so many years, the doctor who had delivered all four of his children, his own first cousin—he was wrong. He had to be wrong.

"She wants to see you, but she wanted me to give you this first."

There was a letter in William's hands, and he wondered how it had gotten there, a letter folded into an envelope and addressed in Martha's hand: Mrs. Janson Sanders, it said, with a tremble in the script that should not have been there. Mrs. Janson Sanders, with an address in Alabama.

"She wants to see Elise, and she wants to see her grandchild—you need to send for them, William, and soon." Matt looked at him with eyes filled with sympathy. William wanted to tell him that he did not want his sympathy, that he did not need it—Martha would be fine.

"Martha wanted to write Elise herself, to tell her, and to ask her to bring the baby as soon as she can—she had the letter ready before I got here, William; she already knew."

The words seemed difficult for him, painful to speak or even to think about. Matt had been a good friend for so many years—but he was wrong just this one time.

"I think you should post this to Elise today, William, and, to be honest with you, I think you should telephone as well. It would be easier for her to hear it from you instead of reading it in a letter, and, there would be more of a chance she might get here in time." Matt seemed to look at him closely for a moment. "I'll be happy to call Elise for you, and to post the letter as well, if you would like." He held out a hand, a hand William just stared at for a moment before shaking his head.

"No," he said, straightening his back and meeting Matt's gaze levelly. "No—I'll take care of it myself—"

Matt looked at him for a moment, then moved to get his black bag from the sofa where he had set it upon coming downstairs. He took up his hat and looked at William again, then asked, "Will you be all right, William?"

"Yes—of course, I'll be fine. Thank you, Matt. Thank you very much." He walked the doctor to the door, then stood on the veranda and watched as the doctor descended the steps to the yard below.

Matt turned back to him. "Don't forget to post that letter, William, and to telephone Elise—"

"I won't." William turned and went back into the house without waiting for the doctor to drive away. He closed the door and looked toward the staircase and up, toward the upstairs where Martha slept under the watchful presence of Mattie Ruth. After a moment he looked down at the letter in his hands—Matt had to be wrong; he was mistaken. Martha could not die. She could not—

He stared at the envelope with his daughter's address written on it in a hand that seemed a shaky imitation of Martha's own careful one—Elise was gone to him, as gone in life as Alfred was in death. When she had first left, he had thought she would return, that she would get tired of the life her farmhand could give her, and that she would come home, but, after months had passed and she had stayed away, he had tried to put her out of his mind. He could not face seeing her now, not her, or the child she had borne by her half-breed farmhand. Bill was gone from the house, living on his own in town, having divorced himself from his father and his family, and William worried now to think of the kind of man his eldest son had become. Stan was silent and distant, looking at William with distrust after what had happened with Elise and the half-Cherokee dirt farmer. Martha was all that William had left now—she could not be dying. She could not be—

He stared at the envelope for a moment longer, then ripped it in half—Martha was ill now, but she would get better. She needed all of his energy and strength to help her—he could not be worrying about Elise and the farmhand. He could not allow Elise to come home with her child to tire her mother out. Later, when Martha was better, he would tell her what he had done, and his reasons for doing it. Later, when Martha was better—

He shoved the torn halves of the envelope beneath the family Bible on the nearby hall table, the Bible where generations of Whitley births and deaths had been recorded, then took up Martha's needlepoint from the tabletop where she had left it in passing earlier in the day. She would want her needlework, he told himself; it would help her to pass the time until she could be up and about again.

He started up the stairs, carrying the needlepoint in his hand—later, when she was better, she would understand why he had done what he had to do. She would understand—she always understood.

# CHAPTER FOUR

A pounding at the front door of the mill house woke Elise and Janson from a sound sleep. She had been awake more than half the night with the baby, and had fallen into a deep sleep that morning with the four-week-old Henry at last quiet between her chest and Janson there on the bed, the daylight showing at the edges of the drawn curtains unable to keep her awake for once.

The pounding came again at the door, waking the baby and setting him into loud wails. Elise hurriedly got out of bed and pulled her wrap on over her nightgown, knowing that Janson's grandmother would lecture her severely for being up and about for at least another two weeks, for Deborah Sanders had already done so twice since the baby had been born. "I'm coming," she called, glancing at Janson as he sat up in bed. They both knew it was out of the ordinary for someone to be knocking at their door at this time of day with the "Day Sleeper" sign nailed so obviously to the front door. Everyone the village over knew never to disturb the house of a day sleeper in the daylight hours.

A knot of worry tightened in her stomach as she pulled her wrap closer and opened the door. She recognized the boy on the porch as the one who worked at the village grocery and wondered what he could want that was important enough to disturb Janson's sleep, much less to set the baby to crying again after he had kept her awake most of the night.

"There's a telephone call for you at th' store," he said, pulling at his cap and shifting from one foot to the other as he stared up at her.

"For us? Are you sure?"

"Yes'm, for Mrs. Janson Sanders—"

"For me?" The knot inside of her increased. Telephone calls had once been everyday affairs at her home in Georgia, but here, in the village, there were few telephones, and few calls. A telephone call had to be important, and that could mean but few things—sickness, emergency, death. "From who? Did they say?"

"Mr. Leon said it was from Georgia, from your brother—" The boy fidgeted from one foot to the other, pulling at his cap again. "You gonna come get it?"

"Yes—yes, we'll be right there." She shut the door in the boy's face without giving him another thought and turned to see Janson pulling on his dungarees. "It's Stan—"

"Yeah, I know," he said, struggling with his clothes.

She moved toward the crying baby where he now lay alone in the middle of the bed, then her clothes, then stopped in the middle of the floor without ever reaching either. "It—it has to be trouble. Someone's hurt, or sick, or—" She turned toward Janson and her words stopped.

She could see on his face that he was thinking the same thing.

Everyone was walking a wide berth around Buddy Eason that morning as he lounged in front of McCallum Grocery. He sat in a straight chair with his legs stuck out before him, trying to obstruct the sidewalk enough to bother anyone who might pass on their way into any of the four stores there on the quiet village street. He found it annoying that the mill families were moving quietly around him, avoiding any contact with his long legs, carefully keeping their eyes averted from his own as if he were not really there, and speaking in quiet tones so that he could not hear what they were saying. Even the three old men whose usual domain he had invaded on this hot summer morning were quieter than usual. They sat as they always sat, in their chairs on the other side of the pickle and cracker barrels, chewing their tobacco, spitting on the walkway, and staring at the village street through yellowing eyes, but today they were silent. Usually they would have been arguing politics or religion, gossiping freely about their neighbors, criticizing their friends and the world in general, reliving their lives in stories that grew grander and more fantastic with each telling—but not this morning. This morning they might not even have been there, except for the wheezing of old man Webber, the smell of rank tobacco from fat old Marcus's cigar, or the occasional streams of tobacco juice from old man Jefferson where he sat tapping his walking cane on the ground at his feet.

Buddy was bored. He had called insults and slights out to the young men who passed, grabbed at the teenage girls, tormented and frightened the smaller children, harassed the old men, and propositioned the women, until they had all begun to cross to the other side of the street to avoid him, and the normally steady foot traffic to and from the stores had thinned to a trickle. He would have moved on to find a more interesting diversion if he had not told Richard and Carl to meet him here. Now he was stuck here, with little or nothing to do.

He turned to lift the lid from the barrel beside him, then reached inside to fish out a pickle before dropping the lid on the ground at his feet. He sat back and chewed on his prize for a moment, looking around, his eyes finally coming to rest on old Amos Jefferson. Buddy glared at him for a moment, until the old man stopped tapping his cane on the ground and stared back. Jefferson looked away and let loose a stream of tobacco juice from the side of his mouth, then brought his eyes back to Buddy—they were gray eyes, old eyes, just like Buddy's grandfather's, and these eyes, just like Walter Eason's, were not afraid of him.

"What are you looking at, you old fart?" Buddy demanded, sitting up to better stare at him.

"I ain't lookin' at nothin'," the old man said, and spat on the ground again. "Nothin' at all—" He wiped at his mouth with one hand and sat back in his chair, continuing to stare at Buddy.

Buddy started to get to his feet, determined to wipe the look from the old man's face, but his eyes caught sight of someone crossing the street coming toward them, and he stopped. Janson Sanders was staring directly at him as he crossed toward the grocery, his wife beside him. Janson kept one arm around the girl's shoulders, and Buddy took the time to look her over, as much to bother Sanders as to satisfy himself—she looked good now that she had lost the belly, the baby now in her arms and wrapped in a faded blanket. Her hair was a bit longer, the bobbed hairstyle growing out, the sun hitting it just right to make it look more red than gold at the moment. She was wearing a cotton print dress that was too long, coming to several inches past her knees, and covering up too much of her legs, Buddy thought as he stared at her—they were nice legs, wasted on that half-Indian millhand.

He raised his eyes back to Janson Sanders as they drew near, tossing the half-eaten pickle back into the barrel he had taken it from without another thought, then he rose to step directly into their path as they approached the front of the grocery. "Where do you think you're going, you red-nigger? This store's no place for red-Indian trash like you—"

"Get outta my way, Buddy. I ain't got time t' fool with you—" There was anger in the green eyes, and hatred as well.

"You'd better learn some manners, boy. You can't go talking to white folks like that."

"Go on, Elise," Janson said, motioning with his head and guiding his wife around Buddy, all the while continuing to stand his ground. "Go on an' take th' call," he told her. "I'll be right in."

Buddy watched her as she brought her eyes to the eyes of her husband, then the girl turned away without ever looking at Buddy directly and walked past him and into the store, the baby held close in her arms. He could see her through the front windows of the grocery, going to the storekeeper for a moment, then allowing old McCallum's wife to take the baby from her as she went to the telephone hanging on the wall near the windows. She took the earpiece from its cradle, and, holding it to her ear, she turned the crank and stood on tiptoe to speak into the small mouthpiece attached to the box on the wall. Buddy could hear her through the screen door at the front of the store. "Hello—hello—could you get operator four in Goodwin, Endicott County, Georgia—"

He watched her for a moment, then turned his eyes back to Janson Sanders. "That's a good looking woman, but she's wasted on you. Who knows, maybe me and a couple of my friends'll show her what its like to have a real man one night while you're at work in the mill, one of us right after the other. She might have herself a white baby the next time—"

The last words had only barely cleared Buddy's lips when Janson was on him, surprising him and knocking him backwards into the chair he had been sitting in, sending it over onto its back, and almost upsetting the barrel nearby as Janson pinned him with one arm trapped beneath him under the chair back. Janson held his right forearm tight across Buddy's windpipe. "I'm gonna break your goddamn neck, like I should'a done years ago. I'm gonna—"

But there was a sudden cry from within the store, then words that were near unintelligible for the horror evident in them: "Mama—oh, God, no—she can't be dead—no—!"

Janson released him and Buddy pushed himself to his feet, then turned to watch the screen door slam behind Janson as he made his way into the store. Buddy watched through the window as the girl collapsed against him when he reached her side. Janson took the earpiece from her hand and spoke into the telephone briefly, then hung it up.

She was crying, shaking with great, heaving sobs that Buddy could see even from that distance, her hands over her face as Janson held her against him. Buddy watched them, watched the sympathy that came to the faces of others in the room, but he could feel nothing, nothing but hatred.

And a determination to make Janson Sanders wish that he had been the one to die today.

The interior of the train that afternoon was a world of heat and sweating bodies. Janson sat beside Elise, staring past her and out the window at her side as the locomotive jerked and started along the tracks on the trip toward Georgia and the home where Elise had spent the first sixteen years of her life. She was crying, silent and staring out the window while the baby slept in her arms—Janson knew that he had failed her today. She had been alone when she had received the news that her mother had died—alone, because he had allowed his temper to get the better of him. He knew that he would never have regretted giving Buddy Eason what he deserved, but he would always regret that he had not been there for Elise when she had needed him. He had failed her, just as he had failed her before back in Endicott County when he had allowed her to stay in her father's house months after they should have left—they should have gone immediately the day she had agreed to marry him, just as she had wanted.

Instead they had stayed as he had worked to earn the money they would need to buy back his land, money they had lost anyway, and he had left her in her father's home until her father had found out about them and had hit her—the memory of her bruised face stayed with him still, even all these months later. The memory of her bruised face, and her father's words when he had at last driven them from his land: "You're both dead to me now. I no longer have a daughter."

Whitley had said that he would kill Janson if they ever returned to Endicott County, but that did not concern him now. Surely Whitley would allow her to return home now, surely he would allow her to mourn for her mother in peace. She should not even be making the trip yet, only four weeks after having given birth, but Janson knew she had to go. He had been ready to give up his job in the card room and the security he had built for them in the village if necessary to go with her, but Walter Eason had surprised him, telling him to be with his wife and that his job would be waiting when he returned.

Now he sat beside Elise, worrying at what they would find when they reached her father's home—she needed her people. She needed her father and Stan, even her brother Bill. She needed to be Elise Whitley again, even for just a time. Surely her father would allow that.

But the words would not leave him: "You're both dead to me now. I no longer have a daughter."

Martha Whitley had come home for the last time, home to the parlor she had loved so well, to the family to whom she had devoted her life. She lay amid banks of flowers in the front parlor, looking as if she were asleep. William sat in a chair near the casket, holding her unfinished needlework in his hands, his eyes on her face, his mind telling him that she would have to open her eyes soon to say that it was all a mistake. She looked so much as she had looked on so many mornings when he had waked before her, so peaceful, sleeping—she could not be dead. She could not be—

Family and friends filled the rooms of the house, moving quietly about him, speaking in hushed tones, talking of what a good woman she had been, what a good mother and wife, how devoted she had been to her family and to the church. The minister and his wife had been in the house almost from the moment Martha had died, trying to console William, trying to get him to eat, but he could do nothing but sit and stare. He could not move from where he was, could not leave her or stop looking at the face that would so soon be shut away—she had to wake up, he kept telling himself. She had to. This could not be real. This could not be—

William had cried, for only the second time he could remember since he had been a small boy, when Martha left him. He had been sitting holding her hand, talking to her quietly, when it happened. He had screamed for help, had tried to lift her into his arms—she could not die. She could not—

The scent of the flowers was overpowering, the presence of the family, neighbors, and friends an intrusion—he wanted to be alone with her, to say goodbye in private if he had to, to cry as he could not before all these people. A knot sat firmly in the back of his throat, a pressure behind his eyes—Martha was dead. His Martha was dead, and, after these days of flowers and condolences from people who could never have known or loved her as he did, he would never see her again. They would put her into the ground, and he would be alone.

Bill was here, for the first time in months, not having come to see his mother even in the last days—he was talking business with someone William had never seen before, talking business as he sat only a few feet from his mother's casket. It angered William that he could conduct business here, today.

But he could not break the spell that held him here looking at her, could not break it even to go and order her son from the house. He knew that he should, knew that Bill had no right here after the pain he had caused his mother. She had spent her last months worrying about him. About him, and about—

The minister was kneeling beside him again, offering senseless words about God and heaven—but there could be no God. William damned the idea of God, damned the idea of heaven, damned even the devil himself—but nothing helped. Martha still lay there, peaceful, serene, dead, looking as if she were asleep.

There was a twittering of feminine voices, a note of lightness that had no place in this room. Stan moved toward him, his young face looking drawn and almost old. "How can they laugh with Mama—" His words trailed off, filled with bitterness. William only looked up at him, and then turned his eyes back to his wife. He wished he could feel comfort in the boy's presence. He wished he could feel comfort in anything, but he knew he never would again. Martha was dead.

There was a light whispering of voices, moving from the open parlor doorway and into the room, a hush, and then a quiet murmuring as people near the doorway stepped aside for someone to enter. William could hear the whisper of gossiped words as he felt the eyes of the room move from whoever had entered to him, then back again. He lifted his eyes, seeing the quiet exchange of words behind lifted hands, then he turned his eyes toward the doorway, his hands clenching tightly on Martha's needlework as he saw his daughter enter the room with the half-Indian farmhand she had married at her side. She held a baby in her arms, a baby wrapped in a light, faded blanket. Her face was pale and tear-streaked, her hair slightly longer, her gray dress neat and plain. She looked older, and so much like Martha.

William felt his breath catch in the back of his throat, the pain rising to choke him for a moment—so much like Martha, before years and children and worry had worn her down and had finally taken the life from her. His eyes moved back to the casket, to the face, to the memories—Martha had looked like that, so much like that. She had once looked at him with nothing but love. She had once seen only goodness in him—until Elise had taken all that from him, Elise and her farmhand. Martha's last months had been filled with pain—Elise had caused that in choosing her farmhand, in breeding her part-Indian brat, in pushing William to do only what he had had to do to try to protect his family. Elise had taken Martha from him even months before her death, causing a distance between them that he would now never be able to bridge—Elise and her farmhand, and they dared come here even now to intrude on his grief.

He slowly rose to his feet, finding his legs were shaking beneath him as he watched Elise cross the room toward him and her mother's casket. She had begun to cry again, her lower lip trembling, as she reached the side of the casket and looked in at her mother's face.

Sanders put an arm around her, standing close at her side, his eyes on Martha as well as Elise reached out to touch her mother's hand—the control within William snapped. A cry of anger and pain escaped him as he took a step forward, bracing his hand on the edge of the casket for support to still the shaking muscles in his legs. "Get out of here! Get out of my house!"

Elise took a step back, looking as if she had been struck, her blue eyes large and bright with tears, her lashes and cheeks damp. The baby in her arms began to cry, and she held it closer against her as she stared up at her father with what appeared almost to be disbelief. "Daddy, I—"

"Get out of my house, goddamn you! Get out of here, and take your squalling brat with you! Get out!" He was shaking with rage, holding out his hand that held the needlework, with one finger pointing toward the parlor doorway.

"Please—I—" She was trembling, crying so hard that she could not speak. It seemed for a moment that she would have collapsed had it not been for Sanders at her side.

"She's got th' right t' be here. Mrs. Whitley was her ma—" Janson said, staring at him as he tightened the arm he held around her. "You cain't keep her from—"

"Goddamn it—I can! Get the hell out of my house! Get off my land!

Goddamn you—you killed your mother, and you dare to come back here to mourn her now! You killed her! You ran off with him and left her here to die! You killed her! Get out of my house! Get out!" He screamed the words, flailing his arm about with the needlework in his hand until he knocked over the nearby flowers and sent them crashing to the floor. "Get out, and don't ever come back!"

The girl collapsed against Sanders as Stan reached her side, the farmhand and the boy both supporting her and the baby she still held in her arms as they led her from the room. She was crying harder, trembling so badly that the baby set into even louder wails.

"Get out of my house!" William screamed again, even after they had left his sight. "Get out!"

Everyone was staring at him, looking dumbfounded and embarrassed, pity for the girl written plainly on almost every face around him.

"Get out!" he screamed again, no longer caring who looked or who heard—he wanted them all out. He wanted—"Get out of my house! Get out, and don't ever come back! Get out!"

The day was hot, the wind still, the heat sitting on her skin and making Elise dizzy as she stood at the graveside staring at the closed casket that held her mother. Janson was beside her, the baby asleep in his arms, but still she felt as if she were alone. Her mother was gone, but Elise could still see her so clearly in her mind, could still see her as Martha Whitley had been the day Elise had left here to be with Janson, her mother standing on the steps that led up to the front veranda of her father's home, waving goodbye to Elise for the last time as Elise had watched her through the rear window of the Model T Ford that had taken them into town that day.

She moved her eyes now toward where her father stood beside the grave. He did not seem aware that anyone else was in the graveyard as he stared at the flowers that covered his wife's casket. He looked old, shaken, barely able to stand, Stan's support at his one side, and that of one of her father's hired men, Franklin Bates, at the other, seeming to be all that kept him on his feet. Elise watched him as the Baptist minister led the mourners in prayer—he did not bow his head to pray, but just continued to stare at the casket as if there were no life left in him as well. She wanted to hate him—but she could feel nothing, no matter how hard she tried, but an aching emptiness that she knew nothing would ever fill again.

As the mourners began to file away, Elise stood watching the family and friends she had known all her life as they cried and hugged and grieved together—but no one moved toward her. They all left the graveyard, walking toward the cars in the church parking lot, Stan and Franklin Bates leading her father away as if he could no longer move on his own, until at last she, Janson, and the baby, were alone at the graveside.

"We've got t' go, Elise," Janson said. He held the baby asleep now on one arm, the other arm held around her.

"Not yet," she said, staring at the casket. "Not yet—"

"Yes—you shouldn't be out in this heat, an' neither should the baby—"

The baby—yes.

The baby who would never know his grandmother.

But still she did not move.

"Elise—"

She could still see her mother standing on the steps, waving to her—

And the men standing nearby now, waiting for them to leave so they could put her mother into the ground.

Her mother waving—

She felt the edges of her vision darkening, her face becoming cold and clammy even in the heat of the day, all sense of the graveyard fading about her as her knees gave way and she fainted there against Janson's side.

It was late that afternoon before Janson would allow her to return to the cemetery. He had taken her back to the hotel and had made her lie down for most of the day, and had only reluctantly agreed to their returning to the graveyard when she had threatened that she would come alone if he would not accompany her—she had to see her mother's grave one last time before they returned to Alabama. She had not been here when her mother had died, and had been driven from her father's house when she had gone there to mourn her passing—this was all she had left, the only way remaining to say goodbye.

Janson stood nearby holding the baby in his arms as Elise sat on the ground at the graveside, her eyes on the flowers that covered the raw mound of earth. Her mother had always loved flowers—but these did little to cover the ugliness of the red earth newly turned, the red earth that now held her mother. She reached toward one of the blooms, but drew her hand back a moment before touching the petals as she realized how badly it had already begun to wilt in the summer heat—there was no life left in it. No life left in the grave that it covered.

She sat for a long time, tears moving down her cheeks until she could cry no more, but still she continued to stare. Janson knelt beside her, saying something that she could not understand, and she realized that the baby was crying—but she could not make herself move. She could only see in her mind that sad, tearful woman who had stood on the front steps waving to her as she had left that day.

She did not realize they were no longer alone in the graveyard until Stan was kneeling at her side. "Elise, are you okay?" he asked, in a voice that brought back memories that choked her. She only nodded, not taking her eyes from the grave. From the edge of her vision she saw him look up to Janson, and then back to her before he reached to take something from his pocket. "I went to the hotel to try to find you. When you weren't there, I knew you'd be here. There's something I think you should see."

He held a paper out to her, but she did not turn to look at it.

"Elise, I think you should. It's from Mama—"

She brought her eyes to him. "But—"

He nodded. "She must have known—" For a moment his words fell silent, and he looked away. "I was going to write the date that—that Mama—" Again, he fell silent, bringing his eyes back to her. "This was underneath the family Bible when I picked it up, torn in half like this. She must have written it right after she found out that she was dying. She wanted you to come home; she wanted to see your baby. She must have thought Daddy mailed it."

Elise brought her eyes fully to the paper in his hands, to the torn halves of a letter she had never received. When she reached for it her hands were trembling, and they began to tremble even more as she recognized the handwriting that she had never thought she would see again. She carefully unfolded the torn paper, smoothing it out on her lap and holding the two sides together so that she could read her mother's words.

*"My dearest Elise . . ."*

She began to cry anew as she read, having to wipe away tears so she could see the words—her mother had wanted to see her. Her mother had sent for her, had wanted her to bring Henry. Her mother had—

There was so much love in the words, so much of the mother she would never know again—and her father had kept them apart during her mother's last days.

Martha Whitley's last words to her daughter were about Janson:

*"I can remember wishing the two of you had never met, because he took my little girl away, but I know now that your meeting was what was meant to be. Janson will take care of you, and he will love you and my little grandson. He is a good man, Elise, and, even though you will never have an easy life for being his wife, I know he will do everything he can to provide for you. I know he loves you, and I know how much you love him—it was so obvious when you looked at each other. If only your father had not been so blind . . ."*

If only your father had not been so blind . . .

Janson was there suddenly, holding the baby, holding her as well as she cried, even before she knew how she had gotten into his arms. He held her for a long time, letting her cry, until Henry began to cry in earnest and she took him.

"We'd better get back t' th' hotel," Janson said, looking at her now, touching her face. "You need some rest, an' so does Henry."

Elise looked toward her brother, and he managed a smile and a nod. Stan walked back to the hotel with them, more silent than she had ever known him in their years of growing up, and he left them once they had reached their room, hugging her and kissing her one last time before he was gone.

Elise slept little that night, as memories of her mother and her childhood came back to her. She was tired when the sun rose the next morning, and did not argue when Janson said she should rest at the hotel until time for them to leave. He reluctantly left her to go to check the train schedule, leaving Elise feeling alone as she sat on the edge of the bed watching the baby sleep. There was a tap at the door and she got up to answer it, afraid that it might be someone her father had sent to drive her from the hotel as he had driven her from his house, but instead she found J. C. Cooper standing there.

"I saw you and Janson at a distance at the funeral, and Stan told me you were staying here," he said. Elise hugged him, tears coming with the sympathy that showed on his face. "I wanted to tell you how sorry I am—"

"Thank you. You don't know how good it is to see you—I was feeling pretty alone." She led him into the room, closing the door.

"Where's Janson?"

"He went to check on the train schedules, for us to go back to—" she caught herself and changed what she had been about to say, "to go back home." Why had she found it so strange to call Eason County home after all the months spent there? This place no longer seemed home, but it had been so hard to say it, to call the village and their half of a house home. It was as if she had awakened from a long sleep, and now Pine seemed less than real, their rooms in the mill house like something from a dream.

She brought her mind back to J.C.'s words and his presence, enjoying his company, looking at his face and seeing there one of the best friends she had ever known.

"I heard you had a baby." He bent over Henry where he slept between pillows on the bed, watching the baby move one fist slightly in his sleep. "He looks like Janson."

"Yes, he does," Elise said, smiling as she looked at her son. She bent to lightly touch the small cheek, then sat on the bed beside the baby and looked up at J.C.. "His name is Henry; it was Janson's father's name."

"Henry—that's nice. I wish we would—" Then he fell silent, seeming somehow distant for a moment. He brought his attention back to her, smiling, rather falsely, she thought. "Phyllis Ann and I are married," he said at last.

"Oh? That's very nice." She tried to make her words show happiness for him, but they rang hollow even to her own ears—she just felt pity for him. Pity for any man who had joined his life to Phyllis Ann Bennett.

"We were married in April; it rained like the devil all day—but I don't believe in old wives tales, do you? She was a lovely bride—" He chattered on, too gaily, as he pushed his glasses up off the bridge of his nose with a finger. Elise had been so happy to see him, as he had been to see her, even in these circumstances—but now the visit was ruined. They both pretended there was not a tension between them, but each knew the other pretended. Phyllis Ann stood between them now, as surely as if she were in the room, straining a kinship that had once been almost as brother and sister. They talked to fill the silence, but both were relieved when J. C. stood to leave.

"I'm glad I got to see you," she said, walking him to the door with her arm hooked firmly through his.

"I'm glad I got to see you, too." He hugged her briefly and kissed her cheek, then turned to leave, but stopped and turned back, looking at her for a moment. "You're happy, aren't you?" he asked, the false gaiety now gone from his face.

She thought for a moment, then answered. "I'm glad that I married Janson. I'm happy that we're together, and that we have Henry."

He nodded, then turned away.

"Are you happy?" she asked, then immediately regretted the words as he brought his eyes back to her.

He was silent for a long moment, distant in his own feeling and thought. "There are a lot of things you don't have any choice in. I guess who you fall in love with is one of them," he said, his eyes on her. "It doesn't always make you happy, but it could be so much worse; it would be worse to live without her—I—" he sighed and looked away, "I don't know." He shook his head.

Elise put her hand on his arm, understanding perhaps more than he could ever know, her mind going to the village, to Eason County waiting for her.

J. C. brought his eyes back to her, a look of understanding passing between them. "Goodbye, Elise."

"Goodbye, J. C." And he was gone, her sympathy going with him.

# Chapter Five

Children filled the front of Perryman Street Baptist Church in the mill village the last Sunday evening before Christmas. There were angels dressed in sheets whose halos looked to be made from coat hangers, shepherds in burlap sack robes, and a Mary and Joseph clothed in what had obviously been curtain material. Elise sat in the third pew on the right-hand side with Henry on her lap, smiling as she watched the tiny Mary give the much larger Joseph his line for the third time.

Janson's cousin, Sissy, sat beside Elise. Sissy had been staying at the mill house with them since the end of summer, when Buddy Eason's trips down their street at last had frayed Elise's nerves to such an extent that she had become afraid to be alone in the house at night with the baby while Janson was at work. At Sissy's other side was Tim Cauthen, whose family had moved into the village over the summer, his father, James Cauthen, having been brought all the way from Florence, near the Tennessee line, to take a job as roller coverer in the mill. Beside Tim was Wheeler James Keith. Wheeler James was two years older than Tim and three years older than Sissy, but, to anyone who saw the three of them, it was obvious that both boys had been interested in Sissy since she had come to stay in the village. Over the past months at least one of them was usually at her side during church services.

The children started a chorus of "Silent Night," one of the angels almost shouting the words, making Elise smile as she watched the mother, sitting a few rows away, at first grin proudly, then squirm noticeably as the loud singing continued—then another sound overlaid the singing, the sound of giggles and stomping feet as someone ascended the stairs, coming up from the basement into the sanctuary at one side of the pulpit.

Iona Walsh and Abby Poole were giggling as they reached the top of the stairs, but were quickly shushed by a third girl, Cassandra Price, as the three made their way to sit on a pew in the little side wing of the sanctuary. Elise saw Abby's eyes move over the congregation, coming at last to rest on Sissy, Tim, and Wheeler James. Abby placed one hand over her mouth, as if to stifle another giggle, which brought Cassandra Price's elbow back into what appeared to be sharp contact with her ribs as if again trying to make her be quiet.

Unease moved through Elise. Over the past months that Sissy had been attending church with her, she had watched Helene Price's only daughter at first ignore the girl, then growingly become jealous as Tim Cauthen's attention moved from Cassandra to Sissy. Elise had seen the whispered words Cassandra had exchanged with other girls in the church during the first weeks, and she had known immediately what was being said; after all, it was not that long ago that she herself had been fourteen, and she knew very well what girls that age could be like. She could also remember her own reaction to Sissy when they first met—Janson had told her that most people considered Sissy to be "simple." At first that knowledge made Elise uncomfortable around the girl, for she had never been around anyone who was thought to be slow—but, as she had gotten to know Sissy, what she had begun to see instead was a goodness within her that was so complete there seemed no room left for anything else. It was true she could not read or write, but, then again, Janson could do little better, a fact that Elise herself had only learned back in Georgia at the cost of his pride in the first months she had known him.

Sissy had been raised by her grandparents, and had spent almost her entire life in their home in the country, her father having died shortly after her birth and her mother not long after her second birthday. Deborah Sanders was so protective of her that it had taken a great deal of pleading on Sissy's part just to be allowed to spend one night in the village, and it had taken the combined efforts of Sissy and her grandfather, and Janson as well, to convince Deborah that she should be allowed to move in with them. Sissy had started attending the village school, and had made friends with several girls, especially with Lynette Pierce, who lived at the far end of their street. Boys her age and older had immediately taken notice of her, for she was undeniably lovely, with long blond hair in curls down her back and a figure already developing well for fourteen. Tim and Wheeler James both spent time with her at church—but that was what had changed Cassandra's disinterest into obvious jealousy.

Elise watched Cassandra now where she sat in the side pew, watched her as she pushed her pale, bobbed hair back from her forehead and then settled a stare on Sissy that did not waver.

Once the play ended, the congregation moved downstairs to the Christmas tree that had been set up in the church basement. Elise took a cup of punch from a table the WMU ladies had set up in a corner, then went to sit down on one of the chairs lined against the far wall. She bounced Henry lightly on her lap, watching the six-month-old's eyes go to the colorful mound of presents piled beneath the tree. She knew at least one of those would be for him, and one for herself as well, for the Sunday school classes had drawn names weeks before to make certain no one would be left out when gifts were exchanged.

One of the two outside doors into the basement opened and Santa Claus came in wearing a thread-bare red suit and a beard made from cotton, "ho-ho's" coming from the tangled mass of white across his lower face as he made his way toward the tree. Elise smiled, recognizing him as one of the deacons, the only man in the church who could fill the suit with a minimal amount of padding.

Dorrie came to sit beside Elise. Sissy was sitting not far distant, Tim on her one side and Wheeler James on the other, both boys having gradually moved their chairs out and turned them inward so they could better see the girl as as they talked.

"Lord, but one 'a them's gonna be hurtin' when she chooses between 'em," Dorrie said. "Tim's a good boy, but I'm pullin' for Wheeler James; that boy 'a mine ain't been able t' see straight since he first laid eyes on her."

Elise laughed, watching the exaggerated hand motions Tim made as he talked, and the disappointment that came to Wheeler James's face as Sissy's attention focused for the moment on Tim—maybe it was a good thing that Janson slept on Sunday morning and never would come with her to church on Sunday evenings. Elise might enjoy watching the two boys vie for Sissy's attention, but Janson was almost as protective of Sissy as his grandmother. He had told Elise that he did not trust Tim or Wheeler James either one, saying that he knew what "fellas that age" were after, as though he were an old man instead of seven months past his twenty-first birthday.

Dorrie took Henry onto her lap as Elise unwrapped the present for him that had been brought to her by Viola Ann Pierce, the little girl helping Santa to hand out presents. The gift went into his mouth the moment she handed it to him, and she sighed—everything seemed to go into his mouth, whether it was meant to go there or not. She kept listening for her own name, and was surprised when she heard Sissy's name called for a second time, then turned to watch Viola Ann hand Sissy another gift, this one more ornately wrapped than the first, which had turned out to be a hairbrush from the girl who had drawn her name in their Sunday school class.

Sissy looked first at Tim and then at Wheeler James, but both boys only shook their heads and looked at each other. She then turned her eyes toward Elise, but Elise shook her head, having no idea who might have brought the gift. She watched Sissy untie the bow and pull the ribbon aside to lay it across her lap, then unfasten the tape and fold the paper back to reveal a box inside. The girl put her thumb under the edge of the lid, a smile on her face as she glanced up at the two boys—but that smile was quickly replaced by surprised disgust. She threw the box down, causing something to fall out of it, Elise realizing that it was animal feces—

Wheeler James quickly gathered up the box, scooping its contents from the floor, and took it out the side entrance, his father, Clarence, following close behind. Tim was bent over Sissy, patting her hand, the girl's cheeks now scarlet with embarrassment. There was a nervous tittering in the room, hushed words, and some much louder—and, above it all, Elise heard the unmistakable sound of laughter. She looked quickly toward the rear entrance just before the door closed on Cassandra, Abby, and Iona, all doubled over with laughter.

The preacher was standing in the middle of the room now, sputtering and indignant, his face red. Elise rose and made her way past him and toward that rear door, wanting to strangle the persons who had done this.

The girls were laughing so hard they did not notice the door opening or Elise standing there. The Walsh girl and Abby Poole leaned against each other as Cassandra Price gave a mock gasp and brought both hands out in an exaggerated imitation of Sissy throwing the box down. Cassandra was laughing so hard she could barely stand, but her words were unmistakable: "Oh, it was worth every minute of picking up that dog shit."

Elise started forward, but suddenly Tim Cauthen was there and then past her, and the girls saw him a moment before they saw Elise, all trace of amusement leaving their faces in an instant as they realized that he had seen and heard everything.

"You—how could you do something like that!"

"We didn't do anything," Abby tried, but fell silent as Tim turned on her, his fists clenched, and the girl looked afraid that he would actually strike her.

"I heard you—if you didn't do it yourself, you knew about it and didn't put a stop to it!"

"It was only a joke," Cassandra said, looking more angry than afraid as she glared at him.

"You rotten little brats!" Elise heard her own words and was surprised at their vehemence, but proud of the look of surprise they drew from Abby and Iona. "You ought to be ashamed of yourselves, every one of you—and you just wait until I tell your parents. You just wait—"

She was surprised to see Cassandra Price start to smile.

If only Elise Sanders had talked to her mother, Cassandra told herself days later, then everything would have been all right. Instead, Janson Sanders had talked to her father at the mill, earning Cassandra Price the first whipping she had gotten in years. Cassandra had known that she could handle her mother, for Helene Price would never believe a word anyone else said over what her daughter might say—but her father could be a different matter altogether. Usually Bert Price gave in to his wife's every whim, but even Helene could not save her this time—it had been only a small whipping, a few licks with his belt, but it had been enough to make Cassandra hate the entire Sanders family.

She did not think they should be attending the Baptist church in the village anyway, for Janson Sanders was not white; he was half Cherokee Indian. He should be attending one of the colored churches on the other side of town, his wife, their part-Indian brat, and his dim-witted cousin with him, and the fact that he hardly ever attended church with his family did nothing to alter Cassandra's opinion.

Cassandra expressed that opinion to her mother—after all, her mother was one of the leading members of the church, a long-standing member of the choir, and the wife of a deacon. Helene should be able to see to it that the Sanders family attended church where they should—but Cassandra made the mistake of expressing that opinion before her father, and got another whipping for it. She would never forgive the Sanders—never.

And it was Sissy Sanders she hated most of all. Not only had Sissy been the cause of the whippings Cassandra had gotten, when she was fourteen years old now and rightfully should be beyond such things, but she had also cost Cassandra the attention of Tim Cauthen. Tim was one of the best-looking boys in the mill village, and he had been interested in Cassandra until Sissy had started attending church with her half-breed cousin's wife and their baby—and now Tim would not pay Cassandra any attention at all. Cassandra, Abby, and Iona had only been having fun at Christmas—and Sissy deserved it in the first place for being so vulnerable and so dumb. Sissy was too pretty, and too simple to know it—and best of all, she was so innocent it was easy. It had been nothing but fun.

But now Tim had become the self-appointed protector of that dim-witted girl. He sat with her in church, and even during lunch break at school when no one but fat Lynette Pierce would sit with her. He could have chosen any friends in the church or school, yet he chose to spend his time with Sissy Sanders—she should not be going to school with normal people anyway, Cassandra told herself, for the girl could not even read or write.

It was a chilly day in late February when Cassandra reached the point where she could take no more. There had been months of seeing Tim with that pretty little halfwit, when he would speak to Cassandra only enough not to appear rude. She had tried to behave as if it did not bother her, as if she had not lost out to a girl so poorly equipped to compete with her, but, on that day, walking home from school with Abby and Iona, with Tim and Sissy just within sight ahead of them, it was impossible to conceal her feelings. She glared at their backs as they walked, filled with anger and jealousy as she saw Tim take Sissy's books to carry with his own—surely he did not really like that dimwit, Cassandra told herself. There had to be some other reason he paid so much attention to her, why he would prefer her company over—

"You're gonna stare a hole through them," Iona said, breaking into her thoughts, and Cassandra turned to see a smile play across her face. Iona stood a head taller than she did, with long, gangly legs and breasts that were already developing well when Cassandra's chest was still as flat as a ten-year-old's. "You're absolutely green—"

"I am not," she snapped, angry that her feelings showed so clearly on her face.

"You are, too. You're jealous and it shows." There was a twangy, nasal tone to Iona's voice that reminded Cassandra of the Northern peddler who had come through the village a few months back. That tone grated on Cassandra's ears, today even more than usual.

"Everybody knows you've been stuck on Tim since he moved here." Abby was grinning openly in her face. She tossed her short, dark hair, obviously liking for once that she had the upper hand—she would never have dared to tease Cassandra if Iona had not started it.

"I am not."

"And he's sweet on Sissy now." Iona stared pointedly at the two walking ahead as Sissy stopped to pet a puppy that had run out from a yard they were passing. Tim stopped and watched her, bending to pet the puppy as well, and again Cassandra wondered—

"She's got him wrapped tight around her little finger. They'll probably even end up getting married—Tim and Sissy Cauthen," Abby laughed, making Cassandra writhe all the more within.

She glared straight ahead, refusing to acknowledge that she had even heard the taunts, much less that they had struck a nerve. She watched as Tim and Sissy began to walk again, the puppy now yapping at their heels. The sunlight played on Sissy's long blonde curls—she had no right to be so pretty and still so dimwitted, Cassandra told herself. She had no right to thick blonde hair when Cassandra's was so thin, pale, and lifeless. She had no right to a pretty smile and blue eyes to hide a mind as dumb as an ox, and no right to breasts that made her look like a woman already when Cassandra was still as shapeless as a child. The longer Cassandra stared at her, the more she hated her, and the more she hated her the more she swore that she would fix her.

"Everybody knows how sweet you were on Tim, and that he'd rather be with Sissy now than with—"

"You know why he spends so much time with her, don't you—she's so dumb she'd let a boy do anything—" Cassandra said, continuing to stare straight ahead as she enjoyed the silence that followed her statement, then—

"You mean she—" Abby began, then fell silent as she turned to stare at the two ahead.

"Of course, just look at her."

"You think Tim would—"

"What else would he want with somebody like her?"

"She's slow," Iona said, "but I don't think she would—"

"I saw it myself." There—so easily said, and Cassandra felt a moment of triumph at their joint gasps of surprise.

"Tim and Sissy—?"

"Really—?"

Cassandra nodded, but did not turn to look at either of them—there, that'll fix her, she thought, although she resisted the urge to smile.

The first time she told the lie it had been on a whim, but the second time it was done deliberately. It worked so well with her friends—if her mother thought Sissy was trashy, then Helene might be able to stop her from coming back to the church again, her and that entire family of hers. She watched her mother's crimson face as she finished the story that same afternoon, celebrating inwardly as she saw the look of shock turn into righteous indignation—oh, yes, that'll fix her, Cassandra thought.

The rumors spread like wildfire. Within a week, almost every female member of Pearlman Street Baptist "knew" that Sissy Sanders was fast and loose. Her lack of morals became the primary topic of discussion on porches and over afternoon visiting from house to house the village over. Ladies said that in "their day" a girl who was "not quite right" would have been kept home and away from other people, so that no one would ever even have known that she existed. A few even said that Janson Sanders was "not quite right" either, and that "mixed blood never resulted in anything good." Several said Sissy should be "fixed" before she could get into trouble and find herself in the family way, and that the world certainly did not need any more "dimwitted people." Quite a number said she should not be living in the village, and they looked at their husbands and sons with distrust, because as the rumors spread first one, and then another, was being named as having been seen with her.

Bert Price was aghast that his wife should mention such a subject to Reverend Satterwhite, the preacher, but he was unable to stop her. Helene told the preacher that Sissy Sanders should be barred from attending services, and her entire family with her—after all, Janson Sanders was Holiness, and Elise, though supposedly baptized a Baptist years before, never really fit in at their church in the village. She was just as Holiness as her husband, Helene claimed, and Pearlman Street Baptist did not need any "Holy Rollers" in the congregation. Elise's child was not white, and neither was her husband—and Janson Sanders smelled, Helene claimed, though she had only seen him once, and then at a distance. She told the preacher that "such people" should attend the "colored churches" on the other side of town, because that was where "such people" belonged—and she also thought, though she would never dare speak of it in public, that Janson Sanders should not be working in the mill right alongside white people, that the Easons should never have hired him to do anything more than scrub toilets or wash windows with the very few black men the mill hired. She would not dare to say that outside her own home, and then only within the hearing of her own husband and daughter, for she knew they would never speak a word of it. After all they were not the sort of people who would ever spread gossip, and it was not the sort of thing one could do openly, to second-guess the Eason family.

The poor Reverend Satterwhite could do nothing but listen and nod, for he knew he could not ask the girl or her family not to attend the church on the basis of rumor and patent dislike. He had heard enough backbiting out of Helene Price in the little more than a year he had been in the village; he well knew the woman could be set off by any little thing. He also knew that whatever she heard she would quickly spread through all the other women of the church.

Within two weeks of Cassandra's talk with her mother, the rumors had reached the ears of Irene Cauthen, Tim's mother, and Tim was forbidden to walk Sissy home, or sit with her in church or during lunch at school—and, for the first time in his life, Tim Cauthen openly defied his parents. Sissy was sweet and good, he told his father, in an absolute rage after his father gave him "the talk" and asked what all had gone on between them. He would not change even one thing he was doing—if anyone told lies on him, they would be as untrue as the lies told on Sissy, he said, slamming the door as he left the house, leaving his father enraged and his mother wringing her hands in the kitchen behind him.

Within a month the rumors had passed through the school. By the time they reached Cassandra's ears again, they had grown and enlarged to such a point that she was not only surprised, but inordinately pleased with herself—Sissy Sanders was going to have a baby, the rumors now said, and she had no idea who the father was.

No more than a week later the gossip reached the ears of the principal of the village school, Mrs. Cunningham, a tall, imposing woman with a mass of iron-gray hair and posture so perfect it appeared she could never bend—she could not have a girl who was in the family way in the village school. It was bad enough that there was no incentive for the children of the mill workers to learn, for nothing was expected of them other than what the Easons would need in the mill—an ability to read and write, to run a column of figures, to operate the cards or drawing frames or other machinery, the ability to follow orders and not to stir up trouble— nothing more and nothing less. She could not have a girl who was in a delicate condition attending the school, and even the thought of that influence on the other girls was almost more than Mrs. Cunningham could bear—something would have to be done, and done immediately, she told herself as she left her office in search of Sissy Sanders. Yes, something would have to be done immediately.

Elise was sitting on her front porch that afternoon, tatting lace for the collar of the new dress she was making for herself while she watched Henry playing on the porch floor at her feet. She would have to go into the house soon to feed him and get him down for his nap, but her mind was occupied for the moment with the lace that was taking longer to make than she thought it should. She had hoped to have the dress finished before Janson got home that afternoon.

The mill had changed from two twelve-hour to three eight-hour shifts late last year. The new schedule allowed additional time Janson could spend with Elise and Henry, and had given him doubles at times, even triples, which meant additional money toward buying his land back one day. He would have to eat and get some rest this afternoon, for he would have another shift starting only eight hours after the double ended, but there might be a little time they could spend together.

She heard Henry laugh at her feet, and she looked down at him to find him bouncing excitedly as he stared toward the dirt street. Elise lifted her eyes in that direction as well, curious to see what had excited him so, and was surprised to see Sissy entering the yard. She glanced down at her wrist watch, not believing she had let so much of the day get away from her, then saw that it was still hours from the time school should be out—a stab of alarm went through her, and only increased as she met Sissy's eyes over the distance between them.

Sissy's face was tear-streaked and filled with pain. Elise set her tatting aside quickly and rose to her feet, instinctively lifting Henry into her arms as she moved to meet Sissy at the top of the steps.

"Mrs. Cunningham said I cain't go to school no more," Sissy said, breaking into tears again as Elise reached out to touch her damp cheek. "She said there ain't no place in school for a girl like me—"

Elise led her into the house and they sat on the bed in the front room—there had to be some sort of mistake. Mrs. Cunningham would not have sent her home. There were only a few more days of school left this year; perhaps Sissy had only misunderstood—but the words repeated to her left little doubt. The principal had told Sissy to go home and to not come back again this year or the next, that there was no place in the school for a girl like her.

Absolute fury rose within Elise—how dare the woman! Sissy could have done nothing to hurt anyone. She might have difficulty learning, but she had actually begun to read and write a little this year with extra help from her teacher and from Elise as well—how dare the principal do this! Sissy had as much right to be in the village school as anyone; she was a member of Elise and Janson's family, and she already talked of going to the mill herself in another year or so.

Elise rose from the edge of the bed and stood staring at Sissy for a moment. "You stay here and watch Henry for me after I get him down for his nap," she said. "I'll go have a talk with Mrs. Cunningham and we'll get this straightened out—"

Visiting the village school that afternoon, Elise did not know what she had expected when she determined to confront Mrs. Cunningham. She only knew she had never expected what she found in the principal's office.

"I am sorry, Mrs. Sanders, but you have to know we can't have a girl like Sissy in this school," Mrs. Cunningham said as she sat behind her desk. She had an unnervinging habit of closing her eyes each time she spoke, and keeping them closed for the entire duration of what she was saying. Mrs. Cunningham was nothing like Miss Perry, the principal of the boarding school Elise had attended in Atlanta with Phyllis Ann Bennett, but in that moment she reminded Elise greatly of Eva Perry. The commanding attitude of the woman was reminiscent of Miss Perry, and made Elise feel again like the sixteen-year-old girl she had been those two years before when she herself had been expelled from school.

"What do you mean 'a girl like Sissy'?" Elise demanded, trying to force the angry tone back into her voice. She did not like feeling like that sixteen-year-old again, and especially not before this woman. "I would bet there is not another girl in this school who works as hard as Sissy does. She may be a little slower to—"

"Come now, Mrs. Sanders, we both know that Sissy was not sent home because she's slow."

For a moment Elise could only stare at her.

"Really—you have to know what kind of girl she is." The woman looked slightly taken aback as she met Elise's eyes across the desktop.

Elise returned her stare. "You can't mean—" The words failed her.

"Well, really, Mrs. Sanders, she lives with you. Surely you must have at least—"

Comprehension came slowly to Elise of the full import of the woman's words. "Sissy is not that kind of girl!"

Mrs. Cunningham looked uncomfortable. She got up from her chair and moved toward the window to stand staring out with her hands clasped behind her. "I would not have thought that I would have to be the one to tell you something about someone living in your own home, but, yes, she is that kind of girl. Surely you must understand now why I—"

Elise rose slowly from her chair, anger building within her to take the place of the initial shock and surprise. "What makes you think that Sissy—that she—"

"I have been told—by more than one source, I assure you—that she has been seen in—well—in improper situations with a number of young men. And she—" The woman stopped for a moment, then seemed to plunge ahead. "She is with child, Mrs. Sanders; I cannot have—"

"'With child'!" Elise almost shouted the words, and Mrs. Cunningham turned to look at her. "Sissy is not pregnant!"

The older woman looked taken aback, and Elise wondered for a moment if it were not more at Elise's use of the word pregnant than her anger.

"Mrs. Sanders, there's no need to—"

"How dare you! Who is spreading lies like that about Sissy? Who?"

"I cannot say, but I assure you that—"

"Who?" Elise demanded, slamming a fist down on the principal's desk and drawing a startled look from the older woman.

"Really, you must control yourself, young lady!"

"Don't tell me to control myself. I am not one of your students to—" But she stopped, took a deep breath, and tried to calm her racing heart.

"I have made my decision, Mrs. Sanders. Just because Sissy is simple does not excuse her getting herself in this situation or her being the sort of girl she is—and you have to know that I cannot have a girl who is in a delicate condition around the young girls in this school. She will not return here, and that decision is final."

Elise held the bare control over her temper, forcing herself to speak more calmly. "Whoever told you such things about Sissy is a liar. Sissy is not the kind of girl who would—" But she could see that her words were making no impact on the woman. "Sissy is not pregnant!"

"Time will tell." Mrs. Cunningham stood for a long moment staring at Elise. "Good day, Mrs. Sanders," she said at last. And Elise knew that she, too, was being dismissed.

Elise turned her steps toward Dorrie's house. She knew Dorrie was home today with a badly twisted ankle and bruised hip and side she had gotten from a fall inside the mill two days before. Elise had already gone by to check on her once that morning, and had planned on going by again later that afternoon. She needed time to think, time to decide what it was she would say to Sissy. She wished now she hadn't been so positive in talking to the girl—what would she ever say to her now?

She called out a greeting as she entered the Keiths' three rooms in the house they shared with the Cofield family. The door was unlocked, as were most doors in the village.

"Come on in," Dorrie called back, and Elise made her way into the middle of the three rooms, where she found Dorrie propped up in bed with pillows beneath her swollen ankle. A mass of single socks lay spread across her lap and the bed beside her. "Amazes me how I can put matched-up socks in th' wash and not be able t' come out with a single pair out 'a th' lot of 'em," she commented absently as Elise sat down in a rocker she pulled closer to the bed. "Where's th' baby?"

"Sissy's watching him."

Dorrie glanced toward the clock that sat on a table across the room. "It ain't time for school t' be out yet, is it?" she asked, and Elise told Dorrie everything that had happened that day.

For a long moment Dorrie was silent. Elise kept waiting for her to say something, waiting for the shock or surprise she had thought to see come to her friend's face, but instead heard: "So, it's got t' th' school now," giving Elise a shock of reality.

"'Got to the school'!—you heard about all this and you didn't tell me?" She almost shouted the words, then forced herself to calm down as she saw the look of pain that came to her friend's face.

"It's all over th' village, Elise. I've been hearin' it for weeks now, people comin' t' tell me, 'specially because Wheeler James is s' crazy about her—folks have been namin' him and Tim both as havin' been with her, sayin' it was one 'a them that got her int' trouble—"

"You know Sissy's not—"

But Dorrie cut her off. "I know she ain't gonna have no baby, just like I know that ain't nothin' out-'a-th' way happened between her an'

Wheeler James, or her an' Tim, or her an' anybody else—she ain't that kind 'a girl, an' anybody that knows her'd know that—"

"But, why didn't you—"

"I thought it'd die down on it's own. I couldn't see how—"

"Who told you?" Elise demanded, too furious to care, too furious at whoever had started this in the first place, and at all those who had spread the lies and kept them going.

"I've been hearing it from a lot 'a different people. There was a group 'a women talkin' about it in McCallum's grocery just th' day before I took th' fall down th' stairs, every one of 'em from Pearlman Street Baptist, so they knowed her and they all knowed better. I told 'em that wasn't a Christian among 'em. Helene even said—"

"Helene—" Elise said, staring at Dorrie, an awful suspicion coming to her mind—but surely—

"Yeah, she was in th' middle of it. She was even th' first that come an' told me about it weeks ago. Come tellin' me Cassandra had told her, an' that since we was family she thought I ought t' know. I told her t' hush her mouth—"

But Elise was no longer listening to Dorrie's words—Cassandra Price and her mother, Helene. Cassandra—and suddenly she understood. She dragged her attention back to what Dorrie was saying.

"She said I ought t' get Clarence t' talk t' Wheeler James, t' see if he'd done somethin' he shouldn't 'a done, sayin' that if she was me she'd be worried t' death knowin' a 'halfwit' might be gonna have her grandbaby— I got her told good, her sayin' those things about Sissy, suggestin' Wheeler James had been foolin' with her," Dorrie's voice was filled with a barely controlled rage now, several of the mis-matched socks clenched tightly in her fist, and Elise could well imagine the confrontation that must have taken place between Dorrie and Helene Price. "She'd be sayin' one minute that any man that'd fool with a girl that ain't just right ought t' have his 'thing' cut off a little bit at a time, an' th' next that a girl like Sissy ought t' be stopped from goin' t' th' church, that it wasn't right for her t' be aroun' good, 'decent' girls like her Cassandra. She said she thought me an' Clarence ought t' go t' th' preacher an' have him tell Sissy t' not come back t' church, an' even that you an' th' baby—"

But suddenly her words stopped, the tirade cut off mid-utterance, and Elise found Dorrie staring at her, her mouth still open, and a look on Dorrie's face that said she had clearly said too much.

"Me and Henry?" Elise asked, staring at her. "Me and Henry—what?"

For a long moment Dorrie only stared at her.

"Me and Henry—what?" Elise prompted again, rising from the chair.

"That uppity Helene thinks she's all high an' mighty. I—"

"What did she say?" Elise asked, cutting her off.

"I didn't want t' tell you," Dorrie said at last. "That was why I didn't tell you what they was sayin' about Sissy—I told Helene t' shut her mouth, that she ought t' be prayin' for forgiveness an' not—"

"What did she say?" Elise could hear her voice now tinged with impatience. She realized her hands were knotted together tightly before her and she forced herself to relax them.

"She said you an' th' baby ought t' be stopped from comin' t' th' church, too, because of Janson—"

"Janson?" For a moment there was only surprise. "Because he's Holiness?"

"That, too, but—"

"But, what?"

"She said—she said she didn't think you ought t' be comin' t' a white church because Janson has Indian blood in him, an' th' baby, too—"

Elise felt as if she had been slapped. She sat down slowly, staring at Dorrie. "How—how dare she—how dare—" She could think of nothing to say. She had never thought that anyone would say any such thing about her, or about her baby—"How dare she—that little—that—" But she could think of nothing bad enough to call Helene Price—she knew now that it had all started with her, with her and with that bratty daughter of hers. Cassandra had been behind this; the lies had all somehow started with her, as well as what had been said about Henry and Janson and Elise as well. Cassandra had started all this, and somehow that made it worse, knowing that it had been done deliberately—the lies that were being told about Sissy had not been built up gradually from misunderstandings and enlarging gossip. They had been begun deliberately.

Dorrie sat staring at Elise, and Elise realized that the older woman was afraid she would be angry because she had not come to her with what she had been told before it had reached this point—but Elise knew now that it had been inevitable. It had been inevitable from the moment she and Tim Cauthen had confronted the three girls behind the church after what they had done to Sissy at Christmas time. It had all been inevitable.

She rose and went to pat Dorrie on the shoulder. "It's okay," she said, quietly. "We'll get all of this straightened out."

Rarely had Elise seen Janson as angry as when he arrived home only to be told that Sissy had been sent home from school and the reasons behind it. He stood for a long moment staring out the screen door, and Elise knew that he was looking out to where Sissy sat rocking Henry in the old rocker on the front porch.

Elise sighed and clenched her hands together in her lap, staring down at them for a moment. "Cassandra Price has to be the one who started it," she said. "She's hated Sissy since Tim started paying so much attention to her, and there's also what she did to Sissy at Christmas. Dorrie said Helene was the first one to come to her with the gossip, and that she was in the middle of it the other day at McCallum's as well."

She fell silent, waiting for him to speak. She could not stop thinking of what Dorrie had said, of what Helene had told Dorrie, that she and Henry should not be allowed to go to the church because of Janson's Cherokee blood. That she and Henry—

"That little bitch—" she said, not realizing she said the words aloud until after she heard them. She looked up at Janson and found his eyes on her now, a look of surprise on his face. She knew he had never heard her say anything of the like in the two years they had known each other.

She looked away again, after a moment feeling him come to stand before her. He did not say anything, but she knew he was waiting.

"Helene told Dorrie that Sissy shouldn't be allowed to go to the Baptist church here," she felt her jaw clench tightly, having to force out the remainder of the words, "and that Henry and I shouldn't, either—"

There was nothing but silence for a moment. "You an' Henry— because of th' talk about Sissy?"

She didn't want to tell him, to have him know the things other people said—she could remember her own mother's words, well over a year before now, when her father had interceded to keep her and Janson from running away together the first time they had tried: ". . . he's only half white, Elise, do you realize what it would be like married to a colored . . ."

But she shook the thought away, watching his green eyes as they moved over her face. She had never once regretted leaving with him, and she knew she did not regret it now.

He knelt before her and took both her hands in his, looking up at her, waiting.

"Dorrie said Helene told her that she didn't think Henry and I should be attending a 'white' church, because you're part Cherokee, and Henry is, too," she told him at last, then felt his hands clench tightly on her own.

He released her immediately, as if he knew his grip hurt her. "I'm sorry," he said, and Elise wondered if the words were for the pain he had caused, or because of what Helene Price had said. He sat on the bed beside her.

"Do you think Sissy ought to go back to the country to stay with your grandparents?" she asked, feeling the need to change the subject. "At least there she could go back to school, and she would be away from all the talk."

"No, she cain't do that," he said. "If she leaves th' mill village, th' rumors won't never stop. She's got t' stay an' face it down; at least that way people'll see soon she ain't gonna have no baby."

She nodded, then stood up from the bed. "I'll go check on your dinner. And you've got to get some sleep. You have a shift tonight, and you're supposed to work straight through another double."

She left Janson sitting in silence on their bed.

⚜

The things she had told him stayed with Janson when he laid down after he had eaten what she had prepared for him, taking from him a much-needed sleep before the double he started that night at ten. Those sixteen hours seemed to drag by more slowly than any he could remember in the mill, and the dullness he felt from the lack of sleep almost caused him to get caught in a card twice during the night as he was stripping it of cotton dust. He thought about Sissy and the lies that had been told about her—but his mind kept returning to Elise and to a growing worry that she might somehow think differently of him now because of the opinions of people like Helene Price.

By the time he left the mill at two on Saturday afternoon he was exhausted. He walked home over the dusty village streets, certain that he was too tired even to eat—but Elise had dinner waiting for him. Gran'ma and Gran'pa were there, the first look at Gran'ma's face telling Janson all he needed to know as to the reason for the visit—the rumors about Sissy had reached the country and her ears as well.

Janson readied himself for an argument, certain Gran'ma would tell Sissy to pack her bags to come home with them, but Gran'ma said instead, "You hold your head high an' show them folks th' kind 'a girl you are—you ain't got nothin' t' be 'shamed of, not like them folks that's totin' lies about you."

Janson picked at the dinner Elise placed before him, then went on to bed even though his grandparents were still in the house. He lay for a time staring at the filtered sunlight that played across the ceiling, but soon fell into a sleep so sound that he never even knew when Tom and Deborah Sanders left the house.

He awoke that night as Elise was getting into bed with him. The house was quiet around them, the rooms dark. She came into his arms easily on the cotton mattress that he had bought for her just before Henry had been born, whispering quietly: "Henry and Sissy are both asleep," just before her mouth came to his.

He finally slept again just before dawn. Afterwards, he had lain in the darkness watching her as she slept, feeling the warmth of her body against his, until sleep had finally taken him as well. It was fully daylight when he woke again to the smell of strong coffee and frying bacon. He got up and pulled on his underdrawers and nightshirt, then made his way through the middle room of the house and into the kitchen to find Elise at the old woodstove.

She turned to look at him, then quickly back to her cooking as she tried to turn over a piece of bacon with a fork, jerking her hand back quickly and dropping the strip over the edge of the skillet as grease popped her skin.

"I've ironed your best shirt and trousers," she said absently, cautiously poking the bacon back into the skillet and then shaking the hand that had been popped. "As soon as you've eaten, I'll fix a bath for you. I've already got water warming on the stove—"

He could only look at her, not comprehending.

"We're going to church together," she said, "you, me, Henry, and Sissy, as a family."

They walked into the Baptist church just after the offering plate had been passed. The choir was just finishing their hymn, as usual more loud than in tune, when Janson and Elise entered, Henry in Elise's arms, and Sissy just behind them. Elise stood in the rear doorway, looking over the congregation, keeping Janson and Sissy from moving forward until a number of the church members turned to look at them, then she put her free hand on Janson's arm and walked at his side down the main aisle. The back pews were almost completely filled, and that suited her—she had intended to sit at the front anyway so no one could miss them.

Shortly after they had settled on the second pew on the right hand side, Tim Cauthen got up and came to join them, settling down at Sissy's side and bringing the girl's eyes to him. Elise could hear the hushed exchange that took place between James and Irene Cauthen a number of rows away, then she reached out to take Janson's hand and smile up at him as the preacher began his sermon.

"First Corinthians, Chapter 13 tells us: 'Though I speak with the tongues of men and of angels, and have not charity, I am become as sounding brass, or a tinkling cymbal.

" 'And though I have the gift of prophecy, and understand all mysteries, and all knowledge; and though I have all faith, so that I could remove mountains, and have not charity, I am nothing . . .' "

When the sermon was finished the congregation sang and the invitation went out over verses of "Just As I Am." The services ended and they rose and made their way toward the back of the church and out the doors, the preacher, standing on the top step that led down to the street, shaking first Elise's hand, then Janson's as he came out just behind her with Henry in his arms. "Mr. Sanders, it was good to have you with us this morning. I hope you join us again next Sunday," Reverend Satterwhite said, a genuine smile on his face, then turned to shake Tim's, then Sissy's, hand, the warmth remaining in his voice as he spoke to both of them. Elise could not listen to him, however, for the words she could hear, just to one side, where Helene Price stood whispering to another woman on the church steps.

"Of all the nerve, bringing that little trollop back to church after she was put out of school just the other day—" she said, obviously intending for her words to be overheard. "And that husband of hers—in my day colored people knew where they belonged, and they stayed there. And what kind of woman is she, anyway, to have intermarried with a—"

Elise turned on her, fury in her voice, her hands clenched at her sides. "If you have something to say about me, I'll thank you to say it to my face and not behind my back."

Helene stared at her, anger coming to her face—not because she had been overheard, for Elise knew she had intended herself to be overheard, but because Elise had dared to call her on what she had said. "Young lady, I'll thank you not to address me in that tone of voice."

"I'll address you any way I please, you gossiping old cat," Elise said, rewarded by the sharp intake of breath that came out of Helene Price's suddenly red face.

For a moment the woman looked as if she would choke on the words that so obviously wanted to come forth, then she stiffened her back, and Elise knew she was trying to summon some dignity about her stout frame stuffed into its slightly too-small dress. Helene turned to the woman beside her, remarking as she took the woman's arm and turned away, "Trash always shows," obviously intent on leaving as she stepped down onto a lower step.

"Yes, it certainly does," Elise said, which caused another sharp intake of breath and which brought Helene up short and turned her back to glare up at Elise.

"How dare you—!" Helene flustered.

"You self-important old hen—you're not any better than anyone else in this church, and neither is that daughter of yours, no matter what you think. The two of you have tried to ruin a girl's life, and you've done it deliberately. You've gossiped about me and my husband and my family—where I come from they would have run you out of town." She was shaking now, she was so furious, and she tried to make herself calm down. Janson was standing beside her, one arm around her waist. The minister was coming down the steps to move in between them, as if he thought the two women would soon resort to blows.

"Now, please, ladies—"

"Well, what can you expect from white trash married to a colored—" Helene began, and Elise opened her mouth to respond, but Janson spoke instead.

"That's enough, Elise," he said, and she looked up at him. Bert Price was suddenly there as well, hurrying from where he had pulled his Chevrolet up before the front steps of the church.

"That was unforgivable, Helen—get in the car, now," he said, the first time Elise had ever heard him raise his voice to his wife. When Helene did not immediately move, he came up the few steps to her and repeated. "Get in the car, Helen—" and she began to move away with him. Elise could hear him still after he had gotten her into the car and slammed the door, then gone around to get in on his own side. "Why on earth would you say such a thing to that girl—"

But she only snapped out: "Don't call me Helen," as a response, then turned to stare straight ahead, not meeting the eyes of anyone left standing on the church steps.

"It really was the most appalling behavior," Helene Price said as she sat in Walter Eason's office there at the mill the next morning. "The things she said to me—why I never!"

She sat in the heavy armchair before Walter's desk, her hands folded over the too-large beige purse in her lap, her legs crossed primly at the ankles and tucked to one side beneath the chair. Her dress was drab, straight and shapeless, as was she, and her beige cloche hat was pulled low over her head with only a few well-planned locks of brown hair escaping onto her forehead, brown hair that was just too brown to be the authentic color.

"Really, Mr. Eason, I hated to have to come to you with this, but I knew you would want to know, especially since that—that husband of hers—is one of your people—"

"Thank you, Mrs. Price." Walter rose from his chair and stood looking at her. She seemed to sense the dismissal for what it was, for she gathered her gloves and purse and rose as well, then made her way quietly from the room. He watched her go, until the heavy wooden door closed after her, then stood there, staring at the polished surface, thinking—he had known she would come to him today; he had known that from the first report he had received of what had happened before the Baptist church there in the village the previous morning. She was not the first to tell him—she rarely was—but she always came just the same, even in the times when she had not been directly involved in what had happened. She thought it was her responsibility to keep him informed of the things that happened in the mill village. She was not the most trustworthy of sources, as he had well learned in the past.

This morning he had no doubt that her story was tinged with dislike, and perhaps with even more, but he knew it to be basically true—Janson Sanders's wife had caused a disturbance before the Baptist church just after services the previous day. There was some connection to stories circulating about Sanders's cousin, Sissy, a pretty girl who Walter had been told was "not quite right," concerning the fact that she had managed to get herself with child even though she had no husband. Mrs. Cunningham had told the girl she could not return to the village school, and Walter was in total agreement with that decision—a girl like that had no place in the village, much less in the school where she could be a bad influence on the impressionable young girls who would one day grow up to be the workers, mothers, and wives in the village.

Janson Sanders apparently could not control the womenfolk in his family, not that alley cat of a cousin of his, or even his own wife—Walter had little doubt that Helene Price had been spreading gossip, just as Elise Sanders had accused her of doing, for he knew that Helene could be one of the worse gossips in the village. But he could not approve of any woman, Janson Sanders's wife included, making a spectacle of herself as she had done before a village church. Women were supposed to be seen and not heard, in church and elsewhere, and such outspoken behavior, even when provoked, was unacceptable from a woman—something would have to be done. Walter could not have a girl like Sissy Sanders in the village, a girl with no morals and who had a child on the way and no husband. Moreover, he would not have it.

He walked out of his office and into the secretary's area, then opened the door to his son's office without knocking and entered, leaving the door open behind him.

Walt looked up from the papers he had been reading, his brow furrowed, a look of anger coming to his face, Walter knew, because he had been interrupted without warning. Walter stared at his son for a long moment, spoke to him briefly, then left the room. The words he had said had left Walt looking puzzled, but vaguely pleased: "Send someone over to Kirk Street; have them bring back Janson Sanders, his wife, and that girl, Sissy—I don't care if he's asleep, have his wife wake him up. I want them here in an hour."

Grace Taylor sat behind her desk later that morning, unable to work for the sounds coming from the sniffling girl who sat nearby staring at Walter Eason's closed office door—at least she told herself that was the reason she could not work. There was such pity within her for the crying, frightened girl that she could think of little else other than wanting to help her.

Sissy Sanders was a sweet, pretty child, and the rumors Grace had heard, that it seemed by now everyone had heard, could not be true. There was an innocence about Sissy that in some other girl might make her fall victim to some man bent on no good—but she was Deborah Sanders's granddaughter, and Grace knew the old woman herself had raised the girl. Deborah Sanders would have reared her with morals and Holiness teachings for a backbone, and Grace knew the girl would never have strayed from that upbringing.

Sissy sat in the heavy, leather chair closest to the office door, a chair that dwarfed her because of its massive size, leaving her feet not even touching the floor, and making her look in Grace's eyes as if she were much younger than her fourteen or so years. She sat crying and unconsciously rocking back and forth as she waited for Janson and Elise Sanders to come out of that room, or for herself to be called back into it. She had been sent out after she had been told stories about herself, stories that had to be lies, and she had begun to cry—that terrible, white-haired old gentleman had frightened her, and she wanted now only to go home. Grace knew that and she sympathized. That old gentleman had scared the hell out of her enough times.

There were sounds of voices, muffled behind the door, interruptions of telephone calls, and once the day boss of the weave shed came in with urgent business for old Mr. Walter—but still Grace could not forget the crying child who sat staring at that closed door. It was not the sound of the sniffles or sobs, or the hiccups that had finally come with the crying— it was a debt owed that kept Grace's mind occupied.

It had been years before when she had gone to see the old healer out in the country. She had been told her husband was dying, and had believed that Deborah Sanders and her faith could bring a miracle— there had been no miracle, but Deborah had stayed with her, and had sat by Jacob's bed on many nights so Grace could rest, and had been with them when the end had at last come.

Deborah Sanders had been so kind that Grace could not forget it all these years later—the old woman would want to know what was happening with her granddaughter, the things that had been said to and about Sissy today. Janson and Elise Sanders had enough to worry about in thinking of themselves from what Grace had seen and heard—the girl needed her grandmother, and her grandmother had the right to know.

Grace sat for a moment looking at the crying girl, then she reached for the telephone on her desk, clicked for the operator, and asked to be connected to the home of the family that owned the land that Deborah Sanders and her family sharecropped—she could only be fired once, Grace told herself, listening to the dull sound on the other end of that line as she waited. She could only be fired once.

It seemed to Janson that he had been sitting in Walter Eason's office for hours, waiting for the old man to finish with his telephone calls and the other interruptions that had come through. Janson was tired and angry, having been awakened from a sound sleep only to be ordered here with Elise and Sissy, with barely enough time to get dressed and to take Henry by to stay with Dorrie.

Elise sat beside him, her eyes straying to the closed door—Janson knew she was thinking of Sissy, as he had been, since the outburst of crying that had caused the girl to be sent from the room. She had not known until then exactly what was being said about her, and Janson knew she still did not understand, as any unmarried girl her age should not have understood, more than to know that she was being accused of doing things she had not done, and that somehow this old man thought she was going to have a baby.

Walter Eason set the earpiece of his telephone into its cradle and settled back into his chair, folding his hands together on the desk before him as he considered Janson and Elise through gray eyes that showed no feeling. His thick white eyebrows, meeting over the bridge of his nose, were drawn down into a scowl, displaying the only emotion that showed on his ruddy face—he believed the rumors about Sissy; he had already made that quite clear, and he was not willing to listen to anything that either of them might say in the girl's defense.

"The spectacle you made of yourself before the Baptist church yesterday was uncalled for," he said, his eyes now on Elise alone. "I realize the gossip about this girl has gotten out of hand, but it is nothing more than what she has brought on herself."

"But, she hasn't done anything," Elise said, interrupting him, and Janson saw her knot her hands together in her lap. "The things they're saying are all—"

"Mrs. Sanders, I know you do not believe—"

"It is nothing but a lie, started by Cassandra Price and that mother of hers. Sissy would never—"

"You cannot accuse someone of something like that without proof!" His voice rose slightly as he stared at Elise.

"They've been accusin' Sissy of all kind'a things without proof," Janson said, drawing Eason's attention to him.

"I want that girl out of this village by tomorrow." Eason's temper was growing, his face becoming only redder. "I will not have a girl like her in this village; she's a bad example to the girls and nothing but a temptation to the boys. Send her back to her grandparents, or to a place for girls like her where they can make arrangements for the child—"

"She ain't gonna have no baby, an' she's better off here where people'll see that. If she leaves now, th' talk'll just keep on—"

"This is not a request. She leaves the village by tomorrow."

There was silence for a moment. "An', if she don't leave?"

Eason stared at him. "Then you'll all leave." The words were quiet, the eyes that Janson stared into absolutely unrelenting. Either Sissy left to return to Tom and Deborah Sanders in the country, or left the county altogether, leaving the rumors behind her to fester and grow so that she could never escape them, or Janson would lose his job, they would lose the mill house, and they would all have to leave the village. Either way, Sissy would be away from the good, God-fearing people of the mill village—and Walter Eason was willing to cost a man his livelihood, and a family their home, to assure that.

"That ain't very fair, is it. Either Sissy leaves us, when she ain't done nothin' t' have t' leave for, or we all have t' leave, just because of th' lies spread by one girl an' her mother—"

"I have already told you that I will not listen to unfounded rumors in this!"

"Damn it, what do you think th' rumors about Sissy are!" Janson demanded, leaning forward in his chair.

"I will not have profanity in this office!"

Elise reached out and took hold of Janson's arm, her fingers digging into his skin through his shirt sleeve, silencing him before he could speak. When he looked at her he found her staring at Walter Eason, and, after a moment, Eason brought his eyes to her as well.

"Sissy didn't even know until today exactly what it was she was being accused of doing," Elise said, very quietly, her fingers digging even deeper into Janson's arm to keep him silent. "She is nothing but a sweet child— you believe everyone else so easily, why can't you at least listen to us? She's just an innocent girl; there is no baby, and she hasn't done any of the things that everyone is accusing her of—can't you at least consider that?" Her fingers dug more firmly into Janson's arm, but he already knew not to speak—he could see that Walter Eason was considering for the first time the possibility that what she was saying might be true, the old man's eyes not once leaving her.

Eason sat back after a moment, his eyes moving from Elise, to Janson, and then back again, and Janson felt Elise release the painful grip on his arm.

After a long moment Walter Eason cleared his throat, seeming to have come to a decision. He did not respond to Elise, but brought his eyes to Janson. "Have the girl examined by Dr. Thrasher. If he says she's—" his eyes moved quickly toward Elise and back again, "still as she should be, then—"

"You cain't ask a lady t'—" For a moment Janson could not even think of what he had been about to say. "You cain't expect a unmarried girl t' let a doctor or nobody else—no!" He looked at Elise, seeing her cheeks coloring, then looked back to Walter Eason. "No, we ain't gonna ask her t'—"

"Yes, you will," a strong female voice came from behind them and Janson turned to see his grandmother standing in the doorway. One hand held the heavy wooden door back and the other held to Sissy's hand as the girl stood beside her.

"Mrs. Sanders, I don't recall asking you into this office." Walter Eason stared at her, the scowl deepening on his face.

"You didn't have t' ask me, I come on my own," Deborah Sanders said, staring at him. "Ain't none of them things bein' said about my girl true, an' if it takes a doctor t' prove it, then we'll go see a doctor—you won't go ruinin' my girl's name in this county. Ain't nobody goin' t' go ruinin' my girl's name—"

The rumors were false, and Elise knew that it would be a long time before some of the good, church-going folk of the village would forgive Sissy for not being exactly what they had accused her of being, and her family for somehow being able to prove it. Sissy was allowed to return to school, and the entire affair was dropped as far as the mill was concerned, though Sissy seemed forever uneasy around Mrs. Cunningham after that.

Elise tried to explain the things that had been said, but that only seemed to embarrass Sissy more, and so they all tried to leave it behind them and go on. Months passed and it became evident that Sissy was not with child. Many of the people in the village who had gossiped so diligently, who had almost ruined a young girl's life, almost cost a man work and a family income and shelter, now were outwardly considerate to Sissy, while at the same time avoiding her as much as they possibly could. Helene and Cassandra Price, however, as well as Tim's mother, Irene, and to a lesser extent his father, shunned Sissy and the entire Sanders family as completely as when the rumors had reigned supreme. They, and so many others, had been accused of gossipmongering, and had been proven of it, and had even been dressed down by Reverend Satterwhite from his pulpit once Walter Eason had suggested the very sermon topic—they would not readily forgive anyone who showed the stains on their robes.

Elise had discovered she was pregnant again before spring was over, and, though she found herself wishing it had not happened so soon, she also found herself hoping for a girl this time. As the months passed, she started to spend more time at her handiwork, gaining skill at doing things she had once hated so badly to learn and do—sewing, tatting, knitting, embroidery, making lovely things for the new baby, and quickly becoming known in the village for what she could do with a needle and thread or a tatting shuttle. Before long other women in the village began to ask her to make something for a child or a grandchild, or for the ladies themselves, and, to her surprise, offered to pay her for the work.

At first Janson objected loudly and vocally to her earning money— she could accept jams and jellies, or baked goods, or home-canned foods in exchange, she was told, but nothing more. The fact that any number of women in the village worked in the mill just as their husbands did, and that his own mother and his grandmother worked just as hard on the land as did their husbands, while at the same time keeping up a house and raising children and cooking three meals a day, still did not lessen the impact of Elise working and making money—he did not like it, and he told her so. He was the man in the family, and he would not have her working. She could make things for other ladies she knew, he told her, if she wanted to and if the ladies supplied her the material, and if they wanted to give her jams or jellies in exchange, then that would be fine— to which Elise asked him if he thought she was a fool, because only a fool would turn down money if it was offered to her.

He refused to allow her to use her earnings toward household expenses, or even to add it to their store of savings for his land, telling her to save it or spend it as she liked, but that it was all her own—and so she afforded herself a few store-bought things for Henry and for the new baby, and nice material to make new dresses for herself and for Sissy. Then on impulse she had her hair, which had grown out more than she liked, bobbed into the newest style and done at the beauty parlor on Main Street, though Janson had said he liked her hair longer and hoped she would let it grow out even more—she was pregnant, and now that she was past the nausea that had plagued the first months even worse than it had with Henry, she was in the mood to "do something," she told him.

She felt foolishly happy over the extravagance of the new dresses and hairstyle, and terribly proud that she had earned the money for them on her own—she even had her own small hoard of savings that she counted and fussed over just as badly as Janson fussed over the savings for his land. They were both absolutely miserly toward those two treasures they had hidden in the kitchen. Janson's savings seemed such a fortune to her now, and they had both begun to fret over it, afraid someone could come in and take it from the house when they were gone, until finally Janson took it, and her savings as well, to the bank up on Main Street just to relieve their minds. There was still a long way to go before they would have enough to buy back his land—but it would be so awful to have to start again, and it made Janson and Elise both sleep better knowing that their hard-fought savings lay safe in the local bank until the day it could help them make that dream come true.

It was a good time for Janson, Elise, and their family. The doubles he often worked took him from Elise and Henry much more than Elise would have liked, but they gave them extra money that could go toward the dream of his land, and also some left over even for the occasional treat. For the first time since they married, they did not have to fret over each dime, although it now was a habit. There were more new clothes for Henry, instead of mostly hand-me-downs from Janson's relatives and things Elise had made for him, a new dress Elise ordered from the Sears and Roebuck catalog, a coat for Janson, and new things for Sissy as well. Everyone seemed to be spending, and most buying on credit—but not the Sanders family: "Cash money only," Janson had said, and that was how they dealt.

Herbert Hoover had come into office earlier in the year promising to wipe out poverty, that there would be "a chicken in every pot and a car in every garage." Hoover said the country had a brilliant future ahead, and Elise could little argue with the thought. She knew the farmers in the countryside, the sharecroppers and landowners alike, were having a difficult time, many losing their land and the farms they had worked for generations because of low crop prices and high surpluses of farm products, but in the village the future looked better than ever. The mill was working three full shifts with doubles, and even triples, available for most anyone who would work them. There was plenty of merchandise in the stores, with money to buy with and credit welcome from all. Credit—that seemed what everyone was dealing on. People bought things they never thought to afford, and they bought them on credit, looking only toward the brighter days ahead. There seemed to be a buying spree going on, and it seemed everyone was getting rich, their little savings in the bank making Elise feel rich even though she had once spent more money on clothes in one day than was in their entire hard-earned bank account.

As October swept in, it seemed to Elise that the entire world was single-mindedly at work to make more and more money. She heard talk in the stores uptown, even in the small grocery in the village and the drug store, of investing and stocks—a bull market, they called it—talk she little understood except to know there was money to be made hand-over-fist investing in the market, and that everyone but their family seemed to be making that money. She tried to talk Janson into investing, but he refused—he did not understand how it worked, and did not like the idea of handing money over to someone in hopes that it would somehow grow to be more money, he said. He preferred it in the bank where it was nice and safe—anything that he did not understand might try to take their money from them, and, though he did not understand the bank and how it took money from some people and let other people borrow it, Elise knew it felt safer to him than some market and things called stocks that he knew nothing about.

As October of 1929 swept to a close, it seemed as if the entire world was investing in the stock market, from the banker in town to the meat cutter in the village, from the wealthy widow who went to the First Methodist Church on Main Street, to the man who worked beside

Janson in the card room at the mill. People went into debt to buy stocks and invest in the market; they bought on credit as they never had before. They spent, they consumed, they drank illegal liquor and spat in the face of Prohibition, celebrating in a mad, giddy rush the brilliant future that lay ahead. Herbert Hoover was at the reins of the country, ready to lead them all on to even better times. There was prosperity and recklessness, a seemingly mad party as the month drew to a close.

But after Tuesday, October 29, 1929, that frivolous, giddy world would never be the same again, not for Elise, or for anyone else who spun through those final dizzying days—that was the day the stock market crashed.

That was also the day that William Whitley ended his own life.

# CHAPTER SIX

To many people, it seemed as if the world had come to an end that Black Tuesday, October 29, 1929. In that one day desperate speculators sold over sixteen million shares of stock in an attempt to get out before the great bull market would collapse, but by then the end was inevitable. By the close of the year the government would estimate that the Crash had cost investors forty billion dollars. Values of stocks listed on the NYSE had dropped precipitously—and panic had set in to stay. People had gone into debt to buy stocks, fortunes were wiped out, jobs were lost forever, and suicide reigned supreme in a nation of people reeling from the greatest stock market catastrophe of all time.

But that day that would live forever in the minds of most of those who had seen it had become even more personal to Elise—on that dark October night, when her father realized that he had lost everything in the Crash that had ruined so many others, William Whitley put a gun to his head and pulled the trigger.

It was devastating to learn that her father had ended his own life, and Elise's mind was stunned at the knowledge. She was unable to think, unable to feel, unable even to realize the import of the words that came to her over that crackling telephone wire at the village grocery that Wednesday morning—her father was dead. He had killed himself—and she was stunned to find herself shaken though dry-eyed at the knowledge.

William Whitley had gambled everything, and he had lost. Old Mr. Bolt had passed away a few months before and Bolt's widow had at last sold William the share in the Goodwin cotton mill that William had wanted for so long. Then Hiram Cooper, his son, J. C., now married to Phyllis Ann Bennett, having no interest in coming into the management of the mill, had sold William his share as well, giving William at last what he had most wanted for so many years—he owned the mill, owned it outright, but now had no one to pass it on to. Stan was more interested in books than business; Alfred had been dead these two and a half years; Bill had left town without a word to anyone; and Elise was off in Alabama with her half-breed and her part-Indian brat—all of his children were gone to him, though Stan still lived under his roof.

William had mortgaged his home, lands, and businesses to purchase the mill and the mill village, and then had taken loans against the mill itself when he had seen what the market was doing—with the way stocks were climbing, he would soon have the mortgages off his property and would be free of debt. He would make a fortune on the stocks when he sold—and perhaps he could interest Stan in the mill. Books were nothing for the boy to be interested in. Books were nothing—

He nervously watched the market sag in September, listening with gritted teeth to assurances that the slump was only temporary—and put more money into the now lower-valued stocks, assured that they would rise again to recoup his losses and bring him the money to satisfy the liens against his property.

Yet the market sagged again, the decline becoming even more rapid as October wore on—but he could not sell now. He took another loan against the mill and village to satisfy the margin calls on his stocks—he would lose too much if he pulled out now. There were loans to be repaid, business to conduct—surely the market had hit bottom, and there was one last chance to buy in—and buy in he did. Scraping together the final dollars he had, borrowing even more, he sank everything into the market—it had to go up. It could not drop any further—it would rise and rise. He would sell at a profit when the shares reached the pinnacle again.

But stocks continued to decline: General Electric was dropping, Montgomery Ward was dropping; United States Steel, Radio, Auburn

Chase—all dropping. He had gone too far; if he sold now he would be ruined. He could only hold on. Wait. And pray.

The panic set in. Everyone was selling before the bottom could fall out. Fortunes were lost, prices dropped lower and lower, and calls for margins to be repaid went out—and William watched in horror as his world was wiped away. It had to get better. Prices had to go up. He could not lose everything—he was William Whitley—people were panicking. Hadn't the big bankers stepped in and formed a pool to support prices? Lamont of J. P. Morgan and Company, Mitchell of National City Bank, Wiggin of Chase National, Potter of Guarantee Trust, Prosser of Bankers Trust—men of such power and wisdom in the financial world could wield wonders. The market would recover and everyone would laugh at the silly panic they had allowed themselves to get into.

For a few days it seemed possible that the bottom had been reached, that the wise men of Wall Street could breathe a sigh of relief, count their losses and watch the market rise again—then the panic began anew and no force short of God Almighty could stop it.

Stock prices plummeted, and in one desperate, last-ditch effort to sell and salvage what he could, William realized that everything was lost—the home where Whitleys had lived, loved, been born, and died for generations; the businesses that had made him a respected part of the community; the money that had wielded power over a county and much of a state; the mill he had wanted for so long—all gone now as completely as if he had never owned them. He could never repay the loans; he could never recoup the losses; he was wiped out.

That quiet October night, as he sat in the silence of the library in the home where he had lived all his life, it seemed that he had nothing left to live for. Martha had been gone more than a year now—no one would even miss him if he died. Everything that had defined who he had always been was gone. Soon he would not even have a roof over his head, he told himself, but would be out in the streets like a pauper—he was a pauper, he realized suddenly, the bitterness inside of him now something he could almost taste.

When he took the gun from the writing desk in the corner of the front parlor, it was with the thought that the world would be better off without him. Everything that had made him the man he had been was gone now—even the Whitley name would be ground into the dust, laughed at and spit on for what he had made of it. There was nothing left to live for, no one to care if he lived or died, no one to shed a tear—no one left now even to talk to.

He sat in the chair before the rolltop in the library and put the gun to his temple. His eyes came to rest on the picture of Martha amid the clutter on the desktop—he hoped she had forgiven him by now.

There was sound, and then there was silence. William Whitley was dead.

At first Elise could not bring herself even to consider returning to Georgia for the funeral. Her father had thrown her out and had denied his own grandson when she had returned upon her mother's death. He had tried to kill Janson and had done everything he could do to keep them apart—why should she return now to pretend a grief that she could never feel, she asked herself. There was a blank space inside her where the love for her father had once existed, and she felt nothing for him now but hatred—he deserved to die, and he deserved to burn in hell, as she was certain he most assuredly was.

In the hours after the telephone call that Wednesday morning, she knew that Janson kept watching her, and she knew that he was waiting for her to cry, for her to show grief or sadness or a feeling of loss, but she did not. She went about the things she had to do at the house, telling him to go to bed to get some rest because he had another shift to work that night—but he continued to watch her as if he thought she was too much in a daze even to know what it was she felt.

"I'll go talk to Eason an' get a few days off t' go with you for th' funeral," he said, watching her as she washed dishes in the dishpan there on the kitchen table, Henry playing on the floor between them. He had offered to do the dishes for her—for her, as if she were not fully capable of doing it herself—but she had refused, and he sat and watched her now as if he thought she would break every one.

"I'm not going," she said, not even looking up from the dish she was scrubbing in the hot, soapy water, hearing it clatter against the side of the pan as well as against another waiting in the water to be washed.

"Not goin'—but you have t' go. He was your pa—"

"My father died a long time ago—he died when he tried to sell me in marriage to J. C. Cooper to try to guarantee himself a part of that cotton mill; he died when he did everything he could to keep you and me apart; he died when he tried to kill you, and when he threw us off his land and told us we were both dead to him; he died when he didn't send for me when Mama asked for me, and when he threw us out of the house when we went back for her funeral." She realized she was shouting at him, but she could not stop herself. She yanked the dishrag out of the pan, sending soapy water out across the table as well as across her pregnant stomach. She squeezed it in her fist now as she stared at him, feeling warm water moving down her arm and soaking through the sleeve of her sweater, realizing she was shaking with fury. "I hate him, and I'm glad he's dead—and I'll thank you not to tell me what I have to do."

He looked at her, his green eyes moving over her face, but she could do nothing but breathe heavily as she stared at him. Then he got up from the table, and, lifting Henry into his arms, left the room without saying a word. She watched him pass through the doorway and into the middle room of their half of the house, and then stood staring at the empty doorway—he had no right to tell her what to do, no right; he was her husband and not her fath—

Not her—

She stared for a moment longer, then set the dishrag down on the table and dried her hands on the apron tied around her, feeling the baby she was almost eight-months along with now move slightly inside of her, then become still again. She continued to look at the empty doorway for a moment, then followed Janson, surprised when she did not find him changing into his nightshirt so that he could get some rest after working all night. Instead he sat in the rocker beside the bed, Henry on his lap. His eyes came to her as she entered the room still drying her hands on the damp apron, and for a moment she could only look at him, then she crossed the room to his side, realizing that her hand was still damp when she reached out to rest it at his cheek.

"You're right," she told him after a time when he did not speak. "I have to go back—for Stan, if for no one else—" Her words trailed off and she realized she did not have to say anything more.

"I'll go see Eason about a few days off," he said. "You won't have t' face goin' back by yourself—"

But she would have to face going back to Georgia alone.

Janson found it almost impossible to get in to see Walter Eason that morning when he went to the mill. He waited in the outer office, leaning forward where he sat in a leather-covered chair, his elbows resting on his knees and his fingers laced before him as he stared at the dark, polished wood of Walter Eason's closed office door. When he was finally allowed in to see the old man, he found Eason preoccupied, shifting papers on his wide desk, not lifting his gaze even once from the pages before him as Janson told him his reason he needed a few days off.

"In times like these, we all have to keep our minds on our jobs," Walter Eason told him, his eyes still on the sheaf of papers in his hands. "You can't go taking time off just whenever you please."

"My wife's expectin' a baby in another month or so; I cain't let her go all th' way off t' Georgia by herself t'—"

When Eason's eyes met his at last across the wide expanse of the desk between them, Janson knew without having to be told that the talk he had heard in the past day was true: the Easons had lost a lot of money in the stock market crash.

He also knew he would not be allowed time off without those days also costing him his job and the security he had built for them in the mill village.

Janson was willing to give up that security if need be in order to go with Elise, but she would hear nothing of it. Now that she was deter-mined to go, she would go without him if she had to, taking Henry and

Sissy with her. Janson had to keep his job, she told him, for, if he quit, they would lose not only their source of income, but also the roof over their heads—and they had Henry to think of, and the new baby as well. She would be fine, she assured him, and so he reluctantly put Elise and Henry, and Sissy, on the train that afternoon. Stan would be meeting them at the station, and he had already made arrangements for them at the hotel in town, for Elise refused to stay in her father's house even now that he was dead.

William Whitley had thrown her out one too many times, Janson knew, and she was not willing to forgive him, not even in death.

He stood on the platform that afternoon at the station in Pine, returning Henry's wave as the train pulled away, feeling as if his entire world was moving away from him as that train started on its way toward Georgia.

The casket was closed at the funeral because of the way in which William Whitley ended his life. There were few mourners to mark the end of a man who had until so recently wielded so much power in the county and throughout much of the state—J. C. was there, and his father, Mattie Ruth and Titus Coates, Sheriff Hill, Old Mr. Tate, who had worked for the Whitleys since Elise's grandfather's time; and Dr. Lester, her father's cousin and the doctor who had delivered Elise and all three of her brothers.

Some of her father's employees and business associates were also there, as were few distant relatives and members of the Baptist church William Whitley had attended all his life, but few of the men he had always considered his friends. Stan said their father had distanced himself from almost everyone in the time since their mother's death, seeming, especially in the last months, to be concerned only with the market and with the mill and mill village he had acquired at last. Stan sat beside her in the church during the funeral, and stood with her as the final words were spoken over their father.

He was the only one who cried.

They returned to the cemetery later, Stan, Elise, and Henry, after the red earth had been freshly mounded over the new grave. Elise laid flowers at the headstone of her mother, but not on the newly turned earth that was her father's grave, feeling strangely drained of emotion as she stood beside Stan. She wished she could cry as he did, but she could feel nothing, could think of nothing but the day her father had driven her from his house after her mother's death, or the day she had seen him beat Janson here in this very graveyard until Janson lay bleeding and unconscious at her father's feet, or the day he had driven her and Janson from his land. She had heard his words that day over and over again, even as she could hear them now: "I no longer have a daughter."

She stood in silence and allowed Stan to grieve, her eyes on Henry where he stood clinging to the bottom of her skirt. The little boy seemed uneasy at the sight of his tall uncle crying—he looks so much like Janson, Elise thought, so much like Janson.

Stan's eyes were red and puffy, and he sniffed as he cried so honestly for their father, that she envied him his grief. All she could think of was that she wanted to be away from here, wanted to be back home with Janson in that half a mill house, even with the noise and the lint and the gossipmongers, and Buddy Eason prowling the streets. Janson had been wrong; she did not need to be here except for her brother Stan.

For a moment she thought she could hear children's voices over the sound of Stan's sniffles, and her eyes followed the sound, coming to rest on a family getting out of a Studebaker parked in the nearby churchyard. There were several children, and a mother and father; the mother leading a little girl by the hand and the father scooping one of the boys up onto his shoulders as they made their way to the church, setting the little boy off into peals of laughter—Elise smiled with the picture, thinking of Janson and how good he was with Henry. He was such a good father, as he would be to all their children.

She watched, even after the family had disappeared through the church doors. She felt a wetness on her cheeks and reached up, surprised to find there were tears there. She watched the front of the church and she cried, feeling Stan's arms go around her, and she knew he thought she was crying for their father, even though she told herself that she was not—she was crying because she was pregnant, and because she was tired and far from home and she missed Janson so terribly.

She put her head on Stan's shoulder as she cried, stupidly surprised that he was as tall now as a man. Henry patted her knee through her skirt and she cried only harder, kneeling cumbersomely in her almost-eight-month pregnant state to hold him to her. She realized suddenly that she was remembering her family as it had been in years past when she had been nothing but a child, remembering her father when he had seemed so tall and strong and her mother when it had seemed Martha Whitley would never change, remembering Bill and Alfred when they had just been her big brothers, and Stan when he had been little Stanny to them all.

Henry reached up and patted her wet cheek, his green eyes reminding her so much of Janson—she could remember her father when he had been much the same kind of man that Janson was. She could remember—and she did not understand what had happened to William Whitley to make him the man she had known in the past years, a man capable of trying to kill Janson to keep them apart, a man capable of doing so much.

It had not just been the knowledge of Janson's Indian blood, or the fact that she had decided to run away with him—something had changed her father over the years, something had made the man who now lay buried in the ground at her feet a stranger to her.

Stan knelt beside her now, allowing her to cry in peace until she was finished, then he gently helped her to her feet. She dried her eyes with the back of one hand since neither of them had a handkerchief, then she looked out toward the pines, out toward the west.

She sniffed and wiped her eyes again. "I want to go home," she said, turning to look at Stan and seeing the concern for her on his face. He was almost a man now, recently turned seventeen, and grown tall and skinny. He looked at her through his round-lensed glasses, and suddenly she could not imagine leaving him here, alone, for Bill was gone from town now, and Stan had never been close to any of their relatives. He would not even have a place to live, according to what they had learned from the letter their father had left, the letter saying he had lost everything—Stan was still her baby brother, and she could not leave him here, alone with no home, no money, no prospects other than to live off the charity of relatives or to leave school and take a job to support himself.

"Can you be ready to leave tomorrow morning?" she asked him, as if the matter had been already settled between them.

"Leave—but you can't mean—Elise, I can't live off of you and Janson. I'll—"

"Nonsense, you're my little brother. I have no intention of leaving you here."

"But, that wouldn't be fair to you—to either of you." He looked worried. "I'll find a place to stay, and I can—"

"You'll stay with us; I won't hear any arguments. It's what I want, and it'll be what Janson wants as well, I'm sure of it—"

But she was not sure, and, after she finally convinced Stan to return to Eason County with her, she became worried at what Janson might say. The three rooms they had in the mill house were already crowded with her, Janson, Henry, and Sissy, and now there was the new baby on the way.

She was grateful for the privacy of the hotel that afternoon, for it allowed her to place a call to Eason County as soon as Henry had gone down for his nap and Sissy had left to walk to the drug store soda fountain a few blocks away, a call to the small village grocery after which she waited for the operator to ring back that Janson was on the other end of the line.

"I asked Stan to come live with us," she said simply, after assuring him that she, Henry, the baby, and Sissy were all fine, realizing belatedly that she had frightened him with the unexpected and expensive telephone call. "Is that all right?"

"Yes, 'a course it is, if it's what you want." His voice came back to her over the crackling wire, and for a moment she could picture him there in the village grocery, standing at the black box on the wall near the front of the store, his black hair less than neatly combed as he stood in his overalls or dungarees and one of his workshirts.

"It won't be too much? I mean, another mouth to feed, one more person to—"

"Don't worry about that, Elise. Stan's family—we'll make it; we'll always make it. We'll be fine as long as we got th' money in th' bank."

When she hung up, she felt reassured—yes, they would be fine, just so long as they had that money in the bank.

By the time Elise had the baby, it seemed as if the country was already pulling itself out of the frightening days of the Crash. Catherine Martha Sanders was born in that December of 1929, with Dr. Washburn handling the delivery and Janson banished to the next room to pace the floor alongside his brother-in-law.

Catherine was a beautiful baby, with a light sprinkling of reddish hair and a quiet disposition that was much different than Henry had been as a baby. Henry, at almost eighteen months, did not know quite what to think of his new sister, staring at her often in the first days as if he did not understand why she was here, climbing into bed with Elise and the baby, or up onto Janson's lap whenever he sat down, trying to come between his parents and this crying, smelly thing that demanded so much of their attention, setting into loud wails of his own any time that she cried, and staring at her often when she did not, as if he were certain she would start up again at any moment.

Much money had been lost in the Crash, and, with it, much of the country's confidence. Hard-earned savings had been lost by many people, massive fortunes by others, and there was a lot of belt-tightening going on. People and businesses began to economize. Where once there had been a mad spending spree going on before the Crash, now no one was buying. There was reduced demand for goods, and reduced need to manufacture them, leaving machines and workers idle.

In the village, there was nervousness in the air. There was no hiring at the mill, and the existing employees worried with each pay envelope that it might be their last. Stan enrolled in the high school uptown, causing quite an uproar because he was living in the mill village—but there was no work for him at the mill, and seemingly little chance there would be any time soon. No mention was made to Janson about his brother-in-law, although the subject had been broached to Walter Eason by several persons—but Walter had more pressing matters on his mind than the schooling of a seventeen-year-old boy. He had much more pressing matters now at hand, matters that not only concerned him, but the entire county.

In the early days after the Crash, a run had begun on the local bank. Fueled by rumor and a general panic, people had flocked to the bank to withdraw their money, frightened of an imminent collapse. Everyone kept hearing stories of banks in other small towns going under, reports on the radio of big city banks closing their doors forever, rumors circulating that local bank officials had invested heavily in the stock market using depositors' money and maybe even contents of safety deposit boxes—the bank was going to fail, everyone was quite certain of it, and they rushed to get their money out before it could collapse and wipe out an entire life's savings.

A disaster had been averted, the run stopped, by Walter's immediate intervention—the bank was sound, he told the people of the county; their money was secure, and there was no reason for panic.

But confidence was holding on by a thread.

Walter knew what would happen if the run resumed—the bank would never have enough cash on hand to redeem every account. There was money out on loans and in sound investments—but the citizens of Eason County would never understand that. They had put their money in the bank, and they believed that there it should stay—if the run resumed, the bank would collapse, and, with it, his fleeting control over the panic-stricken citizens of the county.

It seemed now to Walter as if he were walking a tightrope, just waiting for the right wind to come along and blow him from its surface— and, with him, the entire county. Nerves were stretched taut, in the Easons and in many other of the county's finest citizens who had suffered heavy losses in the Crash. Stock prices were rising again, but the damage had been done, and Walter now waited for the other shoe to drop.

County businesses were already suffering to one degree or another; a few citizens had been completely wiped out in the Crash, and with that, more suicides within one two-week period than the county would normally have suffered in years.

But it seemed the county would survive, though business had dropped, crime had already increased, unemployment was growing, and Walter had had to avert a near-run on the bank. It would survive—it had to survive, Walter told himself. It was Eason County.

Janson did not understand what had happened with the stock market, nor did he really care. He saw no way it could affect him or his growing family, so he gave it little thought. What was happening in the village, however, concerned him greatly.

Houses had been broken into on the quiet village streets while mill workers were working their shifts in the mill, including Clarence and Dorrie's house just a few streets from their own, and even the Baptist parsonage on a day when Reverend Satterwhite was preaching a funeral. People were beginning to look at each other speculatively, and many began to lock their doors at night and ask neighbors to watch their houses while they were away. Blame started to fall more and more on the men, sometimes entire families, who rode the rails through Pine, many of whom were only seeking work elsewhere, much as Janson had done after he lost his land. The men were often caught and thrown off the trains, making small camps near the railroad tracks at the edge of town until they could hop the next freight car out, traveling the country in growing numbers as more and more people became unemployed—and these "tramps," as the good citizens of Eason County called them, were looked at with increasing distrust as being behind the thefts and much of the other trouble in the area.

But Janson knew better. He suspected Buddy Eason and those two friends of his, and had seen them about the village more than usual—and he remained silent, as did others with the same suspicions. No one could . afford to lose jobs now, for they were too hard to come by, and locking doors and watching neighbors' houses was little enough to do to remain employed.

The mill had cut back to five days a week, and was now operating on three reduced shifts. No jobs had been lost yet due to hard times, but there were fewer and fewer hours to work, no doubles, and yet more mouths to feed in the Sanders's crowded three rooms. There was less money to go into the bank each payday, but still they managed to put a little aside each week, the security of that savings making it easier to get by in a world that seemed now unsure.

Like everyone else they knew, the Sanders family began to economize, to cut corners in every possible way they could. Elise lost sewing work from a few of the ladies in town and in the mill village, and was never paid by many others strapped for money.

Stan sought work for after school and on weekends, but had little luck—men with families to support were taking on part-time jobs just to have a wage coming in. Janson began to cut cord wood, weave baskets, and bottom chairs for other mill families in his off-hours from the mill, and Stan helped—anything to increase the family's income. There were six in their three rooms in the mill house—that was six hungry mouths to feed, six pairs of feet to put shoes on, six backs that needed warm clothes before winter set in.

Everyone was saying that times would be better in only a matter of months. There was talk about stock market gains in what was becoming known as the "Little Bull Market," and more and more people began to chant, "Prosperity is just around the corner," until Janson became sick of hearing it and seeing no results—where were the doubles, the "any number of hours you could want" times in the mill? More and more people were out of work as summer approached—but still, they said, prosperity was just around the corner.

It was in Brown's Grocery on Main Street on an afternoon near the mid part of the year that Janson heard President Hoover's voice come over the staticky, crackling wooden box on the counter as Mr. Brown adjusted the dial: *"We have now passed the worst,"* the President's voice said, *"and with continued unity of effort we shall rapidly recover"*—I hope so, Janson thought.

But, however well intentioned the President's words were, the worst had not passed and no recovery was yet within sight. Businesses sagged all the more, and religious and charity organizations, already taxed by the numbers of the unemployed, were burdened even further. There was a general state of worry within everyone, and, with that worry, wild rumor began to circulate again. A run began anew on the bank, and this time not even the power and influence of Walter Eason could stop it.

Janson was leaving the Feed and Seed on Main Street that afternoon after having gone to check on the hoe and mattock handles he had made and left there to be sold—on consignment, Mr. Abernathy had called it, though Janson had never heard the word before. On consignment or not, not even one had been sold, and Janson was leaving the Feed and Seed no better off than when he had come there. He had hoped to make at least a little something from the handles, for the family could use any money he might bring in. As things were, if times did not improve in the mill soon, he would have little choice but to get into their savings at the bank just for them to survive.

As he made his way down the sidewalk toward the heart of downtown that afternoon, he kept trying to think of anything that might allow him to make extra money. There had been less and less sewing for Elise to do over the past months, and even Janson had not been able to collect for her on some of the work she had done, or on what had been due him for several days work re-bottoming chairs for a widow-woman who lived in the village. Everyone was short on cash. That didn't help when Janson's own family was short as well.

He heard thunder in the distance as he reached the corner where he would turn to go back toward the village. He stopped for a moment, staring up at the sky—but then the knot of activity before the bank building at the far end of the downtown drew his attention. Cars were stopped haphazardly in the street. A truck sat in the throughway itself, and a team and wagon as well, even though Janson knew it should be no farther down than the wagon lot at the far side of the Feed and Seed and the dry goods store.

Janson could hear shouts even from where he stood the length of downtown away, the raised voices tightening a knot of worry inside of him as he crossed the street and started down the sidewalk on the opposite side. Men and women moved toward the front of the bank building, joining those already there. As Janson drew nearer, he could see people pounding on the closed doors of the bank—closed doors in the middle of the business day, something inside of him warned. He turned and started to grab hold of the man nearest to him, determined to find out what was going on—but was shoved aside by a cursing woman as she moved to the front of the building, and he felt a momentary shock as he recognized the woman to be Helene Price.

Helene's face was red and her hair poking out wildly beneath her cloche hat. The hat was sideways on her head, dipping down to almost cover her left eye. Her dress was buttoned wrong, gaping open at her bosom, and hitched up on one side, showing torn lace at the tail-end of her slip. Her pocketbook gaped open, spilling its contents as she grabbed someone else and shoved him aside. She was cursing with almost every breath, and Janson kept hearing the words: ". . . goddamn sons-of-bitches, steal my money . . . goddamn sons-of-bitches . . ." though he could make out little else.

He took hold of the man nearest to him, yanked the man around, and then shook him hard enough to almost send the eyeglasses from his face. "What th' hell's goin' on—why're th' doors locked?"

"The bank failed! Our money's gone!"

"'Gone'—what do you mean 'gone'?"

"They gambled it away on stocks. They lost most every goddamn cent we had in there, and they closed the doors to keep us from getting what's left." He tried to jerk free, and Janson released him at last, his mind reeling at the thought. His money couldn't—

He turned and grabbed another man, swinging him around to face him, vaguely recognizing the man's face as that of a deacon from the Baptist church in the village.

"They cain't have lost all th' money," he shouted into the deacon's face. "I had my money in there; they cain't gamble away my money."

"They did, you goddamn fool. Th' sons-a-bitches lost everything. Th' bank's gone. All our money's gone—"

Janson stumbled back, away from the building, away from the locked doors, away from men and women who pounded uselessly for entry they would never have. The police were moving into the crowd now, trying to disperse the people, and he could see Walter Eason arriving—but his mind could register only the one thought: his money was gone. The money he had saved through months and years of work had been stolen again, just as surely as when Elise's brother, Bill, had stolen it. All that work, all that saving, all that hope, all his dreams—gone again. He had made Elise and the children do with even less than he could have given them, had scrimped and saved—and it had been for nothing. It was almost beyond comprehension that the bank could take his money and close its doors and leave him and his family without a cent—why had he put it in the bank in the first place; why try to protect it from small thieves in the village, just to have it stolen by a bigger, more powerful, thief.

Later he walked toward the mill village over the hard-packed clay streets—there was maybe two dollars in coins in a fruit jar at home. How could a family of six survive with only that little money and the next pay envelope not coming for days, and that envelope based on shortened hours this week in the mill? Scrimping, saving, starting all over again—the dream of his land and home seemed distant and unreal now, that red land where he had been born, where his parents had lived and worked and died, seemed so far away, so far from Elise, and from their children. There was nothing left—nothing—and he did not want to start over again.

He had done that twice already.

There was no strength left in him as he trudged toward home. All gone—nothing left—nothing.

Janson stared up at the mill house his family shared with the bickering Breedloves—three rooms under a rented roof, a house only half their own. That was what he had given to Elise, asking her to be patient, telling her there would be better as soon as he could provide it, that white house on those red acres he had been born to. He had promised her so much, so much—he could have given her new dresses and nicer things for the house, could have given the children new clothes and store-bought toys, but he had asked them to wait, to do without—and, now, for nothing.

He could hear angry voices across the street, could feel tangible tension in the air the village over. His family had not been the only ones to lose a life's savings in the bank's failure, but at the moment he felt as if they were. It was personal, very personal.

The noise of the mill's machinery seemed to close about him as he stared up at the house, the sight of the lint floating everywhere—he had lost. That was the one thing he was certain of that day: he had lost. Somehow in a battle he had not even known the world was waging, he had lost—and now the mill would hold him, him and Elise and their children. How could he start over again now. Again.

Janson forced himself to walk up the slight rise and across the yard, then up onto the front porch. He moved through the quiet rooms, then stopped in the doorway to the kitchen, hearing Elise humming to herself as she worked at the woodstove. He watched her in her faded cotton dress and too-big apron, her back to him as she stirred the contents of a black pot on the stove. She was holding their daughter with one arm, while Henry played on the floor nearby, the boy unmindful of him as he banged at the bottom of an overturned pot with a spoon.

Janson thought of the life Elise had known before him. She had lived in a big, fine house; she'd had all the money in the world—he had promised her so much more. So much.

He did not make a sound, but she turned as if she had sensed his presence. A smile came to her face, then her expression changed as her eyes moved over his own.

Henry was suddenly on his feet, rushing across the room with the spoon still in hand. Janson picked him up and into his arms, then turned to look at Elise again—she was staring at him still, her blue eyes moving over his face, and for a moment he could only look at her.

"It's gone, Elise. Th' money we had in th' bank, all of it, it's gone." He watched her set the large spoon aside and hold Catherine even more closely to her. "Th' bank's failed—everythin's gone, everythin'—"

She moved toward him and he drew her close, holding her and their daughter, and their son.

"It's gone, everythin'—" he said again, his face against the softness of her hair, unable to say more. "It's gone—"

It was gone again—the money, all the work, the hopes, their dreams, all stolen again. But this time, added to the anger of loss, was the rage of not understanding, of knowing no one person they could blame.

But, it was not just the Sanders family. It was not just Eason County. There were bank failures, runs and panics the country over. As the months passed, business slacked off even more, throwing additional people into unemployment, and the charity groups could do little now toward relieving even a portion of the suffering, so heavy was the need. More and more farmers, after a decade of low farm prices and high surpluses, were going under. Businesses were closing. People defaulted on mortgages and loans, losing homes and property, and throwing the already suffering banking system into even worse straits for cash.

Entire families, unemployed now and dispossessed of homes, rode the rails seeking work, or camped on the outskirts of towns in shanty-villages that were coming to be known as "Hoovervilles." People looked to President Hoover, some with blind faith that he would pull the country through, others with curses that he had caused this Depression. There were cries for federal relief—but relief was not coming, and thousands looked toward the months ahead praying that prosperity must surely be 'just around the corner.' There was plenty to buy in the stores, but no money to buy with, as more people lost jobs and worry took up permanent residence in the hearts of most.

To Elise, as to many, that worry was never far from her mind, but compounded with the weekly worry that each pay envelope could be the last, was the worry over how Janson had taken the bank failure and the loss of the money he had worked so hard to save. He did not talk much these days, but silently went through the motion of living. There were less and less hours in the mill, and he spent the time when he was not on shift silently working in the garden or playing with the children, chopping wood, bottoming chairs, or making baskets for whatever they might bring. There were few people with cash to spare, and he now often traded work to other village families or families uptown, coming home with eggs or flour, a chicken or ham, a length of cloth, or even a book for Elise in exchange for work he had done. He worked harder now than he had before, but something had gone out of him the day the bank failed, and Elise worried that she might never see it in him again. She knew he was holding onto his dreams by their bare remnants, keeping them silent and locked inside, fighting his own fear for their existence—she knew and she kept her silence, telling herself it would be a long, hard struggle back, but they would do it. They had done it before, and they would do it again—if only times were not so hard.

The mill began to lay off. The least productive, especially the most recently hired, lost their jobs. Some families were left with no wage coming in, and Elise knew that Janson thanked God daily that he still had a job. The mill often ran only three or four days a week, but each penny earned helped lessen the load. A growing number were out of work, and fear lived within those who still held their jobs—if the mill cut back to only one shift—

Everyone was cutting corners, pinching pennies, worrying from one week to the next over shorter hours and what the future might bring. Tempers were running high, and that feeling of impotence, of undirected rage at a world that seemed to be slowly falling apart around them, found direction at first one person, and then another. There were complaints in the village as workers were laid off but continued to stay on in mill houses, Walter Eason telling those newly unemployed that they could remain in their homes and pay rent, though he knew that most would not have the money with which to pay. The unemployed gossiped against those working, looking at their own children and thinking of the cold, lean months ahead when those children might have to go hungry.

Bank officials had fled town amid accusations that bank funds had been mismanaged, just a bare, few steps ahead of angry men threatening violence. Transients near the depot were roughed up, one man nearly beaten to death, when rumors circulated that the hobos were coming in as cheap labor to take jobs in the mill and overall factory. Violence erupted against Negroes and against anyone who seemed the slightest bit different. Everyone seemed to be looking for some other party to blame—but times had to get better, Elise told herself. Things would go back to being again as they had been before. The mill would pick up and begin to rehire. There would be more hours for Janson and the others still working, and Janson would again be able to save toward his land.

It was on a chilly Friday afternoon in the latter months of 1930 when Janson came home at a time when his shift should have just begun. There was a note in his hand, a note that had been attached to his pay envelope, a note he had not had to be able to read to know what it had meant.

The mill had cut back to two shifts.

Janson Sanders was unemployed.

# PART TWO

## CHAPTER SEVEN

What do I do now?—the words kept repeating themselves in Janson's mind, demanding an answer, when he could think of none.

He trudged home along the hard-packed clay road on a November day less than a week after he had lost his job, pulling his coat closer against the chill air. His steps were slow, his mind filled with worry. He had gotten a ride into Cedar Flatts, hoping to find work at the small cotton mill there, but he'd had no luck, just as he'd had no luck at the overall factory in Pine, at Abernathy's Feed and Seed, or any other place he had checked, including a trip he had already made up to the county seat of Wylie. Every day they stayed on in the mill house now was a day of going into debt to the Easons, and he would not be owing and beholden to the Easons for anything.

There was always Gran'ma and Gran'pa, but he could not dump his entire family on his grandparents, or on anyone else in the family, though Deborah and Tom Sanders had already offered them shelter, as had Janson's Uncle Wayne and Aunt Rachel. Families were always there for each other, in the hard times as well as the better, but he could not allow his family to be a burden to anyone. Elise, Henry, little Catherine, Sissy, and his brother-in-law, Stan, were his responsibility and he had to look after them—there had to be something a man could put his hands to, something to earn an honest wage, but where was it? There seemed to be ten men for every opening; ten men who also had families to feed, children to support; ten men who needed the job just as badly as he.

For the first time Janson Sanders allowed himself the thought of sharecropping—but Elise, his Elise, as a sharecropper's wife. Henry and Catherine living in a drafty shanty with the wind whistling through the cracks in the board walls—he had grown up knowing children like that. Not all landowners had houses for their sharecroppers that were as sound as the one his grandparents lived in, or the ones on Whitley's place back in Georgia. Most were small one-to-three-room shacks with rusty tin roofs, poorly hung windows, and ill-fitting walls. He could not imagine taking Elise to a place like that, raising their children in a house like that—and, yet, for the first time in his life, he had to consider it.

But even sharecropping was closed to him for the present. It would take nearly a year for a crop; it was only November, and he knew they would never survive the winter without a wage coming in.

He did not hear the car coming until it was almost on him, and it ground to a halt at his side, too close, making him step away. A man leaned across the seat of the old flivver and peered out at him. "Hi, ya, boy, you need a ride?"

Janson caught himself almost instinctively saying no as he looked in at the man, but instead said, "Yeah, thanks," just before he got into the vehicle. The man was one he had seen in town a few times, at Brown's Grocery and at Abernathy's Feed and Seed. He had heard the name, but could not remember it as he shut the door and settled back in the Tin Lizzie.

The man smelled heavily of sweat and stale cigar smoke, his nearness to Janson making the air inside the car almost unbreathable. Janson knew that he did not like the man, and could remember not liking him from the first minute he had seen him, though he could not now remember the reason, but he needed a ride back into town, and this was as good as any. He leaned his head back, exhausted, and stared straight ahead at the road.

"I seen you in town some. M' name's Floyd Goode, boy," the man held out a dirty hand across the seat, bringing Janson's eyes to him.

"Janson Sanders—" The hand was sweaty when he shook it, with black grime caked under the fingernails, making Janson want to wipe his own palm along the leg of his dungarees when the handshake was over.

"Yeah, I seen you an' your wife an' young'n's in town several times—she's a right handsome woman, your wife. How's she doin'?"

Janson stared at him, not liking the tone in his voice, then answered deliberately: "My family's fine."

"That's good." The man nodded, staring straight ahead as the car made its way slowly toward Pine. "My woman's gone off visitin' her sister down in Montgomery; you don't miss 'em 'til they ain't there, you know; ain't had a decent meal in a week—but I ain't lackin' for company, if you know what I mean." Goode grinned, and suddenly Janson liked him even less. "Plenty 'a women for what I got—too much for my woman by herself, I always say, so I spread it around t' make it easy on her an' give th' others some. They always say a man can take care 'a slew 'a women, you know, same as a bull an' cows—" He seemed pleased with what he had said, laughing with a rattling sound coming from the massive chest. He moved one hand to scratch at the belly that protruded over his belt, the buttons on his grimy shirt near to bursting over it, then reached up to run the hand along the heavy stubble at his chin. "What're you doin' s' far from home, boy? That pretty woman 'a yours thrown you out?"

Janson clenched his fist at his side and took a deep breath of the fetid air within the car, trying to calm his temper before he spoke, but his words came out angry anyway. "I was lookin' for work."

Goode seemed to take note of the tone, for he glanced quickly at Janson. "You got a bee up your ass, boy?"

Janson did not answer, but remained silent, looking straight ahead, expecting to be put out of the car at any moment. Goode returned his eyes to the road.

"You get laid off at th' mill?"

"Yeah."

For a moment Goode did not speak, but reached up to rub his chin again before returning the hand to the steering wheel. "You have any luck findin' a job?"

"Not yet."

There was silence again, then: "Me, I got me a good size place right on th' edge 'a town. Ain't too close t' folks, so I can do pretty much like I want.

It's a little too much work for just me an' my boy, Lionel, now that my older boys're all gone—I could use somebody t' work aroun' th' place, takin' care 'a th' livestock, cleanin' out th' chicken houses, fixin' up some, doin' some plowin' an' plantin'—" His words stopped and he seemed to be waiting. When Janson just stared, he continued, his tone more formal. "I could maybe use you—you ain't gonna be able t' stay on in a mill house an' not be workin' for th' mill, an' me, I got a little place you could stay in. I'll give you a few dollars on th' side, too, along with th' rent. Maybe a little more, if your woman could do some cookin' an'—"

"My wife works at home. We got two children; she don't do no work for nobody else."

"Well, we'll see—you interested, boy?"

A place to live, maybe a few dollars with it—but the offer did not feel right. Something in the man's tone, perhaps in his very presence there in the car, made Janson want to say no. He did not want to work for this man. He did not want Elise or Sissy anywhere near him—but did they have a choice?

"It's just a little place, where my oldest boy stayed for a while before he got—" he paused for a second, then continued, "before he left. Two rooms, ain't got no furnishin's, but I guess you got that. You could move in right off." He waited for a moment, then his voice came again, impatient and demanding. "Well, you want it or not, boy? Men's a dime a dozen right now, an' most'd jump at a place t' live an' some money comin' in. I can get anybody—"

Janson's mind raced, turning over the possibilities, the chance of other work.

"Well?"

He opened his mouth to say no, but the image came to him of hungry faces looking up at him. Winter was coming on; they would have to have warm clothing for the children, food.

He clenched his fist so tightly that his nails dug deeply into his palm, causing pain—but he did not release it. He held it only tighter. "I'll take it," he said, then repeated the words, as if to assure himself that he had said them. "I'll take it."

§

They moved into the house on Goode's property a few days later, crowding themselves and all they owned into two small rooms. Janson told himself that it would only be until he could find better—but there were no jobs to be had, though he continued to look. He had not felt right about the decision to take the house and job, and it worried him that his fears might be justified, for Goode seemed to drop by the house at all times during the day, making Janson swear again that the man would never find either Elise or Sissy alone.

Money was unbearably tight. The wage Goode paid was pitiably small, and it became a struggle each week just to feed the family. There was little call for Elise's sewing, so tight were things with most people in the county, that they could not even count on that little money coming in. Sissy had left school, and Stan had graduated, but neither could find a job, leaving them both at the house during the day to help with the two small children, or to work with Janson on the chores Goode required to be done.

The work took very little of each day with several of them to help, leaving Janson with time on his hands, so he sought whatever work he could find elsewhere. He at last had time he could spend with Elise and the children, but he felt so useless. His dream of the land seemed further from him now than at any time in the past, in the light of the daily need for food and shelter for the family, the daily worry of what lay just ahead. He took an hour's work for himself and Stan where he could find it, two hours, half a day, to patch a roof, burn out a chimney, bottom a chair, or repair a door—anything, just to earn a few extra cents, a hen, vegetables, or eggs in barter for chores done. He walked from door to door, carrying baskets he had made from white oak splits, selling them for whatever someone might be willing to pay. He walked the railroad tracks, picking up coal that had fallen from passing rail cars and taking it home to help heat the little house. He gathered wild plants in the woods, foods his mother and his grandmother had shown him, and taught Elise how to prepare things she had never dreamed to feed her children. He fished and he hunted, teaching Stan to hunt as well, bringing home deer meat, rabbit, and squirrel, or going out at night in the hope of bringing in a possum he could keep in a chicken coop and feed buttermilk to until it could be killed to provide meat for the family—but there was never enough that he could do.

Times were bad. There were so many out of work, so many in desperate circumstances, and so few to help. Gifts of food and hand-me-downs came from relatives and from members of the Holiness church his grandparents attended, and occasionally from the Baptist church in the village that the family had attended until they moved. With each gift that came, Janson felt only worse—he should be the one to support his family; they should not have to live on the charity of others, no matter how small the charity or how well intentioned—so he searched all the harder for work, scrubbing floors in an office for a day, moving machinery at the newspaper building, but often days went by with no work to be had. It was almost Christmas, but there would be little Christmas in their house this year, and that hurt, for Henry was two-and-a-half years old now and he looked at the world with such expectant eyes.

Janson began to check daily at Brown's Grocery for work, stocking shelves, delivering groceries, washing windows, and it seemed more often than not that Edgar Brown could find something for him to do, or that he would have a name for him, and directions to the home of someone else who might have work for him or for Stan. Janson wondered at times if the grocer only masked charity with work that he would normally have done himself, but, if that were true, the older man never gave any sign that he was doing so.

It was on a cold December day a week before Christmas that Janson was cleaning out the storeroom in the back of the grocery, bringing up merchandise to be put on the shelves. Mr. Brown had found work Stan could do for the day as well, sitting Janson's brother-in-law behind the counter at the front of the store with ledger books where the grocer kept track of charges made. Janson had heard them talking during his several trips toward the front, but it was Buddy Eason's voice that came to him this time as he knelt to place tin cans of peas on a shelf.

"I want some tobacco, old man—" Buddy said, his voice rough, demanding. Janson stopped where he was to listen, not returning to the rear of the store and the storeroom as he had been about to.

"I'll be with you in a minute, Mr. Eason. I'm almost finished with—"

"You'll take care 'a me now." The voice was even more demanding, and Janson moved to the end of the shelves so that he could see the front of the store. Buddy stood before the counter, glaring at Mr. Brown across the countertop. A young Negro woman stood nearby, a small girl of about Henry's age clinging to her skirt. The child's thumb went to her mouth as she stared from her mother to Buddy Eason. Janson could see Stan where he sat behind the counter, his brother-in-law now turned around in his chair with his eyes on the exchange as well.

"I said I'd be with you in a minute," the grocer said, though his voice did not change, then brought his eyes back to the young woman. "Now that was a pound of sugar and a—"

"Now, old man," Buddy said, his voice rising, setting the little girl to crying where she clung to her mother's skirts. "I ain't gonna be waited on behind no nigger."

"Go ahead, I can wait," the young woman said, picking the child up into her arms and trying to quieten her crying as she stepped back and away from the counter and Buddy Eason. Buddy turned on her even as she backed away, bringing one finger to point at the child in her arms, and setting the little girl into even louder wails as she found his eyes now on her.

"Shut that goddamn little pickaninny up or I'll break it's neck—and I don't need some nigger gal's okay to be waited on," he said, then looked back at the grocer. "Now, give me some tobacco, old man."

Mr. Brown looked to the young woman, clear apology in expression. "I'll finish your order in a—" he began, speaking to the woman, but he was grabbed by the collar before he could complete the words as Buddy reached across the countertop to draw him up short.

Janson started forward, but the grocer, his eyes meeting Janson's over the distance, quickly shook his head at the same moment he held a hand back to stop Stan.

"You've wasted enough time with that nigger—now give me my tobacco." He released the grocer with a shove. The young woman started for the door, and Mr. Brown watched her go, until at last the door closed behind her. Then he turned an angry look on Buddy Eason. Janson had never seen the grocer angry before, and the look on the older man's face surprised him.

"You ran my customer off," Mr. Brown said, his eyes never leaving Buddy Eason.

"She wasn't nothing but a goddamn nigger—now, get my—"

"She's a good customer, and she pays her bill, which is more than I can say for you."

"You better watch your words, old man." Buddy's tone changed. There was clear threat in his voice.

"I'll watch my words, all right. I'll say something to you that ought to have been said years ago," Mr. Brown said, coming around the counter to stare up at Buddy Eason. "You're nothing but a bully, no better than you were when you were a little boy, and it's a disgrace that you're Mr. Walter's only grandson, because you're not even fit to have his name— and you're no longer welcome in this store. Now, get out." The grocer stared up at Buddy Eason, the older man breathing heavily, his eyes never leaving Buddy's face.

"You better think about that, old man," Buddy said quietly.

"I've thought all I—"

"You old nigger-lover," Buddy said, interrupting his words. "You'd rather deal with niggers than white folks."

"I'd rather deal with the devil than you—now, get out of my store!" The grocer shouted, pointing toward the door for emphasis. "And don't come back."

Buddy looked at him for a moment longer, then reached across the counter and took a tin of Prince Albert from the display there. He walked toward the door slowly, but turned back only a moment later. "You're gonna be sorry you said that, old man," he said, staring at him from the doorway.

"Just get out!" Mr. Brown yelled the words at him, but they did not seem to matter to Buddy Eason.

"I'll be back, old man; don't you worry about that. I'll be back," Buddy said. Then he turned at last and left the store.

"Damn old nigger lover—" Buddy said later that afternoon, drawing deeply on the cigarette he had just rolled. The house was quiet, his mother gone for the day, his sisters probably off with a couple of men, his father at the mill—he, Richard Deeds, and Carl Miles had the house to themselves, but Buddy was restless. Few men had ever dared to talk to him as the old grocer had done, and he knew he would have to do something about it. "Damn old nigger lover," he said again, studying the end of his cigarette.

"That's what's wrong with the niggers now days, people like him making them think they're good as anybody." Richard rolled a cigarette on his knee where he sat in a chair near the sofa, not even glancing up as he spoke.

"Damn right, and I'm not going to let him get away with it."

"You going to teach him about waiting on white folks first?" Carl asked, lounging back against the mantel, out of the swirls of cigarette smoke that hung over the area around the sofa where Buddy sat. Carl always seemed to stay back, never sharing their smokes or their tempers. He was always there, Buddy told himself, yet never really a part of their fun—but Buddy trusted him. They had been friends since childhood, when Carl and Richard had stood lookout as Buddy hassled younger children for coins or for the various other contents of children's pockets—he trusted Carl, and he trusted Richard. If there were ever a time when he could not trust them, he would know, and they would then meet with the temper they had for years coddled and appeased. He knew they liked the money he always had, the nice car and the pretty girls who always hung about, the liquor he never seemed to lack, and the fearful respect he evoked in even the most hardened of Eason County people. They liked the kind of life he afforded them contact with, but they did not like him—and in some way Buddy knew that, but it did not matter.

They were companionship, a mirror to himself against the world, and it mattered little what they thought or felt.

They were nothing anyway, Buddy told himself; they were nothing more than the sons of day bosses from the cotton mill, and he was Buddy Eason—he would someday control much of this county, and then everyone would look up to him as Richard and Carl did now. That day would come, and, until then, these two were always willing to follow, always willing to agree. They looked at him now, expecting him to offer a plan to teach the old grocer a lesson, a diversion to occupy their minds and their hands in this time when the weather was too cold to do much else. "Yeah, I'm gonna teach him, all right," Buddy said.

Richard sealed the cigarette he had rolled with the tip of his tongue. "What're you going to do?"

Buddy brought his own cigarette to his lips, taking the smoke deeply into his lungs, and releasing it in a swirl into the room. He stared at the smoke, and then beyond it as Richard struck a match to light his own cigarette. As the light flared from the match-end, the sizzle and color caught Buddy's eye, the beauty of it, and he captured Richard's wrist in a firm grip, holding it as he stared at the flame, seeing it sputter with the movement of his breath against it.

He could sense Richard's alarm, could feel him trying to pull his wrist free, but Buddy held him still, his eyes caught in the light, his other hand, holding his own cigarette between his fingers, going to press Richard's finger tips together on the match stem to keep him from dropping it as it started to burn down. He could hear Richard's voice, then Carl's, calling his name, trying to draw him back, but he could not listen to them, could not—not until the match burned down to Richard's fingers, making him finally jerk free. Buddy watched with interest and a touch of almost sexual satisfaction as Richard looked first at his burned fingertips before he finally brought his eyes to Buddy.

Buddy took up another match and lit it, staring at the flame for a moment, feeling both Richard and Carl fade from him as the fire consumed his thought. "I'll need you both tonight," he said, though his eyes never left the flame.

♣

Janson picked through the small pile of wilted vegetables outside the back door of the grocery store that evening just before dusk, finding cabbages, bruised tomatoes, and turnip greens turning dark at the edges—his mouth was set in a grim line. The thought that he would be taking home to his family food gathered from the refuse pile behind the store was not an easy one but one he would live with on this day as he had on others. It seemed such a waste to leave entire boxes of food behind the store to be dumped later, when the boxes often contained food that was still fit to be eaten. He had seen men, women, sometimes entire families, behind this and other groceries in the past months, picking through food that had been put out as garbage. He had never thought himself to be one of those men, feeding his family on what others thought too old, wilted, or bruised to serve—but here he was, taking first choice of what Mr. Brown had put out before anyone else could go through it.

Fried cabbage would be good when there was so little else on the table, and Henry liked tomatoes, and the turnip greens would make a meal for the entire family; there would even be cornbread if Elise had any meal left in the house. She never asked where he got the food, seeming to prefer not knowing to what she might learn, for there never seemed to be enough to feed the family. Food was the one thing he had always thought there would be plenty of, but now it was a daily struggle just to survive. Mr. Brown had offered a charge to Janson at the store, saying that he and Stan could work off whatever the family might need, but Janson did not want a store charge sitting heavy on his conscience, a bill he might never be able to pay. They bought the few items they could afford and paid the little cash they had and they made do—and he often thought, when he was tired after walking the streets peddling baskets all day long when there was no other work to be had, of what he had brought Elise to in the three years of their marriage. He had given her two children, and a tiny house that was not their own, and a worry over how they would survive—he had promised her better.

They lost the fall garden when they had been forced to move from the mill house, and the vegetables he had planted there, vegetables they so desperately needed now. His grandparents gave them what they could, his grandmother sending Elise jars of home-canned food she said they would never need, and his grandfather bringing by a ham and bacon from the smokehouse, a ham and bacon that he had said would go to waste if they could not make use of them. There was sometimes fresh game or fish on the table when he could make a catch, eggs when the hens were laying—and, in the past week, the vegetables he took from behind the store. Never enough—but people could throw out food like this without a thought.

Janson found apples under the cabbages, bruised and cut, but edible—fried apple pies, if there was the flour and sweetening. Elise would like the apples, he thought as he dug them out and began to drop them into the gunny sack he had brought along—there would be food enough on the table for the next couple of days. He could go hunting tomorrow, if there was no work to be had anywhere else. Deer meat would be good along with—

The back door of the grocery creaked open and Janson looked up to find Mr. Brown staring at him. Janson dropped his sack and looked away—to the pile of food he had been going through—a man, taking home food that had been thrown out as garbage.

He could not speak; he could only stare at the food, at his sack as the apples and cabbages rolled from it, at the ground—he was less than a man, less than any man should be, less than—

"You're welcome to go through it before it's put out, if you'd like." Mr. Brown's voice was kind, and the pity in his eyes a moment before seemed carefully masked as Janson looked at him now. "It's a waste to throw out so much when most of it is still good food. I'm glad you can use it."

"I just—it's—" What could he say? His pride writhed within him. To gather food from the trash was bad enough, to be caught while doing it was somehow beyond reason.

"You know, there's a sack of potatoes up front that looks like it's just beginning to sprout. I was about to bring it out, but you're welcome to—"

"I don't take no charity," Janson heard himself say even before he thought, his words harsh even to his own ears. He needed the work this man offered; he needed the food rolling into the dirt from the gunny sack; and he needed the potatoes the man spoke of—his pride was screaming inside of him. He was a man, and a man did not take charity—but he did; he had to. No matter how carefully masked, how gently couched, it was charity—from his grandparents, from the churchfolk, from this man in his invented work. He took charity to feed his family—he felt shame in the charity, and shame even in the shame he felt. How could he face Elise after this?

He was aware of a car driving by, a dark Chevrolet slowing as the driver stared at him and Mr. Brown where they stood behind the grocery, and Janson turned away, feeling that the driver of the vehicle saw what he had been doing. A hand came to rest at his shoulder, and he heard the grocer's voice, a voice that did not offer pity or speak down to someone with less. He brought his eyes back to Mr. Brown and he saw a man much like himself, a man with a wife, and family he had come from, and the shame cooled within him as he stared in the falling darkness into the kind eyes of the grocer. "I'm not offering you charity, Janson. You're a hard-working man; there are a lot of hard-working men in this country now, a lot with no jobs, no earnings, no food on the table. I've been lucky to have this store, lucky to make enough to keep it open, to be able to feed my family—it's only by the grace of God that we're not all cold and hungry in these days. I'm not offering you charity, Janson; I'm offering you a sack of potatoes that needs to be put to use. You've done good work for me, can't I offer you something in exchange?"

"You paid me for my work."

"Well, maybe you're worth more than I paid you—come on in the store and at least look at the potatoes. I can show you some other work that may need doing tomorrow while you're here; you can just call the potatoes partial payment. Come on in—" He turned and disappeared back through the door as if the matter had already been decided.

Janson bent and retrieved the apples and cabbages that had rolled from the sack, before he followed the grocer back into the store.

Mr. Brown sent him away from the store that night not only with his gunny sack of vegetables and the potatoes, but also with a five-pound bag of flour, a five-pound bag of corn meal, and a two-pound bag of sugar—it was not charity, the grocer said, for there were shelves to be put up in the store, and a bad patch of flooring that needed to be replaced in the storeroom. Janson left not only with food he needed for the family, but also with a handshake from the grocer, and, somehow, he realized as he walked toward home in the growing darkness, with his dignity.

Edgar Brown was in the grocery that night well after his normal closing hour, counting receipts and straightening up in preparation for the next day's business. He was often in the grocery late, for he loved the work, and was willing to open the store at night, or even on a Sunday, if an emergency arose and someone needed something from his stock.

On this night, he was happy, glad that he could help Janson Sanders and his family, for he had known the Sanders for many years, as it sometimes seemed to him that he knew most people in the county. He could remember Janson as a boy, a dark-haired little fellow who was always nearby if his father were in town, quiet, with hardly ever a word to say to anybody. Edgar had known Henry Sanders quite well, and had known his wife, Nell, just as he knew Tom and Deborah Sanders—they were good people, hard-working people; stubborn, determined and proud, as were most Southerners. Janson Sanders was a good man, and even good men could run on hard times—there were a lot of people in hard times these days, a lot of people with families to support, and little or no wage coming in.

Edgar thought over the times in his life when other people had helped him, and he could understand the pride in Janson—a man deserved his pride; a man deserved his self-respect; and a man deserved help when he needed it. The Bible said that God helped those who helped themselves—and, if anybody had ever in his life tried to help himself, Edgar thought, it was Janson. Edgar could not imagine Janson Sanders sitting still, and he could not imagine him not doing everything in his power to support his family and himself—but these times were different than any Edgar had seen. So many people were out of work, so many in situations they had never dreamed to find themselves in—to help one person, one family, in these times was good, but what was needed was work, a wage a man could earn to feed his family.

There had to be something that could be done, even if it were just for Janson and his family—maybe to buy the well-made baskets Janson wove and put them up for sale in the store, and there were chairs at home that needed to be rebottomed. Mrs. Brown—as he usually thought of his wife—had not had a new dress for quite a while, and Edgar knew that Janson's wife did handsome work with needle and thread. He might even be able to sell some of her tatting to the ladies in town, as well as some of her knitted goods and other dainties she had made with her hands—he was suddenly annoyed with himself. There were so many things he could be doing, things he had never thought of before, things that might help to alleviate even a little of the growing suffering in the town and county—baked goods he could buy from unemployed ladies or the wives of unemployed workers, things that could be sold in the store, jellies and pickles he could stock on his shelves, food every bit as good as what he bought from his wholesalers, handmade hoe and mattock handles he could sell for men with no other wage coming in. It was remarkable to him now that he had not thought of this before—there were so many things he and the other merchants along Main Street could be doing.

He locked away the day's receipts and went to get his hat and coat from the pegs to the left of the doorway. He was tired, and Mrs. Brown would have a good, warm meal waiting at home—bless Mrs. Brown, she was always so patient to keep supper warm for him, no matter how late he might be in the store. She often told him that she had never felt deprived in their not having had children, for she still had him to raise— he smiled to himself; she was a good woman, Mrs. Brown, to have looked after him for the more than thirty years of their marriage.

He put his hat on his head and started to pull on his coat when he heard a noise from the back of the store. He stopped, his arm only part way into the sleeve, and peered down the dark aisle toward the back of the grocery—there, again, sounding almost like the rusty hinges on the back door that led into the storeroom, then the aged floorboards squeaking under a man's weight.

He waited, hearing for a moment no other sound. Was he just getting dotty in his old age, hearing noises that were not there, imaginary ghosts prowling through the deserted store late at night—there, again, and surely that had not been his imagination.

He hung the coat back on the peg, took his hat from his head and did not notice it fall to the floor as he missed the peg—his eyes were set toward the back of the grocery. There was someone in his store, someone moving about in the storeroom—he moved to the cooling black pot-bellied stove that sat near the counter and took up a piece of wood from the stack that rested in its wood bin. Then, clutching it tight in his hand, he made his way as noiselessly as possible, toward the back of the store. His senses were heightened, each sound now coming almost like a gunshot to his ears, his eyes picking out and fixing on the door that led into the storeroom. He knew every squeaky board in the floor, every obstacle that might trip him, and he maneuvered around them—he'd catch them unawares, the little hooligans who had broken into his store.

He neared the door to the storeroom, catching the strong smell of gasoline fumes, and his stomach tightened convulsively within him—not thieves, but vandals, vandals in his store, gasoline on the wooden flooring, on the wooden walls. The front of the building was brick and glass, but everything else was wood, wood that would go up in a second and cost him everything.

Suddenly the door swung inward, catching him off guard, and he looked up into the startled eyes of Buddy Eason. For a moment the two just stared at each other, then an instinct that went beyond thought told the grocer to turn and run—but it was already too late. Buddy was on him, clamping a sweaty hand that reeked strongly of gasoline over his mouth and forcing him backwards. Edgar could feel himself losing his footing, stumbling, being pushed, starting to fall—then his head hit the shelf behind him so hard that the wood cracked with the force of the blow.

There was no pain, just a sudden not knowing, and Edgar Brown sank to the floor at Buddy's feet.

There was a silence as three young men looked at each other in the gloom of the rear of the store. Perspiration stood out on Buddy's upper lip and over his cheeks as Carl knelt beside the grocer.

"He's just out, ain't he?" Richard asked from where he stood nearby, then looked as if all the breath had been knocked out of him as Carl stumbled back, away from the man lying on the floor, his eyes wide and a shocked and frightened look on his face.

"He's dead—oh, God—he's dead!" Carl moved back until he was against the wall near the door they had come through. His eyes were large in the dim light, and he was shaking as he stared at Buddy. "He's dead, Buddy. He's really dead—"

"He just hit his head—he'll be okay—" Buddy said, but did not even look at the grocer as Richard moved to check the body.

Richard straightened only a moment later, wiping his hands on his pants legs, a panicky look on his face as well. "He's really dead. You killed him—"

"Oh—God—" Carl clutched at his stomach, tears starting down his cheeks, and Buddy had the sudden and horrible knowledge that the other man was going to be sick only a moment before Carl turned away and retched onto the floorboards of the store. "Oh—God—no—"

"Shut up!" Buddy snapped. He had to think. "It was an accident— you both saw it. It was only—"

"They won't believe it—us here, the gas and all—" At least Richard was keeping his head, while Carl stood by crying, staring at the man on the floor—useless, absolutely useless.

Richard was right; no one would believe it was an accident—how could they explain being here, the gasoline, the matches in his pocket. He had to think—no one could ever know they had been here. No one could ever know it had been him.

"Get the jug and pour gasoline in here—hurry!" Buddy ordered, but

Richard only stared. "If they get me, they'll get you, too—now, move!"

Richard began to slosh the liquid over everything in the area, moving about the room and close to the front, but keeping hidden from the windows and the electric light on at the front of the store.

"No—you can't—not now—" Carl seemed near hysterics. He shook his head slowly, staring at Buddy through tears that rolled from his eyes and down his cheeks. Trust him to fall apart, Buddy thought. Trust him to cost them everything—he slapped Carl hard across the face, then again, backhanded the second time, and his friend stared at him through shocked, tear-bright eyes, his hand going to his cheek.

"You listen to me—nobody can ever know we were here. Do you hear me—nobody. So help me, you breathe a word about this, you son-of-a-bitch, and I'll kill you myself."

Carl stared, his mouth slack and open.

Buddy pushed Carl and Richard through the door and into the storeroom ahead of him, then went back and sloshed the last of the gasoline over the body of the grocer. He looked around the room, then moved back into the storeroom. Looking toward the open back door he could see Richard and Carl there, dark forms against the less dark of the night outside—the fools were going to be seen.

He took the matches from his pocket, finding his hands steady as he struck one. He stared at the flame for a moment, then tossed it onto the floor, watching it fall until it struck the pool of gasoline. There was a soft whooshing as the gasoline ignited then spread away, toward the doorway and the body that lay beyond. He watched the cloth sacks on a lower shelf start to burn as the fire spread. He could hear Richard calling his name, and feel the cool breeze behind him from the open doorway, but for a moment he could only stare, captivated by the sight before him, and the sound, of something almost alive as it grew and began to consume the wood—then Richard was dragging at his arm, pulling him away and through the open doorway into the night outside.

The fire spread quickly, having engulfed the grocery and spread to the barber shop next door by the time the fire department arrived. The sky was alight as flames shot up from the roof of Brown's Grocery, threatening the cafe on its other side, and the mass of buildings below the barber shop. The grocery was given up as lost, the town's volunteer firemen directing their attentions to the buildings on either side. One entire half of downtown could go if the fire was not contained—stores, shops, businesses, livelihoods, in a town already hurting from unemployment and lack of work. People hurried toward downtown, some to watch, drawn by the excitement, but many more to help fight the blaze. A water spigot ran full open beside town hall, another before the hardware store, and lines of men stretched from both toward the buildings threatened, dousing the wood and brick structures with buckets brought out from the hardware store, Abernathy's Feed and Seed, and the five and dime.

The Sanders had eaten supper, and Janson and Stan afterward went out to the woodpile beside the house to refill the box by the back door. Janson was talking about the work they had the next day replacing flooring in Brown's Grocery, but he suddenly stopped and stared. There was a glow in the night sky beyond the distant bulk of Goode's house, a glow that seemed to be growing brighter as the minutes passed. Downtown—

Suddenly he was running, knowing before he reached Main Street that there was a fire, but he never expected what he saw when he reached downtown. Flames shot up from rooftops, reaching into the night sky. People stood close, fighting the fire, falling back as it edged its way farther and farther down the street. Downtown was jammed with cars parked helter-skelter along the street as Janson reached the sidewalks, the air thick with heavy, black smoke that curled upward into the darkness above the flames, and that floated out over the growing crowd that had gathered to watch. Brown's Grocery was engulfed, the glass windows broken and jagged, fire wildly eating everything behind the bricked front—Mr. Brown had still been at work in the store when Janson had left earlier. If he had not gotten out—

The roof groaned, heavy with fire, and began to crash in, and the flames shot even higher. The grocery was nothing now but a wall, a space, filled with fire—no one could be alive in that. Janson stared up at the orange, yellow, and red—the destruction, the disaster—feeling heat on his face, forcing him back. He thought of the fire that had cost his father's life—then he was moving to the line of men that stretched from the hardware store to the flames, joining the others fighting the blaze the only way open to them. He accepted the buckets, their contents already half slopped out, and dashed at the flames with the water, handing back a bucket, taking another—but it was hopeless, the fire too big, their efforts too small. Buildings were lost, other stores catching, even with the efforts of the men and the work of the pumper truck—one entire side of the street could go, and they could not stop it.

There was a crash from the upper story of Patterson's Drug Store before them, and shards of glass fell on Janson and the other men on the sidewalk below. There was a panic-filled scream and the sound of more breaking glass from the windows above, and Janson looked up—there was someone at the windows of old Dr. Bassett's office, white-sleeved arms thrust out through the broken glass, silhouetted against the dark sky above. Janson threw down the empty bucket in his hand and ran toward the entrance to the building, several other men beside him.

They crashed against the door, Janson and one other man throwing their weight against it, fumbling with the door knob, then Janson drove his shoulder against the wood frame again, splintering it and shattering the glass as the lock gave way and it flew inward. He stumbled inside, coughing with the smoke that was already in his lungs. The fire burned close by, all along one side of the store, catching and consuming more as it moved through the building. He pulled his handkerchief from his pocket and held it over his face, trying to block out the smoke that choked and gagged him as he made his way toward the back of the building and the stairs there already beginning to catch fire. The man beside him grabbed his sleeve and Janson turned to look at him through the stinging smoke, seeing the man shake his head and release his arm to point back toward the doorway then start to move in that direction. There was another sound of a crash overhead, and Janson's eyes moved back to the stairs. The fire was hot on his face and he wiped away the sweat that poured into his eyes. He coughed through the handkerchief, the fire so close now he could feel it, could smell it, could hear it. He stumbled up the stairs, toward the office overhead, almost unable to see now for the smoke and the heat and the hell around him.

Smoke choked the upper floor, flames moving into the wooden walls, rolling across the ceiling overhead, and the sound, hot and deafening, filled his ears. He could no longer see where he was going, but stumbled forward, following instinct toward the windows that would overlook Main Street. He ran into a wall, and felt his way along it to an open doorway, then fell inside and had to regain his feet.

He felt the man before he saw him, and grabbed his arm, intending to push him out the second-story window and then jump himself—but suddenly the man was fighting him, clawing at him, knocking him back, and then moving from the window and the closest means of escape. There was a crashing sound from below, and another, as Janson stumbled after him and through the doorway out onto the landing.

Fire rolled across the ceiling overhead—he could hear it, though he could no longer see anything but blackness, his handkerchief lost in the struggle. There was a high-pitched keening, and Janson followed it to its source, finding the man pressed into a corner near the top of the stairs. Janson grabbed his arm, slapping him hard as he tried to struggle free, then again before he pushed him to the top of the stairs and started down. The man was clawing at him, dragging at him, almost making him lose his footing as Janson shoved him down the last few steps and into the hell of the bottom floor.

He stumbled forward, forcing the smaller man before him. His lungs hurt; there was no air, only smoke and a hot hell that he could no longer breathe in.

Crashing sounds came from behind, a groan as a wall weakened, or the ceiling overhead, ready to collapse. The entire front of the store was burning now, and he forced the man forward, knowing they would both die if they did not push through the flames.

There was the smell of scorched hair and burning flesh, but he forced the man forward, forced him through the flames, through the blackness, through the smoke, and he fell ahead himself, into the open, into the night air.

Alive—he stood swaying on his feet as the man collapsed against one of those nearby fighting the blaze. Alive, alive—

Suddenly he was hit hard from the side, landing hard, sprawling, out onto the brick pavement of the street. Someone was on him, rolling him over, hurting him, bruising already bruised flesh on the hard red brick. He caught sight of open-mouthed faces, but no one would help him. He was too dazed to struggle, but the person would not let go, rolling him over and over on the street—strong, determined, overpowering.

He was released and he lay for a moment on his side, dazed, hurting, then found Stan's worried and smut-blackened face staring into his own, helping him to sit. He was hearing, he was alive, he was breathing, and Stan was there, looking at him, talking, his face streaked with sweat and soot.

"You were on fire. You seemed not to know it—you were on fire—"

The words made no sense. He tried to make himself think, tried to make himself feel. Stan was looking at him, at his arm, at his side, and Janson looked down—I've ruined my coat, he thought. Then—I was on fire; as he stared, in open amazement, at the blackened and burned garment, the burned thing beneath that was his shirt sleeve.

He lifted his eyes to Stan, feeling coming into the scorched and burned flesh, the hurt oddly welcome because it said that he lived, he breathed.

He sat in the street, staring at the line of stores before him, at the fire that had almost ended his life. It was hopeless, the fire out of all control, one entire half of Main Street seeming lost as the flames spread outward. They would be lucky if one building on that side of the street was left standing, lucky if no life was lost. Half of downtown was gone, all the stores and businesses, the places people worked, the jobs that gave money to feed entire families—gone. He realized suddenly that he was crying and sick there on the red brick of the street, as he watched the town burn.

☙

Elise dropped the cup she had been washing when Janson and Stan returned to the house that night. The two children and Sissy were asleep, and Elise had been washing the supper dishes alone at the dishpan on the kitchen table when the door opened and Stan entered the tiny house, followed by Janson—both men were covered with soot, smelling of smoke. Stan's hands were burned from having beaten the fire out when Janson's clothes were burning—but the sight of Janson made Elise feel as if her heart would stop beating. The clothes along his right arm and side were badly burned, his neck raw-looking, and his hair singed along one side—the cup shattered on the floor at her feet, but Elise did not even notice.

She realized she must have cried out, for Janson's first words, as she crossed the room to go to him, were: "I'm okay, Elise; don't wake up Henry an' Catherine—" his eyes large and green in his smut-blackened face.

She was almost afraid to touch him as she made him sit at the kitchen table, and then she frantically searched for the scissors so that she could cut away the burned garments to see how bad his burns were. Her hands were shaking badly as she tried to cut at the material and she knew she was hurting him all the worse, and she kept trying to get him to allow her to send Sissy running for a doctor—but he told her that doctors cost money, and that money was something they did not have, so she cut the burned coat and shirt away herself and cleaned the burns as best she could, gingerly applied salve, and then wrapped them in clean white strips that she cut from the good sheets she had kept stored in the bottom of the chifforobe, sheets Janson's grandmother had given them. Her hands were still shaking as she cleaned and dressed Stan's burns as well, and, when she was finished, they were shaking all the worse, for she realized that she could have lost Janson and her brother in the one hellish fire that they had said had consumed much of downtown.

Catherine cried when she saw what her father looked like the next morning, and would have nothing to do with him. Janson and Stan left the house early, well before breakfast, to do the chores that were required of them in exchange for the roof over their heads and the small security they had in the little two-room house. Elise hardly touched her own breakfast as she tried to keep Henry still long enough to get some small amount of food into him—he looked so much like Janson, with the same black hair, green eyes, and coloring, and she could not help but to think of Janson as she sat looking into those green eyes, and Catherine's as well.

There was sound from outside, Stan's voice shouting her name, and Elise started to get up from the table, her heart rising to her throat at the fear and panic she could hear in her brother's voice. She had not reached the door before it flew inward as Stan stumbled into the room. His hair was in wild disarray and his glasses were almost unseated from his face as he stared down at her, his words gasped out between panicked breaths. "Janson—at the barn, we were working—Mr. Brown's dead. Somebody saw him and Janson arguing out behind the grocery yesterday. The police came and took Janson, Elise; they've arrested Janson—"

## CHAPTER EIGHT

The pool hall on a side street a block off Main was smoky and dimly lit that morning, the light filtering through the grimy windows spotty and almost gray in color. Buddy Eason leaned against a pool table, a bottle in his hand from which he drank openly, the pretense of Prohibition forgotten in the open area of the pool hall, and not just in the dark rooms beyond where the law seldom reached. Buddy was hustling money and stirring up trouble, both of which he often did, and openly enjoyed, in the pool room.

Carl watched from a stool in one corner of the room just beyond the tables, watched as Buddy put down the bottle and took his shot—within minutes he would win the game from the other player, and, as Carl stared at the other man, he knew the money the man would be losing was money he could little afford. The man had lost his job in the fire that had taken much of downtown the night before, but still he had been unable to refuse Buddy's challenge. He was afraid of Buddy, as were many other men who frequented the pool hall. That was a feeling that Carl could well understand.

The night before haunted him now, after having robbed him of sleep, invading his dreams in the early morning hours when sleep finally came—the break-in, spilling the gasoline out, realizing the old man was dead, the fire—Carl had lived it again and again in his dreams, and he shuddered as he remembered the sound of the fire, the smell of the gasoline, the look on Buddy's face of determination and something very near to pleasure. How did we do it? Carl wondered, staring at Buddy.

187

They had run from the store the night before, leaving the dead man behind, leaving the fire set to consume the store and the body itself, the fire that had finally taken half of downtown. In the cold light of day it seemed a nightmare now, a hell of dream and fear, too horrible to have ever been real—but it had been real. The burned-out shells of the stores downtown said it was real; the smell of smoke that still clung to the town; the raw, blackened timbers and collapsed walls and supports, and the charred corpse found in the blackened pit of the grocery said it was real; as did the man who now sat in the jail accused of something that Buddy, Carl, and Richard had done. Carl hated himself, but he had not been able to tell Buddy no, no more than he had ever been able to tell Buddy no about anything even once in their lives. He was horrified of Buddy, and horrified of what they had done, and horrified that he had not somehow been able to stop it, and horrified that he could not now tell the truth.

And horrified of what Buddy planned to do now before Janson Sanders could come to trial for something he had not done.

Carl had gone to Buddy's house that morning—but Buddy had not let him inside, shoving him back onto the porch as soon as he came to the door. Buddy had taken him for a drive and told him what he would do to him if he ever confessed to what they had done, and Carl was all the more horrified now because he knew that Buddy would not think twice about doing to him exactly what he had said he would. They had just reached uptown, driving past the shells of the burned-out buildings, then turning down the side street that took them past the police station where they had seen Janson Sanders being taken into the building by the police—Buddy had seemed to forget Carl's presence in the car as he stared out the window at the door through which Sanders had been taken, and Carl's breath had caught in his throat as he had heard the words, spoken almost to himself, that Buddy had said:

"Maybe the place ought to burn down tonight with him locked inside it. Maybe—"

Then Buddy had fallen silent, sitting there in his car parked in the street, staring at a door through which another man had been taken for something that he and Carl and Richard had done, and Carl had been unable to do anything but sit and stare, knowing how likely it was that Janson Sanders would never live long enough to stand trial.

He dragged his attention back to the moment, watching as Buddy completed the game, watching as Buddy took the little money the unemployed man had, then seeing him go into the back room off the pool hall only to return with another bottle of gin. Buddy rarely got drunk; he only got mean, and he was getting mean this morning as he moved between the pool tables and back toward where Richard stood near the front windows that looked out onto the street. Richard was at the edge of a group of men, listening, having little to say, getting drunk himself as he listened to the talk about the fire, for that dominated conversation in the pool hall since more than an hour before. At first Buddy had listened as well, saying nothing himself, until the first mention of Janson Sanders's name, then he took the lead in the conversation, carefully stoking the anger and rage building within many in the pool hall, until that rage was a physical presence there in the room now that Carl could feel.

"I saw him myself out behind th' grocery, looked t' me like he was goin' through th' trash—" one man began, but another cut him off.

"Probably settin' the fire even then."

"His mama was some kind of Indian; I always heard you couldn't trust no Indian."

"He'd slit your throat as soon as look at you," Buddy said, turning the bottle up, then wiping his mouth on his shirt sleeve before butting into the game going on at the table there, taking the stick from one of the men playing and issuing a challenge to the other—Carl wished that Walter Eason could be here to see his grandson now, Buddy looking so at home as he hustled the little money left in the pockets of unemployed men, Buddy trying to incite violence against a man jailed for something that he himself and his friends had done.

Buddy the killer.

"My wife's brother said he saw 'em arguing—bet'cha he killed old man Brown out there behind the building and drug him inside, and that he set the fire t' cover it up."

"Probably thought it wouldn't leave no trace of what he'd done—"

"Somebody like him's likely t' do anythin'," Floyd Goode said, stepping into the conversation. He had been there all along, listening, keeping silent, for he usually had little to do with the other men who frequented the pool hall—or, that is, they usually had little to do with him. He accepted the bottle Buddy held out to him, wiped at the mouth with one grimy hand, then turned it up to drink before handing it back to Buddy. "Damn no good."

"Ain't you got him livin' on your place?"

Goode's small eyes turned on the man who had spoken. "I done it for his wife an' them young'n's 'a his. That damn no-account would have let 'em starve before he'd 'a done a lick 'a work to support 'em."

"An' his wife's a pretty thing, ain't she Floyd?"

Goode stared at him for a moment, then broke into a broad grin, showing tobacco-stained teeth in the heavily jowled face. "That don't hurt none, ya' know; she might want t' show her appreciation sometime."

"I wouldn't mind some 'appreciation' from her m'self."

Buddy's voice broke over the voices of the other men, bringing silence in the room following the single-word curse he had uttered. He was bent over the pool table, taking his shot, not bringing his eyes to the others, though he commanded attention in the room. "Men like Janson Sanders are what's wrong with this town. He's no better than the hobos down at the tracks, robbing folks, bothering the women, a bunch of no-goods just like Sanders that we're letting take over, and now look at what he's done. He burned half of town and killed old man Brown, and what do you want to bet that they won't do anything to him, any more than they've done anything to those bums and hobos riding the rails that have set up a shantytown by the tracks."

"I lost my store in that fire—they'll make him pay, or, by God, I will."

"Ain't no jobs now, all them tramps comin' in an' takin' work cheap, then stealin' us blind behind our backs—"

"Even more people out of work, 'cause 'a that son-of-a-bitch—"

"And they'll let him go," Buddy said, not taking his eyes from the shot he was about to take. "They'll let him off, just like they'll let the hobos off with all they've done. Nobody's safe on the streets now, and soon he'll be free—"

"We've got t' make sure he stays locked up," Goode interrupted, and Carl noted an intensity coming to his voice that had not been there a moment before. "We cain't have them lettin' him go—"

"They ought t' burn him alive, just like he burned old Mr. Brown—"

"Lynchin' ain't too good for him; I'd like t' see him chokin' an' kickin' at th' end of a rope—"

And, with a sick fear knotting the muscles in his stomach, Carl saw Buddy Eason begin to smile.

Reverend Satterwhite drove in silence, steering the Chevrolet down the wreck of Main Street. Elise sat, quiet as well, staring out at the gaping, burned-out cavity on the right-hand side of the street, at the people moving among the ruins seeing what was left, the smoke-blackened brick, the charred and destroyed timbers, ashes, blackness—death. Clouds hung low over the street, their bottoms the color of slate, speaking of the rain that was to come. Already the air smelled like wet smoke, feeling heavy around them, but the coming rain would never be able to clean the town of what had taken place here during the night.

There was nothing left where Brown's Grocery had stood; even the burned wooden flooring had fallen through. She could not have imagined such utter destruction, having been brought to see Janson earlier in the day along a more circuitous route by Stan in a car he had borrowed to drive her uptown—but she had needed to see this, had needed to see the burned, total destruction that they were accusing Janson of. She and Stan had been able to stay at the jail only a short while that morning, for they had left Sissy alone at the house with the children, and Janson would not allow either of the women to stay at the house alone for long, and both Stan and Janson had refused to allow her to stay at the jail and to walk home later by herself, although Elise had wanted to.

When the Baptist minister had come to the house to see if there was anything he could do for them, Elise had asked him to take her to see Janson, and he had agreed, though he had seemed reluctant. Henry had cried to come with her, but she left him with his sister, with Stan and Sissy to look after them. She could not bear the thought of the little boy seeing his father behind bars. It was a hard enough thing for Elise to see.

The Chevrolet slowed to a crawl at the intersection of Main Street and North, several men crossing the way before them as they waited to make the turn. One of the men's steps slowed as he stared in the front windscreen, and Elise stared back, recognizing a man who had lived near her and Janson in the village.

"Damn bastard, we ought to set fire to th' jail with him in it—"

The words were spoken loudly, deliberately meant to be heard above the noise of the Chevrolet's engine and the sounds of the slight traffic around them. Elise's hands tightened in her lap as she stared through the windshield, meeting the man's eyes, seeing his pace slow even further still as he met her stare—she had seen it this morning, had heard it in the mumbled words of men on the street near the jail, had felt it in the air. The town believed that Janson had killed Mr. Brown and that he had set the fire that had taken half of downtown to cover what he had done. He had been tried and convicted already, tried and convicted over barber chairs and back fences, on street corners where the unemployed gathered, and over coffee among the wealthy at the Main Street Restaurant. Someone had seen him behind the grocery the night before, and another knew of his temper, of the few fights he had been involved in, all of which had been with Buddy Eason—they believed he had been caught breaking into the rear of the grocery, had killed the grocer in a fit of anger, and had dragged the body inside and set the fire. One life had been lost in the fire; others could have been, and Janson's actions in fighting the fire with the other men last night, even in entering a burning building to help save a man's life, were forgotten in the heat of their own convictions, the burns he had suffered little but the mark of a man guilty of committing a crime.

There was a tension in the air as the Chevrolet pulled to the side of the street near the jail, Reverend Satterwhite shutting the engine off and he and Elise getting out of the vehicle—the town felt wrong this afternoon, she thought, looking toward the men who loitered on the nearby street corner. Their eyes were turned to her, and there seemed to be hatred and a self-righteous demand for justice in the stare they directed on both her and the Baptist preacher as they made their way toward the front of the jail. Elise returned their gazes, knowing in that moment that she felt a pure and complete hatred for whoever had set the fire and had killed Mr. Brown, whoever it was that should have been in that jail instead of Janson.

Janson was in one of the cells that ran along the left side of the room as they entered the office. She moved toward him, ignoring the police officer at the desk in the office area as he rose at her entrance. Janson came to the cell door, his hands resting on the bars, his eyes on her, one hand finally reaching out to take her own as she came nearer to him.

"Are you all right?" he asked, not giving her the time to speak.

"I'm fine—are you okay? Did they give you something to eat? Aren't you cold in there? I could bring your coat—no—" she said, interrupting herself, remembering, biting her lower lip as she stared up into his green eyes. "I'm sorry, I had to throw it out; it was burned so bad—"

"It's okay." He squeezed her hand, bringing a smile to his face, though she knew the smile to be forced.

"Are you okay?"

"Yes, I'm fine."

There was little way to touch him but to hold his hand. The officer went back to the paperwork on his desk, and Elise knew he was making a deliberate show to let them know they had at least that little privacy. Reverend Satterwhite now stood with his back to them as well, as he carefully examined a wall filled with wanted posters, advertisements, and notices, as if he expected to find one of the church deacons there. She had asked on her earlier trip to be allowed in the jail cell with Janson, even if that meant she would have to be locked in as well, but the officer would not allow it.

He had apologized even as he explained that there was too much unrest in the town already, too many angry men worried that Janson would try to get away before he could stand trial, that he could not allow them even that small leeway. There had been genuine kindness in the big man's eyes, a kindness that had convinced Elise that Janson would come to no harm from him, though she now worried about those same angry men herself.

She tried to talk of the things she had seen in town, the feelings she had observed in so many, to warn him, to make him prepared, but he would not listen. He kept looking at her as she sat in a cane-bottomed straight chair she had pulled up close to the cell, asking her about the children, about Stan and Sissy, telling her his grandparents had come to see him shortly after she had left that morning, asking if Goode had come by the house, and telling her to be careful. "You make sure that Stan stays at th' house with you. Don't you let him go do no chores, or t' go off for anythin' after it's gettin' dark. You make sure he stays right there with you an' Sissy."

"I will."

"When Stan came with you this mornin', I told him t' get my pa's shotgun, t' get it loaded an' keep it where he can get t' it—"

"I don't really think that's—"

"Well, I do—don't you let Goode in th' house; you hear me?"

"Janson—"

"Promise me."

"I won't let him in the house."

All too soon the Baptist minister said they had to leave. She offered to have him go on alone, telling him she could walk the miles home later, but Janson would not allow it. "Go on, Elise. I'll be fine."

"But, I can walk home."

"No. I won't have you walkin' home by yourself. Go on with th' preacher."

She tried to kiss him, barely able to touch his lips with her own through the bars that separated them, realizing suddenly that she was about to cry.

"It's all right, Elise. Everything's gonna be fine," Janson said quietly, looking down at her, reaching to touch her cheek.

"I know," she said quietly, unable to take her eyes from him, afraid almost that once she left she might never see him again.

"Mrs. Sanders, we need to—" the minister began, coming toward her.

"Okay—" The whispered violence of the word stilled the minister's voice and he moved away, toward the door, putting on his hat and buttoning his coat about him.

"Hug Henry for me, an' give Catherine a kiss from her pa; tell 'em I'll be home in a few days."

"Henry wanted to come with me," she heard herself saying, even before she thought.

"No—I won't have him seein' me here, like this."

She nodded, unable to speak, then reached up to place her hand over his where it rested at her cheek. "The burns, are they all right?" she asked, after a moment, swallowing back tears and forcing calm into her voice.

"They're fine. I can hardly feel them anymore." He moved his free arm, as if to show her the truth in his words, and she watched as he bit back a grimace of pain and turned it into a forced, uncomfortable smile. "Wasn't as bad as it looked, I guess."

"You're a terrible liar." She managed a real smile at his pretense and felt better at the genuine one that touched his own lips. "Maybe they'll at least let me look after your arm next time I come, tomorrow morning. I'll bring some salve, and fresh bandages."

"Maybe." There wasn't much hope in his voice.

"Mrs. Sanders—"

"Okay—" she snapped at the minister, and felt immediately sorry. "I'm sorry. I'll be right there."

He nodded, not even turning to look at her, and went on out to wait by the car.

Janson smiled. "You sleep good tonight."

"Not without you there—"

But he only looked at her for a moment.

"I'll see you tomorrow morning."

He nodded and she reached to touch his face, the bristly light growth of whiskers along his sharp cheekbone and against the angle of his jaw, and she realized he had not even had time to shave that morning before they had taken him away.

"I'll bring your razor, if they'll let me," she promised, not wanting to leave.

He smiled. "Go on; I'll be fine."

She drew her hand back from his face, touching the remembered warmth of his skin to her cheek, and turned away.

She did not want him to see her cry.

The two rooms of the little house were unbearably quiet that night, over Catherine's crying and Henry's loud non-talk as he played, Sissy's soft singing and Stan's reading aloud. Elise's ears strained, listening for the creak of the rocker where Janson always sat, the sound of his voice, the warmth of his rare laughter. She wondered if he was warm, wondered if they had brought him supper, wondered if he had enough blankets, and if they might allow her to bring him a quilt. She worried over his burns, gathering already the things she would need to doctor them, ready to do battle with the police themselves, if she had to, to see to his arm where the burns were the worst. She hadn't even had the chance yet to trim his singed hair.

She stood for a long time, staring at the scissors in her hand, thinking that Janson had needed a haircut anyway, and remembering all times she had cut his hair, the feel of it between her fingers, and his understanding smile after the first haircut she had ever given him those years before, the haircut that had left his hair so ragged that he'd had to even it out himself later, hoping that she would never know—but, she had known, allowing him to keep his masculine vanity even as he tried not to injure the flailing self-confidence of the new wife she had been then. She put the scissors down and moved to sit in Janson's big, straight-backed rocker, setting it in motion on the wide floorboards, comforted by its familiar creak in the little house that now felt so empty. She had put Henry and Catherine to bed already in the next room. Sissy sat sewing quietly now by the fire, and Stan was outside getting wood from the pile by the back door, leaving a silence in the house that seemed almost to seep into her.

Her eyes moved around the room, over the false gaiety of the Christmas tree they had put up a few days before, her mind registering with a degree of shock that not only was it less than a week before Christmas, but that Janson would likely not be home to spend the day with her and the children unless they could somehow find out who had done these things before then. She drew her sweater closer about her shoulders, chill in the lonely room, the house feeling empty and deserted about her, though her children slept in the next room, though her brother was just outside, and Sissy only the narrow distance of the room away from her. Janson had almost been taken from her once before, when her father and brother had both tried to kill him, and a fear sat within her now as she rocked that he might really be taken from her this time.

This night did not feel right.

This town did not feel right.

And the fear would not leave her.

It was somewhere late in the night, the world outside the small police station silent except for the sound of a motor car going along the street outside. Janson lay on his back on the hard bunk, staring up at the dark ceiling overhead. A police officer slept, leaned back in a chair near the cast-iron heater in the office, while the cells lay quiet except for the sounds of the man's snores and of Janson's own breathing. Worry filed his mind, filled the cell, denied him sleep. Elise was at the small house. Elise was on Goode's property. And he did not trust the man.

He should have told her to take the children and Sissy and go to his Gran'pa's. Stan could do the little work required of them to keep the house on Goode's property, and could have Sissy's help during the days in order to get it done—but Elise, Sissy, and the children would not spend another night on Goode's land until Janson was home. He would make sure of it.

Janson lay quiet, staring at the ceiling, hearing the officer's snores, the worry increasing, growing as the minutes ticked by and the night moved past—there was a bad feeling in the air tonight, he told himself. A very bad feeling.

Elise was awakened from a troubled sleep that had been filled with nightmares, demons, and ghosts of people she had known who had died. It had seemed to take forever for her to doze, only to be awakened a short while later by the sound of a car pulling up before the small house. She got up, lit the lamp on the table by the bed, pulled her wrap on and tightened it about her, then went to answer the door. She was startled to find Floyd Goode on the porch, a lantern held high in his hand.

"I need your brother an' th' girl t' help me ketch my cows. Th' fence is down an' they're all over Joiner's property next door."

"But—now, in the middle of the night—"

"Th' damn cows is out now," he said, raising his voice, his eyes on her intently, making her want to back away.

Stan entered the room, pulling his suspenders up over the shoulders of the nightshirt he had shoved carelessly into his pants. "What do you want?" he demanded, staring at Goode with unconcealed distrust.

"Th' damn fence is down. You an' th' girl, Sissy, I need you t' help me ketch my cows."

"I'll help you tomorrow morning."

"You'll help me now or you'll get th' hell off my place," he said louder, glaring at Stan. "It's your place t' help me, with that no-good brother-in-law 'a yours in jail. I don't aim t' lose my cows 'cause you don't want t' go out in th' dark, boy. You help me, or you all get th' hell off my property."

Stan looked at Elise. She knew he felt he should not go, that he and Sissy should not leave her alone in the house with the two small children. Janson had told him to stay with her, not to trust Goode.

"You make up your mind, boy. You get th' gal an' come with me, or you all clear outta this place by mornin'."

"You've got to, Stan," Elise said, telling herself that she would be okay, that Goode would be leaving with them, and that Stan would make sure Goode was not left alone with Sissy, even as she saw the refusal in her brother's eyes. "We'll be—"

"I promised Janson I wouldn't—" he looked quickly at Goode, then back to her, "that I'd stay here."

"We'll be fine—go on. We can't afford to lose this place." She spoke quietly, having moved closer to her brother, but, when she looked back, Goode's eyes flickered over her, sending a chill through her.

"I promised I—" Stan looked at her for a moment. "I don't feel right about going, not after I promised Janson—"

"I know, but you have to. I'll be okay."

Stan stared at her for a moment, then stepped closer, looking at her intently. "You know where the shotgun is—you blow a hole in anyone who comes here who has no business being here."

She nodded. She knew she could pull that trigger if she had to, and she hoped she would be able to steady her nerves enough to hit something if the need arose. Janson had taught her how to shoot the shotgun.

"I'll wake Sissy and tell her to get dressed." She moved out of the room, glad not to feel Goode's eyes on her as Stan went on out with the man. Sissy got up and dressed with no complaint, and left with them. Elise closed the door on the sound of the car driving away, and felt a sudden impulse to lock it—but it had no lock, and neither did the back.

She moved to the chifforobe where Janson kept the shotgun locked away from curious children's hands. She unlocked the cabinet and found the shotgun, glad that Stan had loaded it earlier in the evening, as Janson had told him to, then held it in her hands for a moment before she went to lean it against the washstand where she could reach it more easily if the need should arise.

She checked on the children, finding Henry now with his head at the foot of the bed, laying atop the covers. She turned him around and covered him again, not surprised in the slightest when he did not awake, for he slept harder than any human being she knew, other than Janson himself. She came back to prod the fire in the fireplace and put another piece of wood on it before she laid back down, knowing that sleep was far distant from her.

She stared at the rough, unpainted wall, the light from the kerosene lamp she had left burning, as well as that of the fireplace, throwing the aged wood into shadows. She heard Catherine say "Mama," in the next room, and lay listening for a moment until she was certain she had spoken in her sleep. The house was quiet, except for the popping of the wood as it burned, the night very still, very silent.

After a time she heard feet on the front steps, but no sound of a car as before—Stan and Sissy returning, she thought, sitting up and reaching for her wrap. All that fretting and worrying for nothing—

But the steps did not sound right on the porch; they were heavy, lumbering, the steps of only one man, and not of the two young people returning—she stopped with her wrap in her hands and moved quickly to get the shotgun, but the door opened and she froze immediately, turning, knowing already what she would see there. Her heart caught in her throat as her eyes met the large bulk of a man in the doorway, a man moving into the room. Goode—she started for the gun again, but too late. Goode was on her, grabbing her by the wrist and twisting her back, only inches from the shotgun she cursed herself for putting just out of reach.

She hit him hard in the face, struggling away for the gun again as he tried to hold her back. "Com'on, honey. You been waitin' for this, I know—"

"Let me go!" she screamed, hitting him again, clawing for his eyes, only to have her hands twisted behind her back. He turned her to face him and she tried to slam her knee into his groin, but he blocked the blow, shoving her away, across the room to where she fell against the rough eating table, falling over the bench at its side. He was on her again, pulling her to him, forcing her arms away, behind her back. One arm escaped his grasp and she managed to claw his cheek, digging her nails in and drawing blood. He tried to force his mouth over hers, and she twisted away, spitting in his face and managing to strike him again.

He half drug, half threw her to the bed, and came toward her. She scrambled up, scrambled for the gun, falling to the floor as he grabbed her ankle, pulling her back. She screamed, wishing him dead, damning him to hell if she could only get her hands on the shotgun.

She kicked him as hard as she could in the stomach as he leaned over her, then got to her feet, lunging for the gun as he grabbed her and held her back. She hit him, stumbling away, seeing Henry now in the room, the small boy running up to start pounding at him with his fists. Goode grabbed him up from the floor, shook him hard and hit him across the face, then slung him like a doll across the room, to lie still, unmoving, at the foot of the bed.

Panic gripped Elise as she moved toward her son, but Goode was on her, holding her back, forcing her toward the bed. She screamed, twisting, biting his cheek hard as he tried to bring his mouth to hers again. She kicked and fought, managing to free herself from the bed, and tried to hit him again only to be slung away to land with a hard blow against the wood stove.

She struggled to her feet, bracing against the eating table. Her hand touched the large butcher knife there and she drew her fingers back quickly from the sharp nick of the blade. Goode was coming toward her again—her hand closed over the knife handle. She'd kill him for what he had done to Henry, what he had tried to do to her. He grabbed for her again and she raised her arm, lowering it with all the force in her body and buried the knife to the hilt in his shoulder.

He screamed in pain and reeled backwards, clutching at the knife handle. She stared in horror, seeing the blood, but realizing that she had not hurt him enough to stop him. He pulled at the handle, crying out as he pulled the long blade from his flesh, and he looked at her, spittle on his mouth and chin, and a mad, pained rage in his eyes as he dropped the knife to the floor at his feet.

"You goddamn bitch, I was gonna make it good for you—but I'm gonna hurt you now—" He started toward her, his steps unsure as if from shock, his hands covered with blood as they reached—

She lunged again for the shotgun. There was a scream of rage from behind her as her hands closed over it—turning, twisting, she brought it up into his face, holding her finger over the trigger of one barrel, her heart racing so hard she thought it would burst.

He froze, staring, cautious, then began to move again—toward her, more careful. "Put it down, girl. You won't be able t' use it. You cain't shoot me—"

"I'll blow your goddamn head off—get out of here—" Her hands were shaking, the gun wavering before her.

"Put it down—I only wanted t' show you some fun, what'chu need with your man gone—" stepping closer as she backed away.

"Stop, goddamn it, or I'll shoot—" but he kept moving, inching toward her, the deep wound in his shoulder oozing blood. There was an assurance in his eyes, a damned assurance that made her tremble even more. She moved toward the foot of the bed, keeping the gun up as she made her way toward Henry. The little boy was moving now, beginning to cry.

"You cain't shoot that—just put it down, or give it t' me, an' I'll—"

She raised the barrel, pulled the trigger, and sent a shotgun blast into the ceiling overhead with the load of one barrel, her ears ringing with the sound in the small room, her heart pounding, her hands shaking even more, and her shoulder hurting from the backfire. She could vaguely hear Catherine screaming in the next room over the sound of the ringing in her ears, but she did not move her eyes from Goode as she leveled the shotgun at his chest. "I'll give it to you, all right—right through that fat stomach. Now—get out!"

He had stopped. Henry had begun to cry in earnest, lying on the floor now at her feet, and she wanted to stoop to draw him into her arms, but she could not. She could only hold the shotgun, her finger over the remaining barrel, and stare at the man before her.

"You'll pay for this—either you gimme that gun an' do just what I tell you to do, or you can all get off my place—" His hand clutched at his shoulder, red seeping through his fingers. "How'd you like bein' out in th' road with them young'ns this winter, with your husband behind bars—"

"I'd live on the streets before I'd let you touch me—now get out!"

He stared at her, a muscle working in his jaw. "I want you, your brother, that half-wit, an' them part-colored brats 'a yours out 'a here by morning."

"Gladly—"

He stared for a moment, as if expecting her to change her mind, then began to slowly move toward the door. She watched him, keeping the shotgun up, her finger over the trigger, ready to unload the remaining barrel into him if she had to. He went through the door, slamming it so hard that it shook in its frame, leaving red smears of blood on the knob and the wall beside the door.

As soon as the door closed she collapsed to the floor, laying the gun beside her at easy reach, and pulled her crying, frightened son into her arms. His bravery vanished now, Henry's little face was screwed up in pain, the mark of an angry blow evident on his cheek. She held him to her, rocking him in her arms, and tried to see if he were badly hurt or only frightened.

She stood, lifting him into her arms, then, reaching down to get the gun, she made her way into the other room. Catherine was sitting up in her bed, crying, clutching a home-made rag doll to her, one thumb in her mouth as she stared at her mother in the darkness.

Elise went to her, knowing she had to calm both children's fears, as well as her own.

Stan and Sissy returned half an hour later, having walked home hurriedly from where Goode had driven off and left them, only to find her sitting on Sissy's narrow bed, both children now asleep in her arms, and the shotgun beside her. Stan immediately wanted to go after Goode to administer the beating the man so richly deserved, but Elise would not allow it. She had lost one brother in defending her honor. She was not about to lose two.

They did not wait out the night, but began to pack immediately. Stan left the little house as soon as dawn came, to go to the village, going to borrow the team and wagon Clarence Keith had recently taken in trade, a team and wagon they would need to leave Goode's place. He told Elise later that he ran most of the way, until his side began to hurt, then walked while he clutched at his pained side, until he was able to run again. He had reloaded the shotgun and left it with Elise, who found herself working determinedly in his absence, wanting only to leave the place where the nightmare of the past night had taken place.

When Stan arrived back at the house, he arrived not only with the team and wagon, but with Dorrie and her sons, Wheeler James and Stephen. Elise worked, packing silently, loading, trying to help move things that she knew were much too heavy for her to move. She fretted over Henry and Catherine, worrying over the great, black bruise on Henry's small face, even as the little boy followed her about through the morning as if he could not let her out of his sight now. She knew that Janson would kill Floyd Goode, even if he had to escape from the jail to do it, when he saw what the man had done to Henry, and when he learned what he had tried to do to her. There was no doubt within her of that—and, along with the horror of what she knew would happen, was the knowledge of what would then follow, of the town, further enraged if he managed to get away from the police, of more death, possibly even Janson's own. Then there was her own guilt as well, her foolishness of having sent Stan and Sissy away from the house against his orders, knowing what kind of man Goode was, making this all her own fault.

Somehow in the morning hours, in the midst of the packing and loading to leave this place, in the midst of Henry following her about and her worry over him and Catherine, during Sissy's quiet work and Stan's anger and the help of the Keith family, Elise found herself in charge, packing up her household, vacating the little nightmare house, getting her family moved away. Inside she kept thinking about Janson, wishing that he were here—but she climbed up onto the seat of the wagon and took the reins into her own hands, seeing the surprise that came to not only Stan's face, but to Dorrie's and Wheeler James's as well.

They showed up at Janson's grandparents' house that morning with no warning, her entire family, bag and baggage, all their possessions, even to the huge beast of a woodstove, on the wagon. We need a place to stay, she said, and was taken in. The family was crowded into the small, four-room house with complaints only from Janson's Aunt Belle and his Aunt Maggie, both of whom Elise turned on immediately.

"I've had enough trouble in the last couple of days to do me for a lifetime," she said, staring the two open-mouthed women down there in the narrow kitchen. "I have no intention of listening to either one of you."

She turned to find Deborah Sanders just behind her, Catherine as content in the old woman's arms as she was in her mother's own. Deborah looked at her long and hard, and Elise met her stare, refusing to look away.

After a long moment the old woman nodded her head just once. "You done growed up when I wasn't lookin'," she said, her eyes still set on Elise.

Then she turned on her own daughters.

"You old hens hesh your mouths," she snapped.

Elise later found herself alone with Deborah in the back bedroom she had been given for her and the children, the same room she and Janson had been allowed when she had first come to Eason County three years before. That seemed a lifetime ago now.

"There's some bad men in this world," Gran'ma said after Elise told her what had happened. She took Elise's hand and held it in her own. "There's men ain't 'fraid 'a God or nobody." Then she brought her eyes to Elise. "My boy's gonna kill him when he finds out; you know that."

"I can't let him do that—not to let them put him back in jail, or worse. It was my own fault anyway. I was so stupid!" She turned her face away, only to have it brought gently back by the old woman's fingers beneath her chin.

"Weren't none 'a your fault. It was all Floyd Goode's doin'. An' Janson hisself should 'a knowed better'n t' take you an' Sissy there, anyway. Everybody knows what kind 'a man Goode is—"

"But, I should have known. I shouldn't have let Stan and Sissy leave. I—"

"Hesh your frettin', honey." The woman's eyes were kind as she patted Elise's hand. "It's all right. You don't worry about nothin' now, you hear. You an' my little Henry an' th' baby're welcome here, an' your brother as well, an' 'a course my Sissy—don't you worry none."

"I hate for us to be a burden—"

"You ain't no burden, honey—you're family."

Gran'pa took her into town late that afternoon to see Janson. Elise knew that Tom Sanders would say nothing of what had happened at Goode's, or that Elise and the family were now staying at his place, for she had asked him not to, but Elise soon realized there was no need for Janson to be told. He seemed to sense there was something wrong the moment Elise entered the police station.

She crossed the office area to him, a genuine smile coming to her face, and reached to touch him through the bars. She could see fresh bandages on his neck and arm, and motioned with the supplies in her hand, supplies she had brought to dress the burns. She was disappointed that she would not have an excuse now to enter the cell, but relieved when she was told that Dr. Washburn had been to the police station to see to Janson.

She had brought biscuits and ham from Gran'ma, and told Janson that his grandfather had come by the house to check on them, and that she had asked him to bring her to town. Gran'pa had talked to him for a moment, then shook his hand through the bars and left to go to the Feed and Seed up on Main. The officer who had been sitting at the desk when they entered also stepped outside.

Elise chattered on too gaily about the children, about Gran'pa's arthritis, the Keiths, about things they had done back in Endicott County when they had first met. Suddenly she realized he was looking at her, not eating, but staring at her in a way that made her ill-at-ease.

"What's wrong? Is my slip showing or something?" she asked, trying to smile, failing miserably.

"That's what I want t' know—what's wrong, Elise?" he asked, staring at her, his green eyes on hers with an intensity she realized she had not felt since the last time she had tried to lie to him.

"I know you, an' you ain't actin' like yourself. What's th' matter?"

She got up from the chair she had pulled over close to the cell, and moved away, wanting to make certain he could not read her face. She heard him rise from the bunk within the cell behind her. "Nothing's the matter. I guess I'm just nervous, seeing you here like this."

"That ain't it."

She turned back, finding him leaning against the cell door, staring at her. "Of course it is. What else could it be?"

"I don't know, but I aim t' find out."

"What makes you think there's something wrong? What could be wrong, other than you being in here?"

"You ought t' know you cain't lie t' me; I know you too good. I been married to you for three years now, have loved you longer than that, shared a bed with you—I know you, an' I know when somethin's wrong—"

"There's nothing wrong!" She was upset, and becoming more so—it showed in her voice now and she knew it. "I—I just wanted to spend time with you, and you keep—"

"Come here," he demanded, cutting off her words and looking at her through the cell door.

"Janson, I—"

"Come here," he demanded again, and she could not help but to obey, moving to him slowly, almost reluctantly. He reached through the bars and took her hand, intertwining his fingers with hers and gently squeezing. "You tell me th' truth," he said, more quietly.

"I am. I—" She immediately disentangled her fingers from his—she could not lie to him, not like this.

She tried to turn away but he drew her back, taking her arm to gently pull her up against the bars, as close to him as he possibly could. He touched her hair, her face, then rested both hands at her cheeks, holding her eyes turned to his and making her look at him.

"I want th' truth, an' I want it right now," he said softly, with a finality that frightened her with its import. She began to cry, but still he would not release her.

Like water from a burst dam, the words started to come out of her.

She pulled away from him and turned her back, unable to reveal what Floyd Goode had tried to do while she was looking into his face. She told him how Goode had hurt Henry, of the stabbing, of the shotgun blast through the ceiling, of how the family hurriedly packed up and moved to his grandparents' house, at last turning to find him straining against the bars, the hand of his good arm gripping the metal so tightly that the tendons stood out in his forearm below his rolled-up sleeve, pain and rage in the green eyes she knew so well.

"Is Henry okay?" he asked, his jaw clenched so tightly she could hardly understand the words.

"He's fine. He has a bruise on his face, but he's okay—"

"Did he hurt you?" he asked, cutting off her words.

"I'm fine—"

"And Catherine—"

"The noise woke her up and frightened her, but that was all—"

For a moment there was absolute silence, then Janson's voice came again. "I'm gonna kill that son-of-a-bitch." The words were quiet, no violence in them, just a stilled, deadly rage.

"No—Janson, you can't—you—"

"I can, an' I will—for what he done t' Henry, what he tried t' do t' you. He's dead when I get outta here—"

The tears streamed down her face, even harder than before. "No—I can't have you back in here again! I won't have you in jail for—"

"For doin' what I got t' do?" Anger came into his voice, rage breaking to the surface. He shook the cell door, furious at the bars that held him in while his family had been hurt.

"No—" She broke completely, crying hard, having to hold onto the cell door for support, his arm reaching out, his hand now beneath her elbow to keep her on her feet, a worried expression coming into his eyes. "I—I couldn't live without you. They have to let you go this time because you didn't do it, you didn't kill Mr. Brown or set the fire, but if you kill Goode they'll lock you away for good." She was crying so hard that she knew the words were hardly intelligible. "No—I can't face living if you're in here. No—it was all my fault. You told me—I should have known; I should never have sent Stan and Sissy with him—so stupid. I was so stupid—"

"No, Elise—please stop crying. I won't do it, not if it does this t' you—please, don't cry. Please—I cain't stand seein' you cry—"

"Promise me," she said, looking up at him through tear-clouded eyes, seeing the worried expression on his face.

"I—I promise," reluctantly drawn from him, but she knew he had given his word. He would never break it. "I won't kill him—"

She leaned against the cell door for support, breathing deeply and trying to calm the trembling within her.

"It weren't your fault, Elise—it was mine. I knew what kind'a man Goode was, an' I still took you there t'—"

"No—I should have known. You warned me. You told me to make sure Stan stayed with us, but I sent him off. I was so stupid—"

"Goode'll pay for what he done—"

She looked up quickly. "You promised you wouldn't—"

"I said I won't kill him," Janson said, refusing to meet her eyes, and she found that she could not ask, did not want to know.

"Just be careful," she said, afraid of what could happen to him when he was released. They would have to learn soon that Janson had not done what they had accused him of doing, and then they would set him free— but he could end up back in jail, or hurt, or—

"Please, be careful—" was all she could say, holding on to him for the time they had left.

In the pool room after darkness fell that night, one voice raised above another, shouting to be heard. Liquor was flowing freely; Buddy Eason had seen to that, as had Floyd Goode—the two stood at opposite sides near the front of the pool room, watching, waiting, seeing the rage building within those present in the crowded, smoky room. There were men here tonight who had never set foot in the pool room before, faces Carl Miles had rarely seen in town—and, though he knew what was happening, knew what would happen, he could do nothing but sit on a stool at the side of the door and watch the others, unable to make himself move, unable to make himself speak or even rise to leave.

"Goddamn bastard—I saw that wife 'a his drivin' a wagon out 'a town this mornin' with all their furniture loaded on it. Probably waitin' for him just outside 'a town—"

"She's over at th' jail right now; been there for hours—"

"Plottin' his escapin', I'd say—"

"That bitch is just as bad as he is," Goode said, shouting to be heard above the others. He moved between men standing at the tables, making his way toward the center of the room, then turning to let his eyes move over the others. "Went t' collect my rent from her last night; figured they wouldn't pay it with him locked up. They was already packed up even then, ready t' leave—she met me at th' door with a knife an' had a shotgun right there—" Voices raised to cut him off, but he lifted an arm for silence, holding the other at a peculiar angle, close against his body, as he had been doing all evening. "We ought t' run her an' them colored brats outta th' county, an' then go int' th' jail an' drag him out—"

"A rope ain't too good for him—"

"Yeah, we ought t' hang him—"

"Ought t' get rid 'a th' whole lot 'a them, includin' them niggers an' hobos down by th' tracks, too—"

"Ain't no work now—"

"Goddamn half breed—"

"I knowed it wouldn't come t' no good with a white marryin' a Indian gal. Indian or nigger, colored is colored, an' you can't trust any of 'em. I wouldn't doubt they kilt ol' Henry, too—"

"Son-of-a-bitch, he's gonna pay for what he done, killin' old man Brown, burnin' half 'a town—"

"I catch him outside 'a that jail, an' I'll break his goddamn neck for him—"

Buddy stood to one side of the shouting crowd, a peculiar look to his gray eyes. He watched the others, keeping silent until the fervor threatened to die, then shouting loudly of the need for justice to be served, a look of satisfaction coming to his face when the shouting was again taken up. Carl watched him, as frightened as in the moment he realized old Mr. Brown was dead in the Grocery just before the fire, watched him and Richard as well, who seemed a part of all this. Richard shouted just as Buddy did, just as did many of the others, but his shouts were forced, strained—he knew, as did Carl. They both knew. Buddy wanted Janson Sanders dead before the truth could come out, and, if this angry mob had its way, Sanders would likely be dead before this night was over.

"I say we get a rope an' hang him—"

"Drag him outta th' jail an' string him up!"

"Clean out aroun' th' tracks, too—"

"Yeah—get rid 'a all of 'em—"

There seemed a surge building, moving toward the door. Carl found himself on his feet at last, moving, yelling, stepping into the path of the mob. "Stop! No! This is wrong!" He stood, his arms outstretched, as if he could block them within the building with his presence in the doorway alone.

"Wrong t' give him what he was askin' for—burnin' half 'a downtown, killin' Mr. Brown—"

"He—we don't know he did it!" Carl shouted, trying to make himself heard over the mob.

"Like hell we don't. Move outta th' way, boy—"

"Gonna get rid 'a them tramps, too—"

"If you ain't man enough t' do what needs t' be done, then get out 'a our way an' let us do it—"

"Yeah!" There were shouts from the corners of the room, and the mob surged toward him.

"Stop! Wait! This is wrong! You can't kill an innocent man!" Carl himself was shouting now, trying to be heard, realizing he was shaking as he stood staring at the mob.

"Innocent, my ass!"

"He done it—move boy!"

"Move, Carl—"

"Get him outta th' way!"

"This is crazy! You can't do this!" He backed up, toward the door, refusing to be quietened even as the other men yelled for his silence. "You can't—"

"Move, Carl—" It was Buddy's voice, Buddy standing directly before him, not angry and incited as the others were, but certain of what he was doing, his eyes never leaving Carl's face.

"This is wrong," Carl pleaded, his voice quieter. "Buddy, please—"

"Move, Carl, or we'll go right through you—"

Carl stood for a moment, hearing the words, but unable to do anything more until he was shoved aside, the mob pouring out the door beside him. He caught sight of Richard's face, grim, determined, and scared to death—but he was going along with it. He would watch them hang an innocent man for something Buddy and he and Richard had done. Carl felt sick. His knees shook, and his heart thudded dully in his chest as he stood there—wrong—wrong—wrong—

He found himself moving, following the mob that flowed from the sidewalk and down into the street. Lanterns were being taken from the back of a truck, from under a tarp, the sight of a rope there, and Carl realized with a sick feeling in the pit of his stomach that it was the truck that Buddy had driven up in. He had been prepared. Oh, God, he had been prepared.

Carl stumbled after the others, seeing one group split off and get into trucks to go toward the depot, toward the railroad tracks, toward the shanties and shacks where bums and transients slept, where entire families, robbed of their homes because of unemployment and hard times, lived a bare existence in drafty, unheated shacks. The other arm of the mob surged toward Main and the lower half of North Street where the police station and jail stood.

The mob was growing, men attracted by the lanterns, by the shouts and curses, by the raw surge of violence joined, some taking up the shouting, others, appalled, following, trying to shout above the rest and be heard.

But there was no hearing. The men were tired of long months of no work, no money, no hope. After losses of homes and businesses. After seeing money lost in the stock market, in the bank failure, after seeing half of the downtown area burn—there was no hearing. There was only a mad, insane hunger for blood.

Elise had been about to leave when the sound of voices reached the jail. That sound had grown closer, and she stood now holding Janson's hand through the cell door—she was frightened. Janson could see it in her eyes. It was a look he had hoped never to see there again.

There were shouts from the street, the sound of his name, curses. Gran'pa moved to the window, staring out, his face old and tired in a way that Janson had never seen before. Gran'pa's eyes moved to the young policeman who had been left with them, and they exchanged a look, then the young officer moved to the phone that sat on the desk in the office area as Janson brought his eyes back to Elise.

"It'll be all right," he told her quietly, knowing that it was a lie, and knowing that she knew it.

"Yes—it—it'll be fine—" She looked at him and away, toward the door, toward the voices growing louder outside. She held his hand so tightly that it hurt, but he welcomed the feel of her nails in his flesh—he was afraid as well. Common sense told him that he could die tonight if the mob coming nearer the police station had their way. He could die for something someone else had done. He could die, not see Elise again, not watch his children grow up, not see his land, not—

"I ain't done nothin'—" He whispered the words, to himself, to the world, to Elise who stood with him, the bars of the cell keeping them apart even as he watched the young officer go to the door and out, Gran'pa following only a moment later, the door closing behind them.

Her eyes met his, bright now with tears that he knew she would not shed. "I know." Her voice was soft, a forced smile touching her lips. "It'll be all right. It'll—" Her words stopped and her eyes turned away as she fought the tears—she knew. Little could be done against so many.

All false pretenses of safety, of security, were gone between them. He knew there was no need to make empty assurances to her, no need to say words they both knew could be untrue. "If they—if I don't make it home—hug Henry an' Catherine for me. Tell Henry t' be a good boy, an' you make him mind. He's headstrong, like his pa." He smiled, seeing her tear-bright eyes turned to his, the wetness moving down her cheeks now. "You tell him I said for him t' behave. I want him t' grow up t' be a good man, a strong man, an' I want him t' work for th' land if he wants it, so that he'll have it for his children someday—"

"Janson, I—"

"Tell him." His voice rose.

"I—I will." Her voice broke. She held to the bars of the cell with her free hand, swaying slightly on her feet.

Oh, God—don't let her faint, he prayed silently. He watched her for a moment, watched her until she seemed more steady, then spoke again. "An' Catherine, she's pretty, just like you—you tell her I said that about her when she gets older. She'll have all th' boys heads turnin', but you watch 'em. Don't let her get with th' wrong sort. Boys have got t' be watched; I know how I was."

She managed a forced smile, swaying again on her feet.

"I want 'em both t' finish school, college, too, if they've a mind t'. They'll have t' work for it, for th' money, but they can do it. My young'ns are gonna read an' write just as good as anybody, you hear me—"

She nodded, wiping at her tears with the back of the hand she took from the bars, and then returned it there for support.

"An' you, you'll be all right. You're strong, stronger 'n me. You can go it alone. I never could; I could never live if I lost you—but you can, an' you will—" She shook her head violently, and he released her hand to draw her closer, her face between his hands. "You will—I want you t' find somebody else, get married, have more children—"

"No—!" Violence from her in the word as he had rarely heard before. She pulled away to stand staring at him, swaying unsteadily on her feet. "I'm your wife!"

"But, if I'm gone—"

"No!"

"I don't want you livin' th' rest 'a your life out alone—" The noise from outside, so close to the building now, silenced him for a moment, and they stood staring at each other. "I don't want us t' fight," he begged softly.

"I love you." The words came out in a rush, the feeling. "You said it wasn't 'til death do us part'—you said it—" She would not come to him even as he reached out of the cell for her. She moved across the room, to the window and stood staring out, trembling, he could tell even from that distance. He could see the light of lanterns moving against the front window beyond her as she clutched her sweater closer.

"Elise—"

She looked at him, then back out the window, toward the sound that now seemed to be right before the building. He fell silent, looking at her, knowing that look might have to last him an eternity. She straightened her back, staring out the window, and, with a stiff, determined set to her shoulders, she moved toward the door.

"No!" He shouted, panic filling him and causing him to shove against the bars abruptly. "Don't go out there!"

She turned to look at him, and he could almost feel the blood stop inside of him at the stubborn determination in her face. "I can't just stay in here and do nothing!"

"You'll get hurt—they're crazy; they could do anythin'! In here, at least you're safe, an' if they come in—"

"But, you're—"

"That doesn't matter! You can't go out there—no!" he shouted, shaking the bars in his hands as she reached for the doorknob. "You're my wife! You're suppose to obey me—I ain't never told you t' obey me before, but I'm tellin' you now! Don't go out there!"

She looked at him for a moment, and her chin raised with a look that reminded him painfully of the confrontations they'd had when they first met, all the times she had never listened to him. "I'm not just going to stand aside and let them come in here and beat you or hurt you or lynch you or whatever they intend to do—I will not—" she said, stressing the last two words with a stubbornness that made her for a moment look so much younger than her less than twenty years. "I will not," she said again, then turned to the door, twisted the knob, and started out.

♣

Elise stood staring at men as Janson's gran'pa and the young police-man both moved closer to her. She could hear their words, Gran'pa telling her to go back inside, just as Janson had done, and the officer telling her that help was coming, but she could not listen. She stood, staring at faces in the sharp contrast of shadows and light provided by the street lamps and the windows behind her, as well as the lanterns held in the hands of many of the men. She heard the curses, heard the names hurled at both her and Janson. She looked at faces, silently meeting eyes, staring men down until many grew quieter. So many were familiar— Buddy Eason, loud, demanding; Floyd Goode, staring at her with hatred; a man who had worked in the card room with Janson, another the husband of a woman she had done sewing for; faces she knew.

Shame came to some as she stared, anger and hatred remained on others. A few began to move away. The crowd grew quieter and a voice was raised in a call to disband, for everyone to return home, but someone yelled the voice down, silencing the man's words, and the voice of the mob rose again. There was an orange glow on the horizon, from the direction of the tracks, and the town fire siren began to wail—the transients, the homeless people, they were burning them out, she knew suddenly with intuition born of fear. The mob moved forward, urged on by voices from the back, and the young policeman was shouting some-thing, discharging a gun into the air, but neither Elise nor the men seemed able to hear him above the sound of the fire siren and the shouts and curses around them. They moved forward again, Buddy Eason at the front, and Elise stepped directly into his path to stand staring up at him even as her hands shook at her sides.

"Get out of the way, bitch," Buddy said, staring down at her. She could feel Janson's gran'pa at her side, but still she could not keep the trembling from her body.

"You'll have to kill me before I'll let you in there, and I don't think even many of you are animals enough to harm a woman."

"Damn bitch—git her outta th' way—" someone shouted from the rear of the group, but the other men were growing silent now, staring at her. When the crowd did not surge forward, Buddy shouted:

"You're not going to let some woman stop you, are you?!" He turned to face the other men, shouting to make certain he was heard. "Her husband killed old man Brown and burned half the town—are you going to let him get away with it? She was probably in it with him. Are you worried what some woman says?!"

The men began to stir again toward the building. Voices raised anew, shouts, threats.

"Get outta th' way, lady—we don't want t' hurt no woman—"

"She's just tryin' to protect him—"

"She's no better than he is—and you can't let her stop us from giving the bastard what he deserves!" Buddy shouted, urging the crowd forward, taking his place again at its head.

"Why are you so determined to get Janson hurt, Buddy Eason?" she demanded, turning to confront him directly, stepping into his path as he tried to move toward the door. She hoped he would not try to harm her, a woman, before all these witnesses. "And you—all of you—why do you want to hurt Janson, or are you all just listening to Buddy Eason?"

"Shut your damn mouth!" Buddy looked at her, hatred in his eyes, his words now quieter, meant only for her.

"Janson didn't do anything!" she shouted again, determined not to lose their attention, for they were growing silent now—they were listening. They had to be—"You should be looking for whoever it was that did this, not trying to hurt my husband."

"Listen to her!" someone shouted, and, whoever that person was, Elise blessed him, for she knew that somewhere to the back of these men there was at least one who held reason. "We cain't hang a man without knowin' for sure! Nobody saw it! Nobody knows if he did it or not!"

"We know enough!" someone shouted back.

Elise wildly searched the crowd, her eyes alighting on first one face then another, finally touching on a skinny young man who stood almost a head taller than any of those around him.

Carl Miles met her eyes for a moment where he stood beneath a street light, then quickly looked away, and suddenly she knew—her eyes went to Buddy, to Richard Deeds, then back to Carl. Buddy was too loud, demanding too forcefully for the men to enter the building. Richard was just standing there, staring at the men around him—and guilt had drawn Carl. Guilt had been plainly written on his face in that instant Elise had met his eyes.

She screamed inwardly at her own stupidity—she should have known. The only man she knew who might even be capable of a murder, capable of an arson to cover a murder, capable of letting another man pay for it, of murdering that man in a lynching if he had to in order to cover what he himself had done—it had to be Buddy. Somehow she realized she had already known—she had to have known—she could not have been that stupid. They knew—Richard and Carl both—and yet they were willing to do nothing, to stand aside and allow another murder to take place, Janson's murder, if they had to.

The fire truck screamed down Main Street, delayed by its need for men from the mob, heading to the tracks and the now out-of-control blaze there. Elise looked from face to face, knowing—

"Janson hasn't done anything!" she yelled, trying to make herself heard over the mob and the sound of the truck making its way toward the tracks.

"Sure she'd try t' protect him!" someone shouted.

"Don't listen to her!" Buddy shouted, but his eyes never left Elise. A car came to a rolling stop at the edge of the men, and she looked in that direction, hoping it was the chief of police, or other officers—someone, anyone, who would help her.

Walter Eason got out from behind the wheel of the vehicle, followed a moment later by his son, Walt, and the plump woman she knew to be Buddy's mother. The young policeman seemed to relax visibly where he stood now beside Elise, his eyes on Walter Eason where he moved with his walking cane into the midst of the men, seeing people, even in this madness, part way before him. For a moment a feeling of relief washed over Elise as she watched him move toward the front of the building, for she knew that, of all men in the county, Walter Eason could put a stop to this—then a sudden fear gripped her. If she lost this chance, she would never get the truth out of Carl or Buddy Eason either one. If she lost this chance, they would return, on this night, or another, to try again to hurt Janson.

"Janson hasn't done anything!" she shouted, looking up at Buddy, seeing that his eyes were now set on his grandfather and his parents, then she turned her eyes to Carl, staring at him long and hard, willing him to look at her. "Janson didn't do it, did he Carl?" she demanded, keeping her eyes on him.

Carl's head shot up. He looked at her, his mouth stupidly open, a look of fear evident on his face even in the shadows cast by the street lamp overhead, guilt plainly written on his features. He looked around, looked at the faces turned now in his direction. He closed his mouth, opened it, then shut it again as his eyes returned to Elise, his face a mask of horror as he stared over the short distance between them.

"Did he—you know; I can see it on your face!"

"I—I—" The one word seemed all he could say. Buddy Eason moved through the crowd to his side, speaking a few, hushed words, his head turned toward Carl, and Carl turned away, looking at Buddy, then looking out through the crowd.

"Don't listen to him!" Elise yelled, moving in their direction. Gran'pa moved with her, and Elise knew his eyes were now on the two men as well—he knew, just as she did now. He knew. "Buddy got you into this, didn't he, Carl?"

Carl stared at her, a pleading look on his face. Buddy gripped his shoulder, gripped it so hard that Elise could see the veins bulge out on the back of Buddy's hand.

"We have two children," Elise said, staring at Carl, "a little boy and a little girl, and I don't want to raise them alone—my husband would not have done this."

"Shut your goddamn mouth!" Buddy released Carl quickly and moved toward her. Anger showed clearly in his voice, in his expression, in his manner, but desperation as well. She felt a momentary gasp of fear, but forced herself to stand her ground.

"No—I won't shut up, Buddy, and you can't shut me up, at least not here in front of everybody." Then she turned her eyes back to Carl. "What happened, Carl?"

Buddy moved back to Carl's side, then turned to look at her again. For a moment Elise thought he would speak again to Carl, but instead his voice rose above the sound of the crowd around them. "Are you going to let some woman tell you what to do?"

Men looked at one another, some whispering, some silent. A few moved away. Some only stood and stared. There was no unity among them now, no singleness of purpose. Shame showed on a face here, another there—and absolute horror showed on the face of Carl Miles.

Men stared at Buddy, stared at Carl. The mutterings and whispers began to spread. Elise saw Richard Deeds start to move away, but she called out his name and felt a moment of triumph as men moved to hem him in.

"Tell us what happened, Carl. We'll never hear the truth from Buddy— he'll let Janson pay for what he did, or he'll let you pay for it—" Her eyes caught sight of Walter Eason moving closer, toward them now as she began to move toward Buddy Eason.

"That's enough!" Walter Eason glared down at her, reaching his grandson's side just as she did. He turned to look around him, raising his voice above the rest. "Go home—all of you. Go home! This is over!"

"No, it isn't." Elise stood before Carl, clenching her hands into fists at her sides to still their shaking. She stared up into his eyes, stared up into eyes that were now filled with tears, then the tears spilling over. "Tell the truth where everyone can hear it."

"I—I can't—" He shook his head, the crying making his face now twisted and ugly.

"You can—you've seen one murder, haven't you? Are you going to stand by and watch another one—and you know Buddy will try again to get to Janson, if he doesn't do it tonight? Tell the truth—who was it?"

"It was Buddy," he said so quietly that for a moment Elise was afraid no one else would hear him. "It was Buddy and me and Richard. It was Buddy—"

❧

Janson's knuckles were white where he gripped the bars. There had been no sound from outside the building for what seemed to him to be a very long time. At last the door opened and his gran'pa entered, followed by Elise, and then Walter Eason. Elise stared at Janson as she came toward the cell, crossing the room slowly until she was just before him.

The door had remained open and he could see the area before the building clearing. The policeman came in, a hand closed firmly around the upper arm of Richard Deeds at one side, and Carl Miles at the other. Buddy Eason's parents entered just behind them, the woman saying over and over: "It's a lie. It's nothing but a lie. It's a lie—"

Walter Eason stood near the doorway, the old man's eyes on his son and daughter-in-law. He looked toward the desk in the open office area, then slowly moved toward it, reaching down at last to take something up from its surface. He walked to the cell door.

Walter Eason stood beside Elise for a long moment, staring at Janson. Then he lifted the key in his hand, placed it in the lock of the cell door, turned it, and swung the door open.

"You can go now," he said, his eyes never leaving Janson's face. "Everyone knows you didn't do it. Everyone knows—" Then the blank mask of imperturbation broke, his voice shaking as he moved one hand up to wipe it across his features. For a moment he took a deep breath, seeming to struggle to compose himself, but failing before he spoke again. "Everyone knows it was my grandson, Buddy, who did it. Everyone knows—"

❧

In the face of public embarrassment, Janson was offered a job again in the mill. Walter Eason came to his grandparents' house the next afternoon and asked him to step out onto the porch in the chill December air. The Eason family owed him a debt of apology, he was told, in light of his having suffered the blame for the accident that had taken place—the accident, they were calling it now, not arson and murder as before. Buddy Eason and his two friends had been questioned, but had not been arrested, though nothing had been seen of them about the county since the night before. They would never stand trial, everyone in the county already knew that—would never serve a day in jail, never a minute for what they had done, even though it had cost a man his life, and almost another, even though it had destroyed almost half of downtown, cost innumerable dollars in damage, and even though Buddy had fled the crowd before the police station the previous night before he could even be questioned. Store owners were being compensated for losses in the fire, and Mrs. Brown, who had hardly spoken a word since learning of her husband's death, would be taken care of for the remainder of her life—money, it seemed, could set anything aright.

A place had been made for Janson in the mill, a job in the card room, even with the cutbacks being forced by the lack of work. He surprised Elise beyond speech when he said he had agreed to take the job and the rooms offered in half a mill house on Wheeden Street in the village— they had no other place to go, he told her, anger within him but supressed. There was no other work to be had, no other place to live, if they did not want to live off his grandparents. He had a family to feed, a wife and children to support, and he would support them even if that meant he had to work for the devil.

He was walking the fine line of his pride, and Elise knew that was a very fine line indeed.

He had promised her that he would not kill Floyd Goode for what he had done to Henry and what he had tried to do to her, but Elise feared he was ready to break that promise within hours of his having accepted the job offered by Walter Eason. "You said you wouldn't! You swore to me! You swore!" She clung to him as he pulled on the too-big hand-me-down coat his gran'pa had given him to replace the one lost in the fire.

She tried to block his way to the door of his grandparents' share-cropped home, thinking of the burns on his arm and neck, the burns that were only now beginning to heal. Stan was waiting for him on the porch, waiting to go with him to get both of them killed or thrown in jail or—

"I swore I wouldn't kill him, an' I ain't gonna kill him. I'm just gonna make him wish he was dead," he said, an angry determination in his eyes as he looked down at her.

"You'll end up back in jail, or killed—you and Stan both. I can't let—"

"There's some things a man's got t' do t' be able t' live with himself." He moved her forcibly, but gently, out of the way and went out onto the narrow front porch. She tried to follow, but Gran'ma would not allow it, her hand closing firmly around Elise's upper arm.

"Let him go, child. A man like Floyd Goode needs t' be taught a lesson."

"But—"

"No buts—don't secon'-guess my boy. He knows what he's got t' do, him, an' your brother with him."

Janson and Stan returned to the house hours later, long after darkness had fallen that night. Janson would say little about what had happened, but Stan told her the next day:

"Janson beat him bloody with a buggy whip—"

"But, Goode'll tell the police. They'll come to get Janson again, and you—"

"No." Stan shook his head. "Goode knew Janson was coming after him; he made sure he wasn't by himself, even had the Methodist preacher there—after Janson laid into him a couple of times with the whip, he admitted to what he'd done. He even said he thought he'd killed Henry when he hit him and slung him across the room; there wasn't a man there who would move to help him after that. Janson beat him bloody while the others watched. They wouldn't even help Goode when Janson was through—"

The anger within Janson only slowly cooled. Men avoided him at work, not out of dislike for him, or accusation over anything, but out of shame for some, and caution for many others, as word of Goode's beating spread. Some of their neighbors in the village had been part of the mob that night, and he glared at them, as he glared at others, for Janson himself did not know who had been in the mob, had never cared to ask Elise or his gran'pa, and did not seem to want to know. No one spoke of what had happened, least of all Elise—she just wanted to forget. She wanted to pretend the last months had never happened, that Janson had never lost his job in the mill, that they had never left the mill house, never had to go to work for Goode, never had to live through the nightmare of Janson's arrest, Henry being hurt, Goode attacking her. Janson was working, they were back in one of the many identical mill houses again, they had a wage coming in to put food on the table—but it was not the same. It was not just the atmosphere surrounding them—for there were hard feelings voiced over Janson being taken on at the mill when so many others were being laid off—it was the difference in the times.

The mill was working only two reduced shifts, sometimes for only a few hours a day, sometimes only a few days of the week, only running when there was work to be done—and there was never enough work. There was a wage coming in, but, after the weekly withholding for rent on the mill house, there was so little left to them. They had tried to make an occasion of Christmas, but with no presents except an orange for Henry, a new rag-doll Elise had made from cloth scraps for Catherine, one small, striped candy stick divided between the children, and carved wooden figures Janson had made for both of them—nothing for them to give to each other, nothing to give Stan or Sissy, and just enough food on the table to fill their stomachs.

Every cent from that first pay envelope was counted, worried over, stretched to its utmost limit. Short shifts, only four days that week, even less the second, little better the third, but by then they had received word that made those pennies all the more precious.

The mill was cutting back to only one shift.

All but the old-timers were being thrown off.

Janson Sanders was once again unemployed.

# Chapter Nine

They were calling it a depression—The Depression, capitalizing the words with voices that had grown bitter and sharp from want, need, endless desperation, loss of hope. Over two-thirds of the mill workers were unemployed, over half the employees of the factory that made men's overalls in Pine, at least half those of the cotton mill in Cedar Flatts. Innumerable jobs had been lost along Pine's Main Street because of the fire, and because of business closings and cutbacks. Some people stayed on at reduced wages, reduced hours, desperate to hold on to whatever jobs they did have.

Farms were going under, more and more land going up on the auction block. Bankruptcy loomed over many people, mortgage foreclosures, evictions. Families were finding themselves out on the street, taking whatever they could to live, whatever they had to do in order to survive. Hunger was becoming known to people who had never dreamed to see it, and many parents learned the pain of putting a child to bed with no food in his or her stomach, with little hope for providing more in the morning. People were freezing, in rail cars as they moved about the country in search of work, in back alleys in large cities, and in the Hoovervilles that were sprouting up near the tracks in many areas. Transients and the dispossessed slept in barns, in open areas, in makeshift shelters constructed of whatever could be found handy. Plenty existed in few homes, but usually even in the poorest there was at least something for a stranger, as more and more desperate people began to move from town to town in search of whatever work that could be found.

Individuals tried to help in whatever way they could, charities, church and religious organizations, but there was never enough—and always more and more people coming, wanting, needy.

There was hunger in the village, hunger under the roofs that the charity of Walter Eason allowed the villagers. Few of the unemployed could afford to pay the weekly rent, and little demand was made for it—times will get better, Eason told his people, jobs would return to the mill, and people would catch up on what they owe. They had roofs over their heads, but no food to feed empty bellies, no clothes to put on shivering backs. Villagers did what they could to survive, taking a few hours work where they could find it in exchange for food or money. Many left the village, left the free shelter for the roofs of family and friends. Some left in search of work elsewhere. Some left for the country. The security that the village had always represented was now broken, and even those still working looked on each wage as if it might be their last.

Janson knew that he would have a roof over head for his family in the winter months ahead, knew there would be wood enough to cut in the surrounding countryside to keep their three rooms in the mill house warm—but he was worried. There was food to think of until spring could bring the first vegetables from a garden. There was also next year to think about, and the year after. Better times seemed nowhere within sight. It could be years before the mill put back on the workers it had thrown off. He could not keep on running up a debt in rent to the Easons, a debt that made him angry with himself each time he thought of living on in the mill house. He had been laid off, had seen his family put through hell, had seen his children hungry, his wife abused, his son hurt, himself locked up in jail. He had almost been lynched for what Buddy Eason did, a crime Buddy would never even pay for—he would not now live off Eason charity.

He had to have work, had to have a way to provide for his family. He would not wait for a job that might never come. He and Stan had spent the past days looking for work, checking in town, in Cedar Flatts, even in Wiley and Wells on trips they made partly by foot, partly by catching rides on whatever truck or wagon they could find that was headed in their direction. There were so many unemployed in the village, so many waiting to be rehired, waiting for the prosperity that had been "just around the corner" for so long—he could wait no longer. He had to have more security for Elise and for the family they had made, a way to make sure that months from now he would be able to put food on the table and a roof over their heads that could not be taken from them at a moment's notice—and the need for that security was driven home when Elise told him they were going to have another child.

Janson lay awake long into the hours of that night. Elise was warm against him, having found sleep herself only after they had taken each other. He could feel her breath against his shoulder, but there were no sounds to be heard, not of the children and Sissy sleeping in the next room, or Stan where he slept in his narrow bed in one corner of the kitchen. The mill was silent, and that silence seemed loud to his ears as Janson lay staring into the darkness.

He came to a decision that night, a decision that did not sit easily.

As dawn came he got up to stare out the window that overlooked the village street. After a time he felt a light touch on his arm, and he turned to find Elise there, though he had not even known that she was awake.

"You look worried," she said quietly. "I know times are so bad now—"

"Babies have their own time," he said. Then he moved to sit on their bed—she looked so young, he thought, as she came to stand before him. She was just now twenty years old, and Elise Whitley had given up so much to marry him. He had promised her so many things, and had given her so little. And now—

He turned his eyes away, unable to look at her as he searched for the words. She sat beside him and took his hand, waiting, as if she knew—but she could never know this. He had sworn that he would never, had sworn even to Elise herself—but, then again, he had sworn never to so many things, so many things he had found himself doing. Working for the Easons, living in the village—but this was one never he had not thought to break.

He sighed, holding her hand. "Elise, I don't see no way around it no more. I wish there was. I wish—" His words trailed off. She was watching him, waiting, and for a time he could do nothing as he looked into those blue eyes that he had promised so much.

He looked away again.

"Elise, we're gonna have t' sharecrop—it won't be easy; it'll be a lot 'a hard work without much payback, but I know cotton an' I know I can make a good crop with even halfway decent land. I—" He saw sadness on her face, and something else. For a moment he was afraid that something was disappointment in him.

Resignation came over her features, an expression that tore right through him, making him look away—Elise Whitley a sharecropper's wife, he told himself.

Her free hand came to his cheek and he brought his eyes back to her, unable to read the expression on her face as he met her eyes.

"There'll be fields t' bust up goin' int' it this time 'a year, maybe other work I can do 'til plantin', an' it's gonna be hard—but it'd be hard if we stayed here, an' at least this way we'll have a crop next year, even though we'll lose half of it for use 'a th' land. There'll be space for a garden, enough t' grow what we'll need t' eat, an' we'll have a roof overhead that won't leave us owin'. We can run a store charge once I got a crop in th' ground, but it's gonna be hard goin' for th' next couple 'a months, maybe a day's work here or there for eggs, or a chicken or ham, maybe some vegetables. I'll get us a garden planted first off so we'll have some early stuff comin' in, an' there's huntin' until then. It's gonna be hard t' make it, but I won't let you or th' children go hungry, not even if I have t' steal t' feed this family, not even if I have t' set up a whiskey still myself—"

"Promise me you won't do that!" she said. "Promise me! I won't be worrying about you being arrested again, or shot by bootleggers, or—"

"I won't let you or the children go hungry," was all he would say.

"Promise me," she demanded, squeezing his hand until it hurt. "You have children to think about now, Henry, Catherine, and this baby— promise me you won't moonshine. Promise me."

"I promise," he said at last, reluctantly, and watched the expression in her eyes change, though he was now unable to read it. "But I won't let you an' the children go hungry, no matter what I got t' do t' make sure 'a that. I won't lie t' you; sharecroppin' won't be a easy life, but it's th' only way I can see t' have land enough t' grow what we'll need t' eat, an' t' be able t' have any way t' make it in these times. We could be there for years. We could be—"

She touched her fingers to his lips, silencing his words, and he was surprised to see a smile touch her face. "Let me know when to pack," she said quietly, her eyes moving over his face. "I knew I'd be a farmer's wife one day."

But not a sharecropper's wife, he thought later that morning as he sat at the kitchen table, cutting cardboard to fit into the bottom of his shoe to cover the hole worn there. He knotted the strings and stood to pull on the too-large coat his gran'pa had given him after his own had burned. He knew he made an odd sight, in the baggy, shapeless coat, his worn overalls patched at one knee but neat and pressed, newspapers stuffed into the front of his shirt under the bib of the overalls to insulate him from the cutting January wind.

He tried first one landowner, then another, finding that many other men had had the same thought as he. Many of the villagers, even the townspeople, had moved into the country to sharecrop or tenant farm any place they could find. He tried Cagle Owen, who owned the land his gran'pa and his Uncle Wayne 'cropped on halves, then old Mr. Bishop, Johnny Fred Wilner, and even M. B. Pate. At each place he received the same answer, and asked if they knew of any other land that might be open to be 'cropped on halves. Several times Lester Stubblefield's name was mentioned, along with others, and Janson tried them all, leaving Stubblefield for the last, for he had heard the man's reputation for padding the store charges of his sharecroppers, as well as the poor quality of the houses where many of his people lived. At last he turned his steps toward Stubblefield's place, hoping that he was not making a mistake.

Stubblefield was a tall, rail-thin man somewhere past sixty, with yellowing gray hair and hazy eyes. He smelled of sweat and cheap corn whiskey as he drove Janson in a rattling truck over a rutted red clay road to the farm he said he had open for a sharecropper.

"It ain't been worked in a while, and th' house ain't been lived in for a spell, but it can be fixed up if somebody ain't scared 'a work—"

Janson was not afraid of work, but this farm would take something close to a miracle. The yard was grown high with weeds and choked with brambles, the house a small, decrepit, two-room shack with a hole in the roof of one room caused by a tree branch fallen in a not-too-recent storm. Loose planks shifted and creaked as they crossed the porch and entered the small structure, and an awful scent assailed his nose the moment he opened the door. He coughed and pulled the handkerchief from his pocket to cover his nose, hearing something small and dark moving about the corners of the room. Sunlight shone in through the gap in the ceiling, and part of the tree branch still protruded into the room. There were spaces in the walls and flooring where boards did not meet up adequately, and loose rocks in the chimney at the fireplace.

Janson knelt and looked up the throat of the chimney. It looked to be choked with trash and birdnests, and he doubted little that to light a fire in the hearth would mean only one of two things, either it would cough black smoke back into the house, or it would promptly burn the entire place down—and burning it down did not seem too bad an idea.

Stubblefield led him from the house onto the small, leaning back porch and out into the yard to show him the well there, covered over but rank from disuse. It would have to be cleaned before good water could be drawn from it, cleaned and still even that might not be enough. Another well might have to be dug.

He found the barn in better shape than the house, but that still did not account for much. The roof at least seemed sound, although it probably leaked, or had in the past, causing the rotting planking in the loft that would have to be replaced before someone could safely walk above. There was a creek, running cold and pure along the back of the house, running away down into the fields below.

The land had been lying fallow, growing up in Johnson grass and seedling pines as it curved away from the buildings and toward the dark woods that encroached upon its borders. The place seemed hopeless, the house near impossible to make liveable, the land fertile but wasted—it would take months of work just to repair the buildings and get the land cleared enough to plant. The land wasn't the best he had ever seen, hilly and rolling, rock strewn, dropping off in places to nothing, as did much of the land in the area, but it was decent land that a man could make a cotton crop from—but this was impossible. There was so little promise here, only work, and more work, with little return. The house, the well, the barn—no man could offer that to his wife, to his family.

"I'll buy what you need for repairs, tin for th' roof and all," Stubblefield said, as if the matter had been settled. "I supply th' seed, plow, mules, everything you need t' make a crop, and I get half in return. You can keep th' seed or sell it after th' ginning, and I stake you at th' store after you get a crop in th' ground." He followed closely as Janson walked out into the overgrown field nearest the house. "There's another field that needs clearing that you can work, too. Just needs a couple 'a trees cleared off it and some stumps pulled up, but it's good land, land a man can make a good cotton crop on."

Hopeless, Janson thought as he looked back toward the house. Sharecropping was one thing, but there was not even a chance they could make it on this farm, if it could even be called a farm. There had to be other places open, or maybe the chance of work in town, some place he had forgotten to check.

He knelt and dug his fingers into ground moistened by the previous night's rainfall—red, rich, fertile, not the best cotton land in the South, but it would do the job for some man after the years of lying fallow. A man could clear off the seedling pines, pull up the stumps here and there, turn under all the dead grass and weeds, and he'd have a good place to start a crop.

He lifted his eyes and looked out across the fields, hearing Stubblefield's voice, but not listening—one good crop and a man could be on his feet again, he thought, even with losing half of what he made to the landowner there could be enough, if the price of cotton was good, to take a family through the winter and still leave some left over come planting time the next year.

The land felt good under his fingers, firm and unyielding under the soles of his worn shoes. This was where a man belonged, depending on nothing but the strength in his own back and the work of his own hands to make a crop to support his family. God had made the land to be worked, and man to work the land, Janson told himself—even if that land belonged to someone else.

"Why, the man that used t' crop this place for me used t' make—"

"I'll take it," Janson said, standing, dusting the red dirt from his hands and onto the worn legs of his overalls. "I'll make you a crop on this land."

Janson had been right when he had said that the house was almost not fit to be lived in—Elise stared in open horror at the small, two-room shack the first time she saw it, amazed that something so obviously dead had not already fallen over and been given a decent burial. But, by the time she saw it again a week later, the little house was hardly recognizable.

The roof had been repaired, a few rotten boards in the porch replaced, the rooms swept out and the walls, floor, and even the ceiling scrubbed down with a strong mixture of lye soap and hot water. Janson had whitewashed the fireplace, shored up the falling back porch roof, cleaned out the well, and even chinked some of the more-obvious cracks in the walls. But still it was a sad little house, sitting on its stacked rock pillars in the middle of its newly cleaned-out yard. The scrubbing and airing that Janson, Stan, and Sissy had given it had gotten rid of the odor she had noted the first time Janson had brought her to see the place, but she knew she would always remember that smell and associate the little house with it.

They moved into the house a week after she had first seen it. The two rooms were close-cramped, smaller than those on Goode's place, crowded with the six of them and their bare furnishings. Stan immediately made a pallet for himself to sleep in the barn loft. He said it was because the house depressed him, but Elise knew his reasons were more noble. He wanted to give Sissy more privacy than she had on the other side of a quilt strung down the middle of the room they shared with the two children, and he wanted to allow Elise and Janson more privacy as well. Elise could not help but worry about him, however. It was often bitterly cold in the little house early in the morning before fires could be stoked in the fireplaces and the woodstove, and Elise found herself grateful in the nights for the warmth of Janson beside her in their bed—she could imagine how the nights must be where Stan slept in the barn loft.

Janson had warned her that the winter would not be easy, but she often found it worse than she had imagined. Janson took day work for the neighboring farms, working an hour here or there, a day where he could find it, clearing land for planting, repairing barns and buildings, helping to slaughter hogs, doing whatever he could to help feed the family through the winter, often working for trade in eggs or butter, potatoes, apples, or sometimes meat. Many of the farms in the area were in the same situation they were in, just trying to survive the winter, laying all their hopes on the coming year's crop and the price of cotton at ginning time.

No matter how many hours Janson put in on other farms, there was still land to clear for his own crop, soil to be broken up and readied for the cotton seed that all their hopes rested upon. He and Stan were often in the fields until after dark, ridding the land of the small pines that had taken root there, the tough grass he cursed, the stumps he swore at as Stubblefield's mules strained against their trace chains to pull them from the ground.

He seemed to work non-stop, even working their fields on an occasional Sunday and garnering a stern sermon from Gran'ma in return. He was out before light every morning, home often long after dark, working in his own fields and the fields of others until his back ached and his muscles were sore—but he seemed to come alive in the open fields, under the sun and in the chill air. There was often not enough food on the table to fill his hungry stomach at the end of the day, but he seemed happier just to be working the land, even if it was land that belonged to another man, more content that he had ever been in town.

Stubblefield was more often than not impossible to deal with, and his wife was not much better. But Mrs. Stubblefield liked pretty dresses, though she hadn't the figure to wear them, and she gave Elise work sewing in exchange for milk for Henry, Catherine, and the family, on occasion eggs, or whatever else she hadn't a use for.

Other families that sharecropped Stubblefield's land were standoffish and involved in their own concerns, and Elise could find no friend among them to help pass the lonely winter months. Dorrie was in town, Gran'ma and Aunt Rachel too far away to visit often—there was only Janson, Stan, Sissy, and the children. And never enough food.

There was the baby on the way, making her unbearably nauseated on most mornings, forcing her to eat for the sake of the child, even as she worried whether Henry and Catherine had enough. Somehow Janson always managed to provide, and they had not gone hungry as yet, though often there was nothing on the table for days except for sweet potatoes taken in trade for farm work, and milk taken in trade for sewing.

She could only keep thinking—if we can only make it until spring, then we'll be fine. Once Janson has the cotton planted, we can have a charge at the store to be paid in the fall from the money we make off the cotton. There will be early vegetables from the garden, even our own cow that Janson had promised to buy on credit from Stubblefield. If we can only make it until spring—

The last days of February showed an early warming. Already daffodils bloomed from the flower bed in front of Mrs. Stubblefield's parlor windows. Turnip and mustard greens lay planted in the garden, potatoes, carrots—a few month's time and there would be food aplenty for the family. Janson said that if the weather held and the signs were right, the cotton crop would be planted and then there could be charges at the store. They would buy the cow—things would be so much better. They had survived the worst the winter could give them—hunger, cold, fear— and it seemed to Elise that at last they might make it.

And then she realized she was losing the baby.

There had been no difficulties with the pregnancy, beyond the same nausea she had experienced with both Henry and Catherine, but one afternoon there was blood. She sent Sissy running for Janson where he was plowing, frightening him as the panicky girl spilled out an almost incoherent story.

"Blood—Elise's bleedin'. She thinks somethin's wrong with th' baby—she said you should come—"

Janson flung the plowlines from his shoulders and took off running for home, leaving the mule in the field where he had stopped the plow, yelling back to Sissy to run to Stubblefield's house and get someone to go for Gran'ma in a car.

Elise was lying in their bed when he reached home, a frightened expression in her eyes.

"Does it hurt? Is it bad?" he asked, collapsing to his knees at the side of the bed and taking her hand. He tried to keep the fear from his voice.

"No—it's only blood. It may be nothing—I—I don't know. It's never happened before."

He could do nothing but hold her hand and look at her, but even that was taken from him when Gran'ma arrived and ran him out of the house and onto the porch. He stood staring at the closed door, his heart in his throat at the thought of what could be happening on the other side of it. He heard Catherine crying behind him as Gran'pa loaded her into the wagon to take her, Henry, and Sissy back to their place for the remainder of the day.

"I wanna stay with Pa—" Henry said, tears very close in his voice as well, but Janson did not even turn around. Elise—Elise needed him, but there was nothing he could do for her.

He tried to pray as he heard the wagon creak away from the house, Gran'pa calling to the mules, and both children setting into loud wails, but the prayers would not come. He knew his God, and he knew his God knew him—but words seemed insufficient to give voice to all that was going on inside of him.

Stan strode up onto the porch, looked at him for a moment, then simply said, "I took the mule back to the barn."

Janson nodded. There was no need for words between the two of them. They both had the same concern, one for a wife, the other for a sister.

Stan stayed with him, leaning in silence against the support for the porch roof. After a time that seemed to stretch into forever, the door opened a narrow space and Gran'ma looked out at them.

"You boys draw me some water," she said, then lifted her kind eyes to Janson. "There ain' gonna be no baby this time." Her voice was soft, consoling, but Janson could feel no comfort, just a burning stab of pain through him.

"Is Elise all right?" He tried to push past the old woman, to enter the house, but she held him back.

"It ain' over yet." Her restraining hand on his chest felt like an iron wall between him and Elise.

"But, I want t' see her—"

"No—" Gran'ma shook her head, blocking the doorway with her own squat, rounded body. "This is woman's concern."

She accepted the bucket of water Stan brought.

"But—" The door closed before Janson could get out more than the one word, and he leaned his head against the splintery wood and closed his eyes, his heart on the other side of that barrier.

When it was over and Gran'ma let him in the house, Elise lay in their bed, tears brightening her blue eyes and wetting her cheeks. Janson knelt at the side of the bed and brought her hand to his cheek, wetting it with his own tears.

"Don't cry—" she begged softly. "I can't stand it if you cry."

"Are you all right?" He pressed her palm to his lips and kissed it, closing his eyes for a moment then opening them to search her face.

"I'll be all right—I—I'm sorry about the baby. I know you—"

"All I want is you and Henry and Catherine—"

"I tried so hard. It—"

"No—" He closed his eyes again, burying his face against her palm, crying all the harder out of the worry for her, but not wanting her to see his tears. "You're all that matters—"

"There'll be more babies—"

"She can have a whole houseful," Gran'ma said, moving closer to the bed. "It jus' happens sometime. Most women'll lose a baby one time or another. There ain't nothin' causes it, it jus' happens. It's for th' best. It's God's will."

Elise cried in his arms that night until Henry woke in the next room and came to their bed, pulling on the quilt and saying, "Don't cry, Mama, it'll be all right—" softly before Janson picked him up and tucked him into bed between them, then Janson lay there and watched his wife and son drift off to sleep in the darkness, finding himself wondering at the reasons for God's will.

With spring came work, hard work with seemingly no end, plowing, planting, later chopping the cotton to remove the weeds and thin out the cotton plants, running around the rows with the plow then going back to bust the middles and uproot any weeds still there, poisoning the fields to keep the insects from destroying the plants. The days went from long before light to sometimes long after dark. Life and survival depended on the cotton growing in the red fields. Money enough would have to be made from the sale of the crop to pay off their charge at the store, pay Mr. Stubblefield for the cow they had bought on credit, and still see them through the winter until another crop could be planted and the entire process begin all over again.

As the days passed, Elise watched the maturing cotton plants, knowing that there lay their hope for the future. There were vegetables from the garden, milk from their own cow, eggs from chickens Janson had taken in trade for work. Hunger no longer threatened daily, but worry did not end. Everything depended on the cotton crop, a crop that could be wiped out by storm, or by any act of God, man, or nature, hopes that could be dashed by a drop in the price of cotton when the crop was harvested.

Elise had become pregnant again, and she and Janson welcomed it after the loss of the baby in February, but Elise worried all the more—she knew she could never bear to lose this child as she had the last.

By the last week of June, the cotton crop was lush in the fields, the weather warm and clear. There was talk at Stubblefield's small store, and among people leaving the small Baptist church there in the country on Sundays—times were getting better. President Hoover had proposed a moratorium on war debts to shore up the troubled European economy, with an immediate impact felt in the United States. Everyone had wanted the President to do something, to take some action that would help to pull the country out of the Depression, and it seemed that he was doing something at last.

"Times are gettin' better—" one farmer after another said, as did the storekeeper, the minister, the neighboring sharecropper's wife.

Everyone praised President Hoover. The stock market rose and confidence tried to raise its head—times were getting better.

Laying-by came, and with it a lessening of work on the farms. Cotton crops stood tall in the red fields, waiting only for time so that the bolls would burst open and the picking could begin. There was nothing to do now but wait, hope, pray—and worry.

Elise knew that Janson could not sit idle, any more than could any of the farmers in the county. He began to clear another field for planting the next year, hoping for a bigger crop, more money, a way to get them off of Stubblefield's land and onto land of their own—and Elise knew the dream had to seem farther from him than ever, just as she knew he dreamed it often, just as he always had. He finished the repairs on the house and barn. He worked cutting trees and pulling up stumps. He walked, and he worried. Now time had the upper hand. There was nothing more he could do but wait and see what the hours, the weeks and months of work behind a plow or over a hoe would bring to them.

Elise often found Janson on the porch in the late afternoons, staring across the acres of cotton plants. Their entire life lay in those fields, in the success of that crop, in the price of cotton, in the hours of work ahead for Janson and Stan and even Sissy.

They bought sparingly on credit, doing everything they could to survive on the things they could produce themselves. Credit was a necessity for them, as it was for the other sharecropping families, until the cotton came in, but Elise knew Janson watched every penny charged as if it might be his last. He did not like debt, and Elise knew that he worried himself constantly over every cent—"Credit's what kills most sharecroppers," he told Elise, words his father had often told him. Credit ate up what little profit there might be from the sharecropper's half of the year's work, leaving little to nothing for the winter months ahead when no charge could be run because there was no crop in the ground. They charged so little: soda, sugar, salt, kerosene—only what was necessary—but the bill mounted up, a bill that would have to be settled before they would see any money from the sale of the cotton.

Stubblefield's prices at the store he ran for his sharecroppers and for other small farmers in the area were the highest they had ever paid, higher even than those in the stores in the mill village, but no one else would give them a charge. Even considering Stubblefield's prices, Elise knew the bill could not grow at the rate it seemed to be growing. It was being padded by Stubblefield. She was certain of it, as was Janson, but there was nothing either could do to stop it.

"We're 'croppin' his land," Janson said bitterly when she brought up the subject. "He can do pretty much what he wants, an' there ain't nothin' we can do about it."

The days of laying by crawled along. Gran'ma visited sometimes, bringing Aunt Rachel and at times even the annoying presence of Aunt Belle and Aunt Maggie. Gran'pa or Uncle Wayne sometimes came to help in clearing land that Janson was determined to plant the next year, and sometimes Janson or Stan went to help with work they had to do. It seemed as if laying by would never end. No one looked forward to the aching backs and bleeding fingers of picking cotton, but everyone needed the money the crop might bring. Sharecropping had always been a bad business, and the Depression had made it worse. Selling this crop at a good price and finding better times next year seemed all that anyone could look forward to—and everyone was praying for those better times.

It was a hot, still day when Janson and Stan went to help Gran'pa repair the roof on the old barn on his place. Elise, Sissy, and the children went along to sit on the front porch with Gran'ma, and later to help with the supper they would all share that night after the men were done with their work. Elise sat on the porch shelling peas into a dishpan in her lap, watching Henry and Catherine play in the yard with two of Wayne and Rachel's young grandsons, and a big, clumsy puppy from one of Gran'pa's hunting dogs. Elise had been nauseated earlier in the morning, but was feeling better now, past the time when morning sickness should have bothered her.

Gran'ma was in a comfortable mood, talking of her youth, of long-ago memories of a South in the midst of war when she had been a girl, of a father killed in battle, of men in gray uniforms, and men in blue who had given her nightmares. She talked of children she had borne, the many who had died. Of Janson's parents and Janson as a small boy. Of her people and stories that had come from a long past before her.

The sun was warm, the air still, and only the sounds of insects, the children's laughter, and the puppy's yaps, competed with Gran'ma's voice. Occasionally Elise could hear the sound of the men's voices from the barn, hammers driving nails through tin, the barking of Gran'pa's hunting dogs, the sound of a car, a truck or wagon passing along the road. Cotton grew dense and green in the fields nearby, stretching as far as the eye could see.

Gran'ma seemed to start up from her rocker even before Elise heard the sound—something striking tin, a horrible cry, and the sound of something hitting the ground. Gran'ma was off the porch and running as fast as her age and size would allow toward the barn, toward the sound of the fall, and toward the cry they all knew had been Janson's voice.

Elise slung the dishpan from her lap, sending peas skittering across the wooden flooring and into the dust of the front yard. She jumped from the porch, ignoring the steps and her pregnancy, and ran after Gran'ma, quickly passing the old woman. Her heart in her throat, unmindful of the child she carried who had just begun to change her body, she ran, her mind blank of all things except—dear God, don't let it be Janson. Someone had fallen from the barn's high roof—don't let it be Janson. It had been his cry—but, don't let it be Janson.

Gran'pa lay on the ground, his face turned up toward the sky he loved, one arm twisted beneath him at an impossible angle. His head was turned to one side, and his eyes closed. Janson was descending the wooden ladder, taking two rungs at a time, his hands and body shaking so badly that the wood quaked against the side of the barn. Stan was close behind.

Elise stopped, staring in horror at Gran'pa, at the angle of his neck, at the arm twisted beneath him—at Janson, bending over him for a moment, then looking up at her with hurt and sickness in his eyes.

Gran'ma reached her side, and a small cry escaped the older woman. Elise turned to see her eyes widen in shock and disbelief.

Gran'ma took a step forward, one hand to her mouth, then she fainted at Elise's feet.

The little house lay quiet and still in the hours after the funeral. Deborah, alone, moved from room to room, touching first one thing then another, remembering her husband, remembering the children they had borne only to bury hours, days, weeks, years after life had been given them. Tom was gone. Of the twelve children he had given her, only five still lived—Tom and seven of her babies gone, all buried in the red Alabama clay.

And she wanted to be gone as well.

Deborah knew she could stay no longer in this house where she had loved her husband, where she had raised her children. The house was not hers; the land was not hers. It belonged to Mr. Owen, who would now let his youngest grandson farm it—it had been Deborah's for as long as Tom lived.

Mr. Owen had told them that often enough through the years, and Deborah had always found comfort in the words, for she had never imagined a day when Tom would no longer live. He had produced a crop on this land each year for more years than she could remember. He had worked it, sweated over it, getting only half of the return on what he had grown—but it had never been his, and it was not Deborah's now. She would have Tom's share, if any, of the crop already in the fields, after the store credit was paid and the pickers' wages covered, if Janson and Wayne could not pick these fields in addition to their own—she would have so little left to face the world on alone, just the furniture, a couple of hogs, some chickens.

And her faith.

Belle would move in with Olive, and Maggie would live with Wayne and Rachel. There was only Deborah with no place to go. She could turn to one of the grandchildren—but she did not want to be a burden.. She had always hated old people who had to live off the charity of others, unable to fend for themselves—but, now, with a start, she realized that she was one of these. Just another old woman with no home of her own, nothing but a burden to her family.

She turned there in the kitchen and found Elise behind her. Deborah had thought she was alone in the house, but Elise was there, looking at her from just within the doorway.

"I remember the first morning after Janson brought me here from Georgia," Elise said quietly, moving into the room, looking at the eating table. "You made me sit down here and eat breakfast even though I didn't want to."

Deborah looked at her, then her eyes strayed to the other memories around her, to the years she had spent here in this house, between these walls and under this roof that had never been her own. Her eyes touched on the marks, smudged and faint now, on the frame of the door that led out onto the rear porch of the house, marks Tom had made measuring Sissy as she had grown, and, beside them, fainter still, traces of Janson as he had gone from boy to man. Memories marked into wood that belonged to someone else.

She closed her eyes and turned away.

"What will you do now?" Elise asked, standing still across the room.

Deborah glanced at her briefly, but could think of nothing to say. She did not know what she would do. She could turn to Tom, Jr. in Atlanta, but he had not worked in more than a year now, not since the mills had closed down, and already had too many mouths to feed. Wayne and Rachel had offered, as had Olive and Cyrus—but Wayne and Rachel did not need another person on their hands; they had already four sons, two daughters-in-law, and three grandchildren in the house; and Deborah could not bear the thought of living out her remaining days to the sounds of Olive's carping and Cyrus's daily reminders that she was living on his charity.

"You can come stay with us," Elise said, surprising Deborah with the words. Deborah had thought that Janson might offer, just as she had also known that he hadn't the room or the ability to feed another person. Already Elise's brother slept in the loft of the barn because there was not enough room in the small house, and there was Sissy, Henry, and little Catherine, and Elise was in the family way again. Deborah could not put herself on his hands as well. He had enough—too much—already.

She had never expected to hear the words from Elise, however.

"Janson tell you t' ask me?" she asked, then immediately regretted the words. She knew the girl was trying to be kind, doing what she thought she ought to do, what she thought was expected of her, though Deborah also knew that Elise did not want an old woman on her and Janson's hands any more than did anyone else. She could see it in the girl's eyes— there was no place for old women in the world anymore, Deborah told herself. The world had gotten too wide somewhere along the way, so wide there wasn't room left for old women or anyone else—*wide is the gate, and broad is the way, that leadeth to destruction*, she quoted to herself silently.

"He didn't have to tell me," Elise said. "I know it's how he feels, and it's how I feel as well. You've been there for us so many times."

But Deborah shook her head. "You got enough on you already." She could not make herself another burden for Janson, one more mouth for him to feed, another person to crowd into the already-crowded two rooms. "I won't add even more."

"Where else would you go?" Elise asked, and Deborah stopped short as she started to turn away—where else would she go? There was no place she wanted to go, no place she belonged, no place that belonged to her— that had ever belonged to her, she thought as she stared around the room. "You belong with us. That's what family's for," Elise finished. And Deborah realized, in all her life, that was the one thing she had always had.

♣

Janson stood in the dark recesses of Stubblefield's store late on a Thursday afternoon after the ginning was done, looking over the old man's shoulder as Stubblefield sat working over a long column of figures at the desk before him—Janson's charges for the year at the store, the money owed for the cow, the calculations of what was left of the half of the crop Janson was due. It seemed to take forever for the old man to add the figures, to take from Janson's share what was owed, and Janson watched every scratch of the stubby pencil. A radio came on near the front of the store as Stubblefield's daughter, Nonnie, tuned it. There was a run on gold, the radio announcer said, people hoarding it, afraid President Hoover would abandon the gold standard as England had done. Things were getting worse instead of better. Banks were collapsing in record numbers, bankruptcy was sought more and more, businesses were cutting back hours, wages were reduced to keep as many on the payroll as possible—and winter still lay ahead, Janson thought, watching Stubblefield at his long column of figures.

He ticked over in his mind all the preparations they had made for the months ahead. Sweet potatoes, cabbages, and white potatoes buried in hills or trenches to last for months. Dry peas, corn, pumpkin, and okra. The share of hog meat Janson would take as payment for helping in the slaughter for Stubblefield, for his Uncle Wayne, and for another farmer who had asked. Chickens and eggs, milk from the cow. Home canned foods Elise, Gran'ma, and Sissy had put up. Sauerkraut, pickled beans, and chow-chow waiting for use. Turnip and mustard greens that would be growing throughout the months ahead in the garden. There would be food for the winter—please, God, if the winter weren't too bad. Hunger would not be at their backs this year as it had been the last.

But they still needed money. The baby was due in January. That would mean eight people in the family, not only to feed, but to clothe and to see well through the winter. Henry was growing out of his shoes; Elise's were ragged, and Janson's in such bad shape that the soles had to be padded heavily just to be able to walk in them. A charge could not be run at the store in the winter, not again until a new crop was in the ground, and there were things they would have to have that only money or trade could buy them—sugar, thread, soda, kerosene, so much more. If only he were on his own land—

If there was not half the crop to lose in exchange for the use of pitiful, hilly, rock-strewn land. If there was no store charge that would have to be run in order to survive—how well they could make it. His father had always told him how easily a sharecropper could come out owing at the end of the year, his entire half of the crop taken to cover his bill at the store, and still more owed, forever tied to the land of another, working himself deeper and deeper in debt each year. Credit was something a man was better not to use unless he had to—but he had had to, and each scratch of the pencil clutched in Stubblefield's hand only reminded him of his father's words.

Lester Stubblefield turned in his chair and looked up at Janson. The old man tapped the paper before him with one grimy fingernail and glanced back down at the figures again. Janson did not like the look on his face. "Wish we could'a sold at a better price, boy—it'd 'a helped," Stubblefield said.

Janson looked at him, waiting.

"After my half for use 'a th' land, my mules, plows and all, an' th' cotton seed, and after th' cow I sold you on credit and your bill here at th' store—I do wish we could'a sold at a better price, boy—"

"How much?" Janson asked, hearing the impatience in his own voice. "How much do I have left?"

Stubblefield looked at him for a moment then turned slowly back to the desk, to the small stack of money they had received for Janson's cotton crop. Janson had been so careful with the store charges, so cautious to buy on credit only what was necessary. There had to be money left, money for all the work and sweat that they had endured throughout the year—all that cotton, those fields beautiful and green, beautiful and white, the hours upon hours of picking, the bleeding fingers and shoulders aching from the weight of pick sacks. There had to be money left.

Stubblefield turned back to him with a few coins which he dropped into Janson's open palm. "Price 'a cotton'll be better next year, boy," Stubblefield was saying. "You cleared that new field t' plant, and next year you won't have th' cow t' pay for. You should do better next year, even better the year after that."

But Janson was not hearing. He could only stare at the coins in his hand, stare and think—this is all. After all that work, after all this year—this is all. Winter was coming on. Elise would be having the baby. There were things the family needed, shoes for Henry, so much more—and, this was all. All that work, all that hope—and this was all.

"You're even with me 'til next year, boy. You'll get that crop in th' ground and you can start your charge here again—it'll be better; you watch and see."

Damn you, Janson thought, but clenched the few coins in his hand and left the store without a word.

# CHAPTER TEN

The baby came in the last week of January, 1932, a small, angry, black-haired little girl born on a night so fierce that a quilt had to be hung over the door to block some of the chill wind that whistled through the cracks and crevices. Judith Louise came into life screaming at the top of her small lungs, seeming outraged at the world in which she found herself.

It was a long labor and a difficult birth, and Janson knew that Elise was physically and emotionally drained in the weeks afterward, taking longer to recover this time than from either of the two previous births or the miscarriage. It was a cold, hard winter with eight people crowded into the two rooms as Stan finally had to make a pallet for himself by Henry's bed as the worst of the weather descended. Janson worried for the children, and for Elise, over the cold winter nights as the frigid wind blew under the house and up through the loose, ill-fitting floorboards, coming through spaces in the walls that no amount of chinking could fill.

He and Stan had beaten the cotton stalks down in the fields in the early part of January, and had plowed them under because of the boll weevils, as well as to allow the plants to rot in preparing the land for the new year's cotton crop. Janson had broken up the new field he had cleared, and had already gone back to plow it again, though it soon looked to be packed as tight as if it had never been plowed in the first place.

He made baskets and walked the countryside selling them, worked clearing fields when someone would hire him, did odd jobs, and took whatever was offered in trade—there never seemed enough he could do as the cold days passed. He knew they were on their own until spring came, until they could get another cotton crop into the ground. No charge could be run at the store in the cold months. Now they had only what they had stored for the winter to see them through. If they had misjudged, if they had not planned well enough, they could all be left hungry—that thought was never far from Janson's mind. He had seen too many other people in the same desperate straits. There did not seem to be a sharecropping family in the county who had fared well from the previous year's cotton crop.

But, then again, sharecroppers never fared well.

When spring finally came, Janson and Stan worked from early in the mornings until late in the evenings to get the cotton crop into the ground. Sissy helped distribute the guano and plant the fuzzy cotton seed, and Elise soon joined her, which Janson objected to loudly.

"It's my crop, too," she told him, staring at him stubbornly when he demanded that she return to the house.

"I won't have you—"

"Don't you tell me what you won't have, Janson Sanders," she said, stamping her bare foot on the clay ground. "I'm your wife, not a child you can tell what to do!"

It almost tore his heart out to watch her in the fields, bent over a hoe as she learned to thin out the cotton plants—Elise Whitley chopping cotton for the first time in her life.

Kin came to visit as Decoration Day and Homecoming at the little Holiness church Janson had grown up in approached that year, and Janson could only hope the kin would leave once Sunday was over. The prior year his Aunt Grace and Grace's widowed daughter, Jeanette, had stayed three weeks, and left only after Elise served them a dinner of nothing but scorched potatoes and butterbeans that had been cooked in too little water until they were dried out and brown at the edges, then prepared the same thing for supper that night, and threatened to do it again for the next day's dinner.

"You shouldn't 'a done that," Janson told her, though he too was glad to see them leave.

This year Grace was back, and Jeanette with her, and Janson was wondering how long it would be before Elise started scorching potatoes and beans again—but at least his family was better off than they might have been. His Uncle Wayne had Gran'ma's sister, Nancy, one of Nancy's grandsons and his wife, and all five of their children sleeping on pallets at his house.

Janson rose early on Saturday morning with the intention of getting to the church cemetery and cleaning off the Sanders graves before anyone else in the family could arrive. He was determined to avoid his cousin, Estelle, his great-aunt Nancy's daughter. Janson could not remember a single time when he had been able to pull up weeds and spread fresh sand in the cemetery without being under Estelle's direct supervision—she never did any of the work, but just stood with her hands on her hips and a disapproving look on her round face, telling him what he was doing wrong. Sometimes he thought she would never shut up.

When she did, it always ended with, "Well, if that's th' best you can do."

Stan volunteered to go with him this morning, and Gran'ma as well, though Janson told her there was no need. He and Stan could do the work, and would have the graves ready for Sunday morning, but Gran'ma would have none of it.

"There ain't been a Decoration Day that I ain't cleaned off graves, an' this ain't gonna be th' first—you think I'm gonna have Nancy tellin' everybody Estelle done all th' work?"

Several wagons and one Model-T Ford truck were parked at the edge of the cemetery by the time they arrived. Estelle was there, walking among the graves, hands on hips, disapproving look already in place, though the work had not even begun.

She did not say hello, or exchange any of the typical greetings even a stranger would have thought polite.

"It's a shame how ya'll let these graves go t' ruin every year," she said.

Neither Gran'ma nor Janson responded, though they could have.

Janson had cleaned the graves last fall, and again at the end of winter, and he and Stan had been back no more than a month before to pull up weeds that had come up with the spring showers.

Janson went to work on his parents' graves, pulling out a few stray weeds as Estelle stood over him, the woman leaving him at last with a final: "Well, if that's th' best you can do." He used the wheelbarrow they had brought to haul sand down from the pile at the edge of the cemetery. He could remember doing this so many times as a child, when his parents were alive, and they had all worked together in cleaning their people's graves. It was something you did, something you hoped someone would do for you, when your time came to be buried.

As they did every year, children climbed over the large pile of sand, making the sides collapse, until some of the older folks made them quit. More people were arriving and the day was starting to get hot for May. Janson waved to two cousins he had not seen in years and stopped to visit with them beneath the shade of the old oak tree in the middle of the cemetery. His cousins remembered the syrup cakes stacked with dried apples his mother made every year for dinner on the ground, saying Aunt Nell had always made the best cakes. Other folks stopped to say they sure did miss Sister Nell and Brother Henry, and church singings weren't the same anymore without Brother Tom's voice to join in. Aunt Olive stopped to give him a hug and then moved on to talk to Gran'ma.

Grace had arrived now, as had Jeannette, although they would do more meddling than bend an elbow to any actual work. Aunt Nancy was there, disagreeing with Gran'ma as to who was buried where in the unmarked graves of long-dead kin at the bottom end of the cemetery. It was the same argument they had every year, caused by some woman who was no relation to them but who had gotten herself buried in the midst of their kinfolks. Aunt Nancy said she was buried in one grave; Gran'ma said it was another, between a distant cousin and a great-aunt who died before Janson was born—there was no agreement to the woman's name, her cause of death, or why she was buried in the middle of someone else's family. One year Janson's Aunt Olive slapped Estelle when the two of them joined in—he had not seen that, but he knew he would pay cash money, if he'd had any, to see it happen again.

Brother Sim Leverett interrupted the women as their voices began to rise. He had been the preacher at the church when Janson was a boy, but had moved on years before Janson's parents died. Brother Leverett had come back to help preach both Henry and Nell Sanders's funerals, and, more recently, Tom Sanders's funeral. He would be preaching tomorrow, and Janson was glad to see him a moment later as he shook his hand.

"Brother Sanders—are we going to be seeing you and your family at Homecoming tomorrow?" Brother Leverett asked.

"We'll—" Janson began, but immediately fell silent when women's voices raised a few graves away, followed by the sound of a slap.

Janson turned to see Estelle's hand covering the side of her face, and he was disappointed that he had missed it again. Her mouth was open as she stared at his Aunt Olive. For probably only the second time in her life, Janson was almost certain she could not think of anything to say.

He had to fight the urge to walk over and ask her if it was the best she could do.

♣

The Depression had them down, but Janson knew they were better off than many. The news that came out of the radio at Stubblefield's store seemed to be all grim. A stir had been caused back in March when Colonel Lindbergh's baby son was kidnaped out of his home in New Jersey—and everyone knew of Colonel Lindbergh after his flight to Paris five years before. Shock rode high that someone would steal a baby from under his parents' roof, and that shock only deepened when the news came that the child was found dead. What's this world coming to?— people asked each other, that someone could do such a thing.

In June, fifteen thousand war veterans descended on Washington demanding early payment of the compensation bonuses they were supposed to be paid in 1945. They camped on the outskirts of the city, many having brought their entire families, and they tried to pressure the Senate to pass the Bonus Bill.

But the Bill was defeated, and when President Hoover sent out troops to disperse the Bonus Marchers, a melee ensued in which tear-gas bombs were thrown, people were trampled, and the camp burned to the ground. What's this world coming to?—people asked again. What was the world coming to when war veterans with hungry families are attacked for asking only for their due.

Relief funds were running short, church and charity organizations hard-pressed to handle the numbers needing relief. More and more people lost homes, farms, businesses. Land seemed to be going up on the auction block almost daily, and leaflets circulated announcing when some farmer's land was going up for auction and asking other farmers to try to block the sale—but always the sales continued.

The percentage of the unemployed kept rising. Homeless, jobless people traveled the country, looking ever farther for the prosperity that was supposedly "just around the corner." President Hoover had promised the previous year that the Depression was "only temporary"—but nobody believed that anymore. Times were tough. And they seemed to be getting tougher.

In July, Elise told Janson of hearing a new voice coming over the radio at the Stubblefield's store, that of New York's governor, Franklin D. Roosevelt. Mr. Roosevelt had won the Democratic nomination for President, and had gone on the radio talking of a "New Deal" for the country, a way to pull the United States out of the Depression. This Roosevelt wanted to put the unemployed men to work at nature conservation. He wanted to control the crop surpluses that had ruined the price of cotton, among many other things in the years previous, and he wanted to repeal Prohibition.

In the weeks that followed, it seemed that all anyone could talk about was this FDR—he was calling for relief to help those needy and hurting, unemployment insurance, old-age benefits, help with farm mortgages, and advocating financial reforms, "sound money," and many other things that Janson little understood. Elise seemed to find hope in the words of this Franklin Roosevelt, but Janson could only think that words could not solve anyone's problems, and that maybe not even God Almighty could end the problems the country had gotten itself into.

In that autumn of 1932, words Henry Sanders had often spoken came home to roost on his son's doorstep: "Credit's what kills most sharecroppers." Henry had never wanted his son to have to 'crop another man's land on halves as he himself had done—but necessity had brought Janson to that place.

Janson truly learned the meaning behind those words that autumn. The crop was picked and sold at market, and the proceeds divided, with Janson's share going first to cover the store credit the family had had to run in order to survive—but there was not enough even to cover the charges. The year's work had all been taken, the entire cotton crop, and they were left with no money with which to face the winter. Worse still, there was a balance owing at the store, a balance that hung around Janson's neck like a lead weight.

He sold the hogs they had been fattening for months, hogs they had taken in exchange for back-breaking work he and Stan had done in another man's fields in addition to their own. Stubblefield had threatened eviction, had threatened that there were more and better farmers who could produce better yields of cotton and who would not end the year in debt—he had to be paid or they would be added to the homeless who wandered the highways, or forced to live off the charity of their family, possibly even be forced to give Henry, Catherine, and Judith over to someone else so that the children would at least have shelter and food. He sold the hogs, their source of meat for the winter, and gave the money to Stubblefield to clear the remainder of the charge at the store—not next year, he swore to himself; I'll be damned if next year I'll charge a thing that might leave my family in trouble for the winter. Not next year.

But he had sworn so many things to himself, and each had come true as if to show him that he could not tempt God with promises made to himself: working in the mill, sharecropping another man's land, seeing Elise working in the fields—his Elise, picking cotton. He knew that he would never forget the sight of her dragging the long pick sack behind her, a sack so heavy that her shoulders ached from its weight far into the night—his Elise, her fingers scratched and bleeding, working in the red fields under the hot sun. He had wanted for her a place of their own, a good life for her and the children. It would break her heart in a few years to see Henry picking cotton along with the rest of them. On their own land it would have been different; at least on their own land their children would be working to make life better in the future, not merely working to survive the day, the week, the year. Picking then would be different—it would be their own cotton, worth the hours and hours of backbreaking work.

Many farm families had children in the fields by the time they were Henry's age, but Janson wanted his son, and his daughters as well, to have at least the memory of a childhood, a memory that he, himself, did not have. The boy was only four—Janson had gone into the fields on a row of cotton with his mother when he was four years old. His son and his daughters would not until they were at least six; then there would be both school and work to occupy their minds. Until then the boy would remain a boy, and the girls would be girls, and Janson could pick a little harder, chop the cotton or work later into the dusk each day, to afford his children that. Henry, Catherine, and Judith would have the time to be children, unlike the sons and daughters of most of the sharecropping or land-owning farmers in the area—he had sworn that to himself, and to Elise as well. He had sworn that.

Winter lay ahead, winter on the land of a man he had grown to hate, a man who he believed had cheated him out of the half of the crop due him in exchange for his and his family's work—he did not trust the long column of figures that Stubblefield worked over before telling him there was not even enough to cover the store charge: "Credit's what kills most sharecroppers"—he could now tell his father what truth those words really held.

Somewhere along the way he had made a wrong choice, taken a wrong turn, and had damned his entire family because of it. He could not see where that choice had been made, that turn taken, for he had only done what he had had to do. But somehow he had failed and had set his family in this direction from which they might never escape. Even the food hoarded for the winter did little to allay that feeling—they were all damned. Damned by the Depression, damned by the sharecropping, damned even by this red land they worked, land that would never be their own. Winter was coming, a winter he faced with dread.

Two years—two years on the farm, and they were no better off than when they had come here. But few people were better off than they had been two years before. The Depression had hit hard, and with a fierceness not restricted to the cotton mills and villages and sharecroppers of the South. Elise had told him of tales she had heard on the radio at Stubblefield's house when fitting Mrs. Stubblefield for a new blouse, stories she had heard on the radio at the store, or in the gossip of the Baptist churchwomen on Sundays after services—there were bread lines in the big cities, people sleeping out in the open on street corners, selling apples just to earn a few cents to feed hungry children. People fought over food scraps behind New York restaurants, and murdered other men for a pair of shoes or a coat. The entire world had gone mad.

President Hoover had been defeated in the election, and that man, Roosevelt, was coming into office. Roosevelt promised a "New Deal" that would bring recovery and reforms—all well and good, Janson thought. Hadn't Hoover said he would wipe out poverty, that there would be "a chicken in every pot and a car in every garage?" Hadn't Hoover promised to help farmers who were hurting even back in '28 when he had first come into office?

Well, farmers weren't helped, and neither was anyone else. The country was a mess, uncountable people out of work, thousands hungry, cold, desperate, and Janson felt this Roosevelt would have no more effect on the Depression than Hoover had.

Things got worse. In the months after the election, the country came to a complete standstill. President Hoover could do nothing because Congress waited for Mr. Roosevelt, and Mr. Roosevelt could do nothing until he was inaugurated in March. The business upswing from earlier in the year came to a grinding halt—what Mr. Roosevelt would do seemed to be all that anyone could talk about.

Rumors sent the banking system into panic—Roosevelt intended to play with the currency. Inflation, reflation, panic—everyone whispered. People who could started converting everything they owned into cash, hoarding gold. Runs began and by mid-February the banks were in the worst trouble yet.

"I heard on the radio at Stubblefield's house," Elise said one day after returning from fitting Mrs. Stubblefield for a new dress, "the governor of Michigan declared an eight-day bank holiday in his state because of so many runs—"

All well and good, Janson thought. Michigan was a long way off, and the local bank had gone under years before, taking all their money with it. He did not care what happened to a bunch of folks in some state way up north.

"Someone tried to shoot Roosevelt," Stan announced as he came in from the store no more than a day later. "It was on the radio, some man in Florida—"

"He get shot?" Janson asked, surprised that someone would try to shoot the man who had just been elected to be President.

"No, some other man got shot instead—"

The notion of repealing Prohibition was now with the states to see if they wanted to make liquor legal again—might as well, Janson thought. As many bootleggers and stills as there are in the woods around here, they might as well.

More and more states declared bank holidays, desperate to stop the mad runs that were causing failure of bank after bank. By March 3rd, the day before the inauguration, the banking system had completely broken down. Business had come to a halt. Finance had come to a halt. Farmers waited, shopkeepers waited, mill villagers waited, the men of Wall Street waited—something had to be done. The country could take no more of this.

Saturday, March 4th came, the morning chill, citizens waiting and desperate. Nobody seemed to be moving about on the roads as Janson and his family walked toward the Stubblefield store. Elise wanted to hear what the new President would say once he was sworn in, as did Stan, and Janson had agreed to go along, though he cared little for what some rich man from up north might have to say about anything. Gran'ma appeared to care even less, saying that she thought Mr. Roosevelt was "full of himself," but she came along anyway just not to be left out of the goings-on.

Tim Cauthen had walked to the Sanders house early that morning from the mill village, and he and Sissy remained outside as everyone else went in, the two young people sitting on the splintery wooden steps that led up to the store porch as Sissy watched Henry and Catherine play outside with the other farm children. Janson noted that the store was crowded as the screen door shut behind them. It looked as if everyone in the area had come here for the same reason, to hear what this Roosevelt would have to say.

Cigarette and cigar smoke hung visibly in the air. Stubblefield was behind the counter, for once not seeming to care that so many people were loitering in the store—he probably thought some buying would go on while so many people were there, Janson told himself.

The radio was turned on and Stubblefield adjusted it to bring in the station clearer and the voices from so far away, up at the White House in Washington, D.C. The announcer's voice rang falsely cheerful to Janson's ears as Janson turned to look at the farmers and sharecroppers around him, men whose faces were just beginning to recapture the sunburn they usually wore, at women as worn and faded as their cotton dresses, the skinny children, and the courting young people. It seemed odd to Janson that so many people had come to one place to listen to the speech of one man, a man that so many people had put so much stock in.

To Janson, they were doomed to disappointment. This Roosevelt could work no miracle and end the Depression as so many hoped. Perhaps not even God Almighty could do that, and certainly no one human being could do all the things this man had said he would do.

Elise and Stan seemed to see hope for them all in this Roosevelt, as did so many others, and they stood now, the believers and the unbelievers alike, gathered together listening to the radio in Stubblefield's store, waiting to hear words saying that it would be better, that—really, this time—prosperity was just around the corner.

Roosevelt was sworn into office, Janson hearing for the first time the strangely accented voice.

The room grew quiet and Janson could hear the steady tick of a clock. The voices of the children playing outside came in through the screen door, children who on other days were as likely to be found picking or hoeing or chopping cotton as to be found in a school. A man coughed. A baby began to cry and was taken outside, and everyone waited to hear the words that would come from the box on the counter.

"This is a day of national consecration," Roosevelt began, "and I am certain that my fellow Americans expect that on my induction into the Presidency I will address them with a candor and a decision which the present situation of our Nation impels. This is preeminently the time to speak the truth, the whole truth, frankly and boldly. Nor need we shrink from honestly facing conditions in our country today."

Janson studied the faces of the others in the room. There was hope on the faces of some, hope as he had not seen in these hard, recent years; outright skepticism on the faces of others. Doubt, assurance—but they all listened, everyone listened, their eyes on the radio, seeming to rest their futures in the words that came through in that strange voice.

"This great Nation will endure as it has endured, will revive and will prosper. So, first of all, let me assert my firm belief that the only thing we have to fear is fear itself—nameless, unreasoning, unjustified terror which paralyzes needed efforts to convert retreat into advance . . ."

Elise slipped her hand in Janson's and squeezed, smiling up at him.

"In such a spirit on my part and on yours we face our common difficulties. They concern, thank God, only material things. Values have shrunken to fantastic levels; taxes have risen; our ability to pay has fallen; government of all kinds is faced by serious curtailment of income; the means of exchange are frozen in the currents of trade; the withered leaves of industrial enterprise lie on every side; farmers find no market for their produce; the savings of many years in thousands of families is gone.

"More important, a host of unemployed citizens face the grim problem of existence, and an equally great number toil with little return. Only a foolish optimist can deny the dark realities of the moment."

The voice continued, talking of the need to put men back to work, of action he would take—action which they all craved so badly. Applause interrupted him time and again, but still the voice continued.

"I am prepared under my Constitutional duty to recommend the measures that a stricken nation in the midst of a stricken world may require . . . and in the event that the national emergency is still critical, I shall not evade the clear course of duty that will then confront me. I shall ask the Congress for the one remaining instrument to meet the crisis—broad Executive power to wage a war against the emergency, as great as the power that would be given to me if we were in fact invaded by a foreign foe."

Applause, loud and enthusiastic, came over the crackling radio as those in the room stared.

"In this dedication of a Nation we humbly ask the blessing of God. May He protect each and every one of us," the new President said. "May He guide me in the days to come."

# PART THREE

# CHAPTER ELEVEN

Everyone wanted Roosevelt to do something, and do something he did. The day after the inauguration the new President declared a national bank holiday, closing banks nationwide until each could be looked into and those found financially sound could reopen. By Monday, March 13th, some banks had opened their doors again and action had been taken to cut federal expenses—President Roosevelt was as good as his word, Elise told Janson, though Janson himself could see little effect from this Roosevelt's word.

The Agricultural Adjustment Administration was started to help the farmers, the Civilian Conservation Corps to put young men back to work, the Tennessee Valley Authority to bring electricity to the country-side, and the National Industrial Recovery Act to help keep business in line. Federal relief was instituted, and the blue eagle of the NRA began to appear in store windows and businesses everywhere—things were getting better, people started to say to one another. Men were beginning to go back to work, and relief funds were again available for those still unemployed. Hope was rising, and with that hope also came the complainers—men were being encouraged not to work by relief monies, some said; the unemployed were not going back to work fast enough. Hours were cut so that other people could be employed—prosperity was just not coming back as quickly as it should.

Never did Janson hear the complaints any louder than when the county agents began to talk of plowing up part of the year's cotton already growing in the fields. He little understood the talk of supply and

demand, of reducing the amount of something to hit the market in order
to raise the price it would bring. He only understood that the AAA
wanted him to plow under a part of the crop already planted, cotton he
had worked and sweated over for months. He had expanded the acreage,
planted as much of the land as possible—and now they wanted him to
plow part of it under.

They offered him money now, money he might not make in the fall
if prices fell before he could get the cotton picked—so he agreed, gritting
his teeth and guiding the reluctant mule down the rows of his work,
plowing under the cotton plants he had hoped and prayed over for
months. All that worry, all that sweat—plowed under like it was nothing.
Later the bolls burst open, leaving the destroyed fields peppered over
with fleecy white—but they were not allowed to pick the cotton in the
plowed-under fields even then, and the white cotton lay rotting on the
red earth, unused and wasted.

Janson had been told he would receive a fifty-percent share of the
money the government paid for the plowed-under cotton, but, when the
time came to make the split, Stubblefield faced him once again with his
long column of figures. "You owe me this much for th' charge at th' store,
and this—your share from the AAA'll go t' cover that, and you'll make
your money back in th' fall, boy, when you sell your crop. A big piece 'a
your store bill'll be paid then, and you'll have more t' go int' your own
pocket after my share."

But, it did not work that way. In the fall, after the reduced cotton
crop was picked and sold, his share barely covered the remaining store
charge. "What'd you expect, boy?" Stubblefield faced him, angry when
Janson questioned the amount he was told they owed at the store.
"What'd you expect, selling a littler crop like that—what'd you expect?"

Elise said that the bill at the store had been "padded." They had
watched every cent, charged so carefully—she knew how much they
should owe.

"Are you doubtin' my figures, boy?" Stubblefield asked, angrily rising
from his chair at the battered old desk there in the store. "Are you callin'
me a liar?"

"I'm just sayin' I think you're wrong, that I want you t' double-check your figures."

"I done double-checked them!"

"There ain't no way we could owe that much."

"If you're callin' me a liar, boy, you can get off my property right now, and you can go live off relief like them other lazy bastards in town."

Threatened with eviction, he had to back down. He knew he was right, that Elise was right, but what could he do? If he pushed the point, they would be off the land with no place to go, no way to make a living—what else could he do?

A hatred developed between Janson and Stubblefield that made Janson avoid the man at all costs. He wanted no trouble. He just wanted to support his family—they had just needed the money so badly this year.

Gran'ma had been sick for months, growing progressively worse as the days went by. He had hoped for enough money to bring a doctor if the stubborn old woman would allow it, her claiming that God would heal her Himself if He was of a mind to—but there was no money. She coughed and wheezed, and by Christmas she was unable to move from her bed or the rocker unless doubled-over in a desperate battle with her own body for breath. The Holiness church women came to help tend her, praying through, trying to bring her peace, if not healing. The minister and other church members visited, both from the Holiness church Gran'ma had attended for so many years, and the Baptist church that Elise attended with the children, bringing food and prayer as they did all that they could, but nothing seemed to help. Gran'ma needed a doctor, and a doctor cost money—but there was no money in the little house for a doctor, no money for anything.

January set in with the bitterest cold that Janson could remember. Gran'ma worsened as the days passed, until, in desperation, Janson went for the young doctor who had come in to work with Dr. Washburn, forcing the reluctant man out on a frigid night, promising him money when he had it, and threatening him physical injury if he resisted. The man was silent and cold as he arrived at the house with Janson in the old truck that had been borrowed from a reluctant Stubblefield. He went to

Gran'ma and spent a long time examining her as Janson and Elise waited by the door.

The doctor straightened, then came to lead them into the other of the two rooms when he was finished, his young face different now, the anger of having been dragged out on a night like this by an angry sharecropper no longer evident in his expression. He turned to close the door after them, then brought his eyes back to Janson's. "I'm sorry," he said quietly. "There's nothing I can do for her. If I had seen her sooner—"

"She—she can't—" Elise began, and Janson could hear her voice shake. "There has to be something we can do."

The doctor looked at her with sympathy. "You can pray," was all he said.

Gran'ma's breathing filled the rooms. Elise strained for the sound of each breath, certain somehow that it would be the last. She sat at Gran'ma's bedside, as she had for days, holding the old woman's hand, unable to do anything but watch her—and listen for the sound of each breath that she knew could be the last.

Elise had never watched death come to someone before, but somehow she knew, the sound, the look, the feeling—and Gran'ma knew. The old woman had talked to Gran'pa for hours the night before, looking past Elise and into the room, talking to her husband dead now more than two years.

"Tom'll be back for me," she told Elise later, her eyes bright with fever. "Tom's gonna take me with him."

The rest of the family had been there earlier in the day, Wayne and Rachel, Olive and Cyrus, Belle and Maggie, Tom, Jr. from Atlanta and his family, Gran'ma's sister, Nancy, and so many grandchildren and great-grandchildren that Elise had lost count. The churchwomen had been by to pray for her, as had Brother Harmon, and even Brother Leverett who had traveled from his new church in Randolph County. Elise had tried to add her own prayers—but Gran'ma was not getting better.

As day passed into night, her breathing became more tortured and there was a deep rattle in her chest. Janson had gone into town to bring the doctor again, though he knew already nothing could be done. Stan was outside, bringing in more wood so they could keep the house warm through the night. Sissy lay in Janson and Elise's bed in the other room, the three children with her, away from the harsh reality at work in the room where they usually slept.

Firelight moved in pale orange and yellow shadows against the walls. The kerosene lamp cast ghosts of the chifforobe, the table, the bed, even Elise herself, against the walls. The smell of burning wood, the medicine the doctor had left, the sickness itself, filled the room. It was quiet, except for Gran'ma's breathing and the occasional pop of the logs burning in the fireplace.

Elise was cold in spite of the fire and the closed room, cold from the knowledge of what would happen very soon. She pulled her sweater tighter and eased her chair closer to the bed, trying to reduce the strain on the arm stretched out to hold Gran'ma's hand. She closed her eyes and bowed her head and tried to pray, but no words would come. Gran'ma would not recover. Elise already knew that.

"Tom?" Gran'ma's voice came again from the bed, and Elise lifted her head and looked at the old woman. Gran'ma was looking toward the closed doorway across the room, a look of expectancy on her face.

"Gran'ma, I'm here—it's Elise. There's no one here but me."

"I knowed you'd come back for me, Tom. I knowed—" and a light smile touched her lips, making her look for a moment younger than Elise had ever known her.

Don't let her start hallucinating again, Elise begged God silently. Please, I can't stand that—please.

"I knowed—"

"Gran'ma, look at me. It's Elise, please—Janson will be back with the doctor in a little while—"

"I knowed you'd come—"

Please—please, Elise closed her eyes and forced back tears. I can't cry, she told herself. Not now. Please, don't let her end like this, talking out of her mind, seeing people who aren't here, people who are long dead. Please—

"Elise?"

She lifted her head, startled at the sound of her own name, and startled even more as she found Gran'ma's eyes on her. The old woman smiled and weakly reached to pat her hand. "Don't you cry, honey—this ain't nothin' t' cry about."

"But, you'll be better—you'll see. In the spring—"

She smiled and shook her head. "We both know I ain't gonna see th' spring, child."

"But—" The tears began and Elise turned her face away so that Gran'ma would not see them.

"There—there, honey." The hand gently patted her own again. "Don't cry. I'm goin' where I want t' go."

"But, I don't want you to go—" She looked back at Gran'ma, letting the tears flow freely now.

"It's where I belong—with Tom an' my babies that's already gone on." She smiled past Elise again. "Tom's here for me now—"

"No—he's dead, Gran'ma. He can't—"

"Still s' much t' learn—" She smiled, bringing her eyes back to Elise. "But you're young still, s' young—"

"Gran'ma—" But no words would come; she could think of nothing to say.

"You take care 'a my boy, an' Henry, Catherine, my little Judith—"

Elise turned her face away, her tears flowing now in earnest.

"Don't cry—I'm happy. My work's done, an' I can go home—"

"Not yet—"

"Yes, Tom's come for me."

Elise watched the dear face, the eyes turned toward the empty doorway again, the longing in them, the readiness. There was a prickly sensation along the back of her neck, the same as the night before when Gran'ma had talked out of her mind, talking to her dead husband. Elise looked toward the door, knowing no one was there, knowing—

"I'm ready, Tom. I'm ready—"

Gran'ma lifted her head from the pillow, seeming for a moment as if she were going to get out of bed. Her long gray hair, now with only a few streaks of brown remaining, fell across her shoulder in one thick plait— she looked toward the door, reaching for it with her eyes.

For a moment Elise thought Gran'ma would speak again, but the older woman smiled and closed her eyes, then rested her head back against the pillow. After a moment she turned her face slightly aside, the look of happiness remaining, and the tortured sound of her breathing at last stopped.

It seemed in 1934 that things were getting better. People were going back to work after years of having no jobs. The number of the unemployed stood at about half what it had been the year before. Farm prices were up, and if the price of cotton held steady, Janson hoped to clear enough from the year's crop, barring unexpected freedom with the figures by Stubblefield, to see them well through the winter for once. There were two hogs being fattened for slaughter, and they hoped to have food enough stored as the months went by—times seemed so much better this year than the last, though the two rooms of the little sharecropped house missed Gran'ma's presence.

They began the winter that year with more hope than they had known in the past years, but, as the early weeks of 1935 came in, Elise and all three of the children became ill, and, though Elise, Henry and Judith recovered quickly, Catherine remained sick, crying and feverish into the darkness each night.

Dr. Washburn was called in, taking the little money they had cleared off the cotton, and, as she recovered, Elise and Janson realized they would have to do something if they were to make it through the remainder of the winter. The children did not have warm clothes, and what they did have was so often patched that it was hardly serviceable. There was one decent pair of shoes that might fit Catherine, but none for Henry or Judith. In spite of all their careful planning, food would be running low before winter was out, and no charge could be run at the store until spring came and a new cotton crop could be gotten into the ground.

On a cold night in February of that year, Elise sat brushing her hair before the faded dresser mirror as Janson watched from where he sat on the side of the bed they shared there in the little sharecropped house on Stubblefield's property. The children and Sissy were asleep in the next room, and Stan as well, having again made a pallet for himself on the other side of a quilt hung across the room. Elise watched Janson's reflection in the mirror, seeing an unfamiliar expression on his face.

The shadows cast by the kerosene lamp on the table beside the bed, as well as the fire burning in the fireplace across the room, moved across his features, hollowing his cheeks and making his cheekbones look even more pronounced—but it was the look of almost haunted resolve in his eyes that captured her as she stared at his reflection. At last he looked away, his words coming slowly, giving Elise the impression that he was speaking as much to himself as to her.

"I'll be gone most all day t'morrow," he said, not bringing his eyes back to her, and she stopped in her brushing to wait for the remainder of the words to come.

"Tomorrow?" she asked, sitting the brush aside and turning fully in her chair to look at him.

He nodded as he stared at the floor somewhere between himself and the fireplace. "I'm goin' t' Wiley. I'll start out walkin'; I guess somebody'll give me a ride before I get t' far."

Wiley—the county seat. Elise understood. She did not speak but turned back to the mirror, picking up her brush again—she would leave Janson at least his pride. Through all the hard times they had seen together, that was the one thing in him that had never changed.

"I'm puttin' in for relief," he said at last, unnecessarily, again as if he were saying the words more for his own benefit than hers, as if he were trying to convince himself of what it was he was telling her he would do.

Elise did not turn back to him, but watched him in the mirror. "Should I go with you? Will you need me?"

"I don't know. Maybe—I don't know."

There was nothing more to say. No matter how hard the times had been, they had never turned to relief monies or food. Charity had been given to them—that had been bad enough to Janson, but at least they had never asked for it.

And now, after all that struggle—Janson, her proud, independent Janson, would ask for help. It almost broke her heart to watch his reflection in the mirror, knowing what had to be going on inside of him with the knowledge.

She watched him, not turning back, but staring at his reflection as he lowered his head and shook it slowly back and forth.

She did not let him know that she had seen.

Elise sat beside Janson in the county office the next morning, watching the looks of shame and pride that alternated across his features, then the look of concentration, of determination, as he worked to draw the two words that were his name on the paper he was given to sign, a signature that Elise herself could not make out afterward, not even knowing what the words were meant to be. There was a look of awful pride in his features moments later as he handed the paper to the relief worker, pride that did not diminish even as the woman said:

"You could have signed with an X, you know," her words clipped, though Elise knew they had not been meant to be condescending.

"You told me t' sign my name. I signed my name," he answered, then sat as if frozen as she moved from her chair, not bringing his eyes to Elise even when she reached out to touch his hand.

He would not allow Elise to go with him after that to pick up the relief they were given, going alone instead, sometimes gone an entire day if no one would give him a ride, often coming home late in the night, his feet tired, his back aching, carrying gunny sacks of apples or cabbages or whatever other relief foods were being distributed. At times the food was inedible, bruised, wilted, worm-ridden—they used whatever was good, and threw the remainder away.

He was quieter than usual after each trip into the county seat, and Elise could do little but worry about him in the hours he was gone.

Accepting relief was almost more than he could bear, his pride bowed before the need to ask for charity for his family—and Elise knew what he was going through on each trip, whether she went with him or not. It was hard for him to understand that he could no longer feed, clothe, and support his family with the work of his own hands. He had once told her that he would do whatever it took to see to it that she and the children would not go hungry, even if he had to steal to feed them—and, somehow, Elise realized that stealing would be preferable to him over asking for charity for his family. At least stealing was something a man could do with his own hands. But stealing was not part of Janson's nature, though pride was, and he took the charity with gritted teeth and with as much dignity as was allowed him.

A new cotton crop was planted, vegetables began to come from their own garden, and there was less need for relief as the months passed. People were going back to work throughout the country. Tim Cauthen found work under the Works Progress Administration, and shyly, and with a great deal of embarrassment, he asked Sissy to marry him, leaving at last only Janson and Elise, the three children, and Stan in the little house.

As summer became autumn, Elise suffered a second miscarriage in less than six months, and she was told by Dr. Washburn that it was unlikely she would have more children. Elise had not been at all certain she wanted another baby, but knowing there was little possibility had left her in tears, especially as she worried at how Janson would react to the news.

"I've got you, an' that's all that matters," he told her, "you, Henry, Catherine, and Judith."

"But, you've always said—"

"I wanted you," he said, not letting her finish the words. "We got a son, an' two daughters, an' we're together—what more could any man want—"

Elise had long ago concluded that there was very little of herself in at least two of her three children. Henry, at eight, was so much like Janson that at times it was startling to Elise. Judith, as well, was very much like her father, with the same black hair and green eyes. At four years old, she often sided with her brother against Catherine, and the two of them seemed to delight in annoying the older girl, which Elise knew Catherine oftentimes brought on herself, for Catherine could be high-handed and bossy.

Catherine looked little like either Henry or Judith, for she had her mother's lighter coloring and reddish-gold hair. Even as a baby she had been a "prissy little thing," as Janson's grandmother had often referred to her, and now, at six, that prissiness had become part of her nature. She reminded Elise of how she had been as a child, and for that very reason she irritated her to no ends at times, for she could remember herself doing many of the same things she could now see Catherine doing.

Henry, at eight, seemed more like Janson every day. Tall for his age, with the same black hair and darker coloring that spoke of Janson's Cherokee heritage, he not only resembled his father, but was like him in temperament as well. He was even more outspoken than Janson, with a temper that often surpassed even that of either of his parents or his sisters, and a tendency to speak too quickly and without thinking that reminded Elise mostly of herself.

His temper and quick tongue often managed to get him into trouble in school, where he showed no fear of taking on bigger boys, even if outnumbered, if he were provoked. Elise knew that he was no bully, for he knew that Janson would wear a belt out on him if he were found bullying other children, but there was no doubt within Janson or Elise that Henry would never shy away from a fight when it became neces-sary—and it seemed that it often became necessary. On more than one occasion already in the few years he had been in school, he had come home with a bloody nose or a blacked eye, keeping Elise in a constant turmoil over her temperamental son.

"Who started it?" she would ask, to which she would always receive the same reply:

"He did," without the boy ever supplying a name to his mother—to have done so, Elise knew, would have been less than manly.

"He hit you first?"

"I didn't say that—I said he started it," Henry would answer. Words were as much provocation to fight in Henry's opinion, as his mother had already learned, as any physical threat could ever be. He had his father's pride, and he was never unwilling to respond in his own way to insults or verbal harassment that was aimed at him, his sisters, or his family.

"What did he say?" Elise would ask, hearing the exasperation she often felt now evident in her voice. Or: "What did he call you?"

There were a thousand reasons for a fight: "He called me Geronimo," because Henry's Cherokee heritage through Janson was often the cause for teasing; "He said Pa was a Holy Roller," after a fight with the son of the Baptist preacher; or, "He said there was patches on the seat of my overalls," and even worse yet, "He said Catherine's dress came from the relief."

Janson tried to be stern with his son, disciplining him as sternly as he had been disciplined as a boy, but Elise knew that he always came away from the punishment shaken. The worst problems always brought the boy a whipping with a belt by Janson—but it often seemed to take more out of Janson than it did out of Henry.

"He's just like I was at his age, just as damn stubborn and pig-headed," he would tell Elise later. "My pa'd whip me with his belt, an' I'd go right back out an' do it again th' next day."

Henry was not the best student, unlike Catherine, who took easily to book learning. He did not like to read, and liked arithmetic even less. His cursive writing was barely readable, and his print was little better, for he reversed letters and spelled words in creative ways. His mind was always on fishing, on the outdoors, on the woods, or on something he had planned to do after school—on anything but what his mind should be on.

"I don't see no reason to learn this," he would say when something did not hold his attention. "Won't nobody ever use it."

"You don't see any reason to learn it, because you don't believe anyone will ever make use of it—" Elise would correct with growing impatience. "But, you will learn it, and you will make use of it."

"I just don't see no reason."

"Any reason—" she would correct for the hundredth time.

Janson would sit in silence during the frequent battles over school, not looking at either of them, and never discussing the matter with her later. He wanted Henry, and the girls as well, to have an education, the best he and Elise could provide for them, but that was Elise's domain— she knew that and understood it as clearly from his silence as she ever could from words. The picture of him struggling through that signature would be forever fresh in her mind, as would the shame that had been on his face on the day when she had learned that he could barely read or write—that would never happen to their children. They both wanted better than that for Henry, for Catherine, and for Judith.

Elise had seen the bigger, older children left on the rows with the younger children in the two-room schoolhouse that Henry and Catherine attended there in the country, children forever behind from repeated absences to work the farms, forever behind with no hope of ever catching up, only occasionally passed to another grade, a different row, out of kindness, or from a sheer desire to be rid of trying to teach the same thing to the same child year after year—that would never happen to her children. It had happened to her husband—but not to their children.

Elise knew that Janson was, for the most part, illiterate, but she was the only one who knew. The children did not know, and Stan did not know. Perhaps Gran'ma had known, but, if she had, the knowledge had died with her. He had invented uncountable ways to hide it—his eyes would be tired if the girls asked him to read to them; the light was not good enough; his throat scratchy, their mother's voice much more pleasant, and he would like to hear Elise read as well—then he would sit in silence with Judith on his lap and stare into the fire, not even hearing the words that she read. His inability to read and to write was the one thing Elise knew his pride could not make right. All other assaults on his dignity were from without, but this was from within, something he could not fight, could not conquer. Elise knew the children would never know their father could only barely read or write, and the secret would die with her as well—his pride; his damned, stubborn pride, but it was such a part of him that she knew she could never fight it.

Janson had put Henry to work chopping cotton, hoeing, picking, and doing other work in the fields the year he turned six, and this year he put Catherine to work as well. Judith would join them in a few years. Until then there were chores to be done, but still time for play, still time for being a child. At six there was school, and the fields to contend with as well, but unlike other farmers in the area, Janson did not set a quota of cotton that he expected each child to pick, or punish a child who could not or did not meet the standard.

"You do your best, an' that's enough. You do any less, an' you know somebody else'll have t' make up for it—that ain't th' way things 'r done aroun' here," he told each, and set them to work.

It was the first year that Janson expected Catherine to help pick cotton, but she was of little help in the fields. She spent her time dawdling down the rows, and would end the day with little having been picked into her sack, even on days when Judith and Henry had left her alone, which was not often. Henry picked a remarkable amount for a boy his age, as Janson expected him to, though Henry hated it almost as much as he hated school—picking cotton was something he could not get out of, and the sooner it was done, the sooner he could go fishing, or trapping the rabbits he invariably let go, or doing whatever else that could hold his fancy. School never seemed to end; it was always there, so there was no use for working hard—you couldn't get it over with, and, to an eight-year-old, there were so many other things more inviting and interesting.

It was hard to keep Henry's mind on anything that did not interest him—fishing, being outdoors, exploring the woods, playing with the dogs. Those things interested him. Chores, picking cotton, helping his mother, his father, or his Uncle Stan, were things that had to be done, and things to be gotten over quickly and well enough not to get into trouble over. But school—and, worse still, church—Henry saw no reason for either, and made his opinions evident in his manner and attitude at every opportunity.

The little schoolhouse had closed down for its customary break that fall of 1936 to allow the farm children to pick cotton, which had left Henry and Catherine with their days free to spend in the fields with the remainder of the family. Henry had not gotten a break from learning, however, for Elise had him working problems or reading with her every evening once the work and supper were finished. The boy had enough trouble during the seven months that school was in; she was determined he would not fall behind just because the little two-room school had closed its doors.

That night Henry had been working arithmetic problems his Uncle Stan had for him when supper was finished. Elise planned to have him read with her as soon as he completed the problems. The copy of *The Adventures of Tom Sawyer* they had been reading in the previous evening sat beside his paper now, being shoved slowly farther and farther away, as if he thought distancing himself from the volume would allow him to avoid opening it sometime that night. He sat now, his head in his hands, as he stared at the paper. Elise watched, knowing he would never finish if he did not pick up the pencil, but she also knew it would do no good to push him.

Judith was sitting opposite her brother at the eating table, watching Janson where he sat nearby weaving a basket from white oak splits he had prepared over the past days. Her sister was lying stomach-down on the floor near the fireplace, flipping through the pages of a moving picture magazine that Mrs. Stubblefield had given her, while Stan sat with a ragged copy of *Anthony Adverse* held so that he could better see to read the print by the lamp on the table between where he sat and where Elise worked at her sewing.

The backless and well-worn novel in her brother's hands was one Stan had gotten in trade for a load of firewood he brought in for Mrs. Stubblefield. She had been ready to throw it out, considering the condition of the book when she had gotten it second-hand, and the fact that it did not hold her interest, bestseller or not, as it had been back in '33 and '34. He told Elise that the old woman had thought him crazy to take it in exchange for work, but she could never know the pleasure that both he and Elise received from having something new to read. They took turns with it now, whenever one or the other could find the time, treating the badly handled book as the treasure it was to them, putting it away on top of the chifforobe between readings, out of the reach of children's destructive hands. Everyone was talking now about a new book written by a lady who lived in Atlanta, just as they had talked about *Anthony Adverse* a few years before, and Elise was as curious as anyone to read this new book, but knew it was unlikely she would find a copy of *Gone With the Wind* that could be taken in trade for her sewing or for Stan's split kindling.

Henry had been bent over his problems for a little more than half an hour when the frustration finally got the better of him. He made a disgusted sound, then again when the first received no response. He shoved the paper away and sat back on the bench, folding his arms across his chest and meeting Elise's eyes where she sat sewing in her rocker near the fireplace.

"Henry, get your paper and finish your work," Elise said, looking at him, then returning to hand-basting the seam in the blouse she was making for Mrs. Stubblefield. She heard Henry make another disgusted sound.

"Won't nobody ever use this stuff," he said, giving the paper another push for good measure.

"Henry—"

"It's just a waste of time!"

"Henry, you heard me—"

He gave the paper another shove, and this time the copy of *The Adventures of Tom Sawyer* as well. "What good'll it do; I ain't never gonna use it. Bruce Langford's pa lets him stay out of school until all their cotton's picked, and I could—"

"Henry—"

He gave the paper and book another good shove, this time onto the bare wooden floor. "School ain't no use—ask pa; he didn't go much further in school than me, and he does just fine. Ask him—school ain't no use to nobody—"

Elise saw the look that came to Janson's face. His hands had stilled at the basket he had been working on, but his eyes remained fixed on it, on it, and on the splits still held between his fingers. After a moment his gaze moved to the book and paper lying on the floor, then he slowly pushed himself to his feet, stepping back over the bench there at the table. He bent to pick up the book and sheet of paper. There was a silence in the room, a silence even from Henry as Janson again sat on the bench beside Judith, opposite their son.

Janson placed the arithmetic paper on the tabletop, then set the book atop it, his fingers moving lightly over the worn cover before he finally placed a finger beneath the edge of the cover and laid it open on the tabletop. He turned a page, and then another, then several more. Elise held her breath as she watched, for she knew—

"Th' t-two—" Janson began, slowly and falteringly, as he read from the page before him, "boy—boys f—fl—" He stared at the page a moment, then slowly sounded the word out, "—f—fl—lew on an' on, t—to—tow—ard th'—" His voice went on, missing words, skipping some, sounding out so many that the sentences were unintelligible. Elise stared, the tears beginning to move down her cheeks, unable to make herself look away, even knowing the hurt inside him as she watched—her Janson, her proud Janson, and now—

He went on, stumbling, struggling his way to the end of a sentence. Emotion choked his voice, making it shake so badly at times that it could be little understood—but not one tear was shed down his own face. Not one tear.

"—f—f—fear—feared th—they m-m-mig-t be f—fol—fol— mig— t be f—fol—fol— f-o-l-l-o-w-e-d," Janson spelled the word out, unable to comprehend what it meant, "—mig-t be f-fol—" His voice stopped, and he just stared for a moment at the page.

"—be followed—" Henry said, very quietly.

Janson nodded in silence and closed the book, then stood up, stepped back over the bench, and left out through the front door without meeting the eyes of anyone in the room.

Elise stared long and hard at her son, not speaking, but just staring until the boy met her eyes and held them for a moment. She hoped he understood.

She rose from the chair and laid her sewing aside, then made her way to the front door Janson had just gone through. She found him on the porch, leaning against one of the supports for the porch roof. She had intended to go to him, but found that she could not as she stood in the open front door and watched him where he looked out in the darkness over the unpicked acres of cotton. Henry might never understand what his father had done for him today, but Elise did as she stood in the shadows and watched her husband. She understood, and she knew she had married the finest man she would ever know.

"Them charges ain't right," Janson said, standing with his fists clenched at his sides at the scarred old desk in the back of Stubblefield's store. The year's cotton crop had been picked, sold, the split made, and now Stubblefield faced him with his columns of figures and said he had not cleared enough to cover the charge at the store—Janson fought to control his temper as he stood staring down at the old man.

"You callin' me a liar, boy?" Stubblefield peered up at him through squinted eyes. Not again, Janson thought—you are not going to do this to me again.

"I'm sayin' that we don't owe you that much, an' that you know we don't." A whole year's work—gone, with no money left to show for it, nothing to benefit his family. The cotton they had planted, chopped, worked, picked, sold; seeing Elise, Henry, even Catherine, in the fields— and this man said he was left owing at the end of the year.

"Don't nobody call me a liar, boy." Stubblefield rose and stood staring up at him.

"You ain't gonna do this t' me again this year. I worked hard—my whole family worked hard, my wife, my brother-in-law, my children, an' we had a good crop—"

"Well, it weren't good enough."

Janson grabbed him by the collar of his dirty shirt and shoved him back against the desk. "I'll be damned if I'll let you get away with doin' this t' me again this year! I'll be damned if I—" He was yelling into Stubblefield's face, rage filling him. His hands shook as he clenched the grimy collar of the old man's shirt. "You ain't gonna cheat me again this year!"

"Get your hands off me!" He struggled in Janson's grasp, yelling for help from the front of the store. Janson was grabbed roughly from behind and pulled away. Rage boiled within him and he struggled against the two farmers who held him, wanting to get his hands on Stubblefield again, even for just a moment.

He heard the old man's voice yelling behind him as he was dragged through the store and shoved out the door and bodily thrown into the dirt beyond the store's front porch. "I want you off my land!" Stubblefield stood shouting in the open front doorway of the store, glaring at him as Janson slowly regained his feet. "Get your family and th' rest 'a your trash and get off my land—and don't you ever come back!"

Janson was more silent than usual through supper that night. He sat across from Elise, moving his food about with a fork, but eating very little, and then he got up and left the room only halfway through the meal without saying a word.

Elise found him on the front steps, staring out at the newly picked fields. She leaned against one of the uprights that supported the porch roof, trying to think of a way to ask what was bothering him so deeply.

"We got t' leave," he said before she could speak. "I lost my temper, an'—well—I lost my temper—"

She watched him in silence. She had known all along that at some point Janson would tire of Stubblefield taking the entire crop every year, all their hard work—it had only been a matter of time. His temper, his pride—nothing else could have happened.

And, now the time had come. She sat on the step near him as he told her what had taken place.

"He said we didn't even clear enough t' cover th' credit we run at th' store—I lost my temper, an', well—"

She nodded slowly—it had been inevitable. "When do we have to leave?"

"He didn't say; he was just yellin' for us t' get off his land. I guess soon as we can. I don't know where we'll go. I didn't think. I just got mad an'—I know I shouldn't have, but—"

"No." He turned where he sat there on the step to look at her, his face showing surprise at the feeling behind the one word. "We couldn't keep on going like this, year after year. There has to be something else we can do."

"There ain't many jobs t' be had. They keep sayin' times are gettin' better, but it seems t' me like th' Depression's th' same as its been for years." He sighed and looked back out toward the fields of picked cotton plants again. "I guess we'll go back int' town. I don't know what I can find t' do, but I'll be damned if I'm gonna sharecrop for anybody again." There was a bitterness in his voice that she had heard from many people over the past years. "I'm tired 'a losin' half th' crop every year t' somebody just t' use his land, an' then bein' cheated out 'a th' other half. I'm tired 'a seein' you an' Henry an' Catherine worked s' hard, an' us gettin' only deeper an' deeper every year with somebody else takin' all our work an' us gettin' nothin' out 'a it—I ain't never gonna work another man's land again. I'll crop my own land, but nobody else's—I'll be damned if I'll ever sharecrop for anybody again. I'll be damned if I will."

There was determination in his voice, and a tone she recognized so well—his dream, to have his own place, to work his own land and produce a crop that would be all his own. For years that dream had been crushed beneath work and worry, beneath fighting to just get by, and the need to support the family, beneath the weight of the Depression and the burden of struggle just to put food in their mouths and clothes on their backs.

They had even less now than nine years before when they had run off to be married. Times were hard, money lacking from not only the pockets of themselves but of everyone else they knew, and now it was not just the two of them, but the children and Stan to worry about—but, as she looked at him, he seemed very much like the young man who had sat at the edge of that clearing with her back in Endicott County, Georgia, and told her of his dreams, of what he had lost but would one day have again, a home, land, a place as much him as his own soul was, something that no one could ever take from him again.

Looking back now to those days when she had first known him, before he had told her about his dreams, she realized that perhaps she had fallen in love with him because he made her feel safe and protected in those days after Ethan Bennett had attacked her. As she had gotten to know him and his dreams and the determination and pride, that feeling had deepened into something that was now such a part of her that she could not imagine living without it, or living without him. That girl who had wanted to feel safe seemed so young to her now—but there had not been a day since she had been that girl that she had not loved him. They had been through so much, and his dream had to seem farther away than ever—but it was still there. He was just as proud and just as stubborn, still just as determined that one day he would stand on his own land again. He rarely spoke of it now, keeping it locked inside, but it was there—she could often see it in his eyes, hear it in his voice, and for the first time in those nine years she felt a worry inside of her that he might never touch that dream again. How could he, how could they, when just getting by and living seemed struggle enough to fill their days.

"I guess I should 'a held my temper, but I couldn't. A man can only take s' much. I'll find some kind 'a work in town—anything'd be better'n this."

And Elise could only hope that it would be.

Janson found work with the WPA on the Beautification Project in Pine, raking leaves, planting shrubs, cleaning off graves in the City Cemetery, doing hard work in all kinds of weather. Times were tight, but now there was that steady wage coming in every two weeks. They found a three-room shotgun house to rent a few streets in from the edge of town, a house that now seemed almost lavish compared to the house they had lived in on Stubblefield's place. Elise immediately made a sign that said *Sewing Done* and placed it in the front window. There was little sewing to be had, but she found at least some work, making new curtains for the Baptist parsonage, and then altering a wedding dress for the only daughter of a family who lived just a few blocks from downtown. She had thought the alteration job would be an easy one, but the bride made the job anything but easy as she twisted about trying to see herself in the mirror as Elise struggled to pin a straight hem.

Faith Taggart stood on a low table in the living room of her home one afternoon in December, having ascended to its surface with the help of several friends who stood now talking as Elise worked on the dress. They were a giggling bunch, none over seventeen years of age, making Elise, at not quite twenty-six, feel old by comparison. They were talking, as almost everyone else had been in the past days, on the question of whether Great Britain's King Edward VIII would abdicate the throne so he could marry the American divorcee Wallis Warfield Simpson—as the British monarch, he could not marry a divorced woman and remain king. Faith's mother had voiced her opinion before she had left the room, saying it would be lunacy for a king to give up his throne in order to marry a woman.

"Oh, but it's so romantic," Faith had said, twisting about so that Elise feared she would stick her with a pin.

The radio was on, its sound blending with the voices of the giggling girls as Elise attempted to pin a straight hem in spite of the girl she was trying to fit. Mrs. Taggart came back into the room, stopping for a moment to fuss at the decorations on the large Christmas tree in one corner, bending to rearrange again packages beneath it, and straightening to survey her work before coming to join the conversation of the girls.

Then came words from the radio that hushed for a time the female voices in the room. *"At long last I am able to say a few words,"* came the voice of the British monarch, *". . . I have found it impossible to carry the heavy burden of responsibility and to discharge my duties as King as I should wish to, without the help and support of the woman I love. . . . And now we have a new king. . . . God bless you all! God save the king!"*

"He's a fool to give up so much to marry that woman," Mrs. Taggart declared, her lips set in a disapproving pout when Elise glanced up at her.

"Oh, Mama, you just don't have a romantic bone in you."

"I still say he's a fool," the older woman said, standing now to survey Elise's work even more critically than she had her own. "No matter how much he thinks he loves that woman, there are some things more important than love—"

Not very many—Elise thought, sticking the girl at last and swearing to herself that it had been an accident. Not very many.

Living in Pine seemed strange now to Elise who could not forget the night some of the men in this county had burned the shantytown near the tracks and had wanted to lynch Janson. She could not see the smoke-blackened brick that still showed where stores had been rebuilt after the fire without remembering that night, and with it the anger and hatred and the pure fear that had filled her. With convenient amnesia born of embarrassment and shame, people had forgotten what they wanted to do to Janson, to an innocent man, but Elise could not forget. Janson worked now beside men who just a few years before had stood before that police station and had wanted him dead. "I cain't think about what happened," he had told her when she asked him about it. "If I do, I know I'll break somebody's neck—" Though the same men who would have stood by to watch her husband hang now met her eyes with no visible shame or regret, she could not look at them without feeling anger, and a sense of injustice over what had happened to them all—Buddy Eason was free, though he had been gone from the county now since shortly after that night. Buddy Eason she hated, as she knew she would until the day she died.

There was a bad feeling toward the Sanders from some people in Pine because, like so many others, Janson worked on the WPA. Men who had held their jobs through the Depression, who had not known unemployment, hunger, and desperation throughout those years, looked down now on those working under government aid:

"They could find real jobs if they wanted to work—" Elise sometimes heard.

"It's just a boondoggle—"

"Nothin' but a bunch of leaf rakers—"

"Livin' off the government 'cause they're too lazy t' work—"

But Elise knew that it was work created to busy idle hands, to give needed money to put food in stomachs long empty and clothes on backs dressed in rags, work for proud men who had been too long unemployed through no fault of their own.

The WPA workers planted shrubs, re-bound books for a library, repaired and refurbished desks in school buildings, cleaned off the Pine City Cemetery, landscaped city buildings and county property, and built the new City Hall—but it was "made-up work just to give them something to do," they often heard, no matter how hard they worked or how much they accomplished. There should be no pride, no self-respect in made work, they were told—but to Janson, as to most of the others who worked their hours with the WPA, or the young people who could continue their educations because of the NYA, it was respectable work. Any honest work that a man or woman could put hands to to support a family was respectable. Any work a teenager could accomplish that allowed him or her to stay in school was worthy. Let those more fortunate, those who had not been hurt by the Depression, call it a boondoggle—there was still self-respect and pride in work that gave a man back his dignity.

President Roosevelt had been opposed in the '36 election by Republican Alf Landon, who had pledged that he would see that "relief is purged of politics"—but few people on the WPA were concerned with politics. They were concerned only that their children now had food to eat, clothes to wear, and shoes on their feet against the cold months that had worried them all.

Elise had not expected to hear the speech FDR would give at his second inauguration, but found herself listening to it over the radio in a small store. Janson had been rained out of work on the Beautification Project for the third day that week, and he stood beside her in silence as they listened, for all activity in the store had ceased with the first of the President's words, the now long-familiar voice fighting to make itself heard over the sound of rainfall striking umbrellas at the inauguration.

Elise thought that Janson was paying little attention as they listened, but saw his head rise and a peculiar look come to his face as the President spoke the words:

*". . .'each age is a dream that is dying, or one that is coming to birth'. . ."*

The look permanently settling on his features as the President's voice continued

*". . . In this nation I see tens of millions of its citizens—a substantial part of its whole population—who at this very moment are denied the greater part of what the very lowest standards of today call the necessities of life. I see millions of families trying to live on incomes so meager that the pall of family disaster hangs over them day by day. I see millions whose daily lives in city and on farm continue under conditions labeled indecent by a so-called polite society half a century ago. I see millions denied education, recreation, and the opportunity to better their lot and the lot of their children . . . I see one-third of a nation ill-housed, ill-clad, ill-nourished . . ."*

The hour was late by the time Elise got the children into bed and the house had settled down to quiet around them. She sat at the rough wooden table, a kerosene lamp pulled close on its surface to better light her sewing of a dress she was remaking for Judith from one that Catherine had outgrown. Janson stood just across the room, leaning against the mantel and staring down into the flames that burned within the fireplace.

Elise glanced up at him often, seeing the yellow and orange light moving along the high cheekbones and making small plays of light and shadow in his black hair. He had been brooding for much of the day. He had had little to say since the President's speech, but had watched Henry, Catherine, and Judith with a thoughtful look throughout the evening, and that look was still there even though the children were now long asleep in the next room.

He left the fireplace and went to the rocker where Catherine had sat earlier bent over her schoolbooks. The books remained on the small table beside the rocker, the kerosene lamp showing their worn edges. Janson sat in the rocker and let the fingers of one hand trail along the surface of the book that rested on the top.

After a while he rose, taking the book into his hand, and walked across the room to Elise. He set it down before her as she lowered her sewing and looked up at him, Elise finding a resolved and determined look now in his eyes.

"Someday, when I got my own land again, I want t' be able t' read my name on th' papers, an' t' read th' words good enough t' know that it is mine. Th' old ways won't never be back again, an' I guess a man's got t' know how t' read an' write nowadays t' get along an' t' be anythin'—I hear you tellin' Henry that all th' time, an' I guess it's about time I listened."

"I never meant—"

"I know," he said, a light smile touching his lips. "I know—but th' world's changin'; I guess it's done changed, an' maybe I better change with it."

He stepped long legs over the bench and sat down at the table beside her, and Elise found herself looking at him, seeing shame and pride that battled again for a moment in his features. He put one hand on the book and drew it closer.

"You offered me once, a long time ago, an' I told you no. I'm askin' this time, Elise—teach me, I want t' learn."

# CHAPTER TWELVE

As 1937 drew into its final months, it seemed as if hard times might get harder. Already the year had seen disaster, told on the radio in horror-filled words as the German airship, the Hindenburg, crashed on May 6th in Lakehurst, New Jersey. Already Amelia Earhart and her airplane had disappeared, presumably lost forever. Farm prices had dropped, business had slowed, and people were again finding themselves unemployed.

To Henry and his family, the current economic problems affected them little more than did the Hindenburg disaster or the Earhart disappearance—none of it touched them directly, but it was all around them, on the radio, in the talk of most every person, in the general feeling that seemed to exist somewhat within everyone. Disaster had struck and hard times seemed bent to worsen—but, at least for the time being, Janson still held his job on the WPA, there was a rented roof over their heads, food on the table, and adequate, though worn, faded, and often-patched clothes to cover their backs.

Living in town again and Janson working on the WPA had brought the family more security than they had ever known in the years of sharecropping. The little house they rented was better shelter than the sharecropper's shack had ever been, the WPA wage more reliable than any split on crops that might be sold at a fallen price, the little money that Janson, Elise, and Stan each made at least some buffer against a world they had learned could turn against them all at a moment's notice. But, Henry Sanders was not happy. He hated living in town, hated school, and hated most of the boys he had met since moving into Pine. He had already been in more fights in the months he had been in the town school than in all the time they had lived in the country—he wasn't like the kids in town; he knew that, and he was certain the other kids knew it, because they never missed an opportunity to let him know how different he was.

And Reuben Knott and Teddy Wiggins were the worst. There seemed to be nothing about Henry they could even tolerate, not the way he looked, or the way he talked, not the clothes he wore or where he had come from or what his pa did for a living, and they never missed the chance to tell him so, teasing until he would go after one or both of them. That had happened to him already three times in that first week of November, landing him in trouble with the teacher and at home.

He had to stay after school that Thursday, as he had already two days that week. It had been Reuben and Teddy, as it usually was, and Henry had only defended himself—but the teacher had not seen it that way. The teacher rarely saw it his way.

Henry left the school that afternoon long after the other kids had left for the day. Catherine had walked on without him, as she always did, in the rush of girls usually headed in their direction on the way home from school. He knew his mother would know why he was late, and that would only bring him more trouble—I can't win no matter what I do, he told himself, turning down a dirt street that ran along the edge of the colored section of town, as he usually did in the evenings, for it was the shortest route home. Walking by himself gave him time to think, and to get madder—one of these days he would show Reuben and Teddy a thing or two, he told himself.

He had not expected to hear someone call out to him from the yard of a house as he drew near, so he paid little attention until the voice called out a second time, "Hey, you, In'jun Henry—don't you hear me talkin' to you," the words followed immediately by a clump of dead grass and sod hitting him square in the mouth, leaving him spitting dirt and wiping the mess out of his face.

Reuben and Teddy were in the front yard of the house, Teddy reaching down to dig another handful of grass and soil up from the yard, Reuben taking aim with his own volley—

The rock hit Henry in the ribs hard enough to knock the breath out of him, the second, following a moment later, grazing his cheek with a stinging sensation. He tried to dodge out of the way, only to be hit in the throat with another clump of dirt and rocks, his eyes settling on Reuben and the almost-fist-sized rock now in his hand—

"You boys git on outta here!" a heavy-set black woman was suddenly out on the porch behind them, a broom held high in her hand. "Git outta my yard 'fore I set th' dogs on you—git!"

She came down the board steps and out into the yard with amazing speed considering her size, taking a swing at Reuben with the broom, causing him to drop the rock as he dodged away. She caught him with the broom the second time, swatting him hard along the ribcage, and then again, barely touching him with the broomstraw the last time before he and Teddy took off running down between her house and the next, disappearing into a barking of dogs behind the structures, with the unmistakable sound of, "Goddamn nigger," shouted back in her direction by one of the boys.

The woman made a disgusted sound and shook her head, then turned and started back up the steps, pulling herself from one to the next as she leaned heavily on the banister, as if it were difficult now for her to make the climb. Henry saw a boy of about his age standing in the doorway watching her ascend. The boy opened the door for her as she reached the porch. He looked vaguely familiar to Henry, but Henry did not care. He looked away, feeling the hot sting of tears come into his eyes—he was not going to cry, he told himself. He was nine years old now—he was not going to cry.

He moved back toward the edge of the street, then sat down on the ground with his back to a large tree at the edge of the woman's yard, nursing the pain in his side where the rock had hit him. He felt the tears come no matter what he did to stop them, and he reached up to wipe them away, angry with himself that he could not keep it from happening.

"You okay?" he heard, and he looked up to find the boy now standing over him.

Henry looked away again, wiping at one cheek with the back of a hand, refusing to let this kid see him cry. "Yeah," he said, the word coming out with an angry sound. He drew his knees up toward his chest, resting his crossed arms over them. The boy sat on the ground not too far away.

"You're Henry Sanders, ain't you?"

Henry nodded.

"My name's Isaac. My daddy's Nathan Betts; he used to work in the mill with your daddy—"

Still Henry did not say anything, keeping his eyes set somewhere down the road.

"You were with your daddy one time when he was out peddlin' baskets. You came by our house and we bought some egg baskets from you."

For a long moment Henry did not say anything. Finally he offered, "Ain't your mama gonna wonder where you are?" as he pushed himself to his feet. He was hurting and he was mad and he had no intention of sitting here talking.

"My mama's dead," Isaac said, his words stopping Henry.

"I'm sorry," Henry found himself saying, for that was what grownups said whenever somebody died. He did not know anything else to say.

Isaac got to his feet as well. "I don't know much about her; she died when I was born." He considered Henry. "You wanna come in the house and clean up some before you go home? You got dirt all over you and your cheek's bleedin'."

Henry reached up and touched the stinging sensation at his cheek, drawing his fingers away to find traces of both blood and dirt on them.

"My auntie won't mind," Isaac said. "Come on." He took Henry by the sleeve and drew him toward the house. The woman who had run Reuben and Teddy off was standing just inside the front door watching them as they reached the porch. Her dark eyes stayed fixed on Henry until Isaac spoke. "It was him them boys was rockin'. He needs to get cleaned up before he goes on home." Still the woman stared at him, until she finally nodded and said:

"If them two is got it in for you, then you cain' be too bad."

Henry looked for Isaac Betts on his way home each afternoon after that. Isaac's walk from the colored school at the edge of town usually allowed him to reach his house before Henry could pass on his way from the school he attended uptown. On the days when the weather was good, Henry often found him sitting on his front steps. They would walk together part of the way toward where Henry lived, and then usually join in whatever ball game was going on in the big empty lot at the point where the white and colored sections of town met. Reuben and Teddy at times showed up in the mix of boys, both black and white, who played ball in the afternoons, but for the most part they ignored Henry on those afternoons.

It was during the days at school that the picking would resume.

At times Teddy's mother would come looking for him at the ballfield. She would yank him out of the group of boys waiting to bat, or drag him from his place out on the field, yelling all the while, "You know you're not to supposed to play with those nigger kids—wait 'til your father finds out. You just wait."

Henry knew that Reuben's parents would never think to look for him here. Reuben's mother was too involved with her church group and her charity work, and his father was too busy trying to pretend he still had a job. Jacob Knott had not worked for more than a year now, but he still got up and dressed in a suit each morning. He still drove his car downtown and had coffee at the Main Street Restaurant, and then he sat there all day. Sometimes Henry walked by the restaurant after school in the evenings just to see him inside in his suit and tie. Henry had heard people say the Knotts were living off their savings, and that the savings were close to gone now. Folks said Mr. Knott was too proud to go to the relief people, or to accept a job on the WPA—considering how Reuben and Teddy talked about the job Henry's father had on the Beautification Project, Henry could well understand that Mr. Knott might feel that way. They called Janson a "leaf raker," and more often than not called Henry "reliefer," when they were not calling him "In'jun Henry."

Sometimes Henry found himself wishing that his father wore suits and had coffee at the Main Street Restaurant all day. That way no one would poke fun at him.

Reuben and Teddy and other boys like them made going to school each day the closest thing to hell that Henry could imagine. They loved to get him in the middle whenever they were playing dodgeball, giving them the greatest pleasure in trying to knock him senseless with the ball, bruising him up so badly several times that he was black and blue for days afterward. They would collapse his knees out from under him if they could get behind him in line, bending into the crooks of his knees and sending him to the ground, and had shoved him down the front steps of the school twice by doing it in the afternoons just as they were leaving, then running off before he could get to his feet and lay hold on either one of them.

No matter what they did to him physically, though, they knew nothing would get to him as much as the things they might say:

"Hey, reliefer!"

"Hey, In'jun Henry, why don't you do us a war dance!"

"Hey, Henry—why's your daddy th' only Holy-Rollin' In'jun on the WPA?—'cause they cain't stand t' smell but one?"

"Hey, Henry, you like niggers or somethin'—you're always hangin' aroun' that nigger, Isaac—"

"Hey, reliefer, your daddy ain't nothin' but a leaf raker. My daddy says he could get a real job if he tried—"

Even the grownups made him feel out of place. The new school year began with lessons about how white people had civilized the Indians. That was a far cry from the stories his father told him, of how the Cherokees had been rounded up at gunpoint and marched west, causing many to die. After the lessons in school, Henry felt that everyone was staring at him, because he knew in many ways he looked more Cherokee than white.

He tried—but only once—to tell his teacher the stories his father had taught him.

"That's all nonsense," Mrs. Chappell said, staring down at him sharply from where she stood erasing the blackboard with harsh, jerking motions, her arms jutting outward into sharp elbows, and the bun on the back of her head bobbing up and down with each movement. Henry felt small and dismissed at her side, for, though he was tall for his now ten years, the teacher was much taller by far, taller, in fact, than any woman Henry had ever known. "The Indians were nothing but savages before white people came to this country," she said, disapproval for the subject in every line of her angular body. "Your Cherokees couldn't read or write either one, and they knew nothing of God. They ought to have been grateful for all they were given—"

Henry wanted to tell her that the Cherokee had their own written language, from an alphabet invented by a man who was half-Cherokee and half-white, just like Henry's father. He stared at Mrs. Chappell, remembering instead the story his father had told of how his grand-mother had her mouth washed out with soap in school for speaking Cherokee and not English, and, somehow, he knew a little of how she must have felt.

He had hoped the new school year would be better, but it turned out to be much the same as the last. By December of 1938, he had gotten into more fights with Reuben or Teddy or someone else in their crowd than he had in much of the previous year. There had already been two fights just within that first week of December, the most recent of which had left Henry with a black eye. He had taken a paddling for that fight, but, still, when Reuben had shoved him up against the wall in the classroom this morning, Henry had been unable to keep himself from shoving back. Mrs. Chappell had broken up the scuffle before a fight could break out, and Henry had had to stay after school. He could not understand how she could never miss whatever it was that he did, but never once saw what the other boys had done that had made him react.

"I don't care if he shoved you first," she told him that day, standing behind him as she made him write 'I will not fight' on the blackboards over and over again. "You had no business shoving him back."

He left the school that afternoon long after all the other kids had gone home, having been made to erase and then wash the blackboards before the scarecrowish Mrs. Chappell was finished with him. He thought Reuben and Teddy had left with the rush of others, but they were waiting for him on the low wall near the front of the school, directly along the path that Henry would have to take to go home. Henry did not hesitate, even though he knew what would happen.

"You have to do a rain dance to get the water to wash the blackboards, reliefer?" Teddy asked.

"Hey, Henry, I hear they're putting your father off the WPA," Reuben said, a grin on his face. "They say he's too lazy even for government work." He waited, and Henry knew he was waiting only for him to react.

When Henry said nothing, he continued on.

"They're makin' a rule not to let any more damn In'jun's on the WPA, and then they're gonna run him and you and them little squaw sisters of yours out of town—and your mama, too. I heard tell she ain't nothin' but a whore anyway, to have laid with a damn—"

Henry was on him before he had time to think about what he was doing. He hit Reuben hard in the face with his books, and then went after Teddy for good measure, grabbing him hard around the middle and shoving him into Reuben, sending them both sprawling to the ground. Reuben was back on his feet in seconds, hitting Henry hard in the mouth, leaving him tasting blood and reeling backwards as Teddy laid into him, too.

"Henry Sanders, stop it! Stop it this instant!" Henry could hear Mrs. Chappell yelling as she ran toward them, but he did not care. He was in trouble already, but he would finish this fight.

The other two boys seemed to back off immediately, just trying to fend him away now. Mrs. Chappell pulled Henry away, grabbing him by an ear and twisting it hard.

"Henry Sanders, I've told you—" He was hauled about to face her, giving in to the painful grip on his ear. "And, you boys, I know you know better." She turned on Reuben and Teddy, now looking remarkably innocent.

"We didn't do anything," Reuben said. "We were just sitting here—"

"Yeah, he started it," Teddy said.

"Did you Henry?"

The ear she held in her grasp hurt like hell—but Henry would not whine or try to wriggle away. He looked at Reuben and Teddy, who were grinning at him now that Mrs. Chappell's back was turned to them.

"I—"

"Did you?" she demanded, yanking on his ear for emphasis, and making him bite his tongue to keep from crying out.

"Course he did—see, he won't say nothing—"

Henry found he could not speak—he would not make excuses as Reuben and Teddy were doing. He glared up at the teacher the best he could from the position she held his head in by her painful grip on his ear, trying to keep a look of defiance on his face.

She forgot the other boys altogether with the look he gave her and jerked him forward, toward the school building. He half walked, half ran, to keep up with her, convinced his ear would separate from his head at any moment—he was in trouble, and he knew it. But, he was always in trouble. And he knew the whipping he was about to get would be nothing compared to the one he would get from his pa when he reached home.

Elise was often angry with her son, and only slightly less often exasperated with him. He never seemed to listen, but to do whatever he took into his head, no matter the consequences.

She walked beside him the next afternoon as they left the school building—just like his father, she kept thinking. He's just like his father, with that same temper that would be apt to do most anything. But, unlike Janson, Henry held little control over his temper—more like Alfred, she amended, feeling chilled at the thought of Henry's temper being more like that of the brother who had died attempting to defend her reputation so many years before.

Janson had given Henry a whipping with his belt the night before, as soon as he saw the note sent home by Henry's teacher, but Henry had not cried, and he still would not say what the fight had been about.

Henry walked beside her in angry silence, his dark brows lowered. He was furious that his mother had promised Mrs. Chappell that there would be no more fights, and angrier still that she had apologized for his having gotten into this one—she could read it on his face, and he reminded her even more strongly of Janson. He looked so much like his father anyway, with the same black hair and features, and the green eyes, the pride in his bearing, the injured dignity of the uplifted chin. He had said nothing while she talked to his teacher, just watched the two, refusing to sit down as he stood with his head held high, meeting her eyes with anger in his own over her promise and her words of apology.

He had spoken few words to her since her talk with Mrs. Chappell. His pride had been insulted by her words, as it had been insulted the day before by whatever the two boys had said or done—his pride and his temper. Elise was afraid that one or the other would be her son's undoing.

"Henry, I meant what I said to Mrs. Chappell. There will be no more fights; do you hear me?"

"Yes'm, I hear you." He did not turn or lift his head to meet her eyes, but just walked beside her, staring straight ahead. His voice was even, showing no emotion.

"Henry—"

"You said no more fights."

She looked at him for a moment. He was getting so tall, and almost ten-and-a-half—God, could it have been ten and a half years ago? She was getting older, almost 28—that wasn't old, but Henry could certainly make her feel as if she were old. She sighed and shook her head. "Don't try to get around me, Henry Sanders—I mean there had better be no more fights. Do you understand me?"

"Yes'm."

"And?"

"There won't be no more—any more—fights—"

She allowed herself to feel a moment's relief. If nothing else, her son was honest. If he said no more fights, then—

"There won't be any more fights, as long as nobody says what they said to me again—" He continued to look straight ahead.

"Henry—" She stopped where they were on the sidewalk and put a hand on his shoulder, bringing his eyes to her. He met her gaze without blinking, his head held proud, but with no defiance—he spoke his mind, and to him there was no defiance in that. "Mrs. Chappell said that if you get into one more fight, you will be out of school. She was not joking—did you think she was joking?"

"No, mam."

"Well, if—"

"But, if they say the same thing to me again—"

"Henry—" She looked at him, exasperated, and then sighed—stubborn and pigheaded, just like Janson. "What did they say?"

He met her eyes for a long moment, not speaking.

"Henry—"

Still, he would not speak, but just looked at her instead with Janson's green eyes. Just a year ago he would have told her what had been said. Here in town he was growing increasingly silent. She tried to imagine what the boys' insults had been about—his clothes, his friendship with Isaac Betts, his Cherokee heritage—but she was beginning to wonder now if there was not more to it. What did boys tease and aggravate each other about? Girls? Their backgrounds? Their family? Their speech and manner of dress? She did not know, but she wondered, seeing it trapped somehow within her son.

His manners and behavior were for the most part acceptable, and were the best she could manage from him, as were those of her daughters. His speech was very much like Janson's when he did not pay particular attention to it, which was most of the time, unless she was near; but most of the children in the town talked much as he did. They had little, but few families in Pine had much more, and he and the girls were dressed as well as they possibly could be on what Janson brought home from the WPA, and on what she could make from sewing. His clothes were old, but clean and neatly patched, as were hers, Janson's, the girls', and Stan's, and most everyone else she knew in their part of town the past few years—the

Depression had not affected the Sanders alone, after all.

He was one-quarter Cherokee, but had been reared to be proud of that blood, told the stories that Nell Sanders had raised her son on from the time he had been in the cradle, and Henry could now recite those tales almost as well as his father—but such were the things that children teased about, skin that was darker and a look unlike their own. Henry was proud, and teasing would not sit well with him—but to not talk of it?

Girls—but he was only ten; did boys start to think about girls so young? She could remember her own brothers tormenting each other into fights with teasing about one girl or another—but to not be willing to talk about it?

"What's wrong, Henry? You know you can tell me."

"Nothing's wrong, Mama," he answered, then changed the subject. "Can I go on? I promised to help Mrs. McClarey hang curtains."

Elise sighed. She knew she would get nothing out of him. He was just like his father, she thought. Well, let his father see what he can do with him tonight.

"Go on—but come straight home right after. No playing. Your father will want to talk to you."

"I know." Henry seemed to sigh without making a sound or a movement. "I'll be home in a little while."

Elise watched him cut across the street, after waiting for a rattling truck to pass, and hurry down a way before cutting down a side street. Mrs. McClarey lived only a few houses down from them. She was an elderly widow woman with no grandchildren, and she often plied children from the neighborhood with treats of homemade cookies or cake in exchange for simple chores to be done at her house, mainly, Elise knew, just to have their company.

Elise reached Main Street and turned her steps toward the downtown area. She wanted to check at the drygoods store for the new fabrics that would have come in on the truck from Birmingham that morning. Besides, she needed a spool of blue thread and a paper of pins to finish the dress she had been working on for the past several days for a woman who had already paid her to make two others. The small store near her house sold thread and pins, but the thread was so old that it often broke even when sewing by hand, and thread, like pins, needles, and everything else, was cheaper in town.

She continued to worry about Henry as she walked, but all thought of Henry's predicament left Elise as she crossed the street when she reached downtown and saw Buddy Eason standing just at the edge of the road, blocking the way of a young woman as she tried to get into a car.

It was the first time Elise had seen him since the night he had tried to incite the mob to hang Janson for the crime he and his friends had committed. He had never spent one day in jail for what he had done, or for the burning of downtown, or even for Mr. Brown's death—a cold chill moved down her spine. He was free, had been free since then, and was back in town now, roaming the streets—free to do anything he pleased to anyone he chose with the full protection of the Eason name, influence, and money. And Buddy Eason, she well knew, could be capable of anything.

"Come on—you know you want it," he was saying as Elise drew near enough to hear his words. He blocked the girl's car door with one knee, keeping her from opening it enough to enter the vehicle and escape him.

"Leave me alone. I've already told you—" The girl's hair was short and black, reminding Elise more of the bobs that had been in style ten years before than the way most women were wearing their hair nowadays. She was small, not even as tall as Buddy's shoulder, and looked to be about nineteen or twenty—Elise had seen her in town before, had done sewing for a relative of hers, and thought her name was Peggy.

"You know I could make you feel real good—" Buddy reached out a hand as if to touch the girl's breast through her dress, not seeming to care that they were on the busiest part of Main Street, and she drew a hand back to slap him. He caught her wrist before her hand could make contact with his face and grinned at her as she jerked it away.

A man walking past on the sidewalk had seen what happened, and he hurried on now—Elise saw the man look away just before he had quickened his pace, and she knew the girl had seen as well. They all knew Buddy was safe to harass her or anyone at will, here on Main Street or anywhere else in town. People were just as afraid of him now as they had been years before—Elise had seen it in the man's eyes as he had hurried past her. Anyone who opposed Buddy would suffer, but not Buddy. Never Buddy—and Buddy Eason knew that most of all.

The girl jerked at the car door, making Buddy laugh.

"You sure look good when you're mad," he said to her, his eyes moving over her now openly there on the street. "Now, why don't we—" But he glanced up as Elise came even with them on the sidewalk, and his eyes met hers in a cold, hate-filled stare. The girl took the opportunity to pull the car door open as he was distracted, and slip inside.

Buddy did not seem to notice as the car cranked up and backed away into the street, almost striking another car. He turned his eyes toward the departing car and the girl he had been harassing, then brought them back to Elise, and Elise found her steps quickening, her hurry to be away from him no less than that of the escaped girl.

She glanced back at Buddy, to find his eyes still on her—there had been a horrid promise in that stare.

"Hey, In'jun Henry, I hear the reason your daddy's in Eason County is because they ran him off the reservation," Reuben yelled at Henry on a Sunday afternoon in mid-March, standing at the edge of the ballfield where Henry had spent much of the afternoon after church. "I hear tell he was the worst of all the In'juns they had there—"

Henry had been playing ball with Isaac and other boys and was only just now headed home. Isaac had left earlier, his sister Gloria having come to the ballfield to fetch him to supper, just as Henry knew he would have supper waiting when he reached home—Teddy was there, along with three other boys who often hung around him and Reuben when they were at school. They had been waiting for him to pass, waiting for him safely away from the school grounds in a time and place where no one else would be present.

"Is that the reason he can't do much but rake leaves now, reliefer?" Teddy asked. "Cause he's just a damn drunk Indian?"

"I seen the red son-of-a-bitch picking up trash in the cemetery," one of the other boys said. "He had this big patch on the seat of his overalls, looked like some damn tramp out there—"

"You know why all you Indians and the other coloreds are so dark, don't you, Henry—God made you that way to mark you so everybody'd know you ain't no good—"

"You better shut your damn trap," Henry said, stopped now before them. He clenched his fists at his side, staring at Reuben. He knew he was outnumbered five to one, but if they said one more word he would not be able to stop himself.

"Make me, you red-In'jun nigger—" The words had barely left Reuben's lips when he shoved Henry backwards, and suddenly Henry was on him, hitting him hard in the stomach before the other boys could descend on him.

Several held him down, several pounded at his body, even as he fought to free himself. There were boys all over him, everywhere he turned, hitting him in the face, the side, the nose, his eye, in his stomach. It lasted only moments, and then two men from a nearby house dragged the boys off him and Henry tried to struggle to his feet as the other boys ran away.

"You all right, son?" one man asked, taking him by an arm to help him stand.

"I ain't your son." Henry jerked out of the man's grasp and got to his feet on his own, then left the ballfield and made his way into the street, wiping his bleeding nose against his shirt sleeve.

♣

Elise almost dropped a plate when Henry entered the kitchen that evening. His nose had been bleeding, and dried blood now crusted over his upper lip and stained the front of his shirt. One eye was almost swollen shut, his lower lip puffy, his clothes ripped, covered with grass stains, dried blood, and red dirt. She crossed the room quickly to him, but he jerked away from her the moment she touched his arm.

"Henry—oh, my God—"

Pure anger was in his eyes as he met her gaze, and he pulled away and went out onto the back porch, leaving the door open. Elise tried to follow, but Janson took hold of her arm, rising to his feet from where he had been sitting at the table, and held her back. "Leave him be," he said quietly, his eyes on her for a moment before they moved back to look at the boy through the open rear door, seeing him now leaning against the support for the porch roof.

"But, he's hurt—"

"He's mad as hell worse'n he's hurt—let me see about him."

"But—"

"No," Janson said. "Let me see about him."

Henry did not raise his eyes as Janson walked out on the porch. Janson took up the bucket that rested on the shelf by the door, a dipper and ragged towel beside it, and went out into the yard to draw water from the well, looking back toward the porch and the boy who was now standing staring across the distance with his eyes on Janson.

He returned to the porch to set the bucket on the old straight chair there, then dipped the clean handkerchief from his pocket into the cold water and reached up to wash the blood from Henry's face, but the boy jerked back, refusing his touch. For a moment Janson met a gaze as green as his own, and an anger that was familiar, and, when he tried to wipe the blood from the boy's face again a moment later, Henry allowed it, though his eyes, even the one almost swollen shut, never once left his father's face.

Janson dunked the now blood-stained handkerchief back into the water, squeezed it out, then held it to Henry's nose, tilting the boy's head back to try to stop the nosebleed, the boy's eyes continuing to meet his over the cloth and the hand that pinched his nostrils.

"How many was there?" Janson asked at last.

Henry did not answer, then a mumbled response came from behind the cloth held against his nose. "Five."

Janson nodded, taking the handkerchief away to see if the nosebleed had stopped, then, seeing the seep of blood continuing, he wet the handkerchief again and pinched the boy's nose and tilted his head back again. "Looks t' me like it ain't too smart t' get int' a fight when you're s' bad outnumbered," he said, meeting the anger in the boy's gaze. "They start it?"

"Yeah—" Not "yes, sir" as the boy would have said only the space of a few months before.

"An', you had t' finish it."

"Yeah."

Janson knew that there was more to this than the fights of children. He could see it in the boy's eyes. Could see it, and something more. "What started it?" he asked at last, as he had intended from the moment he had stopped Elise from following the boy out onto the porch.

Henry's eyes, the one swollen until Janson knew he could little see through it, and the other open and angry, met him steadily. The boy did not answer, but he also did not turn his eyes away.

"What started it?" Janson asked again, lowering the handkerchief to stare at the boy—his face was so beaten, the lower lip swollen until it no longer held its shape, one eye almost battered shut, swelling now to the browline, and a trickle of blood beginning to seep again from his nose. "This cain't keep goin' on, Henry. It's got t' stop—now, I want t' know what started it."

"It wasn't nothing—"

"I want t' know." His voice rose in anger, in an impotent rage at something he could not identify. His hand tightened on the wet handkerchief until he felt the water seep between his fingers and run down across the back of his fist.

"It wasn't nothing," Henry said, his voice rising as well.

"Henry—"

"I said it wasn't nothing!" The boy pulled away and ran off the porch, down into the back yard, and across it toward the darkness of the woods until he was swallowed up by the shadows at the edge of the pines.

# Chapter Thirteen

Cassandra Price sat behind a typewriter at the mill office early on the second Monday afternoon in July of 1939. There was a blank sheet of paper rolled into the machine before her, and a hand-written letter in old Mr. Eason's cramped-up handwriting that she was supposed to be transcribing, but she could not keep her mind on the work. She had taken her lunch break early today, taking Grace Taylor's usual time as her own with little warning to the older woman, as soon as she had seen Buddy Eason leaving the mill that morning. Buddy had a habit of taking off in the middle of the day not to return until well into evening, if at all, and Cassandra had made a point of leaving this morning at the same moment, catching up with him on the front steps of the mill office to loop her arm through his, pressing her breast against him.

"Hey, Buddy, how about taking a girl out to eat today?" she asked, staying close against him. In the two months she had been at the mill, he had been all over her whenever she'd given him the slightest opportunity, and she had done her best to keep him at arms-length. It had been an interesting game, but she was tired of the game now.

She had only taken the job typing so she could get close to him in the first place. Keeping him at arms length now was not part of the plan.

They had not even made it out of the mill parking lot that morning. He pulled her toward his grandfather's Cadillac, then got to the point there in the back seat of the old man's car with little preliminaries. It took him little time, but that did not matter; he had accomplished what she wanted with the sound of the mill machinery to accompany them.

Cassandra had found no pleasure in it, but pleasure had been no part of the reason she had taken him. He had finished inside of her and that was the only thing she had wanted in the first place.

If she had her way, Buddy Eason would be a father from that grunting little performance.

Cassandra smiled as she stared at the blank sheet of paper rolled into the typewriter before her. Buddy had money and power and the Eason name, and he could get her out of this mill village. He would marry her once she was pregnant; she had no doubt of that—and, if he did not agree to do the right thing by her, she would simply cry out her story to his grandfather. Walter Eason would never allow his first great-grandchild to be born out of wedlock. Buddy would be made to marry her, whether he wanted to or not—after all, that was the way the world worked, Cassandra told herself.

That was how her own mother had gotten her father to marry her.

Buddy had driven away and left her at the mill not long after they finished, and Cassandra had cleaned up as best she could in the women's lavatory before she returned to her desk. Old Grace had looked at her as if she knew exactly what went on in the parking lot—the old woman's stare was somehow unnerving. She looked as if she thought there was something that ought to be said, and, clearing her throat and rising to her feet, old Grace came around her desk to stand beside Cassandra where she sat at her typewriter.

"Cassandra, you know you're a pretty girl," Grace Taylor said. "There is no reason you have to cheapen yourself just to get a man to pay attention to you."

Cassandra stared up at her. "One of these days I'm going to own this place," she said at last, lifting her chin as she stared into the old woman's eyes, "and, when I do, the first thing I'm going to do is put your fat ass out in the street."

She stared at the surprise that came to the old woman's face, then turned back at last to the work before her.

❧

Buddy Eason stood in the lawyer's office on Main Street the following Friday evening. He had been sent here to take care of business, but
the business was completed now. He had signed his name and pushed
papers about, which was all that it seemed he ever did anymore—but he
continued to stay, even though the lawyer's office was now open long
beyond their normal closing. He knew old man Porter would never dare
ask him to leave, though Porter's secretary and his partner had both left
long before, and the heavy-set Negro woman who cleaned the offices at
night was already at work.

Buddy watched her, this very dark-skinned woman Porter had called
Esther. She was mopping, moving her mop bucket back and away from
them, as if she were certain they were about to leave. Buddy intentionally
tracked the area she had just finished mopping, feeling a touch of
satisfaction go through him as she had to go back to mop it again, and
again a few minutes later as he tracked the area once more.

He lifted his foot and placed in on the edge of the mop bucket as she
started to move it away, realizing that she knew now what he was doing,
and that she had no intention of removing his newly tracked footprints
again. He continued to talk to Porter, discussing his grandfather's plans
for the land he had just bought, but he also watched the woman—she
was angry; Buddy knew that, though he knew she would never dare to
show it. He could see it in her dark brown eyes as they met his briefly, and
even in her stiffened posture as she moved away and began to mop a fresh
area of the floor with a mop she could not now rinse out for the presence
of his foot resting at the top edge of her bucket. She had turned her back
to him, and that made him angry, for he could no longer see her face, or
her reaction to what he was about to do.

He lifted his foot from the edge of the mop bucket and placed his toe
against it, then pushed, intending to spill it over, but it slid slightly on the
floor instead, sloshing the contents up against its sides as it went, then
again as he tried once more. At last he placed his foot again at the top and
tried to tip it. He had intended it to spill out sideways, flooding over the
office floor so that she would have to clean it up, but it turned instead,
rolling back on its round bottom edge to pour out warm water and

soapsuds over his shoes and the lower part of his trouser legs, then it almost tripped him, making him catch hold of the nearby chair as his foot slipped downward and into the bucket itself.

He cursed and kicked the bucket away, sending it to a clattering stop against the far wall there in the secretary's area. He could hear Porter apologizing, the fat lawyer's words of horror at what had happened, even though he had to know Buddy had done it to himself—but Buddy could not listen to him. He was certain the woman was laughing at him; he was certain of it, though she had not made a sound. He could still not see her face, and that made him all the more certain—the goddamn nigger, he told himself, feeling soapy water mush in his shoes as he took a step and then stopped again. The goddamn nigger—I'll show her. The goddamn—

"Are you a crazy white boy or something?" Isaac's cousin, Wilson Jakes, asked Henry the following afternoon as the three boys stood on the sidewalk before Patterson's Drug Store on Main Street. They had been playing ball earlier in the day along with the other kids who frequented the vacant lot between the white and black sections of town, and had only stopped when Teddy Wiggins's father and two other men Henry had never seen before had come to the lot looking for Teddy, and then had stayed, trying to start trouble with some older boys who had been playing at the field. Henry, Isaac, and Wilson had walked toward downtown to pass the time, and Henry had suggested they spend the afternoon at the picture show, never thinking—

"You really think they're gonna let two colored boys and a white boy sit together in the picture show?" Wilson asked, looking at Henry as if he had lost his mind for bringing up the subject.

"I—" He started to say that he did not know, but stopped himself. He did know. White folks and black folks did not sit together in the movie theater, any more than they did anywhere else in Pine. White folks sat in the seats on the main floor of the picture show, and black folks sat in the seats up in the balcony above. Henry had seen the signs that said "White Only" and "Colored Only" posted in the theater, just as he had seen them on lavatory doors in buildings, and above the two water fountains in the back of the Five and Dime there on Main Street. That was the way things were. It was just hard to think of things being that way when your best friend was black. Henry did not see any difference between himself and Isaac. They were almost the same age, and their fathers were friends as well—and both Henry and Isaac had sisters they didn't get along with. Isaac's sisters were older, but that didn't make much difference; sisters were sisters, no matter how old.

Wilson shook his head now as he stared at Henry. He was a year older than Isaac's eleven-and-a-half years, which made him a year and a half Henry's senior, and he had a habit of treating Henry as if he thought he was still a little kid. He gave another shake of his head when Henry did not respond. "You are a crazy white boy," he said at last, a dismissive tone in his voice.

"I'm only three-parts white," Henry said, although he was unsure as to why he was saying it. "My grandma was Cherokee; my pa's only half white," realizing as he said the words that they sounded somehow like an apology.

Isaac changed the subject, taking Henry's arm almost as if he were trying to lead him out of the situation. "I'm hungry, Wilson—let's go on over to Fluellen's and get some cheese and crackers," he said, nodding his head toward the grocery across the way. Wilson agreed, and, as he often did, started just a step ahead of the two younger boys as he headed for the edge of the sidewalk. Henry followed, glad that Isaac had redirected the conversation—Henry had not liked it the times when Reuben and Teddy had called him colored, and he had found out today he did not like being called white if it meant being called crazy at the same time. He looked down at where Isaac's hand rested on his arm, and then at his own hand when Isaac released him—if I was to cut myself and bleed, he wondered, would it be white people's blood, or Cherokee?

And he found himself wondering how it was that anyone could tell.

As he stepped down off the sidewalk just behind Wilson and Isaac, he saw a car door open outward and directly into Wilson, hitting him hard in the side. Wilson stepped back, rubbing at his arm, his eyes on the tall, heavy-set man who slowly got out from behind the wheel of the vehicle. The man looked at him, then turned to examine the edge of the door that had struck the twelve-year-old, and Henry had the distinct impression that the man had hit Wilson deliberately—but grownups didn't hit kids on purpose, Henry told himself.

The man at last turned back to Wilson. He was tall, almost as tall as Henry's father, but much heavier of build. His face was full and close to being jowly, his gray eyes lost in the heaviness of his features—but they were mean eyes, Henry thought, finding himself using a term that his sister, Judith, sometimes used. If ever in his ten-and-a-half years Henry had seen mean eyes, then these were mean eyes, cold and gray, and with almost no feeling in them.

"You goddamn little nigger," the man said, staring at Wilson, sending a shock through Henry, not at the words, but at the hatefulness of them, "you almost scratched my car."

Wilson just stared at him, which seemed to make the man madder. Henry saw the man's fists knot up, and he thought he would hit Wilson, but Wilson only stared up at him in return, then started past him, never having said a word.

Isaac and Henry followed, Henry glancing up at the man as he drew even with him. Recognition seemed to come to the man's features as he stared down at Henry, a look of recognition, and something more.

Henry followed Wilson and Isaac across the street. Just as he stepped up onto the sidewalk at the other side, he turned back one last time—the man was still staring after them.

Henry had never seen such a look of hatred.

The boy was Janson Sanders's son—Buddy Eason told himself a short while later as he stood at the side of the street between his car and the next. He stared after the three boys long after they had disappeared through the door of Fluellen's Grocery. There was no doubt—the straight, black hair; the features; the coloring; the green eyes so like those of the man Buddy Eason hated most in the world. It had been a startling moment, seeing those features on the face of the boy, as if Janson Sanders was made all over again.

Buddy started across the street almost without thought. He intended to find the three boys, to go and cower down Sanders's son and send him home to tell his daddy about the man who had scared him. He paid little attention to the cars as he crossed, and only barely noticed the loud blast of a horn just before he stepped up on the sidewalk at the other side—but that blast brought a face to the window of the office before him there in the line of buildings as he reached the sidewalk, and eyes that met his for a brief instant before the blinds were hurriedly dropped back into place.

He was standing directly before the door to Porter's law office. It was the girl, Esther, who had laughed at him the night before. Buddy smiled, all thought of the three boys leaving his mind now at the prospect of finding her there alone. He knew no one else would be working at the law office on a Saturday morning.

It was time for a little payback.

Esther Tipton tried to thumb the lock on the door before Buddy Eason could reach it. Her hand closed over the knob, one thumb moving up to push at the locking mechanism—but then the knob was twisting in her hands, the door coming inward against her. She shoved against it, trying to force it shut—but Buddy Eason's foot was in the door, blocking it, and he was shoving it inward—

As the door came back into her chest, she moved away, trying to distance herself from him as he entered the room and then turned to close the door after himself.

"Mr. Porter's gonna be back any minute. You better go on," Esther said, hearing the lie shaking in her own voice as he turned back to look at her—she should never have come in today to finish cleaning while the office was empty. She knew that. She should never—

"Lawyers don't come in on Saturdays," he said, very quietly, staring at her, and she felt a knot of fear tightening in her stomach at the look there in his eyes as he started across the room in her direction.

"I mean it; you better go on." She backed away, keeping the desk between them, a table, a heavy chair—she didn't know what he could be capable of doing to a woman found alone on a Saturday morning, but she had heard talk. Her eyes moved toward the door—if she could get past him and out onto the sidewalk, then everything would be fine. He would never dare to follow her outside.

She tried to make it past him, not to run but to push on past, but he caught her with one massive hand and brought her around to face him, then slung her backwards onto the floor so hard that all the breath was knocked out of her with the shock that moved up along her spine—then he was on top of her, his weight pressing her into the wood flooring. His hand clamped down on her mouth and nose, almost ending her ability to breathe as he stared down at her—she could see it in his eyes. She could see it—but still she refused to believe until she felt his free hand yank her skirt up. She tried to bite the hand covering her mouth, tried to get enough air in to scream as she felt him grab hold of her underclothing, her fingers clawing at his eyes, striking him, drawing blood from his hand as she tried to drag it from her face—then he hit her so hard that consciousness started to leave her. Don't let him do it—she begged to God. Please don't let him—then he hit her again and all thought began to fade. There was an awful moment of intrusion as he fumbled between her legs, then pain as he forced himself upward into her.

Then Esther knew nothing but darkness.

She became conscious again only after it was over. Buddy was leaning against the desk, looking down at where she lay on the floor, when the woman began to move, to become gradually aware of where she was and what had happened to her. She moved onto her side, then slid herself back and away from him, to press herself into the corner with her back against the wall—she had not looked at him, and Buddy liked that.

"You'll think before you laugh at another white man again, won't you?" he asked, moving toward her. He hoped that she would cringe away, but she did not, and he found that disappointing. She had moved into a sitting position against the wall, her knees drawn up as she rocked slightly, a stunned look on her face. She did not meet his eyes, though the tears flowed freely down her cheeks now. "Do you have any idea what I'll do to you if you tell anybody what happened here today?" he asked, but still she did not respond. "I'll tell them we were having fun and you like it rough—and who do you think they'll believe, a nigger like you, or me? Then I'll hurt you bad the next time." He waited for her to respond, and, when she did not, he continued. "You can't imagine the things I can do to you if I have to teach you another lesson. You can't imagine—" He stared at her for a moment, then started away at last, knowing that she understood. She would know better than to ever tell anyone.

Then he heard her voice, the words so soft, "*'God himself shall be with them, an' be their God,'*" he heard, and wondered for a moment if she had lost her mind in what he had done to her.

She continued to rock, the stunned look remaining on her features.

"*'And God'll wipe away tears from their eyes; and there will be no more death, neither sorrow . . .'*"

Then her eyes rose to meet his and Buddy felt unease move through him, for there was such an awareness in her features, as well as a hatred sitting atop the shattered look that still remained on her face. "*'But th' fearful, an' th' unbelievin', and th' abominable . . .'*" she continued, her eyes set now on his face, unmoving, "*'. . . will have their part in th' lake that burns with fire an' brimstone. . . .'*"

"Do you think your God really cares what happens to you?" Buddy asked her, and was almost certain for a moment that she had not heard.

Then her words came, and he thought for a moment she was again quoting her scriptures.

Then he understood.

"You're gonna burn," she said quietly, staring at him. "You're gonna burn."

# Chapter Fourteen

Reverend Edward Jakes stood in the front parlor of Walter Eason's home on the afternoon of August 11th, staring into the perspiring face of Walt Eason. He had come here hoping to find some spark of human compassion within this man—but there was no compassion in a man such as this one, he reminded himself, and he knew that he should have known it. What Walt's son had done to a decent, God-fearing woman those weeks before was beyond redemption—Esther Tipton had kept the secret locked inside herself until she could keep it no longer, and had at last turned to Edward because he was her pastor.

Esther had been violently abused by Buddy Eason.

What made the horror only worse was that she believed now she was with child.

Edward had known Esther Tipton since she was a girl, had seen her care for her father after her mother died, and then for a failing aunt after her father passed away. She had always been a big girl and an unattractive one, and Edward knew it was unlikely she had ever kissed a man or been touched by one in her thirty-some-odd years, until what Buddy Eason had done to her—and now it was possible she was with child, by a white man who had used her against her will.

Walt Eason had not spoken since Edward's words. Rivulets of sweat moved down his cheeks, but he did not try to wipe them away. When he spoke at last, Edward realized that he should have expected the words.

"If some nigger gal has gotten herself in trouble, my son had nothing to do with it," he said quietly, at last reaching into a pocket of his trousers to pull out a handkerchief and mop the sweat from his face.

"Your son violated a decent—"

"My son had nothing to do with—" But he seemed to realize suddenly he was shouting.

Reverend Jakes stared at him, no longer knowing what it was he had expected when he had come here today.

"You can go and tell that black whore that she won't get anything out of me or Buddy either one—and if I ever hear even once that she's spoken Buddy's name—"

"She doesn't even know that I came here, but your son has to be held responsible—"

"How do you know he's responsible?" Walt Eason asked, and Edward was surprised to see the ugliness that suddenly twisted the man's features. "I can find ten men, white and colored both, who will say they were with her that day."

Then the ugliness became a smirk.

"I can find ten men who will say you were with her as well."

Reverend Jakes could only stare at him, certain that he was looking into the face of pure evil.

"May God forgive you," was all that he could say. "May God forgive you."

Buddy was with his grandfather at the mill that afternoon when Cassandra Price tapped at the door.

"Yes?" Walter Eason asked, looking up from the ledgers on the desktop between himself and his grandson. Buddy sat back, relieved at the interruption—the old man had to be going senile already, he thought, to think Buddy would even care how the mill was doing. There was nothing of interest in the place anyway, just noisy machinery and mildewy offices, and the fun he had had with Cassandra Price for a time had quickly cooled—she was too ready to get laid now, he told himself, and there was no fun in that.

Cassandra opened the door, smiling as her eyes came to rest on

Buddy. She ran her tongue over her lips to wet them before she spoke. "Buddy, your father wants you to call him," she said, then continued to stand in the doorway, looking in.

"Is there anything else, Cassandra?" Buddy heard the annoyance come into his grandfather's voice as he spoke to her, as it seemed to do often lately.

"No, Mr. Eason, that's all."

"Then you may go."

She closed the door.

Walter Eason rose and took up his cane. "Use the telephone in here if you want. I've got to go check on the new fixer."

Buddy watched until the door was shut between them, then moved to sit with one hip on the edge of the old man's desk, exactly as he knew his grandfather hated, then he reached for the handset of the telephone. Within seconds he heard the door open and close again, and he knew without turning that it had to be Cassandra—she was wearing too much perfume, as she usually did. He felt her arms go around him from behind and her tongue go into his free ear just as his father picked up the telephone.

"What do you want?" Buddy asked him, wasting no time on preliminaries.

"Come home, I need to talk to you."

"What about?"

"Come home, now," Walt Eason said, his voice rising. Buddy felt Cassandra's hand slide down between his legs for a moment before she came around to stand before him. She smiled, then began to unbutton her blouse. Buddy watched until she had it open and had slid her brassiere straps down to expose her small breasts to him.

"Sure, I'll come home," he said, smiling at her. Then he watched the look that came to her face at the remainder of his words. "There's nothing worth staying here to do anyway."

Cassandra hurriedly buttoned her blouse and shoved it down into her skirt as Buddy walked out and left the door open—the goddamn son-of-a-bitch, she thought, anger filling her. She had been certain she was pregnant the month before, but then her monthly had started. She bled and cramped and cursed him every step of the way—it was all his fault; she was certain of it. He had hardly touched her since since that first time, and what he had wanted to do the few times they had been together she had not liked doing at all—she'd never get pregnant doing that, she told herself, but she had been unable to refuse him.

They had not been together in the past week, and if she did not get something out of him today then she knew she would have little chance for this month at all—the stupid son-of-a-bitch; he would ruin her plans if he kept this up. He was eager enough to jump anything else that moved, and it made little sense to her that he would not take what she was offering so willingly.

Cassandra moved toward the heavily framed mirror that hung on a wall near the door, then turned herself sideways to try to imagine what she would look like once she was big with Buddy Eason's child—she would get that baby from him today no matter what she had to do, she told herself.

Walt Eason was waiting for his son in the hallway at the foot of the stairs that rose to the second floor of the house. His face was red, and Buddy knew it was more from anger than liquor at his first words.

"Did you really rape some nigger girl?"

For a moment Buddy could only stare at him, not believing she had told—she knew what he would do to her. She knew—

His father's face flushed even darker. He drew back a fist and slammed it into Buddy's mouth, and then again, sending him reeling backward into the wall. For a moment Buddy tightened—he would kill his father one day for that. He would kill him—he spat blood onto the cream-colored carpet instead, then wiped the back of one hand across his mouth before he turned and started up the stairs. He could hear his father ascending right behind him.

"I won't have you fathering brats all over niggertown—do you hear me!" Walt Eason shouted, only a step behind as they reached the top of the stairs. He shoved at Buddy, almost sending him to his face there on the landing. "Do you hear me!—I won't have—"

"*You* won't have!" Buddy shouted as he turned back. "*You* won't have—I don't give a damn what *you* won't have!" He shoved his father in return, sending him back toward the landing. For a moment he thought Walt Eason would hit him—do it and you'll die, he thought. Do it and you'll—

His father took another swing at him, and Buddy blocked the blow and shoved him away, then again, and his father was grabbing for the banister—

Walt Eason's arms flailed and he started down, his back hitting one of the upper risers. There was a sickening thump as his feet came up and hit the wall over his head, and then he was going down, hitting one riser after another, until he finally came to rest at the bottom with a heavy thud.

Buddy stood there, breathing heavily, feeling nothing, then he started down. Wiping at his mouth and still tasting blood as he reached the bottom, he spat, then knelt by his father—Walt Eason was still breathing. Buddy waited, listening to the rasping sound that came from deep within his father's chest, hearing it falter, come again, then at last stop altogether.

After a time he stood, wiping his hands down along the legs of his trousers. He was surprised that he felt little as he stared down at the man lying at his feet, only the overwhelming urge to not be here when someone else found the body—there was something else he had to do instead, he told himself.

He would scour every part of niggertown this afternoon if he had to, but he would find Esther Tipton, and he would make her wish she had never been born. He would make her—

Buddy Eason turned for the door, all thoughts of the man lying dead at the foot of the stairs left behind him.

♣

It took him little time to find her house. It was at the end of a street that stopped at the edge of her yard, with the railroad tracks and a steep hill just behind it. Buddy drove several streets away and left his car parked at the edge of a field where some kids were playing ball, then walked down into the narrow strip of woods that met up with the side of the field, and made his way toward the railroad tracks that ran behind her house. Some part of his mind kept telling him he should be at the mill when they found his father, for that was where the police and his family would expect him to be, but that part was drowned out by the need to make her pay for telling what he had done—he had not made his mind up yet what he would do to her.

But he did know that she would still be in her house when he burned it after.

He grabbed a handful of briers as he made his way up the embankment, then cursed aloud as he shook them from his hand. A foot slipped out from under him half way up, sending him to his hands and knees on damp ground to stain his trousers. When he reached the top he stood on the tracks and looked down at her house, seeing in his mind already the fire he would start, the fire that would quickly spread to the trees in the yard and possibly other houses nearby—he was so eager as he started down that he hardly noticed when he slipped and then slid his way mostly toward the bottom. He could hear dogs barking from a pen to one side of the house, but they hardly registered on his mind—she was going to pay for what she had done, he told himself. She was going to pay.

He had to duck under a clothesline strung across the yard near the house, then he was stepping onto the porch, his eyes on an open and unscreened rear window over which curtains hung—he did not care if anyone else was at home. At least there would be no husband to interfere, for it had been obvious that he had been the first man to have taken her— but any family she had could suffer as well, Buddy told himself.

She should have been grateful that he had done nothing more than take her the last time.

He made his way across the porch, then he was squatting at the window and pulling the curtains back, eager to be inside. For a moment he was not certain what he was seeing, then he felt cold metal come to rest against his forehead, and he realized he was staring into the eyes of the woman he had come to find.

There was no fear on her face as she knelt at the other side of the opening, a big woman filling up the space on the other side, just cold determination as she held a rifle pressed into the flesh between his eyes.

"You hold them curtains back, white man," she said, forcing the end of the barrel sharply into his forehead as he started to pull his hands away. "I want t' be seein' you good right now."

Buddy pulled the curtains back as he stared at her, knotting the material in his hands—he was certain she intended to kill him. He could see it in her eyes.

Esther Tipton's hands did not tremble as she moved the gun down slightly to press it into the end of his nose. "I'll finish you right off if you let go 'a them curtains again," she said, and he understood exactly what she meant. She stared at him for a moment, then pulled the gun down even with his mouth. "I want you down on your knees, Buddy Eason."

But Buddy could only stare at her.

"Get down on your knees!" she shouted above the sound of the barking dogs, driving the end of the rifle barrel forward into his teeth. Buddy obeyed, afraid to do anything else, then he stared at her. "You ask for God t' forgive you for what you done t' me," she said, her eyes never leaving his, and for a moment Buddy could do nothing but look at her. "I said ask God t' forgive what you done!" she shouted, and he thought for a moment that she would pull the trigger before he could even speak.

"Forgive me," he said, feeling the end of the barrel against his lips as he spoke.

"Louder," she said, jabbing the rifle forward.

"Forgive me—"

"Say 'Forgive me, Lord.'"

"Forgive me, Lord."

"For what, white man?"

"For what I did to you," he said, staring at her, refusing to take his eyes away. For a moment she was silent.

"Do you think He forgave you?" she asked him at last, drawing the rifle away.

"Yes, I do," Buddy said, seizing on the thought—if she thought that her God had forgiven him, then she would have to let him go. He might know there was no God, but he knew she believed in one; he could well remember her quoting scripture after he finished with her that day. She would let him go, and he would come back later to—

"Good," she said, and Buddy was surprised to feel the gun come up hard alongside his nose again. "God might forgive you, but you better know that I cain't." And Buddy suddenly felt his bowels go weak. He stared at her as she forced the gun hard into his teeth. "Open your mouth, white man," she said. When Buddy only stared at her in response, she forced the gun forward harder. "Open your mouth!"

Buddy parted his lips to say something, but she forced the gun hard against his teeth again. When he at last opened his mouth she pushed the gun in until he found himself gagging on the end of the barrel.

"How does it feel t' know I'm gonna kill you?" she asked him, but Buddy could only stare down the length of the barrel to her. She pressed the gun forward, making him gag again. "It don't feel too good t' have somethin' done t' you that you can't stop, does it, white man?" she asked, pulling the gun back slightly only to push it forward again, making him gag once more as it came up against the back of his throat.

Tears welled up in his eyes as he stared at her—he was going to die right here. He felt the hot flow of urine begin down the inside of one leg, but the thought that he had pissed himself barely registered on his consciousness.

"Goodbye, white man," she said, and he felt the gun in his mouth jerk as she pulled back on the trigger—there was a click, but nothing more, and Buddy saw the look of satisfaction that came to her face even as he jerked backwards at what he had thought was the moment of his death.

The end of the rifle came out of his mouth and he let out a wail, then started to scramble back and away from the window, releasing the curtains even as his mind tried to scream out at him that the gun had not been loaded. He looked back to see one side of the fabric being drawn open, the satisfaction still on her dark face as she leaned out the window.

"How did it feel, white man?" she yelled after him. "You know what it's like now—how did it feel?"

But Buddy could not even look at her. He was suddenly off the porch and running across her yard. He could hear her coming outside, and he was certain that she would have a loaded rifle now—there was a sudden, hard constriction across his windpipe, throwing him backward to the ground, and Buddy thought for a moment that he had been shot—

Only when he saw the clothesline moving above him did he realize that he had run into the wire. He tried to force himself to his feet, gagging as his lungs fought for air, almost going again to his knees as a wave of lightheadedness hit him. She was at the dog pen now, lifting the wooden bar that held the gate shut, setting the dogs on him with harsh words:

"Get that piece 'a rotten meat—"

But he was already running, trying to scramble up the embankment before the dogs could get to him, knowing that he would never make it even before he felt one rip through his trouser leg and graze its teeth against his flesh—then he was at the top and falling down the other side, coming to a stop at last in the brambles at the bottom of the incline.

Buddy was certain he was alone in the mill office an hour later as he changed from his filthy clothes and into the suit he usually kept hanging in the coat closet there. He had chosen to use his grandfather's office, leaving the clothes he stripped off in a stinking heap on the floor alongside the old man's desk as he pulled on his clean trousers and then buttoned up the shirt he kept in the office for times such as these. The building had appeared deserted as he let himself in the back door, the lights out, and that told him that it was likely his father had been found by now—the old man would never have left the mill this early on a Friday afternoon unless something had come up.

Buddy finished buttoning his shirt and then combed his fingers back through his thick hair, realizing that his hands were no longer shaking. The knot that had been in his stomach was slowly loosening now, turning into a growing rage—the goddamn nigger, he kept telling himself. The goddamn nigger—he wanted her to die slowly for what she had done today. He wanted—but the thought of returning to her house made his hands begin to shake all over again. He could not go back there.

His grabbed the telephone up from the desk, intending to yank its cord from the wall and shatter the mirror across the room with it to lessen the rage inside of him—then he heard the rear door at the back end of the hallway open and close, and keys jangle in someone's hand. Buddy waited, thinking it had to be old Nathan, the colored janitor who cleaned the offices at night, for there was no reason for anyone else to be here after the office had closed—then Cassandra Price was standing in the door-way, a set of keys in her hand, keys that Buddy knew she would have stolen, for the old man had refused to allow her a set of her own.

"I'm glad you're back," she said, smiling at him, coming into the room, then surprising him as she turned to close the door after herself as if the two of them were not alone in the building. She walked closer and Buddy only stared at her, wanting to snap her neck for her simple intrusion into the room—then her hands were working at his shirt, unfastening buttons he had just done up. "I've been dying to get my hands on you all day," she said, moving closer against him as she tugged his shirttail up and out of the waist of his trousers.

Buddy grabbed her by the shoulders and held her away, then watched the fleeting look of fear that passed across her features as he stared down at her, a fleeting look that was quickly replaced by invitation. "Do you want to play it rough, Buddy?" she asked, her hands reaching out to work at his belt even as he held her away. "I'll play it whatever way you want to—"

When he struck her he surprised even himself—and then he had slung her backward against the old man's desk and was coming toward her. He knew that he was hurting her minutes later as he pushed forward, for there was the bound edge of a ledger and even an iron paperweight under her back, but he did not care.

"That's what I want, Buddy," she kept saying, her hands digging into his back. "That's what I want—"

Cassandra continued to lie there after he had finished, her eyes on him as he dressed.

Buddy was surprised to see her smile.

# CHAPTER FIFTEEN

Henry Sanders sat beside his father on a hot Saturday afternoon in the last half of September that year, trying to slide far enough down on the seat of the borrowed Ford truck not to be seen as the rusty vehicle made its way down Main Street. He stared out the window beside him, wishing he were anywhere else on Earth. He had been forced to give up his Saturday morning to help pick the vegetables and fruit that now loaded down the rear of the truck, and now it seemed his pa expected him to give up the afternoon as well, taking Henry along as he peddled tomatoes, beans, sweet potatoes, and melons to the grocers in town.

Henry watched the people moving about on the sidewalks when the truck slowed as they reached the line of store buildings, then was surprised as they slowed even further still, at last pulling over in an empty space before the glass windows at the front of the drug store. He turned to look at his father as Janson shut the motor off.

"Why don't I buy you a Co'-Cola?" Janson asked, surprising Henry so that he did not answer for a moment, for his pa rarely spent money on anything so frivolous as a soda pop.

Henry followed him into the drug store, then sat on a stool at the soda fountain and watched ice cream being dished up for a girl at the far end of the counter before he and his pa were waited on. He sipped his drink, enjoying the sweet taste and the little bubbles that popped and fizzed on the surface each time he set it down. He watched the soda jerk mix an ice cream soda for someone who had come in just behind them, thinking this had to be the most wonderful place in the world to work—how could anybody ever get paid to work in a place like this, he wondered.

His father was leaning against the counter beside him, talking to Mr. Patterson, the man who owned the drug store, as he made arrangements to deliver a load of firewood to the man's house—more money, Henry thought, telling himself that he knew now why his father had brought him here, so he could make arrangements for a job they would do on another day.

Sometimes working and making money seemed to be all his pa ever thought about.

Henry finished his drink and began to wander about the store, looking into the glass cases at the worlds of things he knew his family would never be able to afford. As he neared the front windows, he was surprised to see that the driver's-side door of their truck was standing open, and that a man was leaning inside.

"Hey—" Henry called out, pushing open the door of the drug store and starting out onto the sidewalk. The man straightened from where he had been leaning into the vehicle, and Henry started, for it was the man who had hit Wilson with his car door on Main Street several months before. "You better—"

But a restraining hand came down on his shoulder, halting his steps there on the sidewalk, and he looked back to find his father now just behind him, Janson Sanders's eyes on the heavy-set man as well. For a moment Henry started to speak again, but the fingers dug even more firmly into his shoulder, halting his words.

"I heard you were back in town, you red-nigger," the man said, shocking Henry as he realized the words were intended for his father. He turned to stare as the man came around the open driver's door and took a few steps closer to them, stopping in the street just short of the sidewalk. "I thought it was you I saw getting out of this truck—who'd you steal it from, boy? I know a red-nigger like you couldn't afford to buy even an old piece-of-shit truck like this."

Henry started to step forward, opening his mouth to speak, but his father's fingers dug even more painfully into his shoulder, making him grit his teeth to remain silent—he could not believe his father would not say something, that he would not at least defend himself.

"You better answer me, boy," the man said, his eyes never leaving Henry's father's face.

"Get away from th' truck, Buddy," his father spoke at last, though his words were quiet, steady. He released Henry's shoulder and moved up to stand just beside the boy.

"You can't tell me or any other white man what to do, you red son-of-a-bitch—"

"You can't talk to my pa like that," Henry clenched his fists at his sides. How dare anyone talk to his father like that.

But the man only laughed, a look of what almost seemed to be contempt coming to his heavy face. He turned back to the truck, and for a moment Henry thought he would walk away—but he only walked around the open driver's door and toward the back of the vehicle, then turned that look of amusement back on them just before he took hold of the side of the truck box, and, with a grunt, pulled himself up to stand in the back with the boxes of vegetables. "Who'd you steal these from, red-nigger?" he asked, looking down on them. "You never were anything more than a thief." The man reached down and took a large tomato into each hand from one of the boxes, then straightened and, with a look of amusement playing around the edges of his mouth, threw them down to splat on the pavement beside the truck. Then he reached down for two more.

Henry snapped. He pulled free of his father's hand and was suddenly past the open driver's door and up onto the back of the truck, reaching for the man's arm, determined he would—

There was a look of surprise on the man's heavy face—but they were too close, and the man shoved at him, trying to back away, and Henry was losing his footing, falling—

He hit the pavement with a jolt, his head striking the blacktop so hard that his teeth ached inside his mouth with the impact, and then his father was there, leaning over him and saying something, though for a moment Henry did not understand.

"Henry, boy—are you okay—?" he understood at last, even as the big man jumped down from the back of the truck to stand laughing at them.

Henry did not say anything, but nodded his head as he sat up, biting his lips at the pain in his skull and down along his backbone.

"Get in th' truck, Henry," his father said, straightening to stare at the man.

"But, Pa—"

"Get in th' truck." Janson's voice rose, but his eyes never left the man before him.

Henry obeyed, getting in the open driver's door and sliding across the seat, then turning back to look at his father and the man through the truck's rear window.

His father met the man's eyes over the short distance between them, then he turned and walked to the driver's door and got in, shutting the door and starting the engine. He brought his eyes to Henry as he put the truck in gear, and Henry could only stare at him, not believing he had walked away. Not believing—

The man moved up onto the sidewalk as the truck backed out into the street, and Henry looked at him, finding him laughing still as the truck started away, then Henry turned back to his father.

Janson Sanders sat in silence and stared straight ahead, not again meeting his son's eyes throughout the trip home.

Walter Eason stood in the front room of a house on Spring Street the first Tuesday afternoon in October, staring into the eyes of a heavy-set Negro woman sitting on a sofa. Her minister, Edward Jakes, and his wife had been in the house when he arrived, and they remained near the door Walter had entered, as if to make certain he understood he had no place being among them. Walter had come to assure himself that what his attorney, Sam Porter, had told him could not be true.

Instead, he had convinced himself of something altogether different.

Buddy had raped this woman and fathered the child Porter said she was carrying.

Walter looked away, unable to speak while he looked into her eyes.

"It would be best that no one ever knows about this child," Walter said.

He tightened his hand on the carved knob of his walking stick, leaning on it more heavily than usual, as he tried to compose his thoughts.

"There have to be places for a colored woman in your situation to give birth, places that will make arrangements for a—" he paused for a moment, "for a mulatto child."

He was silent again.

"I understand from Porter that you're a good cleaning girl. I'll make certain you have enough money to start over once the child is placed, and that you're given a good job with a decent family in Birmingham or Mobile, someplace where you'll never—"

"You cain't buy me," she said, so quietly for a moment that Walter was not certain he had understood. "You cain't buy me," she said again. "You can keep your money an' your good job an' you can tell him if he ever comes near me again I'm gonna send him t' hell where he belongs, even if I go t' hell myself for doin' it."

For a moment Walter was certain her minister would say something at her words. He waited, hearing feet shift on the wooden floor behind him.

The he heard the door open near where the minister and his wife stood, and he turned to see Jakes holding it open, waiting for Walter to leave.

"Get out 'a my house," she said when Walter turned back to look at her. "Get out 'a my house, an' don't you ever come back here again."

Henry could hear the sound of the mill that afternoon long before he and his father reached the railroad tracks that divided the town in half. They finally topped the incline at the beginning of the Eason mill village, and crossed the railroad tracks going down into the village itself, the sound of the machinery, and the sight of the flying lint, seeming to reach out to envelop Henry as they walked—he already hated this place, and could hardly believe his father intended to move them back here if he could get hired on at the mill again.

Henry might have been born in one of these identical mill houses, but he had no desire to move back here now. All it had taken was for his father to learn that the mill was hiring again, on the same afternoon he had been rained out of work on the Beautification Project for the second time that week, and Janson had decided to walk to the mill to apply for a job. Henry had gotten in from school just as Janson was leaving, and Janson had asked if he wanted to walk along—he wished now that he had never agreed to come. His pa had done nothing but talk about the past since they had left the house, and Janson's words had not stilled until they crossed the tracks into the mill village itself.

Henry cared very little for hearing about the past, about a famine in Ireland a hundred years before, or of folks called Huguenots, or people who had been herded west like cattle, or of a fire deliberately set in a cotton field—the past was gone, he kept telling himself. It could not affect him any more than could something that happened at the far side of the Earth, such as when Chancellor Hitler had invaded Poland, and England had declared war on Germany, a month before there on the far side of the world.

Henry's mind was so occupied that he paid little attention to the car that was parked nose-out in the gravel at the bottom end of the loading dock until one of the car doors opened and someone yelled out. "Hey, In'jun—"

Henry stopped there on the sidewalk, certain for a moment the words had been yelled out to him, then he turned and saw the man who had shoved him from the back of the truck up on Main Street several weeks before getting out of the vehicle.

"Hey, you, red nigger—" the man called again, just as the other doors opened and three more men got out.

Henry's father had stopped and turned with him, and he stood staring at the man before speaking. "What do you want, Buddy?" he asked at last.

"That's Mr. Eason to you, boy." His face changed, as did his tone. "I won't have trash like you calling me by my first name, like you were just as good as anybody."

Janson stared at him, and Henry waited for him to respond, feeling the moments slip past and his growing anger and surprise when his father did not say anything to the man, but spoke to him instead. "Let's go, Henry," Janson said, not taking his eyes from Buddy Eason.

Henry opened his mouth to speak, to say something, he did not know what, but his father's voice came again.

"Let's go, Henry," and a burning shame rose to Henry's face as they turned away that his father would take this, that he would not even respond—

"Is your wife at home now by herself, In'jun?" the man asked, halting Henry's father's steps beside him. "Alone there with those two little girls?"

Janson Sanders turned back, and, when Henry looked up at him, he found a different look on his father's face. Janson's words surprised Henry so completely that he could only stare at him. "You go near my wife or my girls an' you're a dead man—"

For a moment Henry did not understand—then he realized this man had threatened his mother and his sisters. Indignation welled up inside of him, and he started to step forward, but a powerful hand came down on his shoulder. He looked up at his father and saw a man that he little knew, and a man at this moment that he dared not disobey. That hand on his shoulder told him this was something he had no part of.

Janson released him and took a step toward Buddy Eason.

"All kinds of things can happen to a woman alone," the man was saying as he stared at Henry's father, his tone as much as his words chilling Henry. "All kinds of things that will make her wish she was dead before it was over, and those two little girls—"

Janson was on him so quickly that Henry did not see it until they were on the ground, his father over Buddy Eason, his hands closing around the man's throat to—but two of the men who had gotten out of the car dragged Janson off and held him between them. Henry tried to reach his father, but was grabbed and held back by the third man, almost lifted off the ground, and then held away to stand staring as Buddy Eason regained his feet.

Buddy reached into a pocket and withdrew a knife, his eyes never leaving Henry's father's face as he unfolded its blade from the handle. There was a look close to pleasure on his face as he stepped closer. "I've been waiting for this for a long time," he said quietly as he wiped the blade on his shirt sleeve. He held it up to look at the edge, then beyond to the eyes of the man held before him. "A long time—" He stepped forward, a smile coming to his face as he prepared to—

"Stop it!" a man's voice commanded, loud and indignant. "I said— stop it!" An old man, white-haired with ruddy complexion, came toward the men who held Henry's father between them. "Let him go!"

Walter Eason held a walking stick raised in one hand, but he did not have to use it. The men holding Janson stared at Buddy for a moment, then allowed Janson to pull away. As Janson moved toward him, the man holding Henry released him without a word.

"What is the meaning of this?" The old man sounded furious, but Buddy only met his stare, answering after a moment in a tone of defiance.

"He's just a damn red-nigger, coming around here, starting trouble—"

"You're a damn liar," Janson said from where he stood now beside Henry. He took a step forward and two of the men moved to restrain him again. "You come near my wife or my girls, Buddy, an' this time I will kill you," he spit, even as the men held him back.

"I'm going to shut your goddamn mouth once and for all." Buddy moved forward, the knife still in his hand, but the old man's walking stick came down hard across his wrist, sending the knife spinning from his hand and into the dirt.

Buddy's hand seemed to spasm and he looked up with fury at the old man, but Walter Eason's eyes were on the men again holding Henry's father.

"Release him!" the old man's voice was commanding, and Henry watched in surprise as the men holding his father again let him go. Buddy turned to glare at his grandfather, but the old man's eyes held nothing but cold resolve. "It's about time you had to face a man without having someone else hold him down for you, Buddy; it's about time you found out what a fool you are." He turned to the men who stood ready to intercede on Buddy's behalf. "If any of you interferes, I'll make certain you regret it the rest of your lives." He looked at Janson for a moment, and to Henry it seemed as if some understanding passed between the two men. Then Walter Eason turned to walk to the car he had left parked alongside the sidewalk.

There was a look of disbelief on Buddy Eason's face as he looked first at the retreating back of his grandfather, and then at Janson Sanders. Henry saw no pleasure on Janson's face, as there had been on Buddy's minutes earlier, just a resolve as cold and determined as had been on the face of the old man. Buddy swung at Janson, but only barely connected as Janson moved out of the way and brought a hard fist upward into Buddy's jaw, sending him stumbling backwards.

It took only minutes before Buddy was backed against his own car, but still Janson did not stop. Buddy's nose looked broken; there was blood everywhere, over his mouth, on Janson's hands, and Henry thought his father would kill him—

"That's enough," Walter Eason said.

His voice was loud, but Janson did not seem to hear.

"That's enough!" There was a nod from Walter Eason, and Janson was pulled away. He immediately jerked free of the men holding him, but Buddy was already on the ground. Janson stood over him for a moment, breathing heavily.

"So help me—you better stay away from my family," he said. He stared at Buddy a moment longer, wiping a bloody lip with the back of one hand. Buddy was trying to push himself from the ground.

"I'll get even with you, you red bastard," Buddy said, his words slurred between split and swollen lips, as Janson turned away. "You'll pay for this. I'll see you dead, you wait and see—but I'm going to hurt you first. I'm going to hurt you—"

But Janson Sanders never looked back.

He walked to the old man and stood, meeting the cold gray eyes as Henry watched him. There was pride and dignity in Janson's bearing, though his clothes were torn and covered with dirt and blood, and his lip still bleeding.

"I come here lookin' for work," Janson said, and, as Henry watched him, some part of him started to understand what it was to be a man.

Walter was sitting at his desk by the time Buddy entered the mill office. Walter heard the front door slam back into the nearby wall, and a moment later Buddy's office door slammed open as well. Walter rose and started from the room, then went back to take something from the middle drawer of his desk, shoving it down into a pocket of his coat before he went out into the hall.

When he reached his grandson's office, he found Buddy had already kicked his chair across the room. The telephone rang as Walter entered and Buddy yanked it up, jerked its cord out of the wall, and shattered one of the windows with it. His eyes came to rest on Walter and Walter stared at him.

"You ruin everything you touch," Walter said, walking further into the room. He stared at his grandson. "I wish you had never been born. I wish you had never taken one breath of life in this county—"

Walter brought his hands up to stare at them. One hand held to his walking stick; the other he clenched and unclenched as he stared at it, thinking of what he could have done, what he should have done, so many times. He could have changed things. He could have—

When he looked up at Buddy, Buddy spat in his face.

Walter Eason snapped. He raised the walking stick and brought it down hard across the side of his grandson's face, then again, hitting Buddy repeatedly until Buddy at last jerked the stick from the older man's hand and brought it down hard across his raised knee to break it.

Buddy grabbed him, wrenching his arm so hard that pain shot from Walter's left shoulder—but he was already bringing the pistol up from his pocket with his right hand, pointing it at his grandson's face, and holding it there as Buddy let go and backed away. Walter wanted to pull the trigger. He wanted—

"Get out of this mill," Walter Eason said, his voice shaking. "Get out of this county; I never want to see you again." He stared at his grandson a moment longer, and then turned and left.

Cassandra Price could hear the sound of furniture breaking after the old man walked out of Buddy's office. She reached the doorway to see Buddy yank a drawer from his desk and throw it, contents and all, directly at where she was standing.

She moved back and the drawer hit the door frame waist high, sending fountain pens, rubber bands, and what looked to be dozens of boxes of matches skittering over the lower part of her legs and the floor near her feet. One hand went to her belly, and she assured herself that nothing had hit her there—she could not let anything happen now. Not when she was this close.

Not when she was going to have Buddy Eason's baby.

She looked back around the edge of the door frame once she was certain Buddy was no longer throwing furniture. He was yanking drawers open, but this time only to grab things from within and place them on the desk. He was cursing, but Cassandra did not take the time to listen—whatever he was saying did not matter. He and the old man had fought. But he and the old man fought often. It did not usually result in thrown furniture or a bloody face, which Buddy had at the moment, Cassandra noted, feeling a touch of distaste as she stared at him—but that did not matter, either. She had not bedded him for his looks. She had not bedded him for his personality. She had bedded him for the baby growing inside of her, and for the money and the Eason name the baby would net her.

"Buddy, are you hurt?" she asked, though she did not care. She was surprised to see him take a gun from a lower drawer and lay it on the desktop. He fished in the drawer again, not answering, and came up a moment later with a handful of something.

When he set the bullets down, she realized what they were.

"Buddy?"

"What?" He hissed at her, and she stepped back.

She did not say anything; she watched him load the gun. He set it down on the desktop, then yanked open another drawer to search inside. He slammed it, then started across the room toward her, and Cassandra shrank away, though he did nothing but take his coat and hat from the hatrack. She walked toward the desk, looking to the open briefcase on the floor at its other side as Buddy came back to toss the hat and coat over one of the leather armchairs before his desk.

"Are you going somewhere?" she asked.

He did not answer. He yanked the chair that usually rested behind his desk back to its normal position and set the briefcase in its seat, then began to rake things from the desktop into it. The gun was dumped in with everything else, and fear surged through Cassandra as it landed aimed at her belly. She moved around the chair to stand at its other side, then watched Buddy cross the room to the credenza.

"Are you—" she began again.

"Yeah, I'm going, if it's anything to you."

"But, where are you going?"

He did not answer.

"But—but, you can't leave—I mean—" Her mind was suddenly panicked. He couldn't leave. Not now. Not with her pregnant. He had to marry her. That was what was supposed to happen. He had to.

She stared at his back.

"Whatever you and your grandfather were fighting about, it can't be so bad—you need to—"

"The old man is the first thing I'm going to settle."

That made no sense. Buddy was squatting, looking in the credenza for something.

"But, why—"

"What does it matter to you?"

"But, you can't leave—I—I'm pregnant," she blurted out. "You've got to stay and—"

"I don't have to do anything." He turned to look at her.

"But, it's yours; the baby's yours," she said, and could hear the desperation in her voice. No, it was not supposed to happen like this.

"So? What if it is?"

She could only stare at him as he turned away again. "But, you can't—you—you have to marry me! You have to! Your grandfather won't let—"

"Do you think I'd marry a mill village whore like you?" he asked, and Cassandra was surprised to hear a snort of laughter come out of him. "Do you think the old man would let me marry you, even if I wanted to?" Cassandra stared at him, feeling as if she had been slapped—and suddenly she understood; he never would have married her.

Those tracks that cut the town in half had decided it after all.

Cassandra was from the village. Buddy Eason was from town.

And he would never marry her.

The memory of something her mother said about a pregnant, unmarried cousin came to her—rather dead and buried than to disgrace the family.

If Buddy did not marry Cassandra, she knew Helene would put her out the minute she learned Cassandra was pregnant. There was no doubt—better dead and buried, Cassandra told herself. Better dead.

Cassandra's eyes moved to the gun lying in the open briefcase before her, and she reached for it almost without thought—better dead. Better not to have people laugh at her and call her trash. She was not trash—she was Cassandra Price—her mother had always said she was better than anyone else living in the village.

She had been good enough for Buddy Eason to bed.

She just wasn't good enough to marry.

She was crossing the room before she consciously made the decision—better dead. But she would take care of something first.

When Buddy turned and stood, Cassandra placed the business end of the gun to his crotch—take care of something. Oh, yes.

Panic came to Buddy's eyes. He was shoving her away with one hand, grabbing for the gun with the other, when Cassandra Price—who would never be Mrs. Buddy Eason—pulled the trigger.

♣

Walter Eason was sitting in his car outside the mill, his eyes closed. The window beside him was down, and he leaned against the door, his arm hurting too much to move, too much even to drive himself to the doctor. His left shoulder was dislocated, and he was too old for this, he told himself, too old to go through having it wrenched back into place, too old to scream like a helpless old man—he was a helpless old man, he told himself, and would be a dead old man if it had not been for the small pistol that still rested in his pocket.

He could hear voices approaching the car and he opened his eyes, for a moment not recognizing the house boss he saw almost every day, much less Janson and Henry Sanders walking at the little man's side.

He had told Bickham to take care of them personally.

"Yes, sir, I will," Bickham had said, looking surprised. The nervous man was as good as his word.

He was telling them about the house they had been assigned in the village as they approached Walter's car.

"It's quite sound. We put a new roof—"

"Bickham—" Walter said, sounding old to his own hearing for the first time. He cleared his throat, and tried again. "Bickham—" and the little man stopped and looked at him just short of the car.

"Yes, Mr. Eason, are you all right, sir?" He poked at his glasses with one finger, rising up on the balls of his feet, nervous habits that always telegraphed his unease, but right now they did not bother Walter.

"You don't need to walk to the house. Get in the car and drive," Walter said, pushing away from the window. "Janson, young Sanders, get in the backseat. Bickham, there's something I want you to do after—"

He had to bite his lip to keep from crying out as pain lanced through his shoulder when he moved, but finally he was on the opposite side of the seat, his back to the door. Bickham looked uncertain, but Walter knew he would do as he had been told. The man got into the car, and it seemed a full minute before the rear doors opened and Janson and Henry Sanders slid in as well.

Bickham choked the car too much—and then they were moving down the street and Walter could make himself breathe again.

His gaze settled on young Henry in the backseat—the boy was very much like his father, Walter thought, watching Henry's eyes move over the interior of the vehicle. Walter could imagine how proud Janson's father, Henry, would have been if he had lived to see this grandson, how pleased he would be to have him carry on his name—not every man was so lucky.

Walter knew he had not been.

He tried to understand what had happened to Buddy over the years. Walter's grandson had never had to worry about food or shelter or any of the other necessities of life that the man and the boy in that backseat had scraped and fought with. Walter looked at Janson Sanders in his faded dungarees and his shirt that looked as if it had once been a guano sack, at his skin darkened by his ancestry and by exposure to the sun, and at the bleeding lip and bruises that were already beginning to show on his face—it had been struggle itself that Janson Sanders had hammered himself out against over and over again through his life. It had been struggle that had beaten into shape the core of the man he was, a man Walter realized he respected as he did few others.

Walter looked at the boy sitting at his father's side, and he could see already some of that same shaping in the boy's dark face—Henry Sanders would grow up to be a man very much like his father, Walter told himself, into a man Walter knew he would be proud one day to know.

"Henry, did you know I knew your grandfather?" he found himself asking, bringing the boy's eyes to him. "He was a good man, your grandfather," Walter said, nodding his head as he stared into the green eyes. "He was a good man."

Janson felt that he was going home, and the feeling surprised him.

He stood with his son on the street before the house they had been assigned in the mill village as Walter Eason's car drove away, his eyes on the front door to the three rooms where they would live, and he could remember years before memorizing the details of a house very much like this one, details that he had taken back to Elise to tell her where they would live. He found himself doing the same thing today—she would be glad to be back here, he told himself, just as he was.

Times were getting better in the county. There would be a decent wage and steady hours, and Walter Eason had said there would be a place for Stan in the mill as well. Electricity would be brought to the village in the months to come, and Janson had already told himself he would buy a radio for Elise—after all these years she would again have some of the things she had given up when she had married him. He had never once heard her complain through that time, even though he realized now that he had not given her one thing he had promised her when she had become his wife—except for their being together and having made a family.

And they had been happy.

He would give her the home he had promised, the land he still dreamed of on so many nights, when he could finally make that dream a reality. That was one thing he would not doubt.

He was only thirty-two years old now and Elise twenty-eight.

There was still plenty of time to have that dream.

He looked at Henry where the boy stood beside him, finding him staring at the house still. He started to speak, but Henry spoke first.

"Pa, what was granpa like?" the boy asked, bringing his eyes to Janson.

For a moment Janson was silent, trying to think of a few words that could sum up a man's life. "He knew what it was like to work for a dream, and to be willing to die to have it," he said at last.

He watched as his son nodded his head, and he knew that Henry understood.